The Case of the Spotted Band

Volume Two of

The Case Books of Octavius Bear

Harry DeMaio

"Alternative Universe Mysteries

for Adult Animal Lovers"

Paperback ISBN 978-1-78092-714-5
ePub ISBN 978-1-78092-715-2
PDF ISBN 978-1-78092-716-9

Published in the UK by MX Publishing
335 Princess Park Manor, Royal Drive,
London, N11 3GX
www.mxpublishing.co.uk
Cover design compiled www.staunch.com

Dedicated to GTP

A Most Extraordinary Bear

Acknowledgements

These books have evolved over a long period of time and under a wide range of influences and circumstances. I am indebted to many people for helping to bring Octavius and his cohorts to the printed page. Thanks most especially to my wife, Virginia, for her insights and clever suggestions as well as her unfailing enthusiasm for the project and patience with its author. To my sons, Mark and Andrew and their spouses, Cindy and Lorraine, for helping make these tomes more readable and audience friendly. To Cathy Hartnett, cheerleader-extraordinaire for her eagerness to see this alternate universe take form. To Jack Magan, Dan Andriacco and Zohreh Zand for their assistance and support.

Thanks to the members of the Monday Morning Writers Group for their help and encouragement. A special thank you to my editor, Coleen (Ms Comma-kaze) Armstrong for her battlefield survival techniques on my punctuation and grammar.

Kudos to Jim Effler, my illustrator, for bringing the characters to life beyond my fondest expectations and to Bob Gibson for his excellent work on the covers.

If, in spite of all this assistance, some errors or inconsistencies have crept through, the buck stops here. Needless to say, all of the characters, situations and narratives are fictional.

The Development of Civilization Volume 2 Part 1

Our Origins

(From "An Introduction to Faunapology" by Octavius Bear Ph.D.)

*"About 100,000 years ago, according to scientific experts, a colossal solar flare blasted out from our Sun, creating gigantic magnetic storms here on Earth. These highly charged electrical tempests caused startling physical and psychological imbalances in the then population of our world. The complete nervous systems of some species were totally destroyed. For example "Homo Sapiens" lost all mental and motor capabilities and rapidly became extinct. Less developed species exposed to the radiation were affected differently. Four-footed and finned mammals, birds and reptiles suddenly found themselves capable of complex thought, enhanced emotions, self-awareness, social interplay and the ability to communicate, sometimes orally, sometimes telepathically, often both. Both speech production and speech perception slowly progressed with the evolution of tongues, lips, vocal cords and enhanced ear to brain connections. Many species developed opposable digits, fingers or claws, further accelerating civilized progress. Some others (most fish and underground dwellers) were shielded from the radiation and remained only as sentient as they were before the blast. This event is referred to as **The Big Shock**. It remains under intensive study."*

The Players in Book 2

Octavius Bear –Narcoleptic war hero; consulting detective, scientist, inventor; seeker of justice; mega-billionaire owner of Universal Ursine Industries; gourmet/gourmand; somewhat sedentary and grouchy just on general principles.

Mauritius (Maury) Meerkat – Part-time narrator; assistant to Octavius; African *émigré* with a French-Dutch background; clever with a shady history.

Inspector Bruce Wallaroo – Irrepressible but brilliant marsupial; an international law and order genius from Down Under; often calls on Octavius and Maury for support.

Imperius Drake – "Moriarty with wings!" Arch-villain; leader of the Black Quack gang; brilliant but loony duck who has developed a serum to make the animal kingdom his slaves; seeks vengeance for ridicule by the scientific community and the death of his beloved mate, Lee-Li-Li; Sworn enemy of Octavius Bear.

Bearoness Belinda Béarnaise Bruin Bear *(nee Black)* – Now wife of Octavius; very rich widow of Bearon Byron Bruin living in Bearmoral Castle in the Shetlands; Owner-pilot of the last flying Concorde SST; Gorgeous polar superstar, with the Aquashow, "Some Like It Cold."

Bearyl and Bearnice Blanc – Belinda's stunning twin polar sidekicks; Actress and singer, respectively. Co-pilot and flight engineer of Belinda's SST.

Otto the Magnificent – AKA Hairy Otter – Once a terrible illusionist magician, Otto, after escaping the claws of Imperius Drake, developed some amazing powers courtesy of Imperius'genetic alterations. He becomes a major player in Books 2, 3 and 4.

Chita - Beautiful, fascinating, clever, sexy, immoral and highly independent feline who is now seeking revenge on Imperius for attempting to kill her. Currently living in Rio and a member of the Spotted Band, Chita reappears in subsequent books as a principal character in her own right.

Cyd – Chita's probably fictional identical twin.

The Spotted Band – A South American rock group of feral cats: **Ozzie**, an Ocelot; **Jake**, a Jaguar; **Lepi**, a Himalayan Snow Leopard and the irrepressible **Chita**.

Frau Schuylkill – Octavius' beautiful Swiss she-wolf housekeeper/cook/pilot/security officer with many other mysterious and military talents. She rescued Octavius from his dive off the Breakurbach Falls while struggling with his nemesis, Imperius Drake.

Wyatt Where – Another wolf. Former military intelligence officer who had retired to a security post at the Bank of Lake Michigan in Chicago and then quit to join Octavius.

Howard Watt – A porcupine, high tech security authority who also left the bank with Wyatt to join Octavius. A laser and particle beam accelerator expert.

Bigg Baboon – The major muscle in Black Quack; the archetypical dumb heavy.

Pontius Puma – Arrogant Brazilian racketeer who controls all entertainment in Brazil and does substantial worldwide trading in stolen military and industrial secrets.

L. Condor - a voiceless Andean Condor cyber-net genius with a 12 foot wingspan. Destroys Pontius Puma's criminal network and meets Imperius Drake in wing-to-wing combat.

The Taurus Brothers – Belial and Brutus; The Chicago Bulls; "facilitators;" classic thugs who do work for both Imperius and Pontius Puma.

Doctor "Odd" Vark – Chief Geneticist at Universal Ursine Industries.

Doctor Chiti BingBang – Chief Physician at Universal Ursine Industries.

Bella Donna Black – Belinda's aunt and Sow of Honor at her wedding.

Wallingford Penniped, Ph.D. – Octavius'scholastic mentor and Best Male at his wedding,

Elijah Elk- Justice of the Peace, Churchill Manitoba.

Juno Bear – Octavius' mother.

Agrippa Bear – Octavius' half brother.

Brazilian Wallaroos – relations and friends of Inspector Bruce Wallaroo

Locations in Volume 2

Cincinnati; Rio and São Paolo; Churchill, Manitoba; St. Louis; Reno and Las Vegas.

Also from Harry DeMaio

Octavius Bear Book 1 – The Open and Shut Case

Octavius

Prologue

The gibbon looks much like an ape

With dark eyes and a long slender shape.

He will tell you his views

As he chatters the news.

Now, let's go to the videotape!

"Mass Assassination Foiled! Genetic Geniuses Jolted! Bear Beats Back Blue Bayou Bombs!" The Nevada tabloids started it and then it circled the world in newspapers, newswires, websites, blogs, twitters, radio, TV and skywriting – the sensational story of the thwarted attempt by Imperius Drake and the Black Quack Gang to kill off the vast majority of the world's genetic science community, all of whom were attending the Quadrennial Worldwide Convention of the Genetics Science Profession – *The Genius of Genetics 2014* - in Las Vegas.

KRAP-TV News, Channel 16, Las Vegas – "All the News While You Gamble and Gambol!!" – said it all.

"Good evening, this is Charles Gibbon with the latest news. This late breaking item right here in our own desert backyard. This evening a major international disaster at the Blue Bayou Resort and Casino was bearly averted when Imperius Drake, the mad genius canard of crime was prevented from triggering off one thousand anti-personnel bombs disguised as musical souvenirs. Only the quick action of Octavius Bear and the phenomenal aircrew of his C-5A, The Ursa Major, saved the evening. The event, a major convention of the world's best and brightest geneticists, was wrapping up with a spectacular Grand Finale when some great detective work by the Nevada and Las Vegas Police, combined with Blue Bayou security and the legendary ursine detective uncovered the unthinkable plot for mass assassination just moments before the bombs were to be set off."

"The duck and his baboon henchman were positioned in one of four huge hot air display balloons tethered to the sides of the Blue Bayou Aquastadium, ready to wreak havoc and carnage during the performance of the world renowned Aquabears, starring the fabulous Bearoness Belinda Béarnaise Bruin*(nee Black)*.

1

Octavius Bear ordered his huge aircraft, on station near the arena, into action and four incredibly accurate heat-seeking missiles took out the balloons and the perpetrators seconds before they were to trigger the bombs."

"Fortunately, no one in the audience was seriously injured in the melee, except for the Chairman of the Convention, *Il Professore* Roberto Rabbito, distinguished geneticist and possible candidate for this year's Noble Prize. He suffered a series of massive heart attacks and is now resting in Las Vegas General Hospital. The doctors say his condition is guarded."

"Although being cited as heroes by the attendees, the press, the public at large, the hotel management and the police, the Las Vegas District Attorney, Bucephalus Burro has nonetheless charged Octavius and his crew with over-flying the city at a dangerous altitude with an armored aircraft and setting off firearms within the city limits. 'The law is the law,' he was quoted as saying. 'The DA is a jackass,' said the mayor of the city in response. *(Which indeed, the DA is.)* It is a foregone conclusion that the charges will either be dropped or reduced to trifling misdemeanors."

"All the musical bombs have been confiscated and destroyed out in the desert, according to State Police Colonel Coyote. There has been no sign or sighting of the duck and his accomplice but from the fiery impact of the missiles, it is doubtful they survived. Nevertheless, a search is in progress."

"Stay tuned for more. And now these messages!"

*****

"Nevertheless!"

"Huh??"

"We said, nevertheless, in spite of what you may have thought, we have survived and we are here in Reno."

"But, Sire, is it really you??"

"Yes, baboon, it is we." The speaker was a mallard with one wing in a sling and a scar across his bill. "We are obviously disguised. By now, the authorities and that obnoxious bear and his underlings might all recognize us in both our Mandarin and Imperius Drake manifestations. So we have humbled ourselves to look like an ordinary mallard. Of course, it is to be hoped that they

2

think that we and you are dead after our Las Vegas misadventure. For which Octavius Bear and that treacherous cheetah will pay fatally. That is, assuming the cat is still alive."

"I don't know if she is, Sire."

"You will notice that, much as it wounds us, we, that is, I will dispense with the imperial 'we' for the nonce. You should only address me as Sire when we are alone."

"What do I call you otherwise?"

"I am Milord Mallàrd, *(accent grave on the last syllable)* an entertainment entrepreneur from the United Kingdom, here in Reno on a search for talent. A simple Milord will do. Obviously you too survived, baboon."

"Yes, Sire, Milord, Imperius, Doctor Yu."

"Be careful, you fool, under no circumstances are you to use either of my real names. Now, come with me. We have plans to make."

*****

For those of you who have not had the exquisite pleasure of reading the prequel to this opus –*The Open and Shut Case* – and for those of you who have read it but whose memories are cluttered up with the whereabouts of car keys and TV remotes, the following brief backgrounder is supplied. You others who are confident that you are up to speed may take this time to try to figure out why the refrigerator is making that funny noise.

My name is Mauritius Meerkat *(Maury)* and I'll be your omniscient narrator today. We have a list of menu specials that I'd like to read for you...ooops, that's my undercover job. I am the trusted associate and field captain of Octavius Bear. As you probably know, Octavius, among his many talents and accomplishments, is a brilliant, self-taught practitioner in the wide ranging fields of biology, physics, ursinology *(bears)* voodoo, teleology, genetics, chemistry, apiculture *(bees)* and oenology *(wine, in this case, honey wine or mead)*. He is a self made mega-billionaire and sole owner of Universal Ursine Industries, as well as a first rate electrical, electronic, structural, maritime, aeronautical, mechanical and chemical engineer. He has a few other interesting characteristics such as falling into brief, deep narcoleptic comas - side effects of his successful genetic experiments to eliminate the need for bears to hibernate.

He is huge - over nine feet tall and 1400 pounds - and like many of his species is given to emotional outbursts.

However, the talent and occupation that should interest you most is his fanatic avocation for criminology. The Bear works in close concert with Inspector Bruce Wallaroo from Australia, of whom more later, and with his own Cincinnati based team:

- Frau Ilse Schuylkill – Swiss she-wolf; housekeeper-cook; jet pilot; detective; and sharpshooter with other very strange and arcane abilities.

- Colonel Wyatt Where – another wolf; military hero; security specialist and pilot; and Frau Schuylkill's equally bizarre running mate.

- Doctor Howard Watt – porcupine; scientist and technologist; laser and weapons specialist.

- Your humble servant – African Meerkat; Octavius' indispensable assistant; operative; scribe; and overall facilitator as well as a pretty clever detective, if I do say so myself.

When we are not out scouring the world for evildoers in cooperation with local, national and international constabularies, we are headquartered in a rambling old mansion near Cincinnati which hides not only the Great Bear's opulent digs but his massive laboratories and shops; his missile silo disguised *(thinly)* as an Asian pagoda; and a large Roman temple that serves as a hangar for his four airplanes, including the Ursa Major, a heavily modified, stealth C-5A Galaxy.

It was the C-5A that played a *major* role in our most recent episode with Imperius Drake and his minions. The Ursa Major is the only one of his airplanes that Octavius can fit into comfortably so it has become his airborne lab, communications center, command post and when heavily armed, his weapons platform.

That's enough background for the moment. We shall cleverly interlard additional appropriate facts, surroundings, conditions, relationships, motivations and history as we move forward in our thrill-packed narrative. Now back to Reno, Nevada where Imperius Drake *(Milord Mallàrd)* has caught up with his subordinate-in-crime, Bigg Baboon. Both Imperius and Bigg were blasted from their perch in a hot air balloon as they attempted to wipe out the thousand-strong members of a genetics convention in Las Vegas. Since not a trace of the two

4

could be found after the heat seeking missiles fired by Colonel Where from the Ursa Major had hit their targets, the police assumed that they had been atomized. Octavius wasn't so sure, but lacking evidence to the contrary, he declared victory *(with some mental reservation)* and decided to take a brief vacation in the Canadian north with his favorite squeeze, the lovely Bearoness Belinda Béarnaise Bruin *(nee Black)*. Obviously, although he doesn't know it yet, Octavius was right to have had his doubts. Are we all back?? Good! Don't bother trying to fix the fridge. Get a new one!

Chapter One

Now, the French word for duck is "canàrd."

Accent grave, like blackguàrd and blowhàrd

But since mállard won't rhyme.

Our dark genius of crime

Claims his name should be "Milord Mallàrd."

"Come, baboon, leave that instrument of impoverishment!"

Imperius and Bigg, who had also been wounded in the missile blast, limped away from the Super Jackpot Slot Machine that had occupied the baboon non-stop for the day and a half he had been there. A little old nanny goat in jeweled glasses, spangled top and Capri pants walked up to the machine he had abandoned, inserted a silver dollar and hit for the Mega Million Payout on the first try. It wasn't clear who or what was making the most noise – the slot machine, the rapturous goat or Bigg, raging at the casino, the machine, goats and *(silently because he was frightened to death of him)* at Imperius for taking him away from his date with destiny. He finally calmed down.

"What are we going to do, Sire..Milord?"

"While recovering from my injuries, baboon, I have hatched another plot to wreak vengeance on Octavius Bear and his crew of cronies. But first, we have some Animal Resources work to do. We must find a replacement for Chita. However, this time, the candidate, while intelligent, must be malleable and capable of being subjected to my will, without question."

"That sounds like me, Milord!"

"Nice try, baboon! But no, you are needed in your critical role of mindless thug for which you are ideally suited."

"Thank you, Milord."

"No, I misjudged Chita. I should have recognized that as she grew more independent and rebellious, she was also becoming a threat to the success of the

Black Quack Gang. Never again! No more Mister Nice Duck! Look, this show lounge seems deserted. Let's sit in here and I will outline what I have in mind."

In fact, the semi-darkened show lounge was not quite deserted. Sitting on a bar stool near the far end of the stage, nursing a kelp juice cocktail, was the most dejected looking otter you never wanted to meet. He was surrounded by all sorts of theatrical paraphernalia and was wearing black rimmed glasses and a short cape. On the bar sat a high silk hat with a rubber chicken sticking out of the top.

A voice from backstage was shouting, "…and don't bother coming back. Magician? Hah! Illusionist, my third tentacle (?!) The only thing you know how to make disappear is an audience."

The otter slumped on the bar, looked down into his bag, pulled out a pistol, held it to his head and shot himself…with a bouquet of flowers. "I can't even kill myself right!" he sobbed.

Imperius turned and was about to leave the room with Bigg. He stopped short. His super IQ brain was having an epiphany *(or reasonable facsimile thereof)*. Could it be? Had his search ended before it had even begun? It was worth a moment of his time. Anything was better than having a conversation with the baboon.

He waddled-limped over to the crestfallen *Lutra Canadensis* and said, "Buy you another drink?"

Taking off his owl-like glasses to wipe his tears, the little mammal looked over at the duck and then, taken aback, stared open mouthed at Bigg.

"Oh, don't let my associate frighten you, my friend. He dresses like that to make people believe he is a famous Latin American generalissimo. Here in Reno, everyone has an idiosyncrasy or two."

It wasn't the combat fatigues that worried the otter. It was the teeth, girth, beady eyes and overall size that set off warning alarms in his head. This guy looked fierce. But what the hell, a minute ago wasn't he trying to kill himself? Who cared if he was going to be mugged? *(And this hombre was definitely a mug.)* The duck, on the other hand was another story. Was this a case of the classic rich bird with his fearsome bodyguard?

"Oh well," he thought, "one last drink before I depart this vale of tears. Especially if someone else is paying for it!"

"Sure, why not? I'm drinking kelp juice and vodka."

"Bartender, another round for my friend here," said the duck, "and I'll have a Singapore Sling." Imperius is in reality Doctor Yu-Aul-Kum, an Oriental genius geneticist who in his natural (?) state is a Mandarin Duck. He still holds on staunchly to his Far Eastern traditions of food and drink.

Bigg barked, "I'll have a Cuba Libre."

"My name is Milord Mallàrd *(accent on the last syllable),* and this is my associate, Commandante Babaloo. We are theatrical entrepreneurs. I am from England. He is from Ecuador. Each year we tour the top American show cities - New York, LA, Chicago, Las Vegas, Reno, Omaha, Hoboken - searching for new acts to highlight in our worldwide touring review – '*Isn't It Beastly?'* I'm sorry we missed your act, but we happen to be in search of an illusionist to round out our talent roster. Am I mistaken? Is that not your profession?"

"I used to think so," said the otter, "but after being fired from five jobs in four days, a little bit of doubt is creeping into my psyche."

"Oh, well," said the duck, "not to worry. Even the Great Whodunit wasn't an overnight success. If you have the basic talent, all it takes is some careful management from an experienced source to polish up your act and of course, a strong will to succeed on your part."

"I have to succeed! All river otters are born entertainers. Some of the greatest clowns, comedians, magicians, jugglers and acrobats are in my family tree. Perhaps you knew of my uncle, Otterino. He could open and eat twenty oysters while juggling them as he slid down a waterfall blindfolded. I can't go back to my folks and tell them I'm a failure. I just can't."

"Well, by sheer good luck," said Milord, "the solution to your problem may be at claw, Mr…er. What is your name?"

"Hairy, Hairy Otter!"

"Well, Hairy. For a start, I think we just might want to change that name. No one could possibly be successful with a handle like that. No wonder you have lost so many jobs."

"What do you suggest, Lord Mallàrd?"

8

"I'm not sure yet. Let's leave that for the moment and plan how best to make you a huge success and make us all lots of money."

"Si," said Commandante Babaloo, "lots of money is good."

"By the way," said the duck, "I should explain our temporary disabilities. I fell off my pony while playing polo and the Commandante fell off a stool while playing the slot machines."

Imperius' brain was running at hyperspeed. Here was the chance to prove that all his genetic experiments were not in vain. As we noted above, as Dr. Yu-Aul-Kum, he was a former scientist at the Pan Asia Institute for Avian Advancement. A brilliant chemist, geneticist, physicist, biologist and psychiatrist, he devoted his early life to the enhancement of beastly brains.

Mocked by his fellow scientists worldwide, shunned by the medical and professional journals and threatened by government functionaries, Dr. Yu-Aul-Kum fled to the highlands of Nepal with his adoring mate and fellow scientist, Lee-Li-Li, to gain inspiration from the Dalai Duck. There, in desperation, he began performing experiments on himself, using a body and mind altering serum he had developed. Just as he believed he was about to achieve total success, Lee-Li-Li, fearful for his life and sanity, swallowed their entire supply of the serum, sacrificing herself to prevent his self-destruction. The serum worked, expanding her intelligence by a factor of 5000, but the overdose burned out her avian brain, and she died in his wings.

Crushed by the loss of his one true love and enraged at the world and science in particular, he re-applied himself feverishly to perfecting the serum and succeeded in creating a genetic change in his nature that turned him into Doctor Imperius Drake – super intellect and arch fiend. Perhaps the most intelligent animal on the planet but also the nuttiest and the most egotistical! Each time he takes the serum, this enhanced state lasts only a few weeks and he then reverts to his Oriental origins, a meek but still maniacal Mandarin. Now, to further confound the reader, he was posing as the British Milord Mallàrd. *(If this is confusing, you can get a scorecard by writing to the publisher.)*

Thus far, he was the only one on whom his serum worked. In the process, he had succeeded in creating a series of very smart but unfortunately, very dead experimental subjects. His dreams of world *(nay, universal)* conquest depended on his ability to develop a race of über-animals with five digit IQs but virtually no independent wills. He had been at his experiments full time for the past several years *(when he wasn't plotting to kill off the entire genetic sciences community)* and he had reached a point where he felt confident he could begin subject trials again. The secret was in generalizing some basic gene chains in the subject before using the serum. Individuality was fatal.

In fact, he had planned to use the serum unmodified on the traitorous Chita who gave him away to Octavius' buffoons. It would have killed her but before it did, she would have become brilliant enough to know that her independent spirit was her fatal flaw. Poetic Justice! Unfortunately, she had escaped before he had the chance to wipe her out. He had heard she was in a terrible auto wreck while trying to flee, but he never learned whether she was alive or dead.

This otter was a different case. Fundamentally, quite intelligent like all members of his species and not at all aggressive. They live in fun-loving families, not like the solitary cheetah. Could he modify his serum and Hairy Otter's genes to create his first super-mammal? It was worth the try. Imperius had nothing to lose but a little time and some serum. And as for the otter, easy come, easy go. He probably was a lousy magician.

"Now, my dear Mr. Otter, I am willing to take you under management and help you establish a new and spectacular career, but you must be willing to put yourself entirely in my wings. I can be a harsh taskmaster, but you will emerge a superstar. Do you agree?"

"What have I got to lose? I wasn't doing anything important anyway."

Where had the duck heard that before? "Oh, by the way, I think we have a new name for you. Otto – yes, Otto the Magnificent. Come, let us go! We have places to be and things to do!"

As they skittered, walked and waddled their way out of the casino, they did not notice the watchful gaze of a Kodiak bear who was dealing blackjack in one of the pits.

Chapter Two

Also known as Red Deer and Wapiti,

You won't find many Elk in a city.

But in this case, you see,

He's the Churchill JP.

Take it up with the Fauna Committee!

Whiiiiine!! Shreeeek! Thump! Rooooar! *(This last supplied by the flight crew along with the reverse thrusters.)* Belinda, Bearnice *(co-pilot)* and Bearyl *(flight engineer-navigator)* looked out over the droop-snoot of The Aquabear, the last Concorde SST in service and cheered. The two hundredth flight by this crew without a miss or a mishap! The SST was a special favorite in Belinda's opulent collection of toys and she and her polar bear flight crew enjoyed taking the venerable jet through maneuvers the manufacturers never envisioned.

They also enjoyed the stares the sylph-like aircraft got every place it went. Not only because it was still flying. *(Its former hangar-mates were all in museums or scavenged for parts coveted by collectors including Belinda.)* But also because of its livery! A running polar bear graced the white fuselage just aft of the cockpit windows; the tip of the droop-snoot nose was painted black in the shape of a polar nose *(pointed but what the hell!)*; on each side of the rudder was a portrait of Belinda complete with bearonial coronet, and four paw pads were painted on the underside of the wings fore and aft. ID letters BBBB-NB. *(Bearoness Belinda Béarnaise Bruin - nee Black.)* And just in case you were still wondering what this Phlying Phenom was, the name "Aquabears" was printed on the fuselage over the cabin windows in art deco fonts. Show-biz at Mach 1.5!

In the passenger cabin were Octavius Bear and eight members of the Aquabear Revue, retired polar show bears who had been performing with Belinda at the *Genius of Genetics 2014* convention finale in Las Vegas. They were all a bit miffed at having their act upstaged and curtailed by Imperius Drake's mega-assassination attempt, but it made for good publicity, material for their scrapbooks and more importantly…they had been paid! Now they were being taken home or to connecting airports but the first stop was Winnipeg International Airport to let Belinda and Octavius off.

Those two were heading for Churchill and a little R & R *(Romance and Reminiscing)* while they watched the annual Polar Bear Migration. Octavius and Belinda Black *(Polar bears have black skin but translucent fur that reflects the light and gives them their snowy white color.)* first met during one of those treks when she was a juvenile and he was doing post-doctorate studies on the polar species. Love bloomed but was promptly stifled by Belinda's mother, Beartha Black, who set the wheels in motion for Belinda to ultimately become Bearoness Belinda Béarnaise Bruin *(nee Black)*.

Belinda Béarnaise *(A white sauce! Clever, huh?)* as she was known in show bear circles became the leading "aqueuse" with the Aquabear review "Some Like it Cold." A dazzling beauty who was also a spectacular diver, swimmer and dancer, she charmed her way into the heart of Bearon Byron Bruin, a rich Scottish playbear, who bought the review, lock, stock and swimming pool and made Belinda its star. They married, courtesy of Bel's pushy mother and much to Octavius' despair, and lived out a short marriage of luxury and opulence until the Bearon was killed in a skiing accident doing a commercial for Pola-Cola. Belinda has since been living the life of a Merry Widow, occasionally reappearing with the original cast of the Aquabear review to perform for charity or some other worthy cause. It was at one of the reappearances that she and Octavius renewed their mutual interest. They have crossed paths a number of times since, most recently in Vegas.

Throughout this northward trip, Octavius had been stretched out on an oversized mattress on the floor of the forward cabin. At nine feet tall standing upright and 1400 pounds, he and the SST had some serious design conflicts. Belinda had modified the doors and cabin arrangements to accommodate his bulk, but it still felt claustrophobic compared to his own cavernous C-5A Ursa Major. As far as Octavius was concerned, the Aquabear's only saving virtue was its speed even if it was banned from flying supersonic over land. *(That speed will come in handy a little later in our tail.)* On touchdown, he was already crawling toward the forward door in spite of the fact that he was supposed to "stay seated until the aircraft came to a complete stop and the captain had signaled it was safe to move about the cabin." Try telling that to a grouchy Kodiak.

Three of the Aquabears were also getting off at Winnipeg and together they created a stir as they all paraded down the jetstairs, through passport control, baggage, customs and out into the reception area.

"What's that Kodiak doing with all those polar bears?"

"Wait, isn't that what's-her-name? You know, the stage and swimming star!" "Wow, they're real beauties."

"So's the Kodiak! He's really hot!"

Octavius and Bel headed to the freight terminal where a modified cargo plane waited to take them on the last leg to Churchill. As they moved toward the building, they could see and hear the SST taxiing back out to the runway. Refuel and go! Bearnice and Bearyl would meet them back in Winnipeg in five days after making a few stops to let off the rest of the Aquabears, and calling at the Bearoness' castle to refresh all their respective wardrobes. Then on to Cincinnati and the Great Bear's mansion, estate and his other assorted arcane and esoteric structures.

*****

Churchill, Manitoba: The Great Polar Bear Migration was on!! The ice was forming on Hudson Bay, and over a thousand bears were on their way to the polar happy fishing grounds. Historians say that there had been a time when the bears made the trek on foot. There are old stories and photos to bear this out. Today a few hardy souls, mostly macho males, still attempt it the old way, but right now Churchill was filled with Tundra Buggies each carrying about 10-12 of the majestic ursines and creating major traffic jams in the process. Rescue helicopters piloted by Siberian Huskies scoured the ice and snow-covered "roadways" looking for breakdowns and hazards while transmitting best route information to the Buggy drivers.

What had been lost in primitive splendor was being made up in good ole fashioned tour bus high jinks. Imagine hundreds of roaring voices in twelve-part harmony, singing out, "The Bear Went over the Mountain." Polars are solitary animals except when they have cubs or are migrating. Then the sociability gene kicks in, and most of it happens in Churchill. Dances, games, mock battles, some romancing and of course chasing after stray cubs were all the order of the day as the buggies paused for a brief time at Migration Central before continuing to the ice floes. Two months of ursine Mardi Gras tucked into a year of bleak, windy, snow-covered cold.

Insanity, noise and frolic held sway. Belinda and Octavius gazed at this exhibition in disappointed nostalgia for the quieter and more romantic times. A Canada Lynx sidled up to them selling souvenirs and hawking a list of the best restaurants. Octavius shook his head. "Not like the old days, is it, Bel?"

"Not at all, Tavi! I wonder if your research station is still here."

"It's probably a snack bar."

"Well, it's still nice to reminisce even if schlock is the order of the day."

"Except, we didn't come here just to reminisce."

"True, Tavi! I wonder where my favorite aunt Bella Donna is. She is hot stuff. She should have been an Aquabear or a standup comedian. She and my mother, Beartha, were twins, but Donna always claimed she was ten seconds older. She could always twist my mother around her paw except of course, when it came to getting me hitched to Byron. Donna didn't like Byron much. 'Take away his money, smooth talk and good looks,' she used to say, 'and what have you got?' Of course it was his money, smooth talk and good looks that had my mother's tongue hanging out. And I was too young and subservient to push back. Oh well, water under the ice floe! Donna's Tundra Buggy was supposed to arrive at noon, but I don't see any sign of her."

"All you polar bears look alike to me!"

Belinda swatted the Great Bear with her paw and said, "Well, if that's the case, go ahead and take your pick. I don't suppose you've noticed how much attention you're getting from the female migrators."

"It's just because I'm bigger than they are. Somebody once told the polars they were the biggest ursine species, and they believed it. I guess they never saw a Kodiak."

"Especially an out-sized Kodiak!"

"Now it's my turn to be offended. Who's that bear waving frantically at us? The one with the big purple floppy hat."

"Aunt Donna! Over here! *(Thump, thump, thump!)* You darling, it's so good to see you again."

"And you too, sweetheart. How's my favorite niece?" (*Polar hugs as only polar bears can hug.*) "And this must be Octavius! My, aren't you a handsome male. One gets so tired of white, white, white. And you <u>are</u> bigger than us! Well, Belinda always did things in a big way. So, you two are getting married. And imagine me as the Sow of Honor! I wonder what Beartha would say. She did so love being mother of the bride the last time. I heard about it for months. It's a shame about her accident. But she always was Type A. Things were Beartha's way or no way. Nobody could tell her not to climb that iceberg. So, *(turning to Octavius)* who and where is the Best Male?"

"The 'who' is Wallingford Penniped. Professor Wallingford Penniped! My university mentor. He was the only walrus on the faculty at Kodiak U. Wonderful animal. One of the few who knew more than I did when I was there. He now holds the Universal Ursine Industries Chair of Faunapology at KU and is also Dean of the School of Animal Sciences. I owe him a lot, and I couldn't think of anyone I'd prefer to be my Best Male. The 'where' is currently an open question. He might be waiting for us at City Hall."

"Do we have all the paper work, Tavi?"

"Everything we could do beforehand."

"Belinda, why aren't you dressed in a bridal outfit? You can't be going like that. I don't care if you are a widow."

"Aunt Donna, this is going to be as quiet and discreet a wedding as we can arrange. No splash, no smash, no sash! We'll explain when we get to City Hall. Is that it, Tavi? The building with the statue of the walrus outside."

"That's not a statue, that's Wally. Professor Pennipen. Wally!" he roared.

"Well," said Bella Donna as the echoes of Octavius' roar ricocheted off buildings, Tundra Buggies and snow piles, scaring a few cubs in the process. "So much for quiet and discreet."

The walrus stopped swinging his head from side to side and stared off in the direction of Octavius' voice. "Poor Wally. Terribly nearsighted. I think his tusks cause him to squint."

"Octavius m'boy. So you *are* here! Would have been a shame to swim all the way over here and miss you!"

"You swam from Kodiak Island?"

"Oh, no! I flew. I just went out for a swim this morning before coming over here. Is this the delightful Belinda?" he said, peering at Bella Donna.

"No, Professor Penniped. I'm Belinda's aunt, Bella Donna Black, but thank you for the compliment. This is Belinda, the Blushing Bride."

"Ahhh, you're lovely, my dear! Octavius, for all his faults has always been a discriminating connoisseur of ursine beauty. Best wishes to you both and congratulations to you, m'boy."

"Thanks, Wally and thanks for agreeing to be my Best Male."

"Wouldn't have it otherwise, m'boy. Besides, in a way, you are my employer."

"Now, Wally, you know that endowment is granted by an objective committee. I supply the money. They decide on the recipient. But I can't think of anyone more deserving."

"Have it your way, m'boy, but the idea of your not making your opinions heard is a bit difficult for this old walrus to swallow. You have never been known to be diffident."

Gales of laughter from the two polars. Sheepish (?) grin from Octavius.

"But I have a surprise for you, Octavius. I didn't travel here alone." He gestured toward a large glass door and through it came a beautifully coiffed and outfitted female Kodiak. Juno Bear was making an entrance.

"Mom," roared Octavius, "you came. I thought you were afraid to fly."

"I am, Tavi," she snorted through the layers of male macho fur that enveloped her. Kodiak bear hugs are something to be seen. "But I'm even more afraid of missing an event I never thought would happen. Imagine you getting married after all this time. Florence *(Juno's arctic fox maid)* is beside herself with excitement, but she absolutely refuses to get on anything that isn't firmly attached to the ground. Wally helped me all the way. I took a sedative and he held my paw and here I am. But introduce me to your exquisite fiancée."

"Mom, meet Bel! Bel, meet Mom!"

"You always were one for flowery introductions." Bel and Juno said in accidental unison. More hugs and laughter. "Please Bel, if 'Mom' is uncomfortable, feel free to call me Juno."

16

Belinda said, "All right, Juno! We all have a lot of getting acquainted and reacquainted to do and Tavi and I have arranged for a post-wedding luncheon at the Two Seasons Churchill. I think we're keeping the Justice of the Peace waiting."

"Before we go in," said the Great Bear, "there is something we want you to know and keep secret."

"Oh dear," cried Bella Donna, "you're pregnant!"

"Donna, for goodness sake! I am NOT pregnant and I'm well beyond cub-bearing age. Look, you've embarrassed Tavi."

"Not in the least, Donna, but we want you, Mom and Wally to keep our wedding a secret."

"Why, for goodness sake?" exclaimed Juno. "An entertainment legend and a zillionaire crime fighter. I'm surprised this place isn't crawling with paparazzi!"

"That's exactly it! I'm a crime fighter, and if my enemies *(and I have many)* find out about Bel being my mate, she becomes extremely vulnerable, and so do I."

"On top of that, Donna," said Bel, "if Byron's family, the moochers, discover I've remarried, they'll be in the Scottish parliament in a shot trying to relieve me of my title and my inheritance. They'd do anything to get their paws on Bearmoral Castle and the Bruin estate. Some day soon I'm going to drive them all out, but not yet. So are we agreed? This marriage is a secret. It's why we're having it here in Churchill, although we both thought it would be a lot quieter here than it is."

Wally barked, "Most of the year it is. Poor timing, Octavius!"

"Well, we met during a migration. Sentiment overcame sense."

The walrus grinned behind his tusks. The thought of Octavius showing sentiment amused him. No doubt he was as sensitive as any bear, maybe more so, but he spent his whole life making sure no one could detect it. Ah, love!

They padded and galumphed into the rural municipal building and looked at the directory. Justice of the Peace - Hon. Elijah W. Elk. First Floor. In fact, that was the only office on the first floor. The doors were glass with his name in gold script and very, very wide. Of course, to accommodate wedding parties and

17

processions! Knocking on the door with his tusks, Wallingford entered into a large room with seats, pads, a decorative tub or two, a wooden rail and a very large stand-up desk. The seal of Manitoba province as well as the Canadian flag and a pennant that must have been Churchill's banner surrounded the desk. A large picture of the Prime Minister, Wexford Wolverine, stared down at them from an adjacent wall. All very efficient and solemn looking. As the rest of the party filed into the room, staring about, a shrill bugling noise came from behind two huge closed doors to the right of the desk. The doors opened and one of the largest sets of antlers any of them had ever seen, floated into the room. Beneath this outsize rack, a medium sized wapiti emerged covered in a black robe with a folio of papers in his pocket.

"Ah, right on time. Don't see much of that anymore. Welcome, welcome! You must be the wedding party from Scotland and the States. Ms Bruin and Mr. Bear, is it?"

He stared first at Octavius who was clearly the only male bear in the group and then at Bella Donna. She raised her tiny eyebrows at him and gestured to her left with her snout. Second time she was mistaken for the bride. Could this be an omen?

"Ah, and of course, the famous Belinda Béarnaise Bruin *(nee Black)*." If he knew she was a Bearoness, he didn't mention it. And you too are famous are you not, Mr. Bear? I'm surprised your wedding party is so small and that my office isn't overrun by the media."

"Your honor," growled Octavius. "One of the major reasons we have come to Churchill to be married is to keep our marriage very low key for exactly the reasons you mention. Although we are public personas, we want to keep our private lives private…very private."

"I understand fully. Now Ms or should I say Mrs. Bruin, since you have provided documentation that you are a widow, are you a citizen of Canada or Scotland?"

"Both. I have dual citizenship. Canadian by birth. Scottish by marriage. Is that a problem?"

"No, not at all and you, Mr. Bear, were born in Alaska and are therefore American. Any other citizenships for you?"

Octavius shook his head – no.

"And these three gracious beasts are your wedding party and witnesses." Hoof, flipper and paw shakes with Bella Donna, Juno and the professor. "You know," said the JP, "it is truly a pleasure to see a mature and refined couple here in my chambers. During the migration, we get all sorts of wild animals wanting to 'get hitched' after an overnight romance. I supposed I shouldn't complain. So few animals get married at all nowadays. But during the migration, it's worse than Las Vegas. Have either of you ever been to Las Vegas?"

"Yes," said the Bear, "and we're not sure we want to return." Visions of crazy ducks, cheetahs, baboons, ferrets, ray guns, exploding balloons and radiating sapphires.

"Can't say I blame you. Shame what's happening to Churchill although it does pay the bills for the rest of the year when we're down to just a few hardy natives."

Wallingford looked puzzled. "Don't the bears all return? Isn't this a twice a year event?"

"Yes, they return, but not all together. They straggle back in small packs and are so full of fish that their energy level is pretty flat. No, this is the time that has the local sheriff and my office pretty busy. Did you know that some polar bears actually drink hard liquor?"

He shook his head in despair and almost flattened the walrus with his huge antlers. Belinda stifled a giggle, and Octavius took the opportunity to take a closer look at the Prime Minister's portrait. Donna was about to reply, but one look from Belinda and *(wonder of wonders)* she shut up.

"Well, let's get you two married. Does anyone here know any reason why these two ursines should not be wed in legal matrimony? Speak now or forever hold your peace."

Belinda looked around at Bella Donna. She was just mischievous enough to say something but for the second time in as many minutes, she was quiet. Her aunt was not quite the nutcake she used to be. Either way, she loved her. Wallingford snorted in a very negative way.

"Well, then, hearing no objections, do you two promise to remain as mates as long as you both shall live?"

"We do!"

19

"Well, then, under the powers granted to me by the Province of Manitoba, City of Churchill, I this day pronounce you...er...bear and bear. Are there any rings to be exchanged?"

"No, your honor!" There were, but like the marriage, they were only going to be worn secretly.

"Well, now, Doctor Bear, I think it is traditional to hug and lick your bride."

Belinda practically disappeared inside the Kodiak's huge grasp. Donna applauded, Juno began to cry, and Wallingford slapped them on the back with his flippers.

"There are one or two documents to be signed by the witnesses, and we are finished. The very best of luck to both of you. I have another wedding right behind this one. Two arctic foxes. I can't see that one lasting, but that's not for me to judge."

Wallingford came forward with the marriage fee and Donna trundled over to the desk to make her witnessing official.

"Well, Tavi, we've gone and done it. I have to add another "B" to my name. Much as I'd like to, I can't drop the "Bruin" or I'd lose my title and estate. I hope you don't mind if it's Bearoness Belinda Béarnaise Bruin Bear *(nee Black)*?"

"Not in the least, Bel, but you're going to have to add another B to the Aquabear's ID letters. BBBBB-NB"

"Oh, you! Only you would think of that at a time like this. Speaking of time. It's time to take your mother, Donna and the professor to our wedding luncheon. And then we have four more days before we have to return to Winnipeg. I don't think I'm as crazy about watching the migration as I thought I'd be. We'll have to find something else to do."

"Don't worry. We'll think of something."

Chapter Three

The huge walrus has tusks in his head.

Science says he's a sea penniped.

His four flippers are feet.

When he runs, he's quite fleet.

And to eat, he digs clams from their bed.

Juno, Bella Donna and Belinda were all delicately slurping champagne from crystal bowls. Wallingford had managed to slide an open carafe past his tusks and was inhaling the bubbly. Octavius was, as usual, taking great snorts of mead from a white, beribboned keg he had ordered for the occasion. Champagne gave him headaches. Assorted fish, splendidly presented, made up the main course and a tiered fish cake with a brown and a white bear suitably attired took up the center of the table.

This semi-secret celebration was taking place in a locked side room off the main ballroom of the Churchill Two Seasons Hotel. The kitchen staff had no idea who the celebrants were and management *(suitably compensated)* had provided two arctic lynxes as servers *(also suitably compensated)* whom they said could be trusted to keep quiet about the newly married ursines.

So, in this relaxed atmosphere, the five of them chatted, laughed and listened to Wallingford making more and more intricate, literary and arcane toasts as the afternoon and the champagne/mead wore down. Bel, aided, abetted and interrupted by Bella Donna told Juno and the walrus her history, especially relating to the Aquabears. She skirted around her prior marriage and everyone had the good taste to stay off the subject unless it related to her aquatic stardom. With his claws crossed behind his back, Octavius invited Donna to visit the Cincinnati mansion, and Bel promised to provide her transportation in the SST. Donna said she was going to continue on with the migration. *("It may be my last!")* But she still negotiated a rain-check on Cincinnati as well as an invite to Bearmoral Castle.

The same invitation was extended to Juno who decided she didn't seem to mind flying as much as she thought she would. She'd never been to The Bear's Lair and not too terribly reluctantly, acquiesced. *(It may have also been the champagne or the prospect of riding in the Concorde. Who could tell?)*

Wallingford said he had to return to the university. New group of post-docs coming in! Truth be told, once he saw Octavius' labs and development facilities, he doubted he would go back to stodgy old Kodiak U. Just as well to leave things as they were.

As the afternoon melted into evening, Donna excused herself. There was a migration party *(and a hunky alpha polar male)* she had promised to join.

Wally and Juno were also about to leave when Octavius said, "I'd like you two to stay for a few more minutes, if you haven't anything pressing on your schedule."

Juno plumped back down on the couch she had been sprawled on and the walrus unceremoniously flopped on the floor.

Bel looked over at the Great Bear, convinced he had something serious on his mind and said, "All right, Mystery Bear, out with it!"

Octavius looked around the room which had been cleared by the wait-staff *(except for a half-carafe of champagne and a small bit of fish wedding cake)*. "I think I'd be happier discussing this up in our suite, Bel. I assume you two can make it to the elevator." Juno was indeed showing a bit of bubbly after-effect and Wally's eyes were drooping. But then they always drooped. With quizzical glances at Octavius, they paraded out of the room toward the elevators. As usual, the Great Bear, this time with Bel in tow, had to find the freight elevator.

When they had all gotten settled in the suite, Juno looked at Octavius and said, "You are so irritating when you play your detective games. What's on your mind?"

"You are!"

"Me? What did I do?"

"That's what I want to find out. Look, all of you. I realize my wedding day is hardly the time to be doing an investigation, *(raised eyebrow from Belinda.)* but I wanted to take advantage of the fact that Mom and Wally are here

22

together. I trust all of you to keep quiet about what I'm going to tell you. Mom, I need you to tell me again what happened to you during your last hibernation. By the way, is the gash on your hindquarter healing?"

"Tavi," cried Juno, "that's nobody else's business. But now that you've blurted it out, it's doing quite well, thank you."

"What gash?" asked Belinda and the walrus simultaneously. "What happened? Were you attacked?"

"In a manner of speaking, yes, I was."

"All right," said Octavius, "let me give you a little more background. Much against my better judgment, I am getting involved in a situation that, if it develops as I expect, could have a greater and longer lasting impact on our world than any other event or phenomenon in our history."

"Oh," snorted Bel, "just as long as it's nothing important. Tavi, you have the most irritating habit of overdramatizing everything. Here I thought our wedding was the most important event in our lives. We're not married more than a few hours, and you're already upstaging it. Oh, all right! Get it off your furry chest."

"Tavi, couldn't this wait?" asked Juno. Wallingford bobbed his head in agreement.

"No, the fact that you're both here right now makes it important for me to check facts and get an opinion, especially from you, Wally. Now, Mom, didn't you tell me that while you were recently hibernating, you felt yourself wake up in a place that was very much like but not exactly your den and its surroundings?"

"Yes, but I'm still not sure I wasn't just dreaming!"

"Fine! Hold that thought. You were by yourself. You searched around for Florence, your Arctic Fox maid, but she was nowhere to be seen. Wasn't that peculiar?"

"Yes, there are times when I wish she'd disappear, but she's always there."

"You went outside, and again, things were almost the same but just almost."

"My den was different both outside and inside, and the woods didn't quite match, but then I had been asleep for well over a month."

"But then you saw some other bears, not Kodiaks, and approached them. You tried to talk to them, but they didn't seem to understand. Instead, one growled at you, attacked you and chased you away. That's how you got the gash."

"I ran back to my den, bleeding, and collapsed. I guess I went back to sleep again."

"The next time you woke up, was Florence there?"

"Yes, and everything was familiar again."

"While you were having this experience, did you see any other animals besides the bears?"

"Oh, I don't know. A snow rabbit or two. Nobody else."

"Mom, do you know what a *Homo Sapiens* is?"

"Of course I do. I'm an educated sow. Scientists believe an advanced species of animal that stood erect and seemed to have social abilities lived long ago but was wiped out by the Big Shock. They've found skeletons and other ancient remains, but that's all. Isn't that right, Wallingford?"

The walrus nodded his head and then stared at Octavius.

"Mom, do you know what an H.Sap would look like?"

"I've seen scientists' drawings and paintings, but of course, I've never met one."

"Let's get back to your experience. What do you think happened to you?"

"I don't know. I thought it was a nightmare, but I couldn't explain the gash or the blood. I just don't know. But, of course, as usual, I'm sure you have a very simple explanation."

"I may have an explanation, Mom, but it's not simple. But, before I do, let me tell all of you about two other stories. The first involves Agrippa."

Juno threw her front paws up in the air. Wally looked askance, and Belinda looked confused.

"You mean your step-brother, Tavi?"

"None other, Bel! Don't look so skeptical, you two. I realize that Agrippa has a hard time recognizing the truth, much less telling it."

"That's being very charitable, m'boy! Where is he, anyway?"

"Vegas or maybe Reno, Wally. I'm not sure. You can never really tell where Agrippa really is unless he's standing in front of you." *(And now, he thought, I'm not sure even that's enough.)*

"He claims he was a witness to murder. He was dealing cards in a high stakes poker game when one player accused another of cheating; a fight broke out; shots were fired; one player fell dead; the others ran from the room, leaving Agrippa to sweep up and keep a very substantial pot before disappearing himself. Now he's on the run from them. They, no doubt, came to their senses after the dust cleared and want their money back. The police may also be looking for him. I don't know."

Juno spoke. "I hate to say it, Tavi but I'm not surprised. Yes, I am surprised. Surprised it didn't happen years ago. Or maybe it did." She shook her head.

"But, Octavius, what has this got do with Juno being attacked by strange bears in a strange world?"

"Just this, Wally. The group he was dealing poker for were all *Homo Sapiens*. He says he had been hibernating, woke up or thought he woke up still in Reno. It was another Reno, dominated by h.saps. They didn't seem to find it odd that a talking bear would be dealing for them in a poker game. He said that after the shoot-out he ran with his loot, hid out and eventually fell asleep. When he woke up, he was back in his original den. Everything was the way it had been, except he had a large wad of cash in strange currency that he couldn't account for. By the way, Bel, he also thinks he saw Imperius Drake in a Reno casino along with a huge baboon."

"Tavi, your step-brother's life is one long fairy story. I should know. I'm his mother, although he thinks I'm the Wicked Witch of the West."

Octavius decided to let that pass. "Now, if these two cases of hibernation gone astray were all I had, I wouldn't be interrupting our celebration to bring it up. But, a new member of my security team, a wolf named Wyatt Where, had been in the military and involved in clandestine security projects before he recently joined me. One of them was called Project Sleepwalker and run by one of the most secret agencies our government has, or thinks it has. He and a partner had been entering periods of controlled sleep and he claims he's been waking up in other worlds, often populated by H.Saps."

"When he surreptitiously left the agency *(No easy task, he thinks his partner was killed to keep him quiet.)* they pursued him for a while, but then they stopped. I suppose they thought no one would believe his story and that he could no longer 'transfer' without their help. They were wrong on both counts. He is still making transits and he has asked for my help to protect him and to help him research out these other worlds. I'm on the verge of agreeing."

The three merrymakers were dumbstruck.

Juno came back the fastest. "You honestly believe there are one or more other worlds, 'parallel universes,' out there. You even think *Homo Sapiens* may still be alive, kicking and occasionally shooting each other in one of them. Oh, Tavi, you do get involved in some crazy things. And…since I seem to have made one of these 'transfers' as you call them, I suppose you want my help in your research."

"Exactly, Mom."

"Well, what the hell, I wasn't doing anything important, anyway."

"Wally, I need your sage advice and assistance, and Bel, I couldn't get involved in a project like this without letting you know."

The walrus squinted, half-rumbled and half-barked, slapped a flipper on the floor and said, "You're right, of course! If it's true and that's a big 'IF,' our world is in for another Big Shock. Of course, I'll help. Can't think of any project that would top this. Besides this mysterious agency you mentioned, who else knows about this?"

"That's the problem. I don't know, and I'm not sure how to find out without starting a major panic. I think the Business *(that's what they call themselves)* believes it has a tight lid on it. They know that Wyatt and I are aware of this phenomenon, of course, but they also think they can control us. Not likely! The other question is: How many hibernating animals are sharing or have shared the same experience as Mom or Agrippa? If hibernation brings on this transfer process, controlling transfers is a lost cause."

Bel raised her residual eyebrows and said, "Octavius Bear, only you could tell a girl on her wedding night that we may end up in another universe. Well, that certainly tops anything Byron ever offered me. Is all this going to happen immediately?"

"No, unless the inhabitants of this other world…"

"Or worlds," interjected Wallingford.

"…or worlds become aware of us, too. Or some other hibernating animal in our world sets off a major blowup. So far as we know, transferring seems to be a limited one- way process. But we actually know very little. And the Business isn't sharing. They want Wyatt and me to share. I don't think *Homo Sapiens* are here yet. After all, they would stick out like a sore paw in our universe."

"Provided they weren't disguised," said Bel, as usual, having the last word.

Chita

Chapter Four

Howard Watt is a young Ph.D.

He's as bright as a mammal can be

But like all porcupines,

He is armed with sharp spines.

So I won't let him sit next to me.

Rio de Janeiro:

The day Carnaval formally begins. And we are here! We being my porcupine friend and associate, Dr. Howard Watt and I, Mauritius Meerkat. We are in Rio on a very well deserved vacation. At least we were until we heard from Octavius, who had just returned to Cincinnati from his romantic interlude with the lovely polar bear Bearoness Belinda Béarnaise Bruin *(nee Black)* in the icy wilds of Churchill, Canada. It was there they had first met, lo, these many years ago. *(Don't say that to the Bearoness-showbear. She's sensitive about her age.)* I learned later that their re-inflamed romance chilled a wee bit with Bel trying to convince Octavius to give up his dangerous livelihoods and retire with her to her opulent Shetland Islands retreat, Bearmoral Castle.

He in turn, has been attempting to get her to move into his mansion in southwest Ohio and join in the fun. They hit a stalemate and agreed to visit each other much more frequently but that was as far as either was willing to compromise their individual lifestyles. When ursines get set in their ways…wel,l anyway! *(Editor's Note: Little did Maury know!)*

As I said, Howard and I had decided to take a vacation after everyone else had taken theirs. Frau Schuylkill and Colonel Where had gone trekking through Transylvania and they had come back spookier than ever. Now it was our turn to chill out. But this morning, we got a call from the Great Bear telling us to stand by for a visit from Inspector Bruce Wallaroo, who was coming over to meet us from Bolivia where he been on a case.

My first adventures with Octavius and Bruce began when I was picked up *(literally)* by the Great Bear on Mauritius while I was playing lookout for several of my family members who were trying to acquire expensive jewelry on the No Pay Plan. Because I was a little kid *(and no doubt, my soooo cute face and long tail helped!)* Octavius decided to listen to my pleas for mercy and set about making me his personal redemption project. I came to the States with him *(I had a choice??),* and rapidly discovered that working with the good guys, especially a very rich good guy wasn't a bad way to spend the rest of one's life. Besides, with my limited but dramatic experience as a criminal, I could think like and anticipate the bad guys. Sometimes! I have now established myself as a skilled crime fighter. Of course, my Meerkat mob back on Mauritius now refuses to acknowledge my existence.

The Inspector, a top flight Australian criminologist and law enforcement officer is on secondment to the International Fine Arts and Jewelry Protective Squad. Since his last assignment, protecting the Deep Blue Sapphire at a Chicago museum show, had not been an unmitigated success *(to be kind)* we fully expected he was going to switch *(or be switched)* to some other unit. Howard and I aren't sure why we're getting together with him. Well, even if we have to go to work, Rio is a great place to do it.

We had already gotten caught up several times in the Banda de Ipanema parades and had managed to get our appendages on several tickets for the Samba Parades. We figured Bruce, being who and what he is, would go crazy at the celebrations. Bruce quite literally cannot sit or stand still. Brilliant though he may be, his incessant bouncing coupled with his unintelligible Strine vocabulary and accent doesn't make for a soothing atmosphere. Octavius has him physically restrained before he will let him into his laboratories. Frau Schuylkill has him on her permanent hit list because of the shambles he always makes of the rooms in the Bear's mansion when he is unfettered. Much as I love the guy, small doses of the Inspector are the best medicine.

While we were busy during the Ipanema parades trying to figure out who were the real males and females and who were in drag *(it's not easy).* Little did we know that soon, we would be right back in the middle of yet another puzzling predicament.

Bruce was to have arrived at our hotel by 5 PM, but that hour came and went and no Wallaroo. There aren't that many evening flights from La Paz to Rio, and it was getting to be time for us to go down, have dinner and head for the Sambadrome and watch the festivities. So we left him a message at the desk telling him where we were and that we had a ticket for him – "Call us on your cell phone!"

Nine o'clock and the parade was beginning. Still no Bruce. We were getting concerned, although the Inspector was a formidable marsupial and could certainly take care of himself. The initial wings of the first featured Samba School were making their way through the runway. The dancers and music gave new meaning to the word, "resplendent." As is generally known, the males of most animal species are more colorfully and elaborately hued than their female counterparts.

This time, it was fun to see the ladies catch up and often go them one better. Jungle cats with iridescent stripes and spots; birds with feathers nature never gave them; a group of chimps dressed up as zebras; a group of zebras dressed as soccer umpires; a collection of outlandishly attired marsupials bounding in every direction to the incessant beat of the samba drums, and one of them looked a bit familiar in spite of a yellow, orange and green ruffled skirt and a hat with a huge basket of fruit that teetered precariously with every soaring leap and skittering jump.

I turned to Howard and pointed. "Look at that hefty dancer bouncing off the light poles. Is that who I think it is?"

Howard's quills went into automatic alert. He stared and then, "It's Bruce! I swear it's him. Do you think he's working undercover?" This assessment wasn't as idiotic as it may seem at first glance. Inspector Bruce Wallaroo was just the animal to disguise himself among five or six thousand dancers in front of several hundred thousand cheering, singing and dancing spectators and then make a complete spectacle of himself.

We were torn between trying to meet up with him at the dispersal area or to stay and watch the rest of the show *(which would run until dawn)*. The show won out. We'd rouse him at the hotel when we got back - assuming he got back.

Music, noise, cheering, fantasy raised to the power of "n." On and on! I was actually beginning to feel exhausted and I looked over at my prickly friend to see how he was holding up when a paw rested on each of our necks. "G'day Maury, G'Day Howard, nice to see you having a happy. Come on, we need to talk." Guess who!

He was out of his costume except for some bright red makeup he forgot to wipe off his nose and a banana wedged between his ears. As we worked our way through the crowd, it was impossible to have a continuous conversation. *(I was going to say a "sensible" conversation but with Bruce Wallaroo, sensible conversations are rare indeed. As I have done in our previous episodes, I will translate his foot-thick Strine into American English for you. No, no, don't thank me. It's part of the service. I myself am fluent in English, French [the Isle of Mauritius] and Dutch-Afrikaans [my Boer upbringing]. Strine does not come easily to me, but then nothing the Inspector says or does comes easy.)*

We finally worked our way out of the "madding crowds" and headed down a street that seemed to specialize in all night bistros. "I need a beer," said Bruce, "In fact, I need a lot of beer."

We settled down at a table just inside the door of a likely looking place and looked around. One or two couples were staring at each other, oblivious to everyone and everything. A rock group was up on an infinitesimal stage disassembling their amps and other gear and a tired looking waiter strolled over and asked the Portuguese equivalent of "What'll ya have??"

Bruce signaled for beer, Howard wanted a scotch and soda, and I had a hell of a time trying to order a fermented coconut milk VSOP. I finally settled for a beer. "Now, I said, "What is going on here?"

"Well, Maury and Howard," he said, "It's a long story." *(They always are.)* "I'm working undercover."

"In front of half the population of South America?" I squeaked.

"Pretty clever, eh? There's a whole Samba School of marsupials here, and my cousin, Jose, is the Grand Marshall. I just joined in the fun. We were the ridgy didge, rip snorters, if I do say so myself."

"But why?" said Howard, "and what were you doing in Bolivia?"

"All in due course, my spiky friend, all in due course. *(Oh great, Wallaroo had been reading Fetlock Holmes, the Great Horse Detective, again.)* But all right, let's dispose of your second question first. What was I doing in Bolivia?"

"That's what I asked," said Howard who had spent less time with the Inspector than I had and was prone to get irritated with him a bit more quickly.

Quill elevation: 30 degrees and rising. It might be interesting to watch a fight between them. Bruce had the mass and the agility but Howard could be devastating with his quills. Right now, my job was to make "nice-nice" all around.

"Bruce," I said, "it's late. We're all tired. Just give us the Page Three version."

"Well, the powers-that-be were understanding but not too pleased with the permanent disappearance of the Deep Blue Sapphire, and we agreed all around that a different type of assignment for me might make sense. I'm now in Industrial Counter-Espionage and Intellectual Property Protection. *(These international law organizations can never come up with short titles.)* And I'm about to start a case here in Brazil, and I may need your help. Oops, looks like I answered your first question first after all, Howard."

"Inspector!!!"

"Any road, on the way here they asked me to stop by in La Paz and clean up a little dust-up at the Archeological Museum. Seems a tenth century Indian idol had gone missing. Last week, it disappeared along with a young curator boar. Big flap! Bolivian police called in! My lot called in! They in turn, ask me to take a side trip to La Paz on my way over from Sydney."

"Turns out, the curator had been examining the idol in his office on a weekend when he was taken with an attack of swine vesicular disease. He locked the statue in his desk and ran out to take a taxi to the nearest hospital. He almost died! No one knew where he or the statue was until he regained consciousness. He's OK. They found the idol safe and sound, and once again Bolivia has its Little Tin God."

Groans! Howard wasn't sure whether he was having his leg pulled or not. He looked at me, but I had only been half listening. Something about that rock group breaking down their gear had attracted my attention. Actually, <u>one member</u> of the band had attracted my attention. The name emblazoned in black and orange across the bass drum said "The Spotted Band." They all seemed to be wild cats, and sure enough, each one had a pelt patterned with rosettes or spots. But one of them was wearing a large diamond collar and looked very, very familiar. I nudged Howard and Bruce and nodded toward the bandstand. Bruce caught it right away but Howard was in the dark.

"Chita," I whispered.

"Rightcheare, Maury," said Bruce.

"Yeah, she's a cheetah, so what?" said Howard.

"Not a cheetah, Chita!" For a brilliant scientist, Howard could be awfully dense at times.

"The Chita?" he blurted aloud.

The cat on the stage heard him, looked over at us and then turned away sharply. But she knew and we knew that her cover was blown. I wondered what she would do. The other three members of the group continued to store their cables and mikes. She turned in our direction and just stared. Face down time! Bruce was the last one of us to see her alive but she had been unconscious at the time. I was the last one she had actually spoken with, and she didn't know Howard from short left field.

We got up from our table and walked toward the stage. I spoke first: "Hello, Chita! Long time no see. You're a long way from home." *(Count on me for clever repartee.)* She looked at me and then Bruce and then back to me. She yawned, showing her impressive and beautifully kept teeth.

"I don't suppose there's any point in saying you've mistaken me for some other cat?"

"Not really." said Bruce.

She looked over at Howard. "Who's your cute friend?"

I introduced them, and then she looked at Bruce and said, "I hope you're not going to try to arrest me or some other stupid wallaroo trick like that."

Wallaroo and I stared at each other and then her. Bruce spoke, "Well, milady, you certainly have a trail of open arrest warrants as long as that tail of yours."

"I'll bet you don't have any with you that would convince the Rio Police, and I wouldn't try extradition, if I were you. I'm legally mated to a very wealthy puma. He's a native Carioca and that makes me a Brazilian national. You can't extradite a national."

Truth be told, Bruce and I, in a peculiar way, liked this larcenous cat. Howard just stared at her, open-mouthed – a not infrequent male reaction.

34

"Well," he said, "I guess we owe you one from Las Vegas." *(cf. Octavius Bear - The Open and Shut Case.)*

"What finally did happen in Las Vegas?" she asked, "I was so busy getting out of town. I never got the full story. Nothing disastrous, I suppose. The headlines said a catastrophe was averted by the quick thinking of Octavius Bear and his associates. I didn't think the Bear could think, let along quickly. Where's the Duck? I owe him one big time!"

"We're not sure," I said. "We think he's dead, but we don't have proof."

"If you ever do get proof that he's still alive," she said, staring at me with her burnished gold eyes, "I'll take a major load off your mind. Just tell me where he is and I will take great pleasure in killing him all by myself. He was hiding right there when I had that conversation with you at the hotel, and he and that stupid baboon slugged me and knocked me out after you left. They took me back to the warehouse, and he was all set to wipe me out after he did his number at the hotel. I beat him to the punch."

"So that's what you were doing in the car?"

"Yeah. I escaped, but I couldn't control that red monstrosity, and I ended up in the ditch where the cops found me."

"I flew you back to the hospital," said Bruce, "The State Police had knocked you out again with sedative darts. You were giving them quite a fight."

"Thanks, I guess. I had a headache for a week after that. Those guards in the hospital weren't very bright and when I woke up I got past them and headed for LAX and the first plane overseas."

"You can't go back to the US," I said. "Octavius and every police department in the country, especially Chicago, would love to get their paws on you."

"And you're going to tell them I'm here, right?"

"We'll have to think about that a bit," said Bruce, "but just head Stateside and all bets are off."

"If the duck is still alive and in the States, I'll take my chances on the police, Octavius, you guys and everyone else. As far as I'm concerned Imperius Drake's goose is cooked and I'm the executive chef."

The band had finished packing up and had strolled over to us. "These guys bothering you, Chita?" growled a jaguar.

"No, I know them from way back. But where are my manners? Bruce, Howard, Maury, *(first names, no affiliations, no mention of law enforcement)* let me introduce you to the other members of the Spotted Band. This is Jake. As you can see he's a jaguar and he plays the greatest set of drums this side of the Amazon."

The jaguar nodded but still was giving us the dubious eye.

She continued, "This rather rare specimen is a Himalayan Snow Leopard originally from Karakorum. Leperello was a member of the Animals' Opera Company of Beijing but got into trouble over an opera he wrote. That's why he's here."

"Call me Lepi!" he growled. "I'm really a singer – a baritone – but I also play keyboard. Chita and I share the vocals. We have a couple of singing gigs during Carnaval."

Chita nodded and raised her paw toward the fourth member of the group. "And this is Ozzie. He says he's an ocelot, but we all think he's a closet margay. He plays the Fender Bass."

"Dammit, No way I'm a margay. I'm an ocelot."

Chita suddenly looked up over our heads to the door of the bistro. Standing there silently with his tail flicking slowly was a large and well dressed puma. "Paolo," she growled and jumped off the stage, joined him at the door and went off, leaving us with the remaining three fourths of the Spotted Band.

"I gather that's her mate," I said.

"Yeah," said Jake. "That's Paolo. Big, powerful, rich and not a cat to mess with!"

Bruce for once in his life was not bounding around or hopping up and down in place. His ears and the banana quivered. But he simply sat there, staring out the door with a very strange look on his red-nosed face.

36

Chapter Five

Kodiaks are remarkably tall,

But Octavius outstrips them all.

He stands nine feet at least.

He's a huge, massive beast.

With a paw like a large volleyball.

The hangar crew had just finished unloading sixteen pieces of luggage and two crates from the belly of the Aquabear – the last flying Concorde SST and the pride and joy of Bearoness Belinda Béarnaise Bruin *(nee Black and now, secretly Bear)*. After leaving off all the Aquabears and before coming back to pick up Octavius, Belinda and Juno at Winnipeg, Bearyl and Bearnice had stopped off at the Shetlands and "packed a few things" for the Bearoness. Supervising and/or observing the offload activity were the Bearoness herself, Frau Schuylkill and Octavius Bear. Juno had wandered into the house, sniffing, staring and shaking her head in wonderment. Sonny-boy was obviously doing quite well for himself.

"I'm glad you decided to stay a while, Bel," rumbled the Great Bear.

"Well, it's only for a fortnight, Tavi, but we did promise we'd see a lot more of each other." She giggled that Belinda giggle, driving him up the wall.

"I should hope so!" he muttered.

"Careful, Tavi!"

Frau Schuylkill, in her dual role of aerodrome manager and housekeeper, growled "Welcome back, Herr Bear! I have seen to your mutter's needs. She has a suite on the second floor." And to Belinda, "Meine Bearonin, your rooms are ready. Your luggage will be sent up immediately. If I can do anything to make your stay more pleasant, please feel free to call on me or the rest of the staff at any time."

"Thank you, Frau Schuylkill! You are such a sweet wolf. I hope we can get to know each other better during my stay here. And thank you for providing rooms for my two flight crew members. *(The two drop dead gorgeous polar bears Bearyl and Bearnice – almost but not quite as lovely as Belinda herself.)* As soon as we finish unloading, perhaps you can have your ground crew make room for the Aquabear in the hangar."

As she was speaking, the columned wall of the pseudo-Roman temple that disguised the hangar rolled open. Inside was the Ursine Luftwaffe, Octavius' air force. By moving the Strike Eagle under the wing of the Galaxy, they could roll Belinda's Concorde inside and out of sight. She had just landed the craft on the runway that was cleverly masquerading as an under-construction Interstate By-Pass.

Octavius operated as much as possible in covert mode, sometimes at great expense. It seemed to work rather well. Few of his Southern Ohio neighbors ever took any notice of what was going on in the old mansion by the River. They were used to jets from CVG Airport and seldom paid attention to the fact that an occasional plane seemed to be landing in the woods. CVG Air Traffic Control knew about Octavius and worked with him at the request of the government.

"Well, Tavi," she said as they entered the house, "I'm here. I kept my part of the bargain. Now, I can't wait for you to come over to Bearmoral. I want you to see the last vestiges of stiff upper lip nobility." She curled her lip and wrinkled her snout at him – a move she knew would drive him wild.

"Bel, you know me. I'm a bear of simple lifestyle and pleasures. *(This as he stood in his forty-room mansion furnished in a mode to turn The Hermitage green with envy.)* I'm not sure how I'd fit in with British nobility."

"Octavius Bear, don't you start that again. You promised, and I'm not letting you off so easily. Bearmoral is a nice comfy palace where a bear can just relax. I'm not sure you know how to relax although... *(Bel was aware of Octavius' narcoleptic excursions.)*"

"All right, all right. I am an ursine of my word. I'll come over."

"Good. Now I'd like to freshen up, and then you can give me that full guided tour of your establishment that you've always been promising me. Where are Maury and Howard and the Colonel? I know the Inspector went back to Australia."

38

"The Colonel is running security sweeps over at UUI. He'll be back for dinner. Maury and Howard are in Rio de Janeiro. They were on vacation, but I think that may come to a premature end. Inspector Wallaroo called and said he wanted to meet with them. He's off trying to stop some new international crime wave."

Bel's tiny ears perked up. Next to "jewels," crime was her favorite subject. "Did he say what it was about?"

"No," said the Bear, "he was kind of mysterious. Now, off you go," smacking her on her shapely rump. "What would you like to drink when you come down?"

"Why, Doctor Bear, you are indeed forward. I will have you know that I am a titled gentlebear and am not used to such familiarity. I'll have the usual – champagne and salmon." And off she padded for the staircase.

"There's an elevator, Bel."

"I see it. A girl needs her exercise. By the way, you did say you had an Olympic pool here, didn't you?"

"I did indeed."

The Great Bear returned to his desk and pried open the keg of mead that Frau Schuylkill had left there for him. As you may know, Octavius is a skilled apiarist and manages a large vintage meadery on the grounds of the mansion. Most of that distilled delight gets no further than his own maw, but he does provide a few gallons occasionally to friends or ursine celebrities with whom he's acquainted. Needless to say, honeycombs in a variety of presentations are frequently on the dessert menu. Frau Schuylkill is a cordon bleu chef who caters to the bear's tastes with inordinate skill.

He pressed the talk switch on his oversized desk phone and placed a call to UUI.

"This is Octavius Bear," he roared. The Great Bear thought he had to shout full volume whenever he used the speakerphone. His employees and friends got used to it. Most of the world did not. "Ask Colonel Where to call me as soon as he can. Thanks."

Frau Schuylkill appeared in front of his desk. The she-wolf always had an eerie capability to materialize out of nowhere but since she and Colonel Wyatt

Where, her co-worker and obvious love interest, had returned from a two week vacation in Transylvania, she had passed through uncanny and was well on her way to out-and-out weird.

"I heard you bellow for the Colonel, Herr Bear. Is there anything I can do to assist?"

"Actually, Frau, there is. *(When the Colonel had casually dropped her given name in a recent conversation, we all learned for the first time that Frau Schuylkill was called Ilse. However, Octavius and none of the rest of us could bring ourselves to use it.)* "I would like the two of you to elevate our security here at the mansion while the Bearoness and my mother are staying with us. I have some reason to believe that Imperius Drake is not dead. I know, besides the ray gun, we found not a trace of him nor that baboon of his. That's what's bothering me. There should have been something. Nothing!! And my half brother Agrippa thinks he has since spotted him and Bigg in a Reno casino."

"If he isn't dead, I'm sure he is even more determined to wreak revenge on me after his debacle at Las Vegas. He's already tried once to reach me through Belinda. He'll try again. I'm delighted she's visiting, but I'd be a lot happier knowing where and in what condition he is."

"Where who is, Tavi?' Belinda had padded softly into the room while he was having his conversation with the wolf. "Are you still worried about that horrible duck? Everyone else including the Nevada Police is convinced he was disintegrated in the blast."

"The missiles were powerful and our aim was true, Herr Bear," said the Frau.

"I know, Frau. I know. You and Wyatt did a marvelous job, but we couldn't find a thing, not one lousy tail feather, and I don't know what happened to the baboon. I'm sure Chita's still around somewhere, because she was the one who warned us. I'm less concerned about her."

"Tavi, you're such a worry-wart. Of course, I'm pleased that's it's me you're concerned about but let's have good time these next two weeks. Speaking of which, where's that champagne you promised me?"

Octavius looked at Frau Schuylkill who in turn pointed to a tray of iced salmon and a large, properly chilled, uncorked magnum of Dom Bearignon '78. He was sure that it wasn't there a moment ago. "Is there anything else you would like, Bearonin? Herr Bear, I shall tell the Colonel of your concerns as soon as he calls back. We will be at your disposal."

She disappeared, leaving both bears staring at the space she had just occupied.

"How does she do that, Tavi?"

"Damned if I know, Bel. Something about '*Höchstgeschwindigkeit.*' "

"Huh??"

Hyperspeed! I've been wanting to check with the Colonel to see if he knows, but now I'm afraid he might be able to do it, too. I wonder what happened in Transylvania."

The phone rang. He waited to see if the Frau picked it up. She did. He held up his keg of mead in a toast to Belinda. She in turn daintily raised a crystal bowl of champagne…and they both almost dropped them. The Frau had reappeared.

"Herr Bear, Wyatt, er, the Colonel is on the line and he says it is crucial he speak to you immediately."

"Put him on the speakerphone, Frau." She did. "Octavius here, Wyatt. I have the Frau and the Bearoness here with me. What's that noise?"

"Hello, Octavius, Ladies! I'm here in the mailroom at UUI. A package arrived a few minutes ago addressed to you, Octavius. When they took off the wrappings, the box fell open and a big, black egg started quacking so loud we had to evacuate the mailroom. Is this what I think it is??"

(The Colonel had never actually seen nor heard the Black Quack, the deafening decoy of that dire and dastardly demon, Imperius Drake. He leaves it as his autograph at every crime scene or anywhere he wants to issue a challenge.)

"Yes, it is, Colonel, yes it is! It's the signature of Imperius Drake. He's telling us he's still alive! Dump the thing in the Ohio River. There's no way to turn it off."

The noise of the egg quacking over the speakerphone was almost drowned out in the mansion by the enraged howling of Frau Schuylkill.

"I'd better call in the troops. I hope Maury and Howard are still in Rio. I wonder if Wallaroo is free. There you have it, Bel. No more doubts! He's alive…and dangerous."

Chapter Six

With long whiskers and fur tinted brown

And a face that belongs on a clown,

Hairy Otter's no name

For a beast who can claim

The Magnificent Otto's renown.

Just north of St. Louis near the merge point of the Missouri and Mississippi Rivers sits Pelican Island, an innocuous place, home of a county park and, carefully hidden underground, the North American headquarters of Imperius Drake. Late in the evening, a black hydroplane rumbled up to a dock on the island and disgorged three figures – a river otter, a baboon and a mandarin duck disguised as a mallard.

They had just completed an arduous, high speed journey from the banks of Lake Huron and the Mackinac Straits, down Lake Michigan, through the Chicago Sanitary and Ship Canal and via the Illinois River, into the Mississippi.

Otto the Magnificent had just completed his first great illusion. He convinced the dock master at Pondscum, Michigan where the hydroplane, Miss Lee-Li-Li had been impounded awaiting an auction for unpaid wages and bills, that he was Admiral-in-Chief of the US Coast Guard. They had come to take possession of the speedy craft for use by the CIA. *(Imperius had to abandon the boat during his last adventure, but swore he would recover it, named as it was after his one true and sacred love, now deceased.)*

Weary and jolted by the high velocity river run, they slipped down a cleverly disguised ramp that opened into a large and well appointed lab and living quarters.

"Welcome to the Duck Blind, Otto," said Drake. "This is where Commandante Babaloo and I have our US base of operations."

"Gee, Milord Mallàrd *(accent on the last syllable),* this is impressive, but why would a theatrical entrepreneur want such an elaborate technical setup?"

"My dear Otto, what is theatre today but special effects, computer imaging and illusions? Much of this technology is well ahead of state of the art, and the Commandante and I take special care to keep it from getting into competitive hands. I must congratulate you on your performance as the admiral. Well done!"

"Gee, Milord. I felt a little funny pretending to that old river rat, but if you say the boat belongs to you, I guess it was OK."

"Otto, do you know the many hours, nay, days of red tape we avoided in recovering what is rightfully mine? Think nothing of it. Now for a little dinner, sleep and tomorrow morning, we will begin your training. Come into the kitchen, and we'll see what we can find. Baboon, er, Commandante, tomorrow we shall have to stock up on provisions and necessities."

Bigg headed for the food locker and began tossing things out helter-skelter. "Now, now, Commandante, control that Latin blood. I'll have a small portion of mixed grain and I'm sure our new found friend would like some shellfish."

"I'm not being selfish, Milord," said the baboon. "There's plenty for everyone."

"No you idiot! You must forgive the Commandante, Otto. His English is not always the best. Shellfish – oysters, clams, mussels." He knew the minute he said "mussels" he had gone too far. Bigg immediately dropped into a body builder pose waiting for the applause.

"Here, Otto, let me help you." The otter didn't notice that the mallard was carefully exchanging the clam shells as he finished them and had switched his glass of kelp juice several times. Imperius was gathering DNA samples for his great experiment. "Now, when you are finished, off to bed. You may sleep late in the morning. I have some catching up to do. Paperwork, an experiment or two, but I will see you in the early afternoon."

"Do you have any problem if I go swimming, Milord? I haven't been in a river for quite a while."

"Just as long as you stay undercover, Otto. We don't want our competitors to see you or know this lab is here."

"Oh, we river otters are the stealthiest aquatic mammals there are. We're expert swimmers and divers. I hardly make a ripple when I swim or a splash when I dive. I can move at an average speed of seven miles per hour and stay underwater for up to two minutes. My ears and nose close up and keep me watertight underwater. Swimming really IS something I can do right, even if I'm a klutz at magic."

Imperius was enthralled. Here was a potential he hadn't considered. A very important potential! "Well, Otto, we'll have to make sure we take full advantage of those skills when we begin your training. You remember the Great Whodunit used to escape from tightly sealed containers underwater. Who knows? You may put him to shame."

Otto dragged his paraphernalia off to his room and Imperius turned to Bigg. "Well, Baboon, I think we may have struck gold here."

Bigg looked around the room for a glittering pile of coins. He was still upset about that nanny goat and the slot machine.

"Otto may yet exceed all of my expectations in my war against that infernal bear. By the way, while we were up in Michigan reclaiming the boat, I threw down the gauntlet."

"Did you lose it, Sire?"

"No, Baboon, that is a figure of speech. I stopped by the Pondscum Courier Service and sent a Black Quack egg to Octavius Bear's company, Universal Ursine Industries. I'm not sure where his lair is but UUI will do for the moment. I want him and those other idiots to know that Imperius Drake is still alive."

"So am I, Sire."

"That's as may be, baboon. That's as may be! I wish I had been there when they discovered my quacking herald. Oh, Bear, I will bring you to your massive knees and inflict a fatal wound upon your heart. I swear it on the ghost of Lee-Li-Li. But that's enough frivolity. I must go to the lab and work on my formula for the otter's metamorphosis."

He waddled-limped off, testing his wounded wing as he went. He could flap it. He was recovering, and not a moment too soon. Bigg had piloted the hydroplane from Michigan and brought some attention upon them by forcing two barges and an ore carrier aground. to say nothing of swamping a Chicago Police boat. Fortunately, the hydroplane is one of the fastest crafts afloat. Chita would have handled the helm with much greater finesse. He wondered where Chita was. There was another score to be settled. So much to do and so little time!

Through the night, Imperius analyzed the otter's genetic structure and created a prototype serum that would alter his character and intelligence but *(hopefully)* leave him otherwise intact. The duck would, no doubt, have to make refinements, especially to "breed out" the otter's sense of morality and independence. He must become the duck's slave, superior in every way to all others of his kind *(and most other species, as well)* but subservient to the commands of Dr. Imperius Drake, Ruler of the Universe.

 Tomorrow, he would reveal himself to the otter in his true form, black of feather and black of heart but most of all supreme in intelligence. *(He never seemed to realize that his tragic flaw was his own hubris — an arrogance and ego that again and again had meant his downfall. Fortunately, his enemies were counting on it.)*

Morning came, and Bigg had already polished off half the contents of the food locker for breakfast and was making a shopping list. He'd have to remember to stock up on fish for Otto. Strange what some animals would eat.

A sodden Otto slipped down the ramp, shook himself off and looked over at the Baboon. "Boy, Commandante, that was fun. I haven't had a morning swim like that in months. *(Bigg didn't care for swimming, either.)* I was out for over an hour. Did you know there's a big city down river from here. They have this huge arch on one side. Where are we, anyway? I got completely disoriented on that boat trip yesterday."

Imperius had come out of the lab and was having trouble believing his ears. Did Otto swim all the way down to St. Louis and back in an hour? This was interesting. "Good morning, my boy, we are on an island at the confluence of the Missouri and Mississippi Rivers. That city is St. Louis. You must have been making good time to get all the way down there and back so rapidly."

"Actually," said Otto, "I was just loafing along. It felt good to be in a river again. The best I could do in Reno was a swimming pool. I never even got near Lake Tahoe, much less the Truckee."

"Well," said the duck, "I'll bet all that exercise has given you a big appetite. Here, we have some special fish for you and a tonic to help enhance your coat and whiskers. We want to make you into a matinee idol, you know."

"Gee, Milord, you're certainly taking good care of me. I don't know how I can repay you." He dug into his breakfast with zest, occasionally flipping a fish in the air and catching it in his mouth while sitting up on his tail.

"Oh, don't worry about repayment," said Imperius. "As I told you in Reno, we'll all profit from this venture."

Otto didn't notice them staring at him. For several minutes he didn't notice much of anything. "Gee, this tonic has a real kick, Milord. What's in it?"

Imperius replied, "Oh, all sorts of healthy things. It will take your system a little while to become acclimated to it, but the results will be astounding. Wait and see!"

Suddenly, Otto fell over on his back, his paws held stiff in front of him.

"What happened, Sire?"

"We are not sure, Baboon. *(Back to Imperius-speak and the Imperial 'we'.)* We did not anticipate this strong a reaction. See if he is breathing."

Bigg leaned over the stiffened otter. "I think he's dead, Sire."

"Let us get our stethoscope." He held it to the otter's chest. Not a thump, not a pit-a-pat, not a sound.

"Curses, the formula was carefully worked out, and we mixed it with the greatest precision. He must have had some physical flaw that wasn't apparent. A pity! We were beginning to have great hopes for this one. Drat, this means we'll have to find another subject."

Bigg looked the other way. Somehow, he didn't feel motivated to volunteer.

"Back to the drawing boards, yet again! Start up the hydroplane. We'll tie him in a sack and weigh the body down with a steel anchor and toss it overboard out in a deep spot in the river. We don't want a trace of him to appear for a long, long time."

The engine of the boat was softly rumbling as they *(actually Bigg)* carried out Otto's body and dumped it in the aft hold. Looking around carefully to ensure no one was nearby, they briefly revved up the engine to get away from the dock and then cut it, drifting out into the current. Imperius pulled out a fishing pole and told Bigg to do the same.

"I don't like fish, Sire, and neither do you. Why are we fishing?"

"It's a ruse, Baboon, in case anybody sees us. Now let's drift a little bit further and then you very carefully lift the cover of the aft hold and when we say so, dump the sack and anchor over the side and don't make a splash."

Bigg, amazingly, got it right and the otter's body disappeared into the deep and swiftly running current.

"Now, let's get back to the lab. We must consider our alternatives."

They pulled up to the dock, and Imperius for the first time attempted to fly on his mending wing. He got aloft *(just barely)* and made it out of the boat and onto the dock. "Baboon, hurry and tie up the boat. Bring the keys and unlock the door to the ramp."

Bigg arrived with the keys and rolled up the heavy steel door. Imperius waddled up to an inner door and stepped on a foot reader to open it. He quacked several times to convince the voice print reader. They stepped inside and turned on the lights.

"Hi, where have you guys been? I was beginning to wonder about you." It was Otto. Sitting at the table, munching a fish, soaking wet with a small piece of burlap stuck on one of his ears.

Chapter Seven

Is he mountain lion, cougar or puma(r)?

Is he nasty, or is that a rumor?

But he has this distinction.

He is nearing extinction.

That can impact a cat's sense of humor!

<u>*Rio*</u>

Dawn was breaking, and Chita had just bounded out the door to meet Paolo, a not too savory looking puma. I glanced over at Bruce who was staring at the doorway. He turned away, caught my eye and shook his head gently. Translation: "Not now. We'll talk later."

I turned back to Lepi, the opera star-keyboardist and asked, "Are you guys here every night? We'd like to catch part of your act."

He did some mental calculations. "Yeah, we'll be here two more nights, and then after we do the float in the Samba Parade, we go back to São Paolo. That's where the group is from."

Typical question: "How long have you been together?"

Ozzie chimed in, "The Spotted Band has been around for years. This particular version is only about three months old. Players come, players go. For a while we were a sextet. Now we're down to four, and I doubt Chita will be with us for long."

"Why is that?" asked Howard.

"Lots of reasons. Chick singers tend to float from band to band. She just showed up one night a few months ago, and I suspect she may just not show up some night and that'll be the last we see of Chita."

"You're not crazy about her, are you?" I asked.

"Well, she's a great cat, and she certainly has this distinctive voice – she can run from a scream to a growl like you've never heard before. And she's sure easy to look at. It's just that we have to go through all these rehearsals to bring a new 'talent' on board every time one of us disappears. That, my friend is a big pain in the tail."

Jake did a quick paradiddle with his paws on the table top and barked: "And there's Paolo."

The other two nodded their heads, "Yeah, Paolo!"

"What about Paolo?" asked Bruce, breaking his silence.

"That's what we'd like to know." said Ozzie, "We think he's bankrolling our group, and it makes us nervous. Our manager won't talk about it but we have strong suspicions."

"He showed up about the same time Chita joined us, and suddenly we have these gigs in Rio during Carnaval," said Lepi. "As I told you, Chita and I are singing at a couple of big clubs over in Ipanema, and day after tomorrow, the band is going to perform on a float with one of the biggest samba schools. It's the final night and some acts would kill *(or worse)* to be on one of those floats. We're good, but we're not that good."

"Yet!" That was Jake.

"Yet!" said Lepi and Ozzie together.

"So you think he's the reason for the upswing in your careers?" I asked.

"He's the reason for the upswing in *her* career. We're just along for the ride but what the hell, if he wants to spend money on making the group famous, that's OK with us. The minute she leaves, he'll drop us in the ocean like a sack of kittens."

"How did he get so rich?" asked Howard.

"Don't ask, don't tell," said Ozzie. "All we know is Paolo swings a lot of weight in Rio and São Paolo. Hey, maybe the town is named after him."

Laughs all around. Bruce yawned and said, "Nice chatting with you, mates. We'll be by tomorrow night to hear you blokes. Right now, it's time to hit the swag."

Strange looks from the band. Strine is not taught in most Brazilian schools. We got up and headed for the door. Bruce went over to settle up with

50

the waiter who was dozing near the bar. When he joined us outside, I poked him and said, "OK, Fetlock, what's the big mystery about Paolo?"

Bruce looked up and down the street. Empty except for the three of us. "Paolo isn't Paolo," he said in a low voice as he hopped from one foot to the other. His red stained nose twitched, as did his ears. Somewhere along the line he had lost the banana.

"Well, who is he?" shouted Howard, who was no doubt tired and irritated with Bruce.

"Shhh! That cat, my dear porcupine, is none other than Pontius Puma, a one cat South American crime wave. He's looking pretty sleek and prosperous nowadays but that peculiar way he twitches his tail – one, two – one, two, three – is a dead giveaway. He started out life as a bongo drummer. He could play five drums at one time - one for each paw and his tail doing the baseline. He made it big time by literally taking over the entire South American music industry in a not too legal way. Not a gig gets set, not an act gets booked, not a show gets aired, not a CD or DVD gets pressed without Pontius' say-so."

"So how come the Spotted Band didn't recognize him as Pontius?" I asked.

"He's usually a recluse. Pontius doesn't want be recognized. Too many outstanding grudges against him. I'm surprise he ventured out at all. That Chita must have some attraction. He's also a sucker for Carnaval."

"How do you know all this, Bruce?" asked Howard.

"Pontius Puma is the reason I'm here in Brazil," he replied, "but not for his music industry extortion. The Brazilian Police, if they ever want to, can handle that. Our feline friend seems to be branching out into more global and dangerous fields like stealing high tech weapons information and selling it to the highest bidders."

"Wow, that's a stretch from pushing around piano players."

"Not as much as you might think. Pontius has one of the largest computer networks, disc pressing and distribution systems in the world. To say nothing of his booking agencies and studios. Smuggling defense information in some of his shipments is no problem at all. He gets the data from a ring of industrial spies on his payroll, downloads it to several of his secure storage facilities and begins the bidding. A few million can buy you a special edition DVD with all the how-to's, diagrams and backup data for an advanced hand held rocket launcher."

"Does Octavius know about this?" asked Howard.

"Too right, my quilled friend! That's why Ocko asked you to stay on and work with me."

Stupid question time: "If you know this much about Pontius/Paolo, why don't you just move in and shut him down?"

Bruce sighed wearily, reminding me of how tired I was. Howard looked completely out of it. Fortunately, we had arrived at the hotel. "Maury, m'boy, knowing and proving are two different things. And Pontius has friends in very high places. I think something more dramatic is called for."

I didn't like the sound of that one bit but was too weary to protest. "Goodnight Howard, goodnight Bruce and oh, Bruce…"

"Yeah?"

"Wipe your nose!"

*****

I was chasing three beautiful meerkats dressed in practically nothing down the beach at Ipanema when the phone in my room rang. *(Howard snores, so we got separate rooms.)* Searching for the warbling monster with one eye and trying to get the sleep out of the other, I ended up on the floor, but the noise wouldn't stop. I finally found it and always debonair and suave, muttered, "Hullo??"

"MRAUREE!?" *(Guess who! And full volume!)*

"Octavius, do you know what time it is here in Rio?"

"Yes, you lazy gerbil, it's one hour later than it is here in Cincinnati, and that makes it 9AM."

Well, that ploy wasn't going to work. "What can I do for you," I asked, stifling a yawn *(and nearly choking to death)*.

"Imperius is alive!"

"Octavius, I'm not fully awake, and I'm sorry about that, but I thought I heard you shout: 'Imperius Drake is alive.' "

"I did. He mailed one of his signature black eggs to UUI, and all hell broke loose. He's no doubt coming after us, and we need to close ranks here at the mansion. Bel and my mother are with us and that makes it all the more important that we get together and strategize how to protect them and put him out of business."

"Look," I replied, "Bruce arrived last night. *(I left out the part about the samba parade. The Great Bear is already convinced that the Inspector is a Class A Flake.)* He's up to his floppy ears in that Pontius Puma weapons thing. He's spotted his target already, and we're getting together in half an hour to plot our next moves. Suppose we call you back then, and we can sort this all out."

"All right, I'll ask the wolves to stand by, too. We can have a conference. I'll expect you in half an hour."

And he will. Not thirty-one minutes. Half an hour. I shall have to awaken our merry band. Which I did to great protestations from Howard and imprecations on my head in Classical Strine with a little aborigine tossed in from you-know-who. We agreed to have some food sent up to my room and to meet in twenty-eight minutes.

Twenty-seven minutes later, I started to place an overseas call to the Bear's Lair. Boop, beep, buzz, buzz, beep, beep, boop. Ring, Ring. "You're late," he roared as he snapped on the speakerphone.

"No, we are not late. The phone companies are slow. Bruce and Howard are on extensions here in the hotel."

"You should have accommodated for the phone companies." It was clear that the Great Bear was in a mood and a half. No doubt out of concern for Bel. "Frau Schuylkill and Colonel Where are here with me. Juno, my mother, Belinda and her two crew members are swimming in the pool."

"Hellos" all around.

"So what happened?" I asked.

"Just as I told you. The Colonel was over at UUI headquarters, reviewing security when a package arrived at the mailroom addressed to me. No return address, Michigan courier origination. They took off the wrappings, and the box fell open. It was another one of those Black Quacks. We have two of our mail clerks in a trauma center and some dead catfish at the bottom of the Ohio."

53

"Are you sure it's Imperius and not Bigg? I think we can be sure Chita's not involved. She's here, by the way."

"What??? Nab her, Inspector, and bring her in."

"Not sure I really want to, Ocko. She's really super cranky with that duck and she wants to get her paws on him and tear him apart. The reason she ran off with the Ferrari in Vegas was he was planning to kill her – long and painful, as she tells it."

"So?"

"So, maybe she knows where his hideout is in the States. I'm thinking maybe we let her know he's alive and maybe we can get her to cooperate with us in tracking him down."

Frau Schuylkill interrupted, "Your pardon, Herr Inspector, but she seems like a lone wolf to us. I do not think she will cooperate with anyone if she's that angry. Revenge is very personal. We know." *(Now there was an interesting comment! I wonder if Bruce knows how much he bothers her.)*

"Yer may be right, Frau, but I think we'll take the chance. What the hell, even if she's doing a solo, that's one more way he could get taken out. What do you think, Ocko?"

"I don't trust Chita as far as Maury could throw her, but what you're saying has some logic. Follow your own instincts, Inspector. Now, how soon can you get back here? Frau Schuylkill, the Colonel and I have been enhancing the mansion's security, but Bel is not going to be content to sit around here for two weeks. She and her two crew bears want to hit the Cincinnati night life and won't take no for an answer. Neither will my mother. We could use some more help up here. I don't want to warn the authorities, at least not yet. The Duck will make another move and probably soon."

Howard asked, "What do you make of that Michigan postmark? Do you think he sent it when he was up in Pondscum (*cf. The Open and Shut Case - Volume One of The Case Books of Octavius Bear*) and it just got there? You know post offices, especially in a little town like that."

"No, he knew we would be in Las Vegas. There was no point in sending it here. Besides the postmark is dated three days ago. And it was sent by courier."

"What was he doing back in Michigan?" I asked.

The Colonel spoke up. "I have a theory. He left a very valuable and powerful hydroplane docked up there when he escaped by plane. He might have gone back to reclaim it."

"Good thinking, Colonel," said Octavius, "We'll check with the Michigan police. I believe they impounded the boat."

"That boat fascinates me," I said. "Why does he need a hydroplane, and what was it doing in Chicago when he went after the Deep Blue Sapphire? Do you think he has a base somewhere on the Great Lakes?"

"It could be. It's one place *(a damn big place)* to start looking. We'll check and see if the boat is still in Pondscum, and if not we'll find out if anyone reported seeing it in the last few days. It's not an ordinary boat, so it shouldn't be easy to mistake. Now, about you three coming back."

"Ocko, we're on the verge of making some serious progress on this case down here. I really don't want to walk away from it. In fact, I'm sure the powers-that-be would skin me alive if I did without settling it."

"I understand, Inspector but what about Maury and Dr. Watt?"

Howard spoke up. "Look, Inspector, I'm just about 'Braziled' out. Why don't you and Maury go on over to São Paolo and check out this puma's operation, and I'll catch the next flight back to Cincinnati?"

"Sounds good to me, Howard. How about you, Ocko? We'll come up as soon as we wrap this up. I have a plan that shouldn't take very long."

"Agreed! Doctor, you can help us enhance our security measures with the Colonel and the Frau. Let us know when you'll be arriving at CVG and Maury, keep in touch." Click!

"Well, that's that. Howard, have some breakfast and make your reservations, and Bruce and I will plan out tonight."

Ten o'clock the same night:

The porcupine had long since gone and was no doubt ensconced in a first class seat downing 20 year old Scotch on his way back to the States. The thing I really like about working for Octavius is all the perks. But some perks are better than others.

For example, Bruce and I were back, squashed into the same small table at the same small bistro – The Splenda Loaf – drinking beer. *(I was no more successful tonight in getting a fermented coconut milk VSOP than I was the night before.)* This time however, the place was packed solid and Ozzie from the Spotted Band had to talk to the head waiter about getting us a table, preferably inside the bar.

We'd been drinking and listening to the band throughout their first set. They were good. The beer wasn't. Jake's drums had the place vibrating along with Ozzie's Fender bass. Chita had just finished a smoldering Latin love song and now she and Lepi were doing an up tempo duet that had the audience shouting the refrains. Lepi was having a wild time at the keyboard, and Chita was playing a Gibson Flying V. They were veeerry good! One of these days, I'm going to take up electric guitar if I can find one small enough.

That number brought the set to a close, and the band took a break. I looked around to see if Paolo was in the house, but he wasn't. At least, I couldn't see him. I doubted whether he would make such a public appearance. He probably had a special enclosed box to watch the Samba Parades, one of which was going on right now a few blocks away. Or he might be here backstage, such as it was. Chita and the band came over to our table, working their way through admiring fans and drunks advising them on musical technique. They finally got to us and squeezed in with Bruce and me.

"So you did come," said Jake the jaguar.

"You bet," I said, "and it was well worth the trip." I called the waiter over and told him to put whatever the band wanted on our tab. "You cats are terrific!"

Chita blew out her breath and sagged a little. She put her all into the act, as did the others. "Thanks! Where's your cute little prickly friend?"

OK, here we go! I looked over at Bruce, and he nodded.

"He's gone back to the States. He's a security techie and Octavius needed him to help boost the protection around our base."

"Why, what's the big deal?"

"Well," said Bruce, "he just got a Black Quack in the mail. It seems Imperius is still alive."

"Say that again!!!"

"Imperius survived. I don't know about Bigg."

"I don't give a damn about Bigg." With that she rose from the table and knocking over a waiter and a few patrons, she shot out the door.

"What's that all about?" asked Lepi. "Who's this Imperius?"

"Someone Chita hates very much. I was hoping to get her to work with us on it but I'm not betting on her coming back."

"Well," said Ozzie, looking wistfully out the door, "which of you guys can sing?"

Chapter Eight

They're a beautiful sight to behold,

With their shimmering coats of white gold.

Polars rule in the North.

Over ice they set forth.

But they never seem bothered by cold.

Octavius had just ended his conversation with his Trio in Rio when Belinda and her two crew members padded into his den. They had just finished their swim and were still a bit damp. *(Wet fur on three gorgeous polar bears. His cup runneth over.)* Juno came in, toweling herself off.

"Tavi," said Belinda, "I don't think you've had much chance to chat with my two flight crew members. They were in the cockpit during most of the run to and from Winnipeg. They went straight to bed last night after the trip. Even at supersonic speeds, polar bears get jet lag, even if we don't hibernate." She looked at him archly with a wicked grin.

Octavius stood, all nine feet of him and held out his paws. "Welcome, ladies! Thanks for all your help in making our arctic run possible. The Aquabear's a bit too cozy for a bear of my build but I do enjoy the idea of supersonic speed and luxury. A shame they retired them all."

"All except ours, Dr. Bear, and I think the Aquabear has enough replacement components in it from other ships in the fleet that we can claim that we're flying some parts of all the Concordes ever built. We also have warehouses full of spares and a crew of mechanics who worked with the SSTs when they were in service. The Aquabear should be in service for a long, long time."

Bearyl chimed in, "Unless, of course, Bearnice here flies it into a mountain."

Giggle, push, shove, swat! Belinda did not share in the jollity. That plane was one of her most prized possessions.

"I hope you're enjoying your stay with us. Is there anything we can do to make things more comfortable?"

"Oh, things are just perfect, Dr. Bear. Thank you so much!" said Bearnice, the co-pilot. She'd been coached by Belinda. Always lead with the Ph.D. The Bear has an ego.

Belinda pointed at the speaker. "This is Bearnice Blanc, my co-pilot, and this lovely ursine is her sister, Bearyl, my flight engineer and navigator."

"One of these days I hope to hitch a ride with you all on the Aquabear over an ocean," said Octavius. "I've never flown supersonically." *(From Las Vegas, Belinda and Octavius had taken the SST to Winnipeg and then a shuttle to Churchill. Easier to handle on the ice. Same routine in reverse when they came back. But since the flights were over land, even if it was the Arctic, the Concorde had to fly subsonic. The sonic booms would have created havoc with the indigenous fauna and probably the ice.)*

Juno blanched at the idea of exceeding the speed of sound. "Not for me, thanks! I'm off for a short nap. Don't worry. No hibernating."

"Actually, once we've taken off, the sensation is no different from regular flight, Dr. and Mrs. Bear," said Bearyl. "It's not very exciting."

"Ladies, please. We don't stand on formality here. Please call me Octavius, and my mother is Juno. May we call you Bearyl and Bearnice?" Nods. "Would you care for something to eat or drink?"

"Some champagne would go very nicely, thanks," said Bel.

Without even a "whoosh," Frau Schuylkill appeared with five bowls and an uncorked bottle of Bearrier Chewy '89. Four ursine jaws dropped simultaneously. Bel raised her eyebrow at Octavius. He shrugged back. Some things are better left unknown.

The Frau announced that lunch would be served shortly. At the sound of lunch, Juno who had just about exited the room turned back into the room. "Did I hear someone mention lunch? Do I see champagne? I think my nap can wait a little while."

"Ja, Frau Bear. I will fetch you a bowl." *(Watch out for flying glassware. The wolf made a crystal bowl appear out of thin air and poured some bubbly into it.)* "You may come into the dining room at your leisure."

"Good," said The Great Bear, "Frau Schuylkill, I'd like you and the Colonel to join us. We all need to discuss the latest developments about Imperius Drake."

Bearyl and Bearnice looked puzzled. They knew who Imperius was from their time in Las Vegas but they weren't aware that anything involving him had happened since. In fact, they too believed he was dead…until this moment, that is.

"Ja, Herr Bear. Wyatt…er, the Colonel and I will be happy to join you. That *verdammte* duck doesn't know how to die. Perhaps we should give him some lessons."

Juno shouted, "Right on, Frau!"

Now Bearyl and Bearnice looked positively taken aback. First at Juno and then… Who was this sweet *canis lupus* housekeeper that Belinda liked so much? They looked at Bel, and she just winked. "Fasten your seatbelts, ladies. You're in for a ride."

Around the lunch table, a simple meal of river trout with wild blackberries garnished with fresh honeycombs topped off with more champagne produced a festive air that was in sharp contrast to the subject under discussion.

"For the benefit of the Three Bears and you, too, Mom, I'll go back very briefly and outline our history with Imperius Drake. Not to make too great an issue out of it, the Black Duck advertises himself as the most intelligent creature in the world and also the greatest criminal mind that ever lived. There is some argument about the first of his claims." *(Short pause for someone to speak up about Octavius' phenomenal mental prowess. No takers.)* "But he may well be correct in his second statement. He has concocted some of the most diabolical and fiendish schemes for world conquest that history has ever known. Fortunately, so far, they have all been flops."

Giggles from the Three Bears.

"However, that doesn't mean he is not a serious threat. He came within milliseconds of wiping out the entire genetic science community in Las Vegas. And that's what has me concerned. Up to this point, Imperius was content to seek power through financial manipulation, fraud and extortion. He was quite good at it. But even though he has that thug, Bigg Baboon with him, and also had Chita for a while, we have never known him to resort to deadly violence."

"With one exception! The time I caught him exploiting UUI's facilities for some wild, expensive and clearly illegal genetic project he was developing. He was posing as a lab assistant. I tossed him out bodily, and he fought back with amazing strength for a duck, wrecking a good part of the lab and taking with him parts of the prototype particle beam weapon the UUI Defense Contracts Division was working on. He obviously salvaged and developed the weapon, as did we on separate tracks, and he demonstrated a whole new phase of his criminal career when he began to use it. Fortunately, we did recover his version of the gun in the wreckage at Las Vegas. He can probably manufacture another but it won't be easy."

"Now, here are my concerns:

- This is a new Imperius Drake. He transforms himself from a mild mannered Mandarin maniac into a full scale Black Death by taking a gene altering serum he concocted himself. The serum seems to be eating away at his personality, making him more and more deadly and demented with each ingestion. We don't know who or what he is anymore.

- He has a special hatred for me and has already shown he wants to get to me through you, Bel. I'm not sure how safe you would be either, Mom.

- I'm sure he wants his weapon back or failing that, he knows we have the only other one in the world. He'll be coming for one or both of them.

- He still has that muscle bound baboon that follows his every order.

- Chita escaped from him. If she knows he's alive she'll want to revenge herself on him for trying to kill her. That could create all sorts of complications.

- He may have acquired other associates. Chita left a significant gap.

- Finally, there's that hydroplane. The Colonel is right. That craft is an important link. He's located someplace accessible by that boat. Have you tracked anything yet, Colonel?"

"A few things, Octavius! The Michigan Police had impounded the boat to pay the wages of the Pondscum villagers who helped build those egg bombs. The villagers thought they were making music players. Imperius ran off without paying anybody anything for anything, including the hotel and their meals. Several nights ago, an Admiral from the Coast Guard appeared and persuaded the dock master holding the boat that the government wanted it released to the CIA. I'm pretty sure that admiral was one of Imperius' cronies, although I'm not sure who he is.

We picked up a track again in the Chicago Sanitary and Ship Canal, where several ships and a police launch had been run aground or swamped by a black, high speed hydroplane plowing through the water and heading southwest. Nothing since. I think he was heading for the Mississippi River and might have been planning to go south to Mexico, but that's only a guess."

"If he sent a Black Quack to UUI to announce his resurrection from the dead and to challenge us, do you think he'd go so far away, Colonel?" asked the Great Bear.

"Damned if I know! Sorry, ladies!"

Bearnice and Bearyl chuckled. "Colonel, we've been in show biz, and we fly a supersonic airplane. We've heard *(and we say)* a lot worse than that."

"What do you think, Frau Schuylkill?"

"I think we need to put the particle gun under very heavy security, Herr Bear. Without it, he is a very dangerous and *verdammte* duck. With it, he can become a one duck *blitzkrieg*."

"Good thought. What else can we do to protect it, Colonel?"

"We're already doing it, Octavius, but I'll be glad when Howard gets here from Rio. He's the expert. It might make some sense to disassemble the gun and hide pieces in separate places, unless you want to use it in defense."

"I'm not sure, Colonel. I'm beginning to rue the day we developed the thing. Howard should get in early tomorrow morning. Now, Bel, you and the ladies, I'm afraid, are going to have to curtail your wanderings. That goes for you too, Mom."

"Just because I'm a female Kodiak, doesn't mean I'm a pushover Kodiak."

"Oh Tavi, this is ridiculous," cried Belinda. "We didn't come all the way here just to sit quietly by while you prepare for open warfare."

"Maybe you should go back."

"Octavius, any cub could locate Bearmoral Castle. And while we have the normal guards and security systems any rich widow would have, it's not a fortress. If, as you say, he's after me, why would we be any safer there?"

"Unfortunately, you're right."

"And we are polar bears, Octavius, not cute little kittens." This from Bearyl. "We're pretty good in a fight."

The thought of these three beautiful creatures battling off an enemy reminded Octavius of his first meetings with Belinda Black, as she was then called. He was doing research for his Ph.D. in ursinology and was studying the migration of the polar bears at Churchill, Canada. She was a migrating polar bear. He had seen several polar fights, not to the death but to serious damage. Males and females. They could rough-house with the best of them, but when it was a serious point like rivalry for mates or protecting cubs, they didn't kid around. Yes, Bearyl was right. They could be formidable.

Bearnice chimed in, "And we have and know how to use sidearms. We double as the Bearoness' bodyguards."

"I'm not exactly a slouch in self-defense either, Tavi," said Belinda. "In addition to what comes naturally, Byron, my late husband made sure I took karate lessons. I'm black belt."

"And while we're at it, Sonny-Boy, your Mom isn't exactly a slouch at self defense, either. That damn bear in the alternate world caught me off guard, but I'm still pretty good with my paws, and oh yes, I can shoot, too."

Well, so much for demure little ursine maiden ladies having quiet champagne brunches in the early afternoon. Octavius looked over at the two wolves who in turn were staring at the bears with new admiration. What the hell! No deranged duck was going to make recluses out of them. They'd have to be careful, but they were not exactly undefended or without resources. Bel was here, and duck or no duck, they were going to have a good time.

"Well, in that case, I have something to show you." He trundled over to the Frau and Colonel and whispered something in their ears. They disappeared. *(literally!)*

"Do you ladies feel like taking a short stroll down to the riverside to walk off lunch?"

The Three Bears rose as one *(part of their showbiz act was synchronized swimming)* and started toward the door. Juno sidled along. Bearnice raced back and gulped down the last of her champagne. *(A bear after Octavius' heart.)*

Octavius walked slightly ahead of the polars who were taken up with sniffing and staring. Juno did her own reconnaissance. The Ohio rain forests were new to them and they were on their guard against any exotic creatures that might suddenly appear. For example, they had heard about the Cincinnati Bengals, but had never seen one up close. Very few creatures had.

Suddenly there was a break in the foliage, and they could see the Ohio River. Just ahead was a small but beautiful paddle wheel river boat docked at the end of the path. Standing at the starboard railing to welcome them on board was Colonel Where, and up in the pilot house, resplendent in a blue and white uniform was Kapitan Frau Ilse Schuylkill.

'Ladies," boomed Octavius, "Welcome to the Belinda B."

'Oh, Tavi!"

The Development of Civilization–Volume 2 Part 2

Psychokinesis, Telekinesis, Teleportation

(From "An Introduction to Faunapology" by Octavius Bear Ph.D.)

Psychokinesis is the umbrella term used to describe the paranormal movement of objects, animal groups or individuals. Little rigorous scientific process, evidence or proof exist to support the idea that such movement can be initiated strictly through the power of the mind. However, there are enough anecdotal reports to keep interest alive.

Among the many sub-categories of psychokinesis, two stand out: Telekinesis and Teleportation. The first applies to causing targets to move without any application of physical forces. Essentially, the target is willed to another location or has its state changed such as turning a switch on or off. Imperius Drake makes claim to this capability and some say he has provided examples to back up his claim.

Teleportation is another matter although many argue that teleporting is just an expanded form of telekinetics. In the most common case, individual animals are capable of disappearing and reappearing in different places. Movement between parallel universes, if such exist, may be a specialized form of teleportation, although in this case, anecdotes suggest the movement is not always deliberate.

Unlike telepathy (direct mind to mind communication) which seems to have developed among certain species to compensate for their lack of a voice box, labial skills or aural capabilities, psychokinesis seems rarer and more haphazard in its occurrence. Some claim it can be produced through artificial enhancement of mental faculties. Experiments have been conducted in the past and, no doubt, continue to be performed. It has become a subject of great interest to us and will be further examined throughout this narrative. We invite you to read on.

Imperius Drake

Chapter Nine

The baboon is aggressive and tough.

Fighting him can become pretty rough.

His huge paws and big jaws

Make his enemies pause

And decide that they've just had enough.

As Imperius and Bigg stared, Otto finished off his fish and grabbed a bottle of kelp juice. He reached up and peeled off the wet burlap clinging to his ear and smiled. "That was a good test, Milord, it took me a few seconds to figure out what you had done. But here I am."

It was Bigg who spoke, "How did you do that? We thought you were dead."

"No, no, no, my boy," interrupted Imperius, staring down the baboon. "The Commandante merely meant many other illusionists would have been dead as a result of that test but I had the utmost confidence in your abilities. But between a performer and his coach and manager, how did you do it??"

"Do what?"

"Get out of that weighted bag!" Had the serum made him even denser?

"Oh, I just decided I'd be better off on the outside without the ropes you had tied around me, and there I was swimming back to the Duck Blind."

"How did you get back in here?"

"I opened the doors and walked in. What's so strange about that?"

"They were locked."

"I didn't notice," he said taking a swig out of the bottle.

Imperius was thunderstruck. Could it be? Had he succeeded beyond his wildest imagination? More tests would be necessary but if it were true that Otto could not be restrained or excluded by locks, walls, bars or shackles, world conquest was his. With Optimized Otto, it would be child's play to reclaim the particle accelerator weapon from that accursed Bear. That would be just the beginning. He would construct a huge center for producing copies of the ray gun and a research and development facility for perfecting, experimenting and injecting the Super Serum. Then, at a training ground where he would build an Imperial Army of Optimized Ottos *(as well as more formidable beasts)* equipped with the unstoppable ray guns and hyper-intelligence, he would reign triumphant and invincible. The Bear would be atomized before his very eyes to say nothing of the rest of his despicable crew. And then,. on once again to all those geneticist frauds. Oh, sheer delight!

But first another test. Would Otto obey the duck's every command? Did he still have any individuality left in his psyche? Could he be Imperius' slave, even more than the baboon?

"Otto, come over here!"

"Why?" *(Not a good start!)*

"I would like to examine you after your adventure."

"I want to finish my breakfast first, if it's all right with you." *(Didn't sound much like a slave.)*

"Otto, do you have any realization of what your…er, talent can mean? You may be able to get into or out of any confined space in the world."

"Wow, that would make a great act, Milord, but I wouldn't want to do anything illegal like sneaking into a show without paying."

"Uh, oh," thought Imperius, "his ridiculous sense of morality and justice is still intact."

This was going to take much analysis. He must also observe him closely to see how long the effects of the serum would hold on. Even if Otto was not ready to give up his free will, he could probably be tricked into doing what Imperius wanted. He wasn't the sharpest quill on the porcupine. Bad metaphor!

He turned to Bigg and said, "Commandante, let us leave Otto to finish his breakfast. We have things to discuss."

The baboon looked at Imperius quizzically but shuffled off behind him to the lab area of the Duck Blind.

When he was sure that Otto was out of earshot, he turned to Bigg and said, "Baboon, we are going to have to continue our masquerade as theatrical promoters. I thought the serum would not only enhance his illusionist's powers but make him my abject slave. I suppose one out of two ain't bad, but I cannot reveal myself or you in our true guises as long as he is in his present state. His ridiculous sense of ethics may make him rebel. We must trick him into doing our bidding. So, I am still Milord Mallàrd *(accent on the last syllable)* and you are Commandante Babaloo. Understand?"

"Yes, Sire!"

"No, you idiot, I'm Milord! He doesn't know how totally the serum has changed him. To his foolish mind, it was just a tonic. We know differently, but indeed, we do not know how differently. There are obviously other forces at work besides his genes. I shall have to study this further. Meanwhile, I want you to take him through a series of challenges and see how he does. DO NOT TRY TO KILL HIM!!! For instance, let's call him in and lock the door before he gets here."

Bigg yelled, "Hey Otto, got a minute?" As the otter got down from the table *(that tonic certainly was making him hungry),* and walked toward the lab, Imperius sprang forward and locked the door. He jumped back in pain. His wounded wing was still hurting him.

Otto opened the door and executing a double back flip, landed in front of them. "Ta-da! Wow, I don't know what's in that tonic you gave me, but I feel great!"

"Just something to help your energy, my boy! Show business can be grueling and we must make sure you can handle it. Now, I would like you and the Commandante to go outside and go through some illusion and extrication exercises for a while. Try your best to outwit him."

This wouldn't prove much. It didn't take a lot to fool the baboon, but it would give him time to work out a plan, and they needed to know how long the serum worked.

Bigg *(pardon, the Commandante)* and Otto walked out of the Duck Blind and up the ramp to the river.

"Wanna play hide-and-seek?" asked the baboon.

"I don't think that's what Milord Mallàrd *(accent on the.....aw, you know)* had in mind. Let's see if I can make something disappear."

He walked down to the hydroplane and reached into the cockpit. He came back out holding one of the fishing poles that Bigg and Imperius had used earlier in the day as camouflage while they dumped Otto over the side. He waved his hand over the pole and ...it disappeared. Bigg gasped.

"Where did it go? Where did it go?"

"Look behind you, Commandante!"

Bigg turned and got slapped in the face with a huge catfish hanging on the end of the line attached to the fishing pole he had just seen disappear.

Otto laughed. "I could have done that a bit faster, but I had to make sure I had caught the fish securely." He walked over, picked up the fish and struggling with the weight, removed the hook and dumped it still flailing, over the side of the boat. "So long! Thanks for your help. Sorry about your mouth."

He turned to Bigg. "What'll we do next, Commandante?"

The baboon thought for a minute and said, "Make something appear. How about a nice pile of silver dollars." He was still thinking about the slot machine and the nanny goat back in Reno.

Otto closed his eyes, waved his hands and strained. Nothing! "I'll try again." More nothing! "I guess I can just transport nearby things like the fish or the pole. The nearest pile of silver dollars must be outside my range. I can't make things out of nothing."

Imperius was watching and listening to all of this over a spy camera network and furiously taking notes. "He can't make things that don't already exist. There is a limit to his sphere of influence. We'll have to measure that. I wonder how large an object he can manipulate?"

As if in answer to the duck's last question, Otto walked over to the boat, waved his hands and the dock was empty.

Bigg went ballistic. "Bring it back, bring it back! The emperor...er Milord Mallàrd *(accent on the etc.)* will go out of his mind. He worships that boat. It's named after his old girlfriend. She died. Bring it back."

They heard a huge splash about one hundred yards upstream. Running in that direction, they spotted the hydroplane, serenely flowing with the current. Otto dove into the water, swam to the boat and grabbing the bowline, tossed it to Bigg as he and the boat came drifting by. Bigg gave it a huge tug, and the boat started to crab along toward the shore. Otto grabbed the stern line and swimming with it in his teeth secured it to the dock. Bigg did the same at the bow. Except for a little water in the cockpit, the boat was unharmed and unchanged.

Imperius, watching over the closed circuit system, was torn between having a nervous breakdown after almost losing the Miss Lee-Li-Li and leaping in ecstasy at the otter's capabilities. He settled for fainting.

Otto looked at Bigg and said, "Your turn!"

"Don't make me disappear," shouted the baboon, "I have two sisters to support."

Otto said, "No, it's your turn to break out of chains and handcuffs." Bigg found himself hanging, bound to a sturdy limb of a tree in chains with hand and foot cuffs.

"I'm tired and hungry." said Otto, "I'm going inside for some lunch. Come on down from there and join me."

Imperius had recovered from his dizzy spell and stared unbelieving at Bigg bound and hanging upside down. Had he heard right? Did the otter just think what he had been doing was normal and that any beast, even one as stupid as the baboon, could do the same thing? The duck must think all of this through very carefully. Meanwhile, he shouted over the external loudspeaker system, "Commandante, stop fooling around. Come down from there and meet me in the lab. We have much to discuss."

Bigg naturally screamed his head off.

An hour later, after Imperius had cut off the chains and handcuffs *(Otto had almost immediately fallen off into a deep, hypnotic sleep, perhaps brought on by the serum),* he and the baboon settled down in the lab. Imperius prepared to examine the evidence. Talking with the baboon was like talking to himself. No, not true. The only way he could get an intelligent conversation nowadays *was* to talk to himself. There were times he missed the cat. She at least had a brain but a treacherous brain.

"Now let us review the bidding!"

"I have three spades and a heart."

"Let-us-now-consider-the-situation!!"

"Oh!"

"We know that:

- The otter can make very substantial objects move to different places. They do not disappear. They are transported. Telekinetics!

- The otter does not seem fazed by restraints. He can get out of personal bonds like chains and cuffs without even seeming to notice they exist.

- Likewise, he can open any enclosure in which he is placed. He does not go through walls. He defeats locks and tied ropes and other access controls.

- We do not know yet whether he can be detected while doing this. That will be test #1 when he awakens.

- He clearly is not behaving in a subjugated way. In fact, his respect for us seems to be minimal while under the effect of the serum. This is a very serious drawback.

- But he is a pleasant and not too bright young fellow whose intelligence does not seem to be enhanced by the serum. Another unexpected result. Most subjects' IQs rose dramatically *(before they died)*.

- However, his talents as an illusionist at the moment are magnificent.

- We must continue to make him believe he is being prepared for a life on the stage. You, Baboon and I, we, I will carry on as his showbiz mentors.

- Finally, we must see how long the effects of the serum last and then determine whether it is worthwhile to alter the mixture or work with what we've got.

Bigg, who had been following *(sort of)* this one-sided conversation, interrupted, "I think we ought to get him some new costumes. He looks like a real jerk with that cape and hat. No wonder the audiences leave."

Imperius kept his temper. "There will be no audiences, Baboon. He will be working in secret with us. But wait, you may have hit on another way to convince him that we are going to promote his talents theatrically. Congratulations, Baboon!"

"It was nothing, Sire."

Imperius agreed. "We must come up with a costume that makes him believe he is indeed Otto the Magnificent."

Bigg, whose personality ran in those sorts of channels, asked, "Why don't we call him the Big 'O'?"

"I think not, Baboon but an O would be appropriate on a streamlined motorcycle helmet with a dark visor. A matching shirt might finish it off nicely."

"Yeah, in fluorescent green and yellow!"

"No, you idiot, we don't want him to stand out when he's working a job with us."

"OK, how about clear? That doesn't show at all."

"I think a dark purple. I reserve black for myself. Yes, we'll tell him about it when he wakes up."

Bigg looked out through the lab window. "He just woke up."

Otto sat up, rubbed his eyes, adjusted to his surroundings and then looked around for something to eat. He spied Imperius and Bigg inside the laboratory and waved. He got up and walked over to the lab door...and walked *into* the lab door. It didn't open. He tried the knob. It was locked, and he couldn't turn it. He rapped on the frame.

"Well," said Imperius, "that answers one question."

The Development of Civilization - Volume 2 Part 3
Quantum Leaps?

(From "An Introduction to Faunapology" by Octavius Bear Ph.D.)

I regard myself as one of the few members of the scientific community to have a comprehensive grasp of quantum mechanics, the scientific principles addressing the infinitesimal. I also am deeply steeped in Newtonian physics (Phigg Newton 1643-1727) as well as Albeart Einstein's (1875-1955) remarkable work expanding Newton's pronouncements dealing with the nature of the infinite but tangible universe. However, somewhere between the very, very small and the unimaginably large, there is a major disconnect among the theorists. Quantum mechanics and Newtonian physics don't match up! There have been attempts to patch over the gaps with approaches like string, thread, rope, cable, twine, wire, filament, chain and cord theories. In the process, the theoretical multiverse has acquired as many as eleven dimensions including space - time.

There is one principle of quantum theory that should interest us at this point in our narrative. Quantum superposition at the sub-atomic level.

In 1935, a cat named Schrodinger showed how superposition would operate in the every day world. As long as we do not observe or measure it, an object can exist in any number (a superposition) of states. It is only when we turn our attention to the object that the superposition is lost, and the object appears in only one of its potential states. This situation is sometimes called quantum indeterminacy or the observer's paradox: the observation or measurement itself affects an outcome, so that the outcome as such does not exist unless the measurement is made.

Can this explain the possibility of us visiting parallel universes? If a witness, after shutting down all sensory perception through sleep or coma, totally withdraws from observing the current world, can this same sense-deprived observer then somehow "change channels" and have a different universe appear to his reawakened senses? Is this how hibernating bears and deep sleep subjects like Wyatt Where make quantum leaps from one parallel world to another? Can we all do it? Do we want to? Can I do it during my narcoleptic outages? Do I want to? Damned if I know!

Bearoness Belinda
Béarnaise Bruin
(nee Black)

Chapter Ten

On an afternoon cruise without care,

Up the river, just taking the air.

What a paddling delight,

Not a problem in sight.

Well, there's always Octavius Bear.

Aboard the Belinda B, paddle wheeling up the Ohio River

Bowls of champagne were clinking. Fish snacks were being delicately snarfed. Five bears and a wolf, leaning over the taffrail, watching the stern mounted blades churn a sparkling spray into mini-rainbows as they propelled the glistening boat against the current. Just an afternoon of merry makers enjoying a carefree outing. Well, almost!

Count on Octavius! Galumphing toward the pilot house where Frau Schuylkill was busy keeping the huge steering wheel on course, he shouted, "Would everyone please join me up here on the Texas deck. I have a few important things to tell you."

Juno snorted, "I wouldn't know a Texas deck from a Delaware deck. Where are you going, Tavi?"

"Right up here, Mom, near the pilot house. I want Frau Schuylkill to be part of the conversation."

He moved his considerable bulk around to avoid blocking the she-wolf's lines of sight. That's all they needed. To run aground on the Ohio while he was having a confidential meeting.

The three polar bears, Belinda in the lead, took up station on the starboard side of the deck. Juno, still holding on to her champagne bowl, flopped on a bench that ran the length of the deck rail. The Colonel slid into the pilot house with the Frau. Octavius stood in the middle of the group. No problem hearing him. Octavius could make himself heard over the roar of a jet engine. In fact, he had to be careful not speak too loudly, or the entire population of Southwest Ohio and Southeast Indiana would be in on the game.

"I suppose you're wondering why I summoned you all here." *(Oh lord, not that threadbare line!)*

"Well, Tavi," said Belinda, "up until a few seconds ago, I thought it was to enjoy a beautiful afternoon on my lovely namesake boat. You are not going to spoil it with a serious discussion, are you?"

The Great Bear, taken aback, was puzzled by her reaction. As Juno had often said of him, "Brains ten plus, Sensitivity zero."

"In fact, Bel," he said, "I do have something serious to discuss. *(Groans in unison.)* But first I want our two wolves to become aware of what all you ursines already know. The Bearoness has done me the honor of becoming my blushing bride. We were married while we were in Churchill. My mother, Belinda's Aunt Bella Donna and Wallingford Penniped, my professor at Kodiak U, were the witnesses. I think Bearyl and Bearnice already know about it, too."

The polar twins laughed, sending echoes across the river and stirring up a flock of birds.

Rounds of applause. The two wolves who had already been informed, pretended to be surprised and howled their delight. The Colonel hugged Belinda and then, taking the wheel from Frau Schuylkill, stepped aside as she threw herself at Octavius with a tail wagging snarl.

Then, "Oh, your pardon, Herr Bear," she said to the amazed Octavius. "I overstep myself *(blushing)* but I am greatly overjoyed for the both of you. Will you be coming to live with us now, Bearonin? Who will occupy your castle?"

Belinda looked at Octavius, and he stared back. Bel broke the ice. "That's a matter that is still in the discussion phase, Frau Schuylkill. Each of us has been trying to convince the other to take up residence at our respective homes. We're both rather set in our ways. Octavius has UUI to run here in Ohio and if I leave Bearmoral Castle, which I adore, my ex-husband's relatives will no doubt try to take it over. They may even try to strip me of my title since I've remarried. I'd rather blow the castle up than see it in their greedy hands. Right now, we've settled on each of us commuting to be with the other. We'll see how that works out."

"Well," said the Colonel, "owning an SST should certainly help things along." Turning to the two polar pilots, he inquired, "Could Ilse and I interest you two in learning to fly the Ursa Major in exchange for us being checked out on the Aquabear? With your agreement of course, Bearoness...and Octavius!"

"You know, that sounds like a really good idea; having flight crews on both sides of the ocean that can handle both planes. What do you think, Bel?"

"Fine, Tavi! Just as long as you don't get any ideas about trying to fly either one of them yourself. But I forgot, you can't fit in either of the cockpits. You even have some trouble with the main cabin of the Concorde." She took a playful slap at Octavius and said, "Now that that's over with, can we return to our champagne and sightseeing?"

"Not yet. I do have something else to discuss, and I think it may become serious very shortly."

"Oh no," said Juno, "Not that crazy duck again. Do what I told you, Tavi. Kill him off and get it over with."

The wolves looked at Juno with expressions of awe on their faces. Now, she was their kind of bear.

"No, not Imperius! Although I shudder to think what he might try to do if he caught on to this information I'm going to pass on. I'm talking about the fact that two of you, Mom and Wyatt, as well as my half-brother, Agrippa, seem to be having experiences in alternate universes either while hibernating or in induced sleep."

The twin polars blinked in unison. "Alternative universes? Sometimes you go too far, Doctor Bear!"

"Yes! Alternative universes! Parallel worlds! Just listen for a few minutes! I don't think this can wait. I wanted to use this boat to ensure we could meet without being overheard."

Bel was obviously miffed that her trip on her "bridal barge" was being preempted by a "Save the World or Worlds" strategy session, but she was concerned enough not to protest. This was what married life with Octavius Bear, the Great Detective, was going to be like. Oh well, a little lightweight on the romantic side, but never lacking for excitement.

"Now," said the Great Bear. "Some of you already know parts of this story, but I want to get us all reading from the same script. I'm sorry Maury, Howard and Inspector Wallaroo are not here. I'll bring them up to speed as soon as I can meet with them face-to-face. Let's review the bidding on special locomotion. Telekinesis usually refers to someone being able to move or otherwise affect objects strictly through the power of the mind and will. Imperius Drake claims he can start or stop those damned Black Quack eggs telekinetically."

"Teleportation is a form of paranormal movement of individuals or groups. It's like telekinesis, I suppose, except it's not always an act of the individual's own will. According to the semi-scientific literature, you can be teleported deliberately by another being or by unintentional consequences of another event. Here one minute, somewhere else in another with no apparent physical effort."

Bearnice: "You believe this, Dr. Bear?"

"I don't know what I believe, Bearnice, but I do believe the animals who are telling me about their adventures or misadventures. Now there are other forms of movement that can mimic teleportation. For example, you, Frau Schuylkill, can move about at hyperspeed and give the impression you're teleporting or moving things telekinetically. In fact, you're locked in this reality, and when those kegs of mead conveniently appear out of nowhere you are actually carrying them faster than the eye can catch. Is that correct?"

"Close enough, Herr Bear!"

"So that's how she does it," said Belinda.

The wolf blushed and shrugged, causing the helm to shift to port. "Ach, sorry!"

"Wait," said Juno, "Let me get something straight. Teleporting, if it's possible, doesn't mean you end up in another world. You could teleport around the block or below this deck for another bowl of champagne which isn't a bad idea. We're talking about several different things at once here."

"Good catch, Mom! You are absolutely right and I want everyone to hear your story in just a minute. But you, Colonel, you have made a substantial number of trips into at least one other universe where *Homo Sapiens* seems to be the dominant species. Right?"

This was new news to the twin bears, and they stared quizzically at Wyatt. Belinda along with Juno and Wallingford had heard a version of the story from Octavius when they were at Churchill. Frau Schuylkill was no doubt aware of Wyatt's adventures.

He replied, "I was part of a top secret defense program run by The Business, a supposedly non-existent organization headed up by a paranoid horse named General Turmoil who I wish *was* non-existent! They were attempting to induce prolonged suspended animation in test subjects for use in a variety of offense and defense situations. Somehow, through processes not clear to the scientists running the project, things took a strange turn. Some of us started to cross over to other locations while we were under deep sedation. The best guesses were that it was somehow linked to fundamental changes in our bodily structure while our metabolism was practically at a halt. Only a few of us, two to be exact, actually transported. My partner died in mysterious circumstances and after that, I took the earliest opportunity to get out of Dodge. They chased me for a while but I eluded them. I think they gave up and are now content with just discrediting anything I might say about the program. At least I hope so!"

"I wouldn't trust General Turmoil as far as I could throw him," snarled Octavius, "even if it's into another world. But you told me you can still teleport between worlds in spite of escaping from the project."

"My body is permanently altered in ways I don't really understand and I can still slip into a deep inanimate sleep with the help of an extremely small shot of hydrogen sulfide. If I transport *(it doesn't always happen)* I have no control over my destination or duration. By my estimates the longest I have traveled is six days. Most excursions last less than an hour. The only reason I knew I was no longer in this world was that I met up with a couple of *Homo Sapiens*. I assume I was somewhere off our earth. As far as I know, none of them survived here."

"Let's hope not!" said Juno, "but I wouldn't bet on it."

"I managed to travel around a bit while I was in the teleported state. I wasn't detected, even when I stowed away on a cargo plane. But I covered enough ground to see that this wasn't an undiscovered part of our own world. This place was different, big and widespread."

Bearyl looked at Wyatt. "Can you also do Frau Schuylkill's hyperspeed trick?"

"Not nearly as well as she can. But yes! I learned it when we vacationed together in Transylvania."

Bearnice shook her head. "And all I can do is pilot a supersonic airplane."

"But you do it very well, dear!" This from Belinda.

"Colonel, what happened when you met these *H.Saps*?"

"For one thing, Octavius, we never actually met in the social sense. I'm well trained in eluding discovery and while observing them, I stayed out of their sight. Even if they did see me, they probably assumed I was just another wolf from their world, a semi- intelligent but non-communicating species. At least their wolves don't communicate the way we do. They don't seem self-aware, either."

Juno stared at him. "They have species of animals like you that haven't developed the same way. Are there bears?"

"Yes, there's a full complement of less developed fauna. I have no idea how many different species there are but there must be thousands. I saw a large selection in what the *H.Saps* call a zoo."

"A zoo? What's a zoo?"

"A place where the *H.Saps* keep samples of these animals captive for study, protection and entertainment.

"Why that's absolutely unbeastly! But that might explain why the bear I approached on my excursion didn't reply to me and then chased me and took a swipe at my hindquarter. She looked like a Kodiak, but she certainly didn't act like one."

"Tell us about your experience, Juno!" Bearyl sat down, laid her elbows on the bench Juno was sprawled on and rested her head on her paws, all attention.

"I thought I had just woken up from hibernation. My den looked the same…almost. My maid Florence, an arctic fox, was nowhere to be seen, and I went to look for her. I walked outside and things looked the same…almost. The stream that runs through my den had dried up, the trees were different, and so were the smells. I decided to take a little tour and I found myself staring at another female 'Kodiak' and her two cubs. I said 'hello' as any sociable bear would, but instead of returning my greeting, she charged at me and took a chunk out of my hindquarter. I ran back inside my den, hid and I guess passed out. I don't know how long I was under, possibly weeks but when I did wake up, everything was back to normal. My maid was there, and the stream was running through the bathroom like always. But when I tried to move, I felt this pain, and there was this deep gash in my rump. That's when I knew it wasn't just a dream. I guess I had been sleepwalking, but now I'm not sure where."

Octavius intervened. "Your story gibes with the one Agrippa told me. Only in his case he said he awoke from hibernation and found himself dealing a high stakes poker game for a group of *H.Saps*. They didn't seem to think anything was wrong with a Kodiak bear being a games dealer. He got the impression that other intelligent, self aware species were commonplace along with the *H.Saps*. Unfortunately a fight broke out among the players, shots were fired, one of the *H.Saps* was killed, and the rest ran from the room. Agrippa, true to form, took the opportunity to grab the high stakes pot and make a run for it. When he woke up, he too thought it was a dream, but then he found several decks of cards and a large pile of cash in denominations he didn't recognize scattered by his bed. Now he's convinced those card players are coming after him. He's convinced he was in another world and he's hoping the inhabitants can't bridge the gap."

"Wait a second, Octavius!' said the Colonel. "Something doesn't fit."

"Something??" growled the Frau. "Nothing fits! The worlds you're describing don't sound the same. In one case, the bears are undeveloped. In another, the bears deal poker and the *H.Saps* don't seem to notice anything unusual. In another, the *H.Saps* treat the animals like wild creatures. Assuming any of this sleepy-time travel actually happened, and I'm not sure about that, it sounds like you all went to different universes. *Himmel!*"

During this tirade, she had gesticulated enough while gripping the helm to turn the Belinda B. perpendicular to the current. "Ach, I am so sorry, Herr Bear. I apologize, everyone."

"No problem, Frau. We should be heading back anyway. I think my on-board supply of mead is just about used up. But you make the same point that is troubling me. Let's establish a working hypothesis! *(Polar eyebrows raised!)* From all of the experiences discussed this afternoon, there seems to be some good evidence for teleportation while in a deep soporific state. It may happen at random, even though the Colonel seems to be able to induce it."

"Not reliably, Octavius. I miss as often as I hit."

"Fine! In any case, none of you could deliberately direct yourself to a specific time or place. The destination and duration happened to you. You didn't control it. We're not sure *H.Saps* were at all the destinations you reached. Even you, Colonel! Are you convinced you always journeyed to the same world?"

"Not at all! I'm not sure where I go. I tried to leave some traces of my visits, so I could pick up on them again but so far, it's never worked."

"OK! Now there are several real issues we have to deal with:

1. How do we explore this further without giving ourselves away?

2. Who else knows about it, here and in those other worlds?

3. How do we avoid causing a panic or even more important, stop some damn pernicious fool like Imperius Drake or General Turmoil from using this phenomenon for world, no, **worlds**, conquest?

4. What do we do about the very real possibility that *H.Saps* who create zoos and kill each other over games of chance might suddenly show up in our midst?

5. …

…"I think you've made your point, Tavi." said Bel. "We obviously have a lot of research and protective measures to initiate. I'll be glad to see Howard, Maury and Bruce back here. We need all the brainpower we can get."

"Right, Bel. Well, I see we're approaching the dock. I hope you all enjoyed our little cruise. Especially you, Bel! I want the Belinda B. to be a real pleasure boat for your use!"

'Oh, yes, Tavi!" The Bearoness forced a smile and strongly resisted the urge to push the Great Bear overboard.

The Development of Civilization-Volume 2 Part 4

Electronics, Communications, Computing, Miniaturization

(From "An Introduction to Faunapology" by Octavius Bear Ph.D.)

Electronics *deals with the flow of electrons through semiconductors such as silicon. By altering the state, flow and direction of the electrons, it is possible to create effects that can be used in the construction of communications, computing, regulating, amplifying and similar devices. It is unlike* **Electrical** *science and technology, which deals primarily with motive and heating power by directing the flow of electrons and other charge carriers through metal conductors such as copper. This distinction was first established with the invention of the vacuum tube by the scientific genius lion, Leo De Forest. Today, we are surrounded by all manner of semi-conductor circuits and devices that have made possible most of the communication, computing and control functions that we employ so routinely.*

Radio, television, signal recording and reproduction of all types as well as computing systems all rely on electronics. Radar applies the principles of measuring electronic signal behavior when bounced against an object. Electronic locks are simple variants of computing devices which use solid state calculation circuits to create encoded combinations. The computer and the computer network based on digital devices are key to our crime fighting abilities.

I am especially proud that Universal Ursine Industries, under my direction, invented and developed the Internet. We are also extremely grateful to Arachnid Associates for their brilliant addition to the Internet's global reach and versatility – The World Wide Web. It is impossible to measure the profound changes that this technology had made in the lives of every male, female and cub throughout the world.

Finally, with the advent of micro and nanotechnology, many of these functions and more still to be imagined, will be implemented at molecular, atomic and sub atomic scales. Major technological advances will be available to all creatures, regardless of size and physical characteristics. Our highly intelligent colleagues, the ant and the bee will have new and more powerful devices at their disposal. Physically deprived species, such as the condor will have voice capability inserted directly and unobserved into their systems. There is still much to be done.

Maury Meerkat

Chapter Eleven

Condors fly through the Andean air.

In the States they're incredibly rare.

They can endlessly soar

On wings ten feet or more,

Climbing thousands of feet with no care.

Hi! Maury again! Were you wondering about us down here in Brazil? Now we're in São Paolo *(population 18 million plus two)*. Bruce and I took a train west from Rio this morning in time to catch the last night of São Paolo Carnaval here in this super huge metropolis. Working our way out of Barra Funda Station, we arrived at our hotel in time for lunch.

Last night at the bistro in Rio, we had to "fess up" to the remaining members of the Spotted Band that we were international law enforcers and that while we were not pursuing her directly, we were hoping to get Chita's cooperation on a case back in the U.S. We also told them the cat had quite a few "wanted" posters with her name on them on post office walls around the world. This didn't seem to bother them much. In fact, I got the impression that somewhere there might have been one or two with Jake's name on them, as well.

Bruce also mentioned that he shared their suspicions about Paolo being a bad 'un. He said nothing about him really being Pontius Puma, and we didn't give them any hint as to why we were going down to São Paolo.

We told them where we'd be staying and to give us a call when they got to São Paolo after their performance on the float *(sans Chita)* at closing night at the Sambodrome in Rio. I wasn't taking bets that they'd contact us.

So, here we are, and Bruce is acting mysterious again. He was on the phone all through lunch sending text messages. He looked over at me with a sly smile on his hairy face and said, "Maury, m'boy, you are in for an interesting afternoon. I want you to meet an old friend of mine. He's a bit unusual, but I think I can get him to help us cut Pontius Puma off at the pass. Finish your meal, and we'll go."

87

No amount of wheedling would get him to say anymore. So I hopped on his shoulder *(the way we usually travel together, especially in crowds where Bruce is prone to knock other people prone with his bounding, jumping and bouncing)*, and we headed for the cab stand.

Sitting in a taxi, stuck in a traffic jam watching the "paulistanos" passing us by on foot while Bruce went through his own shifting gyrations is not my number one recommended tourist activity. But then, I kept reminding myself, I was no longer a tourist. We were here to deal with a very dangerous, influential and nasty international criminal.

We finally reached a building in the outskirts of the city that looked more like a warehouse or airplane hanger, except its base was supported by columns that lifted it about thirty feet off the ground. Underneath, an elevator shaft and stairway surrounded by a garden led up into the building's base and what I surmised was a living area. All told, a pretty remarkable looking place.

Bruce bounded into the elevator. *(My second least favorite activity is being in an elevator with Bruce, especially when he is excited or nervous. He was both).* The lift rose, and the door opened into a wide corridor, and in the center was a pair of even wider doors. The ceiling was about twenty feet high. Working with Octavius, you get used to unusual architecture, but this one was pushing toward the top of the oddball list.

Bruce walked up to a coded keypad and paw print reader and identified himself. The doors opened, and we walked into a huge, unbroken space that was loaded floor to ceiling on every wall and in standalone columns in the middle of the floor with electronic equipment. I looked up at a huge skylight that dominated the ceiling. It was open.

I wasn't quite sure what I was looking at. Some of the equipment looked like conventional computers. There was a mass of connecting cables and power supplies. The thing that puzzled me was the work surfaces. You normally expect desks to be set on the floor, right?? Well, there were plenty of horizontal work surfaces but they were at several different levels. Curiouser and curiouser!

I looked back up to the skylight and a head peered in at me. A big and, not to be coy about it, ugly avian head. Suddenly, there was a thumping sound and down through the skylight flew one of the largest Andean Condors I have ever seen. I take it back. I have never seen an Andean Condor before in the feathers. Only on the Geography Channel. This guy had at least a twelve foot wing span, which he stretched fully as he hovered slowly to the floor of the room. Bruce strode forward, extending his arms and the condor enveloped him in his wings.

"Condo, my mate." said Bruce, "It's great to see you again." The condor said nothing but folding his wings, he stepped over to a nearby table and came back carrying three smartphones. He gave one to each of us and on the screen appeared, "Senhor Bruce, the pleasure is all mine. Welcome, *amigo*, welcome!"

Bruce looked at me and said, "Maury, say hello to L. Condor, one of the true geniuses in computing and communications."

I waved and said, "Pleased to meet you, Mr. Condor. Bruce has told me a great deal about you." *(A rotten, bare-faced lie!! This bird was a complete and shocking surprise.)*

"Maury, Condo is an Andean Condor, *Vultur Gryphus,* a native of the South American wilds. He's come in from the mountains and established himself here in one of the world's largest cities to pursue his passion for telecommunications. It started out as compensation for the fact that Andean Condors have no voicebox and can't make any kind of vocal sound. *(You could certainly hear his wings.)* Nature really dealt him a rum hand. He's not telepathic, either. That's why he handed you the text phone. He can hear you perfectly but he has to speak to us through the keyboard and screen. He's very good at it."

The screen lit up again and across it scrolled, "I've been working on a voice synthesizer, but I haven't decided yet what I want to sound like. The first version was a sexy fox, but that seemed a bit out of character. I'll try it out for you later. Meanwhile how about a drink? Beer for you, Senhor Bruce and for you, Senhor Maury? Let me guess! I have some twenty year old fermented coconut milk VSOP. Can I interest you?"

I had achieved nirvana! I looked at Bruce and asked, "Did you tell him what I drank and that I couldn't find it in Brazil?"

Before the Inspector could answer, another message flashed across the cell screen. L. Condor was fast on the keyboard. "No, No, Senhor Maury! *(LOL)* I knew another Meerkat once and that was his favorite. I kept the bottle in case he ever came back to São Paolo but since you're here..." He half flew, half hopped over to a refrigerator and shortly came back with Bruce's beer. It took

89

him a little longer to find the coconut milk. He was having a caipirinha. It looked green, tasty and potent. I made a mental note to try one before I left the country.

"Now," he flashed, "what can I do for you, *amigo*?"

"Condo," burped Bruce as he took a substantial swig of Brazilian beer, "We're on the trail of an international intellectual property thief by the name of Pontius Puma."

The condor's head swung up and he looked at Bruce out of one eye. "I congratulate you on your ambitious choice of targets. Are you sure you don't want to take on all the Mid-Eastern terrorists while you're about it?"

"We've heard he's pretty tough and ruthless," I said. "We had a brief chance to see him the other night in Rio. He was using another name, Paolo, and he was enjoying Carnaval and the company of a cheetah who's got a pretty impressive criminal record herself. We've had some pretty serious dealings with her, as well."

The condor typed, "Paolo? Not a very original alias but it fits his arrogant nature. Pontius Puma, as you may know, is a one cat crime wave. He hides behind legitimate businesses and he has a wide range of good friends in government, the police and especially the army. He's seldom seen in public. Are you sure it was him you saw?"

"Dead certain," said the Inspector. "I'd know that distinctive tail twitch anywhere. I was on his trail once before when he was a bongo player working in low-down dives and smuggling anything he could get his claws on. Nowadays, he's wearing fancy clothes and driving super-luxury cars, but he's still a thief."

"All very true, Inspector, but he is a very powerful thief. I doubt very much you will be able to bring him to justice inside this country, and he seldom leaves."

"Right now," said Bruce, "I'd settle for putting one of his businesses in the dunny. He has been using his recording and on-line music trade as a blind for dealing in military and government information. He has a global network of industrial spies, many of whom we're about to close in on, but his center of operations is here in São Paolo. I want to shut him down."

"And you want my help?"

"Too true, Condo! No one I know has the mastery of computer and communications hacking and attacking like you do. It's a good thing you're one of the good guys."

"Or you'd have to kill me, true??"

"Never crossed my mind, Condo, never crossed my mind! Maury, Condo has helped us a number of times to both protect vital information and to break into supposedly uncrackable electronic data banks and services. He's a ridgy-didge genius."

Watching a condor blush is an interesting experience. "*Amigo*, you can cut off the flattery. You know I will help you any way I can. What do you have in mind?"

"I want to take down his entire network and data storage facilities and make sure they stay that way for a long, long time."

"Oh good, nothing difficult! How much time do we have…in microseconds, of course?"

I didn't think he could sound that sarcastic when he was communicating by keyboard but the irony was dripping from my display.

"How much do you need?"

"Give me forty-eight hours. I have to ensure I've got his entire network and backup locations identified before trying anything. I have developed an attack that works in stages. The more you try to counteract it, the more virulent it becomes. I assume you would want them tied up for months and have to start over and over again from scratch."

"That would work beautifully, Condo! If we can shut down his sources, and you can wipe out his current capability, it would give us breathing room to go after him personally. Right now, there are some pretty important assets in his possession that don't belong there."

"All right, check in with me tomorrow and I'll give you a progress report. In the meantime, enjoy the last day of Carnaval."

"Aren't you a reveler, Senhor Condor?" I asked.

"Since my mate died, Senhor Maury, I don't go to the festivities. My Conni was a great dancer and flyer, and she could soar in great circles and keep

91

exact time with the samba band. Each year the bands would compete to have her join them. She was lovely...such gorgeous red eyes. Unfortunately, she wasn't looking carefully enough one night and flew into a press helicopter that was televising the event. Ever since, I can't go back."

We both expressed our sympathies, but he had already hopped up onto one of his intermediate perches and was booting up a major array of hardware. We said good-bye, and he waved at us distractedly.

"Once he gets on a problem, it occupies him completely. I worry about him. His entire life is tied up in those techie toys. Any road, we'd better get back to the hotel and check in with Ocko. And then, on with the dance."

"Where do you suppose Chita went?" I asked after we finally found a cab. "And what do you suppose was Pontius' reaction when he found out she had split? Coming to think of it, what's Octavius' reaction going to be when he hears she's on the loose?"

"I'm sure Chita went back to the States. Probably not directly. She's smarter than that, but that's her destination. She's going to find that duck. We'd better tell Ocko to be on the lookout for her. She knows where the duck's major hideout is. She operated out of there herself for quite a while. If they can find her, they may be able to find him, assuming he's still working out of the same place."

"Since no one seems to know where it is, it's likely he's still using it," I said. "I imagine he has quite an investment in laboratory equipment and experiments, to say nothing of weapons. I hope he doesn't have a second copy of the particle beam gun."

"The other question is: Did he get another partner? Chita was quite an asset to him. I'm glad she's on the other side of the fence now, although exactly where she stands on anything except getting back at Imperius is anybody's guess."

"Yeah,' I replied. "That baboon has all his brains in his arms and legs. He must drive Imperius nuts, but he sure follows orders, and he's damn strong and agile. Imperius needs someone who can think, but of course, isn't as smart as he is. His ego couldn't stand the competition. Do you really believe he becomes the smartest animal in the world when that serum of his kicks in?"

"He thinks so! So far he hasn't convinced me, but I'll give him a few points in the game."

More of the same conversation until we crawled back to the hotel. Early revelers *(or were they holdovers from last night?)* were already out in force. We got up to the room and called the Great Bear.

Frau Schuylkill answered the phone. It was a good thing I was calling and not Bruce. She said Octavius was out showing the Three Bears his apiaries. If one of those bees stung him *(or any of them)* he would not be in a good mood. I could hear her calling him and I could hear him coming to the speakerphone. I braced myself. Here it comes: "MRAUREE!"

"Greetings from São Paolo, Octavius. Happy Carnaval!!'

"Why haven't you called in?"

"We were changing cities!"

"Is Bruce with you?"

"I'm here, Ocko," said Bruce from the extension.

"Well, what's going on?"

We told him about seeing Pontius/Paolo. We told him about our plans with L. Condor. He bought off on everything and then, we told him about Chita doing a bunk, in Bruce's words. That did not sit well.

"When did she take off?" he asked.

"Late last night. She can't have reached the States yet unless she flew direct and knowing her, she'll come in through some indirect means. Possibly by way of Europe."

"Did she show any signs of being willing to work with us?" asked the Bear.

"The minute she heard Imperius was alive, she was out the door before we had a chance to say a word, and you know how pointless it is to try to follow her on foot. For all I know she may have run halfway to North America by now."

"We've got to find her before she gets to his hideout. We need to be able to trail her. I want to get the duck where he lives, not the other way around."

"Why?" I asked. "Just let her kill him off."

93

"Suppose she fails, and he kills her. He came damn close once already. I know you two have developed a perverse affection for that feline felon, a feeling I do not share, but I don't think any of us wants to see her getting killed by the duck and his baboon henchbeast."

"Let's change the subject for a minute," I said. "Let's talk about extricating good old Bruce and sweet little Maury out of here. This Pontius Puma has a lot of friends and a lot of influence. When he discovers we've wiped out his operation, he will not be pleased, and he has a tendency to be violent toward those who have displeased him."

"Does he know you're in São Paolo?" asked the Bear.

"Not as far as we know, Ocko, but we can't guarantee he won't find out. On top of that, L. Condor is really sticking his neck out for us. I don't want Pontius unleashing his heavyweights on him."

"Well, I guess we can send the Ursa Major down for you in stealth mode, but it will take at least a few days, possibly more. Frau Schuylkill has pulled two of the engines for maintenance."

Suddenly, a new voice came over the phone. Belinda! I wasn't even sure she had come in with Octavius.

"Why not let us take the Aquabear, Tavi. We can get there in about seven hours."

"Nothing doing, Bel. One of the reasons we're doing all this protective build-up is to keep you, Bearnice and Bearyl out of harm's way."

"Tavi, don't be ridiculous. We're big bears *(true),* and we have been in dangerous situations before. We could be down there and back with Maury and the Inspector before Frau Schuylkill can get the C-5A's engines back in their nacelles."

"You'd have to get past the airport authorities, and the Aquabear is hardly a subtle piece of hardware."

"Let me think," she said, "Got it. Our troupe is known in Brazil. We can say that we had loaned out some of our costumes and equipment for Carnaval and we're coming in to retrieve them. Maury and Bruce can handle the materials. I assume you gentlebeasts can get your paws on some spurious Carnaval props and costumes."

94

"We can get the real thing," I said. "L. Condor needs forty eight hours to pull off his little prank. That's about noon day after tomorrow. We'll be there at the airport just about then, and when he tells us Pontius Puma's world has collapsed, we can take off."

"Wait a second, Maury," said Bruce. "I don't want to leave L. Condor here to take the heat if PP should figure out how and by whom he got torpedoed. I want to give Condo the chance to leave town with us and stay away until this thing dies down."

"You're right! Sorry! OK, Bearoness, still plan on being on the tarmac here at São Paolo at about noon day after tomorrow. We'll be in contact about clearing customs and other stuff and you take care of the flight plans. Let's touch base again this time tomorrow."

"It is exactly 4:28 PM Eastern Standard Time. I'll expect to hear from you again at precisely the same time tomorrow," boomed the Bear.

It's a good thing we weren't on video. It's amazing the things that Bruce can do with his face.

As soon as we hung up, Bruce called his cousin Jose in Rio and asked whether he knew where we could get our paws on some Carnaval costumes, float decorations and any other stuff that we could use as cover for our rather abrupt getaway day after tomorrow. Jose told us to stand by, and he would make a call or two. A half hour later, he called back. Today, the last day of the celebration, we could get nothing. Tomorrow, we'd be deluged. He gave us the name of a company owned by another cousin, Jorge, who would be happy to bring an assortment of paraphernalia out to the airport for us, assuming of course, that we could reach agreement. I let the wallaroos negotiate.

Bruce hung up with a smile on his face and said, "It pays to have relatives." I smiled back, thinking of my own mob on Mauritius and how close my relatives came to having me turned into Meerkat fricassee when I was young and restless *(and lawless)!*

São Paolo is a great town for eating, and I was hungry. It's also a great town for celebrating if you don't mind doing it with 18 million of your closest friends. We went out.

95

Chapter Twelve

The species that's called Wallaroo

Is a wallaby plus kangaroo.

His large feet - (macropod!)

Make him look rather odd

But I bet he moves faster than you.

I think this is still São Paulo. Overfed, over-libated and over celebrated, I stared at the ceiling of the hotel room and tried to remember who I was. Finding that too difficult, I tried to figure out the meaning of life. That wasn't working too well either, when the phone on my hotel end table chirped away at me. "Hello," I croaked, expecting it to be the illustrious Inspector Bruce Wallaroo who together with yours truly made complete jackasses of ourselves last night among the merry revelers.

It was a voice I didn't immediately recognize. "Maury, this is Lepi." *(Lepi? Lepi? Lepi! The singer keyboardist from the Spotted Band! My brain WAS working!)*

"Hey Lepi, *que passa?*" *(Wrong language but what the hell!)*

"I just got off the train from Rio, and we have a big problem, a Paolo problem."

"Paolo as in rich, powerful, nasty thug?"

"You got it."

I was sobering up very quickly. "You said 'I.' Where are the other two cats?"

"We're traveling separately. We agreed to meet later this afternoon at a small café that Ozzie sometimes works at. We'd like you two to be there as well. Paolo sent some pretty heavy muscle after us last night at the Sambadrome in Rio. He's convinced we know where Chita is. We talked him out of beating us to death by telling him about you guys and your interest in Chita. Now, he's after you."

(Oh boy. I was really sobering up now.) "Lepi, can you call me back in about ten minutes. I want to get a hold of Inspector Wallaroo, so we can talk with you together."

"Make it twenty. Kat, we are in bad shape. I may never play the keyboard again, and Jake has a broken foot."

"OK, call back at the same number. Twenty minutes. We'll be here."

I hung up and dialed Bruce's room. After about thirty seconds of non-stop abuse in Classical Strine, I got a word in edgewise and told him what little I knew. He too, sobered up pretty quickly. Houston, we have a problem!

As I tried to drown myself in the bathroom, I could hear the shower running in his room next door. I think we both were trying to hydrate ourselves inside and out, so we could deal with this issue. It had been a fifty-fifty proposition that Paolo/Pontius would find out about us. I was kind of hoping it would happen after we had left the friendly skies of Brazil tomorrow. Time for Plan B, whatever that was.

Bruce semi-bounded into my room. We both looked like poster children for the Society for Prevention of Cruelty to Animals.

"You realize this could be a set-up," he said.

"The thought has skittered across my mind," I said, "I don't think I want to meet with them in some cozy café where Paolo's gorillas can jump us."

"I'm not sure I want to stay here either, if the band told them where to find us," said Bruce. "But I don't think Paolo's musclemen will get here this soon."

"I hope you're right. How many more cousins do you have in town?"

"A bunch. Good idea, Jorge can probably put us up somewhere, and I want to make sure we take care of L. Condor."

The phone chirped. Bruce picked it up, and I got on the extension. "Allo," he said in a French accent you wouldn't believe. No one would believe it.

"Maury? Is that you? This is Lepi, and I have Ozzie with me."

"No, Lepi, this is Bruce. Maury's here. Where are you?"

"We're at the house of a friend. Look, we need to tell you what happened, and then we're splitting."

"Splitting where?"

"We don't know yet. We have to wait for Jake, but São Paolo isn't too healthy for us or you, and neither is Rio."

"OK," said Bruce. "Calm down and tell us what happened."

"Last night when we showed up for the parade minus Chita, two of Paolo's gorillas came up to us and said, 'Before you go on, Mr. Paolo wants to talk to you.' That was enough to scare the hell out of us right there. They led us to a box in the grandstand that had a private entrance and thick concrete walls. I guess that's where he watched the parades. Anyway, he wanted to know where Chita was, and naturally we told him we didn't know. She had run off the previous night, and we tried to call her but no luck."

"Go on," I said.

"Paolo wasn't in any mood for us not knowing. So the gorillas started roughing us up. That's when we told him how you two guys said something to Chita to set her off. He got very interested and wanted to know who you were, why you were in Rio and where you were now. When he found out you were the law, he went ape…no, the gorillas went ape. We told him you had gone over to São Paolo but didn't give him any more than that. He's looking for you. I think he thinks you're after him and are using Chita to get him."

(Smart cat, that Pontius.)

I said, "Actually, seeing Chita was a complete accident, but I doubt he would believe that. He's probably had you followed to see if you contact us."

"That's why we took separate routes back here, but you're right."

Bruce interjected, "Look Mates, you're nice guys and all that, but animals do funny things when they might be about to get their heads torn off. How do we know you didn't agree to set us up?"

Lepi thought for a minute. "I guess you don't. But we didn't. "

"Any road, my spotted friends, much as we'd like to believe you, I think we're going to play it safe. We are NOT going to meet you this afternoon at that café, and we are not staying here at the hotel. After we hang up on you, we're outta here. Now, you can give us a number where we can reach you and if it turns out you're telling us the truth and you want to disappear, we may be able to help you. But if you're deliberately leading them to us, you're gonna have two angry mobs to worry about."

Long pause. "If we're leading them to you, it's not deliberate. Honest! Hey, if you can help us become scarce, that would be cool."

"Nothing's gonna happen today," said Bruce, "but be ready to move very quickly tomorrow morning. After we figure out what's going on and get ourselves set up, we'll call you. We may have to cross the border so have your papers with you."

"Which border?"

"The less you know, the less Paolo can beat out of you. What's the number to reach you at?"

He gave it to us. It was a cell phone. Bruce took it down and said, "You may hear from us tonight but more likely early in the morning. Don't get separated unless one of you wants to be left behind." He hung up.

"Now, my little mate, we are going to change our digs. Get packed and meet me at the elevator in ten minutes. I have a couple of more calls to make."

When we met at the elevator, Bruce was wearing a dress and makeup. He said, "We go out separately. My cousin Jorge is going to meet us in twenty minutes at the fountain we were splashing around in last night. You go down first and take the front door, and I'll take the side entrance. I checked us out of the hotel over the phone. Jorge drives a BMW and looks like me. *(Amazing!)* Keep a look out to see if you're being followed. If the Spotted Cats didn't tell them where we're staying, we're in good shape. If not, some evasive maneuvering will be called for."

I got an A+ in evasive maneuvering at Meerkat Crime School. Oddly, neither one of us would stick out in the streets as much as you might believe. São Paolo is a very cosmopolitan city, and there's a small but recognizable population of Meerkats here. There are quite a few Wallaroos…Australian emigrants.

The elevator came, and I skittered in and went down to the lobby. In the corner, there sat a rather nasty looking gorilla behind a newspaper. He was reading it upside down. Great help Paolo hires. I headed for the door slowly and purposefully and joined a group of tourists heading for their sightseeing bus. While I stood in the boarding line I called Bruce and warned him. The tail might have missed me, but Bruce was a lot bigger, even if he was dressed as a woman. As I got to the head of the line for boarding the bus, I walked around the front, crossed the street *(almost getting killed)* and dodged my way into a department store. I stopped at the first counter I came to, Cosmetics, and looked around. No one seemed to be after me. A smiling sales fox was coming my way and before she could start a conversation, I smiled back and sauntered off toward the side door. No gorilla.

About ten minutes to contact time. I strolled around the edge of the small park and fountain, trying to look nonchalant with a backpack and a valise. I was about to walk away for a few minutes when a BMW pulled up to the curb, and a voice called, "Senhor Maury?"

It must have been Jorge. He did look like Bruce but all Wallaroos look alike to me. I walked nonchalantly over to the car, looking over my shoulder and got in.

"Where is Bruce?"

"We separated. He'll be along in a minute."

And he was, skirt flapping, bag swinging and moving like a Wallaroo afire. I looked past him and could see why. The highly literate gorilla from the lobby was galumphing along behind him. Jorge put the car in gear, moved in Bruce's direction and just as we reached him, I opened the door, and he sprang in, landing on top of me. We shot past the ape so fast that I doubt he got a good look at the car's license plate. Jorge went through side street traffic the way Bruce flies a helicopter – swoops and swerves.

After about a half hour of Formula 1 competition with the rest of the traffic, we turned down an industrial street and into a warehouse. There were several trucks and crews unloading all sorts of Carnaval decorations and rolling a float through the doors. Bruce had changed out of the dress and with a little help from my pocket handkerchief, got most of his makeup off. It must have been power of suggestion from the handkerchief, but I started sneezing. It happens when I am nervous. And at this point, I was nervous.

Jorge pulled the car into a far corner of the warehouse and signaled us to get out. He opened the door to what looked like a security room for valuable stuff and got us inside quickly. "I trust most of those guys," he said, "but better to be safe than…" "Sorry!" we all chorused.

"*Obrigado*, Jorge, you're a '*bom amigo*,' I said and sneezed producing a laugh from the Wallaroos."

Jorge said, "Who said you have to sneeze when you speak Portuguese?"

"Bruce, of course!" I turned to my bouncing buddy and asked, "Great escape, but what do we do now?"

"We make some calls. First to L.Condor. Then Jorge has some organizing to do. We have to call Ocko and make sure the plane is going to be here and then we call our feline friends and tell them they're on their own. There was only one way that gorilla knew where we were. Our spotted mates!"

Bruce picked up his cell phone and dialed the condor. Many rings as I watched the expression on his face go from neutral to concerned and then…relieved. They started text messaging, and I could make out parts of what was flashing across the cell phone's screen. It looked like Condo was ready to lay it on our *amigo* Pontius/Paolo. Then a lengthy argument about him leaving town and going to the States with us until things cooled down. Bruce was losing until I said, "Tell him about UUI and Octavius' labs and Howard."

That seemed to interest the great bird. Perhaps a little vacation in *América del Norte* might be a nice diversion after all. He would like to bring some of his specialized gear.

Bruce typed, "One small crate is all we can handle. UUI will get you all the standard and not so standard kit you could want. Be ready by 10:30 tomorrow morning. We'll be by in a black unmarked truck. I'll call you at about 10:00 to check and do me a favor. Don't go up on the roof to check the antennas again. I thought Paolo's apes had gotten to you."

While this text conversation was going on, Jorge was engaged in what sounded like a longshorebeast's shape-up. He was calling out to the other roos in the warehouse and giving them orders. I heard the word, "amanhã" *(tomorrow)* several times and what sounded like "Meerkat" as well. When he had hung up the phone, I jerked my thumb toward Jorge and said to Bruce, "What's he doing, organizing next year's Carnaval?"

"Close, Maury, close. We have a diversion planned for Paolo and his crew if they come after us. We may not need it, but we'll see. What time is it?"

"Almost time to call Octavius. He's one time zone behind us."

"OK, Jorge do you have a couple of phones we can use as extensions?"

We got the Frau who was no doubt concerned about us. "Herr Maury, are you all right? What has that bounding bungler gotten you into this time?" *(Clearly no sympathy for Bruce. There's a limit to how many end tables you can accidentally smash before you bring down the wrath of Frau Ilse Schuylkill.)*

"I heard that, you lupine menace!" said Bruce on the other extension.

Not wanting to referee a long distance fight, I intervened and asked the Frau to get Octavius and Belinda. Belinda got on first.

"Maury, you sweet little thing, you. Are you and Bruce all right?"

"Yes, Bearoness, we're fine, but we're being chased by a very nasty group down here and we think the time has come to say *saludos amigos.*"

"The Aquabear is all ready to go. It should take a bit less than eight hours with the right winds. We can't fly supersonic all the way, and we might stop in Miami to refuel."

Bruce came on. "G'day Bearoness, G'day Ocko if you're there. *(A rumble in the background. He was there.)* If you can be at the freight terminal at São Paolo International with the cargo bay open before noon tomorrow, we'll be coming in with a truck loaded with crates and Carnaval costumes and float characters. Be careful with the crates. We'll be in them. We will definitely have one additional passenger with us. L.Condor. I think I mentioned him to you, Ocko. The bird's miraculous. He's a computer and communications jackaroo like you've never met. Things will be getting a bit hot down here, and he thought he'd like to come north for a little climate change."

"Bring him up, Inspector. We'll make arrangements with Immigration to let him in considering what he's doing for us and the country."

"There may be three more passengers, Ocko. I'm not sure. They're the remaining members of the band Chita was playing and singing with. Pontius Puma beat them up pretty badly trying to find out what happened to Chita. They told him about us and that's why were on the run."

"Let me understand this, Maury," said Belinda, "These cats ratted on you, and you want to give them a holiday trip to the States?"

"Don't know yet, Bearoness. I do believe the information was beaten out of them and if they stay here, they'll get killed by Pontius, especially after he discovers our big surprise."

"It's your call, Inspector, but don't jeopardize the mission over them," said the Bear. "I'll be flying down with Bel, Bearyl and Bearnice in case you need some moral support on the tarmac."

"Gotcha, Ocko. Bring some weapons just in case...Ocko? Ocko?"

"He's asleep, Inspector. We'll plan to be there well before noon in case there are in-flight delays, and we'll be ready to button up and roll out again as soon as you're on board. We'll check in with you on the way down, and if you have to reach us..." She gave me a ground to air number and signed off.

"OK, Bruce, let's talk to the cats."

"The inspector dialed the number they had given us, and this time Ozzie answered the phone. "Sing Foo Laundry," he said.

"I've got some imported shirts I need cleaned right away before I go on a trip."

Sigh of relief, "Inspector Wallaroo, good to talk to you."

"Maybe not so good, Oz m'mate! Maury and I have had a run-in with Paolo's pals. They knew we were at the hotel. Now how do you suppose that happened if you didn't tell them?"

"Oh, geeez, we were afraid of that. Jake, you *were* followed. Here, get on the phone. It's Inspector Wallaroo."

Jake the Jaguar picked up the phone in the middle of a stream of latino cursewords and said, "Hey, Inspector, You guys all right? Hey, look, my bad. We split up and came to the city by different routes. I took an overnight bus, and it took a lot longer. There were a couple of unsavory looking characters on the bus but that's what you get on overnight buses. Anyway, when I got off, I tried to reach Ozzie and Lepi, but no luck."

Lepi interrupted, "We had turned off our phone and were going to call him."

"Anyway," Jake continued, "it didn't look like I was being tailed, so I thought I couldn't hang around the bus terminal, and I'd better go someplace where I could stay for a while. Then the thought struck me. I'd look for you guys. So I went over to your hotel, hoping Lepi and Ozzie were there with you. When I got there your phone was busy and they wouldn't tell me your room number. Then I saw a big gorilla just like the ones that roughed us up in Rio coming into the lobby, and I lost it. I got out of there so fast I stomped over a bunch of Japanese tourists. I don't think he followed me out of the hotel."

"No," said Bruce, "he didn't need you anymore. He knew where we were, and he knew what we looked like."

"We never told them your names," said Jake, "just that you knew Chita and were with the police."

"Not entirely true but close enough. Hold on," said the Inspector. He put the telephone in his pouch and said to me, "What do you think?"

"These cats are either very clever or very dumb. I'm inclined to think dumb. If we leave them here, Pontius will take it out on them without question. But they may get us all in a mess of trouble."

"Not if they're in crates!" said Bruce. He pulled out the phone and said. "OK, you guys, here's what we're going to do, but if you screw up we will have you hand delivered to Paolo, the Thug. Understand?"

The Development of Civilization - Volume 2 Part 5

Transportation and Travel

(From "An Introduction to Faunapology" by Octavius Bear Ph.D.)

It interesting to note that during the period before the Big Shock, many of today's surviving animal species seemed destined to be the primary modes of transportation for Homo Sapiens. From early cave paintings and other primitive art, we see that H.Saps began to develop methods of "harnessing" animals larger and more fleet than themselves and training them to convey them on long and difficult journeys or in hunting or warfare.

The concept of "being transported" did not disappear with the extinction of the H.Saps. Rather, it seems to have been imbued in the enhanced psyches of many species. Some animals rebelled forcefully at the prospect of being "beasts of burden" or "pullers of the plow." Others, citing ancestral examples, took more willingly to the prospect but also worked out complex schedules of rates and tariffs for their services. Transport began to develop as a business.

Slowly, as development of implements took hold, [see our discussion - Tools and Toolmakers] the application of basic technologies such as the skid, the ramp, the raft and most important, the wheel advanced the state of travel. Going long distances in search of food and water was mapped into the genes of most herd animals and birds well before the Big Shock. But now the more gregarious species began to see travel as a means of widening their knowledge, their relationships and as you might expect, their influence.

The wheel, of course, ranks as the number one invention that advanced animal kind into its current state of mobility. Millennia later, with the advent of the internal combustion engine and its complex attachment to the wheel, self propelled vehicles made their way into our lives, relieving many animals of their onerous roles as haulers and carriers. For example, the chariot and the ox cart were transformed into the automobile and the truck ["lorry" for our UK friends] with all sorts of variants suited to the needs, sizes and configurations of the animals involved.

*Water travel for the non-amphibious first began through the use of hollowed out or strung together logs. We are not sure when wind power was first used to supplement the use of rowing implements. It may indeed go all the way back to the H.Saps. Of course, once the internal combustion engine was introduced, its application to sea-going vehicles was not far behind, first through the paddle wheel and then the screw propeller. Today of course, some boats are driven by jet reaction. Oddly enough, while many experiments were conducted to mechanically emulate the movement of fish **in** the water, they proved to be inefficient for mammals to move **on** the water. And now we do have submerged vehicles such as submarines, but these are usually highly specialized.*

The other form of transit that had for the longest time fascinated the advancing fauna of earth was flight. Birds, with their unique construction, seemed to be the applicable model but reproducing the flapping, soaring, diving, turning, take off and landing configurations of the avians proved to be no easy task, even with the cooperation of the birds themselves. Indeed, most birds didn't know how they flew any more than most fish know how they swim.

Fortunately, unlike most of their undersea brethren who were not affected by the Big Shock and thus did not move up the sentient scale, birds were enhanced and while the insulting epithet, "bird brain" still persists, many of them have tested at the highest ranges of earth-wide intelligence. Witness our new friend, L Condor. Nevertheless, it has only been a few hundred years since scientists and engineers from the Ornithological Institute of Applied Aviation invented machines that can fly. Indeed, the world owes a great debt to the famous female aeronautical designer, Kitty Hawk, whose successful prototype aircraft, The Golden Goose, set the world on its way to universally accessible flight.

Rocketry, leading to space travel and a brief sojourn on the moon just a few years ago, may be our final step in aerial propulsion. Unless, of course, teleportation turns out to be real and commonplace, making most of our transportation vehicles redundant.

Chapter Twelve

The Snow Leopard's also called "Ounce."

And his presence he'll never announce.

He's quite beautiful, too.

But don't let him near you.

Without warning, he'll suddenly pounce.

Mach 1.5 at 45,000 feet over the South Pacific Ocean *(it's down there somewhere.)* The Aquabear was making good time. Taking a direct route due south from Cincinnati; over the Gulf of Mexico; making one refueling stop in Central America and then on to the Pacific and the west coast of South America *(to maximize the over-water supersonic time);* the Concorde with the Three Bears plus Two *(Octavius and Juno who had come along for the ride)* was plotted to turn east over Chile and fly subsonically over Bolivia, Paraguay and finally into southern Brazil and São Paolo. Arrival at about 11:15 AM local time looked good.

Bearyl, the navigator-flight engineer dropped back into the cabin to see how Octavius and Juno were doing. He had been asleep for most of the trip. Belinda and Frau Schuylkill had modified the seat used by the late Bearon Bruin to fit the somewhat larger girth of the Great Bear. He could not stand erect in the fuselage, but could maneuver quite easily on all fours in the almost empty cabin. An airplane once designed to hold one hundred medium sized animals was now down to sixteen widely spaced seats.

Octavius woke up, looked around and saw Bearyl. "Are you Bearyl or Bearnice?" he asked.

"I'm Bearyl. Bearnice wears an ankle bracelet."

"Right, sorry. Have we left the US yet?"

"Oh, Doctor Bear…."

"Octavius!"

107

"Oh, Octavius….a long time ago. We're coming up on the coast of Peru. When we get to Chile, we turn due east toward São Paolo. Welcome to supersonic flight. We'll be there a little early."

"Not too early, I hope. I don't want us sitting around there like fish in a barrel. This airplane's not exactly inconspicuous. Speaking of fish, do we have anything to eat?"

"There's a buffet set up near the aft galley. Help yourself. You too, Mrs. Bear! Actually, the fact that this airplane is something of an attraction sometimes works in our favor. Everyone is usually so taken up with its uniqueness that they pay little or no attention to what we're doing. To help things along, on this trip we three will be wearing modified Aquabear costumes when we arrive. That usually gets the attention of the customs officials and the ramp gangs. But you're right. We want to keep our ground turnaround time to a minimum."

"I should check in with Frau Schuylkill, Howard and the Colonel," said Octavius. "I'm sure they have everything under control, but with Imperius, you never know. Also, please let me know when you plan to call Maury and the Inspector.'

"Not for another hour or so. Want to watch a movie in the meantime?"

*****

São Paolo, early morning: Bruce and I stayed overnight at the warehouse. Not the Ritz, but they did have a couple of cots. Our first run was to pick up L. Condor. Since Pontius/Paolo didn't know about him *(yet)*, we could be a little less circumspect in our approach. We told him to be ready with his crate of equipment inside the elevator to his home-lab-computer center-attack base-whatever.

We sent an unmarked truck on a circuitous route with a large German Shepherd driving. In the back were two more dogs, a Doberman and a Pit Bull, and me. I was in command. *(Ta Da!!)* Bruce stayed back at the warehouse to avoid any unnecessary exposure, but I was small enough to hide in the truck, if necessary. When we got there, the two dogs in the back plus the driver all dressed as freight haulers walked up casually and rang for the elevator. The door opened, and there was L. Condor almost covered with portable electronics devices along with his crate. We hustled him and the very h-e-a-v-y box into the back of the truck and took off.

He handed me a text cell phone and began laying out for me what was going to happen to Pontius and his pals' empire of stolen information. *(Phase One)* I asked him to hold off until we got to the warehouse, so he could tell Bruce and me at the same time. In the meantime, I gave him a run down on UUI, Octavius and Howard and how I hoped they could give him a real boost in getting his synthesized voice going.

I also thought he could be a great help to us with Imperius Drake. He was free to stay with us as long as he pleased, but certainly until we were reasonably convinced that nothing that had happened to PP could be traced back to Condo. He actually seemed eager to make the trip and join us for a while. Maybe we could get him out of his depression over his lost mate. It would also be very interesting to see him and Imperius in "wing to wing" combat. Probably wouldn't happen, but it does make for interesting musing.

Anyway, we pulled up to the warehouse, the dogs opened one of the rear doors, and Condo and I hopped out. The truck and its crew stood by for its next pickup: The Spotted Band minus One.

When we got inside, Bruce was on the phone, as usual. He was talking to the Aquabear which had just passed over Chile and was approaching subsonic on a due east vector to São Paolo. They expected to be on the ground around 11:30 and would check in with us again just before they entered their final approach. We had a little over two hours to put phases two, three and four into action.

L. Condor handed a text phone to Bruce and proceeded to tell both of us the basics of the death and destruction that would be unfolding in Pontius Puma's computers, databases, networks and back up storage units. Essentially the attack encrypted every piece of data it ran into. The algorithm was L.Condor's super secret invention, as was the extensive crypto key. It would take years to break. It demolished all the network addresses and killed off each computer's applications, operating system(s), registry and registry backups and then just sat around and waited.

The real beauty of the attack was that most remedial action by PP's staff would set the whole process off again. The condor estimated they would be down for several weeks or longer and that they would never recover their data. Unfortunately, because of the way they were tied together and used for camouflage, the Puma's music businesses and the stolen military and scientific data both had to be destroyed. Some musicians would be very upset, but it couldn't be helped. With any luck, Pontius' income stream from all sources would be getting a good deal drier.

Bruce picked up the phone and called through to his headquarters in Australia, telling them to start the global roundup of Pontius' ring of industrial spies. Now, if we could get away from São Paolo unscathed, this would go down as a rather upsetting day for the Puma and a pretty good score for us.

Phase Two: Pick up the cats. We had told them to be ready at three different locations and to stand by for an unmarked truck. Actually there were three different trucks. Each one being driven by one of the dogs. We had told them no baggage, but Lepi talked us into bringing his keyboard sans amplifiers, and Ozzie had one guitar. We drew the line at Jake's drums. He was so beat up he couldn't play them anyway, and the other two weren't in much better shape. One by one they arrived at the warehouse looking spooked and very tired.

When they got inside, Bruce asked them, 'OK, which one of you has been having the conversations with Paolo?"

No response.

"Let me ask it a different way. If one of you were to call him, whose voice would he recognize?"

Lepi looked up and said, "I guess me, but what are we going to call him for? Isn't all this cloak and dagger stuff supposed to keep him from finding us?"

"Right," said Bruce, We want him to find *Maury and me,* and we want you to tell him where we're going to be – at the airport."

"Are you guys nuts?" yelled Jake. "I thought we were going to be safe with you but it sounds like we signed up for a suicide pact."

"Nope," said Bruce. "Just a deucedly droll diversion." *(Fetlock Holmes was back on the scene.)* "I want you to call him now and tell him in exchange for laying off you three, you'll tell him where to find the two of us today. At the intercontinental terminal at Guarulhos International Airport at 11:45 AM ticketed on Vireo Airlines Flight 98568 to Los Angeles."

"Do you honestly think he'll lay off us if we tell him that?"

"Of, course not, you twit. He'll still try to kill you. That's why we're taking you with us when we leave on a private aircraft from the freight terminal on the other side of the airport. We hope they'll be looking for us at the

110

intercontinental terminal at just about the same time. He's probably had the airports, bus stations, railroads and rental car agencies covered since yesterday. Just as a precaution, we want to get any of his gorillas who might be at the freight terminal moving over to the passenger side of the airport. We'll have a few friends there to keep them busy while we take off. Now here, take this phone and make the call."

Lepi called Paolo/Pontius' office. He used a phony business name. Enterprise Enterprises! *(The three cats still didn't know who Paolo really was, and we didn't plan on telling them until we were well out of Brazilian airspace. They probably got some of their bookings and CDs through his agencies. We didn't want to tell them yet that although they were still alive, their musical careers in Brazil were toast.)* He got a secretary who called an assistant who went through a song and dance, no doubt trying to trace our cell phone that would soon be at the bottom of the Morro do São Paolo estuary courtesy of Jorge and his friends.

Finally, Lepi just said, "Look, take a message and make sure he gets it right away, or I wouldn't want to be in your paws. You can grab the Wallaroo and the Meerkat at the Intercontinental Terminal at Guarulhos. They're catching a 13:45 flight to Los Angeles on Vireo and should be arriving at the airport any time after 11:00. Tell him that makes us all square; we still don't know where Chita is, and we don't want to have anything to do with him from here on in."

"File that last part under fat chance," I said.

"What the hell," said Lepi. "I figured I might as well give him some guff while I was at it. My front legs are killing me from that beating."

OK, on to Phase Three: We loaded up the truck inside the warehouse with some large Carnaval figurines, eight medium sized crates of costumes *(six of which were only half filled)* and the three cats, Condo, Bruce and me. We also had Condo's equipment crate. In short, a sizable but not outlandish load to be putting on the Aquabear. We drove off at a normal rate toward the airport, checking to see if we were being followed or assuming these guys had the brains for it, being tag teamed. No sign of them. If they were tailing us they were better than I thought *(but I have been known to be wrong)*.

As we neared the airport, we pulled over into an industrial parking lot, and the three dogs who had been in the front seat came back with some hammers, nails and official looking seals. Bruce took the opportunity to call the

111

Aquabear. They were on course for a touchdown in five minutes. He told Octavius to wait until we had the plane loaded up and then to call Jorge to set off Phase Four. *(We were going to be inside the crates and in no position to see what was going on. Once the Aquabear was buttoned and rolling, Bearyl and Octavius would open the Concorde's passenger cabin floor to the cargo hold and get us all out before we got airborne.)*

The cats weren't crazy about getting in the crates and being covered over by the costumes. Ozzie was afraid he'd suffocate. *(He wouldn't. There was enough ventilation in the seams of the crates.)* Lepi was concerned about how hot it would get. *(Tough! It might be hotter for him if he were dead.)* Jake just muttered something about crazy cheetahs and %#$&-ing Pumas and nutty wallaroos and pesty meerkats and his lost drum set. *(Bitch, bitch, bitch!)* Condo, of course said nothing, but hopped into his crate taking one last look at his equipment box. *(We were going to palm that off at customs as electronic show gear for controlling lights and fireworks.)* Bruce and I got into our box *(I was small enough to fit in there with him)* and felt the dogs hammering lightly on the top of the crate.

The three dogs were real pros when it came to dealing with customs and airport security. We had one moment when one of the inspectors wanted to open a crate and almost picked the one with Jake in it. Ten to one he would have snarled or made some other noise, if they had. The dogs slyly and I suspect with a little monetary incentive, got them to open the crates that were full of costumes and no passengers. Condo's equipment rated a security check but the Carnaval show story worked. I could feel the truck being closed up, and we took off again. We zigged and zagged a bit. I assume we were dodging other trucks and ramp equipment when we finally came to a stop.

The door opened and I could hear Octavius' booming voice giving the ramp crew directions on how to load the cargo on the Aquabear. I was told later that all three Polar beauties were on the ground in their Aquabear costumes supervising the refueling and loading and checking out the airplane before taking off again. In their show outfits, I'm surprised any fuel got in the tanks. I'm also surprised two or more of the ramp trucks and tugs didn't crash into each other.

We could feel ourselves being beasthandled off the truck and onto the cargo loading belt. Finally with a metallic thump and some pushing around, under Octavius' command, we settled in for what we hoped would be a very short confinement in the belly of the Aquabear.

While all this was going on, Phase Four was well into its full scale epic production. Over at the intercontinental terminal, PP had placed his gorillas at the cab and bus drop off points, ready to grab us and dump us in a limousine that was waiting across the roadway. Inside the limo, behind darkened windows surrounded by a bank of phones and a lynx secretary sat Senhor Puma. He was giving directions to the welcoming committee. There was one false alarm when a mother Wallaroo and three joeys going back to Australia crossed their paths.

Suddenly a bus marked Brazilian Fiesta pulled up to the curb. There was a Wallaroo framed against one of the windows. The gorillas converged on the bus. Out stepped a Wallaroo and a Meerkat, and as the apes swooped in for the grab, out stepped another Wallaroo and another Meerkat and another and another.

The head gorilla yelled into the cell phone, "Senhor, they're all Wallaroos and Meerkats. We don't know which ones to grab. What do we do?"

Pontius was not pleased. "Idiots, look for one that looks like an Australian cop."

"They all do!"

Before he could respond, the red phone rang, and his secretary picked it up. She handed it over to Pontius. "You'd better take it. It's Rinaldo." *(The Chief information Officer.)*

He picked up the phone. "This better be important!" And as he listened, any thoughts of capturing a Wallaroo and a Meerkat faded from his feline brain. His screams of rage were drowned out by the screams of the engines of a Concorde SST leaping into the sky.

The Development of Civilization - Volume 2 Part 6

Science, Engineering, Tools and Toolmakers

(From "An Introduction to Faunapology" by Octavius Bear Ph.D.)

Many scientists and philosophers agree that the design and fabrication of tools is one of the most distinguishing characteristics of a developing civilization. There are other civilizing traits, of course, such as widespread communication, economic structures, codes of ethics, care for the weak and defenseless and widespread cooperation within and among species. But operating paw in glove with all of these are the enhancements that technology can bring to each process.

It is unclear which animals first demonstrated tool making skills. There are many examples of the early use of sticks and rocks to assist in retrieving food or constructing basic forms of shelter. Slowly, more materials were brought to bear as the tools and protective cover became more sophisticated and elaborate.

Weapons, of course, are something of a conundrum. They were probably accidental in their origin. The discovery that a well aimed rock could permanently settle a dispute must have come as a shock to all the participants. Sharpening that rock into a pointed spear blade made it a purposeful tool. Weapons became necessary for self defense and hunting but unfortunately, all too often were also implements of aggression and destruction. The proverbial two-edged sword! Arms and armament reach back well before any transcribed history. They, no doubt, will outlive our civilization, perhaps even causing its demise.

What we speak of today as science and engineering are probably the results of the Big Shock creating among the enhanced species the first real instances of self-awareness and the urge to question. Who, what, where, when and perhaps most importantly, how and why! "How?" primarily for the engineer! "Why?" primarily for the scientist! Homo Sapiens seemed to have been making strides in these areas, before their sweeping extinction. Wall paintings, images and rudimentary religious artifacts left behind bear out the existence of the inquiring mind at work. Only in recent years have faunapologists and archaeologists come to appreciate some of the rather complex concepts that H.Saps were wrestling with before their mass demise.

There are other great strides that have propelled the tool making characteristics of our society:

The discovery of electricity. Although fire had been known, used and for the most part tamed by early post Shock species, it had many limitations as a power source, not the least of which was its destructive consumption of fuel. When magnetism and then electricity were first introduced to the scientific community by a team of ocean explorers, the true importance was not understood or felt for many years. Magnetism first showed itself to be useful in navigation, although the makers of the first compasses did not have any real appreciation as to why their instruments insisted on turning to the North.

Electricity itself first became known as a potential source of power when some early ichthyologists made the shocking discovery of the electric eel. They spent nearly a century before they could harness and reproduce this source of power. Along the way, many great scientists including Nils Boar, Albeart Einstein, Nicator Tesla, Sir Isaac Newt and Tortoise Edison contributed to the explosive growth of electric and then atomic energy. We will talk about the evolution of electronics in a later discussion.

Tools for making tools. A true sign of technological advance is the ability to use and make additional and more advanced tools. One spear is useful, but many spears greatly enhance the offensive and defensive capabilities of the pack. Even more useful are devices that enable the rapid, easy and repetitive production of spears, wheels, shafts, rafts, boats, vessels for eating, drinking and storage and components for shelter. The combination of these devices with a variety of materials including the first metals opened the path to more sophisticated devices for transportation, heating, pawufacturing and protection. The internal combustion engine, first proposed by Galapagos Galapagi has, of course, altered civilization for all time.

Chapter Thirteen

They spend life as a loyal, faithful pair,

Full of love, deep devotion and care.

But if one of them dies

Then the other one cries.

The lone Mandarin lives in despair.

Meanwhile back at the Duck Blind on Pelican Island, Imperius reached over and opened the door to the laboratory. He looked at Otto. "Notice anything???" he asked.

"Yeah, you locked the door. Why?"

"You got through before."

"It wasn't locked."

"No, my dear Otto." said the duck. "It was indeed locked. You just opened it as if it wasn't. And that thing you did with the fish and the boat. Let's go outside and see if you can do it again."

They walked up the ramp. Imperius had to unlock the door and identify himself to the access system as they left. Out on the dock, he looked at Otto and said, "Make the boat disappear like you did before."

Otto waved his paws, and the hydroplane responded by doing absolutely nothing. "Wait a second, let me try again." he said. More waving, this time with a very determined look on his whiskered face. No movement.

"Try the fishing pole." said the Baboon. "You caught a big catfish the last time. Maybe he's still swimming around out there."

Otto waved at the pole which sat unstirring in the cockpit of the hydroplane. Then he waved at the river, trying to raise the fish. Finally he jumped into the river and swam out into the center of the current. Suddenly the water churned and boiled. First an otter tail appeared, then a fish tail and then

116

with a sharp smack, Otto came out of the water and landed with a huge splash right by the dock.

He spat out some water, climbed up on the dock and shook himself off. "The fish didn't want to play any more." he said.

"Otto, my boy, we need to talk." said Imperius. "First, you must realize that not everyone can do what you did earlier this morning. You are a remarkable swimmer and very agile, but breaking out of bondage or making boats disappear and reappear is not normal behavior. Neither is walking through locked doors and yes, in spite of what you thought, they were locked."

"Well, why can't I do it now?"

"The answer to that, Otto, lies in the tonic I have been giving you. It enhances your illusionist and escapist talents to the point where you can make things disappear and break through all sorts of restraints."

"Wow, that's really something, Milord, but it doesn't seem to last that long."

"Once again, you have put your clever paw on exactly the problem that needs to be solved. I have some more work to do in my laboratory, and we'll be ready to try the new, improved version with Vitamin E. Results may vary. Do not drive or operate heavy machinery. Do not take if pregnant, allergic to ragweed or suffering from congestive heart failure."

"I don't have any of that!!"

"I know. It's a government requirement for me to say that. Now, why don't you take a nice swim while I go in the lab and the Commandante takes the boat to get supplies. You've been eating enough to feed a herd of otters."

"Bevy!!"

"Pardon!?"

"A group of otters is called a bevy or a family."

"Thanks!"

"You're welcome, Milord. Yeah, I think I would like a swim."

"But, Otto," said Imperius, "stay in the immediate area. I may want to try a few variations on the tonic on you."

"This won't be dangerous, will it?"

"Otto, my boy, you must learn to trust us. Have we led you astray or done any harm to you? Are you not on your way to a new and spectacular career? What possible good would it do the Commandante or me to cause you harm? I'll be blunt, Otto, you're going to make a lot of money for all of us. We want you in the very best of condition and at the top of your form." *(Unspoken Fiendish Villain's Aside: So you can help me to bring Octavius Bear to a fitting end, and then on to world conquest! Followed by cackling, no, quacking laughter.)*

"OK, I'm sorry. I guess I'll have to get used to traveling in the fast lane if I want to be a big hit on Broadway and Vegas and TV and the Catskills and Cruise Ships and London and Paris and Tokyo and…"

"Indeed, my boy, indeed, you just keep thinking that way!"

"…Miami and Cincinnati and Omaha and Hollywood and …" Splash!

"Baboon," said Imperius, "when you go downriver for supplies, keep a watch out for any strangers or boats that look like they're searching for something or someone. That accursed bear is no doubt looking for us now that I sent him my little *billet doux*."

"Who's Billy Doo?"

"Not who, you idiot, what. The Black Quack! I told you about it. It probably created quite a stir at UUI headquarters. Now get your list, and go shop and stay out of the gourmet aisle."

The fact that his uncontrollable ego may have precipitated that search never occurred to the Mad Mandarin. Poking his finger in Octavius' eye, to say nothing of the eyes of law enforcement in general, had such compulsive sway over his actions that he often came perilously close to self-destruction. Close but not close enough. We can only hope.

Once again Imperius felt the pangs of loss of his beloved Lee-Li-Li. What once was despair at her demise was now transmuted into a raging lust for vengeance. His Great Plan for eliminating the genetic charlatans of the world came so close, so close. Once again, that hated ursine interfered. Every turn he made, that odious bear stood in his way. Unbearable. Yes, the world must be made un-bear-able. And he was the duck to do it.

Otto was floating along on his back, watching Commandante Babaloo maneuver the hydroplane away from the dock. He wondered why Milord Mallàrd kept such an expensive and high performance boat. A small outboard would certainly do for shopping, but that's the way it is nowadays. Everything has to be oversized and glitzy. He paddled out into the mainstream of the Missouri river and then decided he might do a little exploring on the opposite shore.

Sloshing up the river bank, he shook himself off and decided to sit for a minute to dry off before going on his mini-expedition.

"Hi cutie!" a sultry voice whispered near his right ear.

He turned and, oh gee, there was the blackest, slinkiest looking panther he had ever seen. In fact, it was the only panther he had ever seen. He started to shake. There went his showbiz career before it began.

"Don't worry, Sweetface! I'm not going to hurt you. What's your name, honey?"

"Errr, Otto, no, Hairy, no, Otto."

"Are you having an identity crisis, darling?"

"No, my real name is Hairy Otter, but my stage name is Otto the Magnificent."

"Oh ho! And what are you magnificent at, Otto?"

"I'm a magician and illusionist."

"Are you famous?" asked the cat.

"Not yet, but Milord Mallàrd and Commandante Babaloo are helping me to become famous. Oops, I wasn't supposed to mention that."

"Why not??"

"Well, there's a lot of competition in show business, and we're working out my act in secret over there on the island."

"Well, don't worry about me. I'm not in show biz anymore. I used to sing a little. but I'm retired. Too stressful!"

"Who are you and why are you over here?" asked the otter.

"You can just call me Catt, with two t's. Catherine Catt, and I'm just out touring around, seeing America and all that. I thought I'd walk along the river a little. Where did you come from?"

"The St. Lawrence River originally, but I'm staying on that island over there for a while with Milord Mallàrd and Commandante Babaloo."

"Just the three of you?"

"Yup, but not for much longer. We're going on tour soon."

"Well, I wish you a lot of luck. You know, I think I once did a gig for Milord Mallàrd. His name was different then but so was mine. We didn't part under the best of terms, so I'd appreciate it if you didn't mention meeting me."

"No problem, Ms Catt. Nice talking with you." With that he slipped back into the water and swam off downstream.

Chita *(Aw, you guessed!)* watched him paddle off and sat down to ponder, plot and plan. She knew the Duck Blind very well. She used to operate out of there with Imperius and Bigg. It was from there they launched the Deep Blue caper. *(cf. The Open and Shut Case - Volume One of the Case Books of Octavius Bear.)* She wondered if her access identification was still on the security system. It would be just like Imperius to overlook a detail like that while he contemplated the destruction of the world.

The otter was a new development, one that might play right into her claws. She had come back to Pelican Island and the Duck Blind looking for Imperius and just waiting for the first opportunity to get him alone and kill him. But what was Imperius planning this time? This whole illusionist thing with Otto piqued her curiosity. Yeah, she knew *"Curiosity killed the Cat."* But it might be worth waiting to find out what Imperius was up to. Maybe she could use this otter against the duck *(and if she was feeling really perturbed, the baboon too. Bigg was stupid, but he was nasty stupid, and the world could do without both of them.)*

Down in his laboratory, little knowing his second nemesis was lurking just across the river, Imperius worked away at improving the formula. He must be careful. Certainly, he didn't want to kill the otter, seeing how close he came the last time. Not only did he need to improve his formula; he had to gain a better understanding of the otter's makeup. Was he so unique that thoughts of generalizing the serum were once again going to prove illusory?

But Otto's abilities when "under the influence" were astounding, better than the duck had expected. Even if he was unique and required a specially tailored serum, the results might indeed be worth it. With Chita gone, Imperius needed assistance – powerful, intelligent, preternatural assistance. The otter showed strong signs of having all of that and more. He must be especially attentive to keeping or enhancing those characteristics. Now, if he could figure out how to make the effects last longer and most importantly, how to make Otto more compliant, his job would be complete.

He looked up from his work. The baboon was coming down the ramp with the fruits of his shopping expedition, and Otto was giving him a paw. They dragged the food over to the locker and Bigg *(Commandante Babaloo)* went back out for more while Otto arranged the stuff in the refrigerator, freezer and pantry. Imperius called him into the lab.

"Otto, my boy, I have improved the tonic for you. I think this will make your unique talents last far longer, but we must test it very carefully. Are you ready for another test?"

"Gee, Milord, I think I'd rather have something to eat before I do."

"Of course, my boy, of course. By all means, have a fish or two and come back when you're finished."

He stared after the otter and thought about his cunning plan of retribution against the bear and his underlings. Oh, how sweet it will be to invade his bastion of self-proclaimed justice and harmony and to wreak devastation on UUI as well. But first, he had to find the bear's center of operations. He was pretty sure it was in reasonable proximity to UUI Headquarters in Kentucky, but he did not want to waste time on a long and painstaking search.

The first order of business after he had gotten Otto to the state of performance required was to attack UUI again and to smoke the bear out of his den. He would then follow him back to his lair, recover the particle beam weapon and based on the situation, stage the *coup de grace*. It would be lovely to strike at all his hangers-on especially that worthless slut of a polar bear. How dare she foil his master stroke in Las Vegas! He would bring disaster on her and her stupid swimming entourage if he had to track her around the world. But enough! Otto was wiping his whiskers and coming back into the laboratory.

"I guess I'm ready, Milord."

"Good lad, good lad! Now just lie here on this table, and this time instead of having you drink your tonic, I'm going to inject it in your rump."

"Are you sure this is necessary?"

"Remember, Otto, stardom awaits."

"Yeah, I guess so…Ouch! That hurt!"

"It will only sting for a moment, Otto…Otto, Otto? Egad, here we go again. Commandante! Come quickly."

Otto had immediately stiffened up and assumed the position of "playing dead" only he wasn't playing. The baboon ran through the door and said, "Gee, did you really kill him this time?"

"I don't think so. We must wait and see what happens. His system is reacting to the genetic changes, and he is rebooting."

"Did you make a back-up just in case?" asked the baboon. "That's what you always tell me to do when we work on the computers."

"No, baboon, careless of me as it may seem, I do not have a backup otter. Now just sit there and watch. He may become violent when he wakes up."

Minutes passed *(after they were seconded and voted upon by the committee),* and Otto showed no signs of recovery. Bigg sat in the corner looking in turn concerned, puzzled and mournful. "Gee, Sire, I kind of liked the little guy. But maybe you can use the tonic to kill people, if it doesn't work out."

"Good, Baboon. Always look on the brighter side of things." Imperius was composing a Help Wanted ad in his head as they waited. His dreams of empire required more effective staffing than the baboon and even the otter *(if he survived)* could provide. Shame about the cat! She was a real talent. He might have been able to subdue her sense of independence if he had more time to work on her. Perhaps he was too hasty trying to kill her off in Las Vegas **but she had betrayed him!!**

He looked over at the table on which Otto was lying and noticed an anomaly. There seemed to be something different. What? Of course……there was **NO** Otto. The Otter was gone!!!!

"Baboon, where is Otto?" he shouted. "Can't I trust you with anything?"

Bigg added total confusion to his menu of expressions. "He was here a second ago. Out cold!"

They were interrupted by the sound of running water coming from outside the lab. Then they heard a squeaky voice singing, "Rubber Ducky, you're the one. You make bathtime lots of fun. Rubber Ducky, I'm awfully fond of you; Woo woo be doo!" alternating with "Splish, Splash, I was takin' a bath."

"He's in the shower, Milord," said Bigg.

"Yes, I know, Baboon, and he's singing that ridiculous Rubber Duck song."

Bigg started to hum along. "You make bathtime lots of ……"

"Baboon!!!!! I hate that song. Shut up, and get him out here."

Otto came out of the shower, rubbing himself down with a towel. "Gee, that Missouri River has all kinds of nasty stuff in it. I really needed that shower."

"How did you get out of the lab?"

"I walked out. Why, did I do something wrong?"

"Otto, I want you to go out to the dock. The Commandante is going to tie you up in the boat while I stay here inside watching over the surveillance system. I'm going to lock all the doors with the highest security and when I say "go" over the loudspeakers, I want you to untie yourself and meet me back here in the lab as fast as you can. Got that?"

"Sure, are we doing speed trials?"

"Exactly, my boy, exactly. Commandante Babaloo will tie you up as tightly and with as much complexity as he is capable of *(not much, but what are you going to do?)*."

Out they went. While the baboon was tying Otto up and then securing him to the steering wheel of the boat, Imperius put the Duck Blind on maximum security shut-down, turning off all the entry systems, activating the electronic locks and bringing down the corrugated steel shutters that sealed the ramp and the windows. "Wave when you're ready, Commandante!" he called.

The baboon checked all the knots and for good measure handcuffed Otto to the steering column. He waved at the cameras.

"All right, Otto." The duck's voice boomed over the speakers. "Go!!"

A swirling wave of motion in the cockpit of the boat and then over the speakers, "Egad, Otto, three seconds and you're in here!"

"Was that OK, Milord?" echoed a squeaky voice.

"Yes, Otto, that was OK. Now we will have to see how long the effects last."

Out on the dock, Bigg scratched his head in disbelief. On the other shore, a stealthy black cat was also scratching her head and staring at the Duck Blind.

Chapter Fourteen

There are ocelots found in Brazil

Where they spend their whole day lying still.

But they come out at night.

When they eat, mate and fight.

Getting near them requires great skill.

"Somewhere over the Pacific, way up high!" I'll say this for Belinda and her flight crew. They're right up there with Frau Schuylkill and the Colonel as high performance jet jockeys. Let's just say we made a noticeable exit. I'm not sure whether Paolo/Pontius noticed our howling departure. He was probably too busy howling over his data debacle.

I felt but saw nothing of our exodus, still being stuck in a crate in the cargo hold. We were supposed to emerge from our captivity before takeoff but the Bearoness sweet-talked the ground and air controllers into making an immediate exit, and we all stayed in storage.

As soon as the thrill ride leveled off, and we were in cruise mode, I could hear thumping and bumping, an occasional swear word from Octavius or one of the polar bears and the sound of containers being unlatched. Each one of us traveled in a separate box *(a luxury perk)* except of course, for me. I had Bruce as a roomie. We were cushioned by Carnaval costumes to keep from hurting each other if we fell over or slid. That's the second time in as many days I have had Close Encounters of the Fifth Kind with the Inspector. *(Yes, I am feeling sorry for myself.)*

Several boxes were stored in each Concorde cargo container. Needless to say, as usual, I was one of the last to be extricated. As the side of our box was popped open by someone being none too careful with a crowbar, I was treated to a picture of Bruce Wallaroo once again in dance costume. I'm beginning to worry a bit about him. One by one we crawled through the cargo bay ceiling onto the floor of the passenger cabin to be greeted by bowls of champagne and some lavish munchies.

Belinda came back from the cockpit and greeted everyone. Bruce and I did the introductions, explained about L. Condor's speech situation and his technology-assisted communications system. The cats had not met him either. He was boxed before they were loaded on. Octavius took an immediate interest in L. Condor, and they were engaged in a text chat fest in nothing flat. I could see that something very fruitful was going to come from this. I wondered what would happen when Howard Watt met the condor.

After a few rounds of stretching and bitching, the three cats started to come around. The fact that they were on the last "living" Concorde impressed the hell out of them and even though we weren't flying supersonic yet, they were awed by the prospect. They were super-awed by Octavius who looked even more massive in the confined space of the airplane's fuselage. His booming voice ricocheted around the walls.

"Frankly, gentlebeasts, we were of two minds about bringing you along on this Great Escape. You can thank Maury and the Inspector for interceding for you because I still have some strong suspicions that our hasty exit was a result of you three talking too freely to Pontius Puma."

"To who????"

"To whom" said the Bear. "Oh yes, your friend Paolo is in reality Pontius Puma and I can see from the expressions on your faces that you are familiar with him or at least his name."

Lepi recovered first. "You don't perform in Brazil and most of South America for that matter, without Pontius Puma's approval. We've never met the guy, but some musicians we know have been under contract to him for years and aren't even sure what he looks like, except of course, he's a puma."

Bruce broke in, "Too right, your leopardship, very few beasts have seen him in the flesh….at least as Pontius Puma. Paolo is one of his many guises, and I guess he was crazy enough about Chita and seeing the Carnaval hoopla to risk a little public exposure. We've been after him for a different reason. An espionage and terrorist support sideline that he had going on an international basis. We won't go any further on that for security reasons except to say that Pontius will be out of all of his businesses big time for a good long while. When he puts two and two together and comes up with five, he'll have you guys on his list along with us as disposable occupants of time and space. You three can't go back to Brazil any time soon or at least not until we get him locked up. Our best bet is to

126

try to tempt him out of the country, but the odds on that are slim. Maybe we can use Chita for that if we can find her. You may be able to help."

Jake moaned, "You mean we have to start our careers all over."

I looked at him and said, "Consider the alternative. A memorial concert in Brazil from some of your many musical friends no doubt paid for by Pontius."

Jake was silent. Ozzie looked up and said, "Well, maybe he personally won't reach us but he has a lot of goons all around the world, if what we hear is true."

"That's right!" said Octavius, "We'll give you a hand in hiding out for a while but we're making no guarantees, and if you screw up or attempt to reach Chita without telling us, we'll dump you in the front lobby of Pontius' headquarters with big identifying signs hung around your spotted necks. So you can cooperate, change your ID and even enjoy yourselves building a new career in the States or you can 'Keep On Runnin'."

Jake looked up, "Hey Bear, cool. You're one hip ursine. Who'da thunk?"

Octavius, about as unhip as they come, hadn't the slightest idea what they were talking about until Ozzie started singing a few bars of "Keep on Runnin." The light dawned.

This set the three of them off improvising with available resources. Seat backs as drums, their surviving keyboard and electric guitar plugged into the aircraft entertainment system and feline howls. Octavius retreated, not sure whether his message had gotten across but there would be more time for impressing it on them.

Suddenly, Bearnice, the co-pilot stuck her head out of the cockpit and started singing along, harmonizing and doing obbligato riffs. The cats were impressed. Belinda waved her into the passenger compartment and then took back the command seat herself with Bearyl flying shotgun. Bearnice sat down with the band and continued singing.

Lepi looked at her and said, "Hey lady, you got a voice. You ever do any professional singing?"

"Well, for a few years before I joined the Bearoness, I was a polaratura soprano with the Northern Light(s) Opera. I had the lead in *Lucretia Beargia.*

"Hey, you do opera? So do I. In fact I've written an opera. That's why I got kicked out of China and ended up in Brazil. It's called, *Comrade Carmen's Carbuncle*. It's a study of civilization's futile call for understanding and brotherhood."

"It sounds avant-garde." said Bearnice.

"It's actually Avant Red Guard, and that's why I was deported." said Lepi. "Would you like to hear some of it?"

"I have to get back to the flight deck but maybe after we land we could try a few things together."

This was not as suggestive as it may have sounded since feline-ursine relations are just about always platonic for a lot a reasons we will not discuss here. Lepi looked at the other two cats. "Our next Chita? We have to change our names anyway. How about the BearCats. Do you think that would play in Cincinnati?"

Jake broke into a 50 BPM groove on the snack tray table and promptly broke the supports. Ozzie twanged his guitar once or twice and said, "Ya know. It just might work. Let's see."

Belinda's voice came over the intercom. "Please sit back and relax with your seat belts on. We are about to enter supersonic flight. We will be passing Mach 1 very shortly. Watch the Mach Meter in the front of the cabin."

This quieted the band down and left Bruce and me staring at each other. We wanted to corner Octavius and get the latest on the Imperius Drake situation, but an airplane is not the best venue for a confidential chat. On the other hand, the Bear and L. Condor were text chatting away furiously. To my amazement, although his paws were the size of blue-ribbon pumpkins, Octavius could be quite dexterous with his claws. He too, chose not to speak out loud but we could both see that they were engaging in very serious talon to claw conversation.

Juno had been asleep since takeoff but awoke from her nap and came back to our seats to say hello! Bruce vaguely remembered her from a case he and Octavius had pursued in Alaska and I had been sent up to her den several times to take care of some estate paperwork between the Great Bear and his mother.

"You boys lead pretty exciting lives, don't you?" she said.

"All in a day's work, Mum," replied Bruce in his best stiff upper lip Australian copper tone.

"They'll probably get even more exciting."

"Oh, you mean the return of Imperius Drake, Mrs. Bear!" I said. "He's almost getting to be routine." *(If you could call an attempted mass assassination of over a thousand animals routine.)*

"No, no, no! I'm talking about teleportation and *Homo Sapiens* and alternate worlds, not that psychotic duck! Octavius should just kill him off and write finish to that story."

Bruce and I stared at each other. Teleporting? *Homo Sapiens*? Had Juno Bear gone ga-ga in her advancing age?

"Well, Mum, we hadn't heard about any of that. I guess that *would* be exciting."

"I'll leave it up to Tavi to tell you about it but I'm one of the principal parties to the events. It seems I have actually teleported and returned to tell the tail. But so many others are involved. Tavi said he also wanted to make sure Howard was brought on board as soon as possible. Who's Howard?"

"He's a recent addition to our team, Mrs. Bear. He's a porcupine. One of the smartest porcupines, no, one of the smartest animals we've ever met. He's a physicist!"

Juno was about to ask if Howard was smarter than Octavius but thought better of it. "A physicist! Well, that explains why Tavi wants his thinking on the problem. This teleportation stuff seems to violate all the rules of physics, or maybe it actually validates them. Although I studied it, quantum mechanics and I have never quite gotten along."

Never quite gotten along? This lady wasn't over the hill. She, like her son, is no doubt an ursine intelligence to reckon with. After all, all those smart genes running around inside Octavius had to come from somewhere. He never spoke of his father. May not even know who he is. But Juno Bear and teleportation. Never a dull moment working for the Great Bear.

So the flight passed. Frau Schuylkill checked in from the Bear's Lair, confirming our arrival time and also told us Howard had arrived safely.

We later learned that Pontius Puma's empire had taken a very serious shot. Not only was his information system down for the count, but Bruce Wallaroo's compatriots had rounded up seventeen agents around the world who had been supplying him with industrial and military data. We were too cynical to believe that's the last we would hear of the Ponderous Pontius, but he would need some time to recover. Time we could use to pursue our other unfinished business. The Demon Duck and now, alternate universes? I curled up on a large polar bear sized seat and headed off to dreamland at Mach 1.5.

Chapter Fifteen

Most animal experts insist

Black panthers don't really exist.

But they're being puristic

If a cat's <u>melanistic</u>.

Then "Black Panther" is hard to resist.

Chita, still in her black panther disguise, was clearly fascinated as she sat and stared across the river at the Duck Blind. She thought back to the printed signs the Black Quack Gang would always leave at the scene of a theft. "Now you see it, now you don't!" embossed on vellum in classical script. This otter gave a whole new meaning to that nasty greeting. Under Imperius' tutelage, he could turn out to be one formidable weapon. Chita knew she was fast *(yes, that way, too)* but this guy could blow her right off the track.

Funny though! He didn't seem to be the criminal type. He was actually rather sweet and goofy. Of course, that could be a guise or...or...or, of course, Imperius and his crazy serum. Had the nutty duck succeeded? Had he created a superbeast, a superlative otter? Otter. Otto! Otto the Magnificent? Yeah, that's what he said his name was. Otto the Magnificent. Well, if that last demonstration was any indication, the kid wasn't lying. But he seemed to think he was heading for big time show business. The duck at his double-dealing best, no doubt.

Well, Chita my dear, what do we do about this turn of events? With Bigg and this whiskery, high speed Houdini both in the duck's thrall, knocking Imperius off isn't going to be that easy. Let's think this through.

- Imperius seemed crazier than ever from what she could see. The serum seemed to be slowly pushing out any residual sanity or ethics Yu-Aul-kum may have ever had. She'd have to watch carefully. She had planned to wait until he reverted back to his Mandarin Duck state and was weaker but while the physical change might still take place, the personality now seemed the same in either state. At least, that's what she thought. A quick commando raid on a weakened opponent may or may not be the way to go.

- Bigg was still Bigg, dumb and now limping, but still as strong as a...baboon and still obeying Imperius to the letter.

- Otto! This was the puzzle piece. Could she put him out of commission when and if whatever Imperius was pumping into him faded out? From what she could see, they were still experimenting. Well, maybe she could assist in the lab work. Would the otter tell Imperius he met her? Probably. She'd need to act soon.

- Paolo! He's probably looking for her, too. *(Narrator's Note: It isn't clear whether Chita was aware of Paolo's true identity as Pontius Puma. Being his legal mate and having her singing career boosted by him might lead one to believe she knew who he really was. But some things remain a mystery.)*

- The Bear, the Wallaroo, the Meerkat and their goody-two-shoes team. They were a pain, but they weren't stupid. It wouldn't have taken them long to figure out that she was probably heading for the U.S., last known headquarters of Imperius Drake. It also wouldn't take them long to start tracking her in hopes she would lead them to the duck. Now, there's a thought. Could they work something out together? Bruce and Maury seemed to like her, although the bear certainly didn't. Is there a card in that deck she could play?

Well, she had options. Too damned many options, in fact. She snarled and shook in frustration. Oh, how she hated that duck. But whatever she did, it would have to be quick.

She looked across the river. Bigg was still sitting there next to the boat. She waited to see what he'd do next. If he went off down the river on another supply run, she might take a chance at crossing over *(much as she hated swimming)* and giving the security system a try. If the duck hadn't killed off her credentials yet, she might be able to sneak into the lab and get a better feeling for what was going on. "Come on, Bigg, you stupid jerk. Go for a boat ride. Come on, stupid! Move!"

He did. She saw him jump into the covered cockpit and start up the engines. As the boat pulled away, she slinked down to the river bank and stuck her paw in the water. Ugh! Cold and slimy.

It was starting to rain, and that would help her stay low visibility. Either way, she needed to get wet so she could get rid of the black panther makeup. The Duck Blind ID system wouldn't recognize her as anything but a spotted cheetah. Into the water she slipped, a black piece of flotsam gently floating across the river.

After paddling about and getting very unpleasantly sopped, she crawled ashore near some overhanging bushes, slipped out of the panther suit and rubbed her face, paws and tail with the river water to get rid of any traces of black. Let's make sure it's all off. The scanners had to believe it was her. Providing, that is, they still had her profile in the authorization database.

Looking around for any movements and checking from memory the positions of the surveillance cameras, she approached the entry. Bigg had left the corrugated steel barrier up, but the front doors were fully secured. OK, on to the access panel.

Let's see – the recognition sequence was full face, profile, paw, voice and access control number. If the system didn't identify her as authorized, it would set off all kinds of alarms. But even if it did, she was counting on Imperius still being somewhat disabled and the otter not knowing what was going on. So any responses from them would be slow. She could easily outrun them, and Imperius no longer had the ray gun, according to the Bear's buddies. So, provided Bigg didn't make a sudden reappearance, if the alarms did go off, she could probably get to the other end of the island and disappear before they could do anything. But she would have also telegraphed that she was here.

Well, let's give it a try. She crept up to the ramp and through the opening of the steel overhead portal to the walk-in door with all its security sensors. OK, she'd used this entry hundreds of times before. Rubbing her face with her paws once more to make sure she'd gotten all the black dye off, she sauntered up to the video camera and staring straight ahead pushed the access button. No response. Then suddenly a green light went on and the screen read, "Show Profile." So typically Imperius. Not even a "please."

She turned sideways and pressed the access button again. Another green light. OK, so far so good, but these were the generic controls. Any number of cheetahs could have passed. Now came the specifics. Right front paw print. She checked to make sure there weren't any things stuck under her claws from the river. Then she placed it on the pad and pushed down. Amber light. "Try Again!" Uh, oh! Get ready to run, cat. She looked at her paw again. There was some mud on one of the pads. She licked it and wiped it on her fur. One more time. Yes!! Green light. The voice check was simply her name. Chita Cheetah. So far so good.

Now what was the code? If he had changed that, she was sunk. Oh, of course. He'd never change that. IH8BEARS. She typed it into the keypad, the door swung open and she peeked around the jamb. No lights in the entrance or main area. Imperius was back in the lab at his work bench turned away from the entryway.

Where was the otter?? Light snores coming from what used to be her room. Well, he's welcome to it. She was in. She ran over to the utility closet that housed the computers and network gear and shut the door. It was warm inside, but after the involuntary bath she got in the river a little warmth was welcome. God, she stank from that water. She hoped the otter's sense of smell hasn't been souped up by the serum or whatever Imperius was feeding him.

What to do? Not like her to get into a situation without an exit strategy or two. That much she learned from the duck. She was being impulsive again like the first time she met Bigg. That almost ended up in a kamikaze run. "Calm down, Chita, and think. What's the objective here? Kill the duck and split. Simple. But wait! Maybe there's a way to parlay this into something even better. The serum. Kill the duck, swipe the serum and split. Better! But what to do with the serum? *(She didn't know genetics from gendarmes. Actually, she had operated in Paris and knew too much about gendarmes.)* Concentrate, dammit."

Maybe she could solve her other problem. Octavius Bear! He's a geneticist and he and the duck hate each other with a passion. Could she strike a deal with the bear? The serum and notes in return for a clean slate and maybe a small contribution to the kitty. Probably not. He's such a noble pain in the ass. But Wallaroo and Maury. Now there's a thought. She could work with them. They'd probably look the other way and let her get back to Brazil and Paolo, especially if she brought them the serum and a dead duck. Or would they?

This Socratic exercise was interrupted by the heavy thumping and scraping of boxes being dumped and dragged along the floor. Only one animal could make such a raucous racket out of bringing in lab supplies. Bigg! Time for new tactics yet again.

The bad news was that Bigg was back. The good news was …so was the hydroplane and she knew how to pilot the hydroplane better than any of them. Now while the confusion and noise was on, she'd run into the lab, take a *(hopefully fatal)* swipe at Imperius, grab the serum and his lab notes and take off like a bat out of the Duck Blind and onto the Ms Lee-Li- Li.

OK, open the closet door slowly. Bigg had left the outer doors open. Probably going back for another load. Imperius was still at his bench. Here we go! She was out like a shot, through the lab door, hit Imperius hard with a glass retort, grabbed the serum and his notes and ran like hell…right into the yawning otter who was coming out of the bedroom. Instead of shoving him out of the way, she grabbed him and carried him struggling out of the doors, up the ramp and into the boat.

While the panicked otter was shouting for help, Chita pushed him into the cockpit, hit the starter and throttled away from the dock. The stupid baboon hadn't even secured the boat properly. Bigg, after tripping over several boxes, came charging up the ramp just in time to see the hydroplane's high tail wake heading up the river.

Total time: 13 seconds. Not bad. Now to shut this guy up. She wasn't quite sure why she had kitnapped him. Grand theft Otto! Maybe she just wanted to get the poor sap away from the duck. Milord Mallàrd!! Yeah, sure! And Commandante Babaloo, the dope.

Otto was yelling and pushing and shoving and trying to head for the rail. She cuffed him hard on the side of the head, and he fell backwards, hitting his skull on the bulkhead. Down for a short count. Hopefully long enough for her to pilot the boat into open water. How could she subdue this guy?

And then it hit her. He could be subdued. He didn't escape when she grabbed him. The serum wasn't working anymore. Aha!! What does that tell us, class? The duck was only meeting with marginal success. The duck!? Had she killed him? She'd certainly hit him hard enough. She'd know soon enough. Or maybe not. No one knew whether he was alive or dead after Las Vegas until he chose to show himself again. Nothing's easy anymore.

Meanwhile, she had to idle the boat, tie up the otter and make for a deserted section of shore. She took one of the short ropes from the cockpit storage locker and tied the otter's feet and front paws together. She ran a loop around his jaw and just behind his nose to keep his mouth shut. It wouldn't last for long, but she just needed enough time to talk to him without interruption. She wasn't crazy about his big tail still being loose, but it was the best she could do with one eye on the river and one paw alternately on the wheel and throttle. She had put the sealed beaker of serum and the notes in the locker among the ropes to cushion any sharp movements. Those were her ticket back to Brazil....she hoped.

They were several miles upriver from Pelican Island. The river took several twists and turns and while the rain had slowed to drizzle, a mist was rising off the water, and the sun was hidden behind the clouds. Good! Lo-viz is our motto. Black as it was, the hydroplane still stuck out like an island in motion. She had to ditch it fast. Better yet, she'd scuttle it. The sinking of Ms Lee-Li-Li. Right up there with the Titanic. If he was still alive, that would drive Imperius nuts. If he wasn't, at least Bigg would be left high, dry and stranded. Now, where to pull in?

What looked like an abandoned loading facility for barges was hulking by the riverside about half a mile up ahead. If she could get up to it and get ashore with the otter and the serum and notes, she could hide away for a bit and figure her next move. Otto was coming to. He looked up at her, startled, and started to flail about.

She pushed him into a corner and said, "Hello, Otto. I'm not going to hurt you provided you stay still long enough for me to maneuver over to this dock up ahead. I may let you loose once we're tied up and after I explain a few facts of life to you. You are in no danger. In fact, you're in a hell of a lot better position than you were with those two. Yes, I'm Miss Catt. We talked the other day. I looked like a panther then, but I'm really a cheetah. In fact, that's my real name – Chita." She spelled it for him.

Otto stared at her wide eyed and kept twisting his head and flipping his body to try and break loose.

"Otto, you're a sweet little guy. At least I think you are, and I don't want to have to belt you again, but I will if you don't calm down. Now let me concentrate here. I'm not going to let you get near the water. For all I know you could try to swim away just using your tail. I wouldn't advise it. I'm no swimmer, but I could probably run you down with the boat. But, as I said, I really don't want to harm you at all. In fact, after we've had a nice little chat I have a proposition for you that you may find very interesting. OK??"

Otto nodded his head nervously. Nothing was making any sense. In fact, very little had made sense since he'd left Reno with the duck and baboon. Right now, all he wanted was a ticket to the St. Lawrence River and his family. That didn't seem too likely. He didn't really have much in the way of options. So he'd listen to the cat, at least to satisfy his curiosity and then take the first chance he had to get away.

She maneuvered the boat over toward the dock. Overhead, a very unreliable looking ore loader vibrated in the wind. Definitely a safety hazard! They'd have to talk fast and get going, or that thing might come crashing down.

"OK, Otto or whatever your name is. Here's the story, short and sweet. I'll fill in the blanks later. Your two 'friends' are not what they seem. In fact, the duck is never what he seems. He is a criminally insane, genetically assisted dual personality called Yu-Aul-Kum when he's in his relatively mild mannered state and Imperius Drake when he's a super maniac. He becomes Imperius when he takes a serum not unlike the stuff he's pumping into you."

Otto's eyes almost popped out of his furry little head. He starting grunting and making indistinct sounds that may well have been screams.

"All right, I'm going to take the rope off around your mouth so you can talk…..talk, understand, not scream or yell. Agreed? Remember, dear, these claws can do a lot of damage in a very short time to say nothing of my teeth and jaws." To make the point, she yawned. Otto started to shake.

"As I said, I'm not going to hurt you unless you try to do something stupid. In fact, you're quite a likeable little guy. So let's make nice-nice. OK?"

The otter nodded, and she reached over and none too gently pulled the rope from his mouth and jaw. She left his extremities tied.

"Now we can talk. To continue. Bigg on the other hand is not a Latin American show biz entrepreneur or revolutionary. He's a South African baboon. Strong as they come and twice as dumb. I know. I worked with both of them for several years. Yes, dear heart, I too, have a very shady past – mostly fraud and theft – but I have never killed anyone. *(Not anyone I didn't intend to eat, at*

137

least.) We were called the Black Quack gang. You may have seen us mentioned in the newspapers."

Otto gaped. "You're the Black Quackers? Didn't you steal that big sapphire in Chicago a few months ago? That was Milord Mallàrd and the Commandante and....you?"

"Correction! I *was* a member of the Black Quack organization but then Imperius tried to kill me because I attempted to stop him from wiping out an entire convention of geneticists in Las Vegas. I draw the line at mass murder. But this little caper is all part of my revenge for his attempt to knock me off. Details will follow at a later time."

"But, what does he want with me?" squeaked the otter. "I'm just an incompetent magician and illusionist!"

"That may be so when you're not technically augmented but I was watching you during your last test runs and let me tell you, when that serum kicks in, you are one impressive illusionist and escape artist. Now ask yourself the question. What would a sociopath duck want with an animal who could get in and out of locked rooms, could shed bonds, move like lightning, swim like a torpedo and disappear at will? Get the picture?"

"But I'm not a criminal. I wouldn't do anything illegal. We were going to create a smash act."

"Imperius' idea of a smash act is to smash something, steal valuables and run like hell. I repeat: He is not a theatrical producer *(although he can get pretty theatrical when he is juiced up with his own serum).* Another thing. I've been with him for quite a while and he's been experimenting with this genetic enhancement stuff for years. Of course, he uses it on himself. But now the serum has gotten to him. He's completely insane at this point. He used to have moments of rational lucidity. Not anymore.

Now here's another thought for you: The stuff in that beaker that he's been giving you is basically the same as his own formula, but it's modified to match your DNA. If it didn't match, you'd be dead by now. In fact, that's how he intended to kill me off. By feeding me his formula. Query: How long before you go completely nutso?"

"Ohmigosh, he's fed it and shot it to me three times, and he keeps saying it still needs work. What's he trying to do?"

"He hasn't been able to alter your personality...yet. He wants a super otter with no willpower. Has he tried to give you commands?"

"No, yes, I think so."

"They start as suggestions and work up to auto-suggestions. He obviously hasn't succeeded yet. Now look, this is all very chummy, but I'm going to give you a choice. I belted Imperius with a heavy lab beaker, and he may be dead, but he may not be. Either way, there's no telling what he's done to you. Now, I know a couple of people who may be able to help and oddly enough, they're with the police."

"The police??? I didn't do anything. Will they arrest me? For what?" Otto started shaking again.

"Calm down, Whiskers. These guys hate the duck just as much as I do, and they want to put him out of business permanently and mop up Bigg as well. Now, to be truthful, I'm not sure where I stand with them, but if I deliver the serum and his lab notes to them *(one of them is a top geneticist)* they may be willing to help you and let me get out of town, hopefully with a handsome reward for my efforts."

"Or I can let you go here. You're no threat to me even if you go back to the Duck Blind – a strategy that I think is strongly counter-indicated. But neither one of us is sure just what long term effects that serum is going to have on you. Imperius doesn't care. You were just going to be hired help or another experiment gone wrong. Of course, if he succeeded, he'd be back trying to conquer the world with you as his primary weapon."

Chita had long experience in telling convincing stories. *(Oddly, this one happened to be true.)* She could see that the otter was buying her pitch.

"OK, at least for the moment. I'm not sure I have many choices. All I wanted to be is a headline entertainer."

The cat looked up. "You know, Ms Lee-Li-Li was a mandarin duck and Imperius' love life. She's dead, but this boat's named after her. I thought we could use it but now it's a liability. Too many people know about it including Bigg and Imperius if he's still alive. Maybe, if there is anything left in that ore loader up there we can reverse the old proverb and kill one bird with lots of stones. I'm going to release you. Let's tie up here under the loader. You find

139

someplace to hide and I'll move up to the loader's control cab. I'll take the serum and the notes with me. I like you, but I'm not sure I can trust you yet."

Otto looked at her. "You're not sure you can trust ME?"

"Yeah, I know. Ironic isn't it?"

Otto skittered down the dock and hid behind the abandoned shed. It looked like there had been a fire recently. Cheetah scrambled up the ladders to the control cab. There were still some rocks on the conveyor belt. Now if she could get it moving maybe she could drop enough ore on the hydroplane to scuttle it right there by the dock. She looked around at the controls. Pretty complex. There were the power switches. Were they still active? Yes!! Now how to get the belt moving so it would dump on the boat. First try–wrong direction. Second try–right direction but the ore was held back by a chute gate. Where's the switch? No! No! No! Gotcha!

The gate flipped up and several tons of heavy rock came thundering out of the chute and down onto the hydroplane.

"And now, tourists," she thought, "as our boat sinks slowly into the west, we bid farewell to the lovely Missouri islands and set out for our next port of call – Octavius Bear Land. Wherever that is! Hey Otto, c'mon out. I got a call to make and then we hit the road."

Chapter Sixteen

The Jaguar's a spotted cat too.

And a car as I'm sure you all knew.

But pronouncing his name

Isn't always the same.

In England, they accent the "U."

I felt a none-too-gentle push at my elbow and woke from that same dream where I was chasing those luscious meerkats down the beach at Ipanema. Some deep psychological meaning there. I needed some female companionship. Maybe it was seeing Bruce in a skirt too many times.

Speaking of female companionship, Octavius and Belinda had earlier broken the news to Bruce and me that they had gotten married while they were in Canada. Bruce went ballistic, literally, bouncing around in the confined fuselage and shouting all sorts of well-wishes that were unfortunately covered by a ton of Strine. All I picked up for sure were half a dozen "Good on-ya's" and "Brilliants!" He bounced over a couple of seats, knocking one of the cats to the floor, and climbing over Juno, he reached out and hugged the Bearoness. He tried to hug Octavius but ended up being suspended by his ears at the end of Bear's massive arm's length. I imagine hugging Octavius is sort of like burying yourself in a fur-covered bean bag. I'm sure the Bearoness can manage it but I have no incentive in that direction.

I offered felicitations to both, but in the back of my mind a debate started. Was I happy or not to see the Great Bear married? What was this going to do to our own relationship? Would the Bearoness become his operational Number One? She's certainly smart enough, and she outweighs me by at least five hundred pounds, to say nothing of her sharp teeth. And she's weapons trained and a pilot. She could be formidable!

On the other hand, I am an experienced sleuth *(and former criminal),* and she is not. Maybe the Bearoness and I could team up, and together we could smooth out a few of the Bear's rough edges. That might have some fascinating possibilities. Options! Options!

Then Octavius motioned Bruce and me to the back of the plane past the cats and Juno. In a low voice, remarkable for him, he proceeded to tell us all about the alternate universe – teleportation – ultra high speed – telekinetic stuff that we had been missing out on while we had been lolling around Brazil. Several times he had to shove a paw in Bruce's mouth to keep him from shouting out some form of down-under expletive. Everyone else at the Lair had been briefed, was part of the briefing or both. We seem to have been the last two of the team brought on board. Bruce and I stared at each other. No teleporting talent here.

Aha! That also explained why Juno was still with us. I began to wonder where Octavius himself went when he drifted off in his narcoleptic fits but since he never admitted they happened, it was not too politic to bring the subject up, at least not yet. Shaking our heads to absorb all this news, Wallaroo and I headed back to our seats up forward. Many things to ponder upon as I drifted back to sleep.

Anyway, that dream-destroying shove was Octavius informing me that we were on final approach for the Bear's Lair. I looked around at my fellow passengers. Octavius was staring at the three cats. They in turn, were looking out the windows at the Midwest landscape. Juno was still asleep. Bruce was all tangled up in his seat belt and L. Condor was trying out different fastening positions to accommodate his twelve foot wingspan. The three bears were all up in the cockpit.

Belinda got on the speaker system and told us we were arriving. The road and ground crews had checked out the ersatz interstate for obstructions or debris; CVG air traffic control knew we were coming and was figuratively looking the other way, and with any luck Frau Schuylkill was preparing one of her culinary extravaganzas. I had been snacking all through the flight when I wasn't asleep, but right now my stomach was rumbling and not from airsickness. Psychological as well as physical decompression. I still can't get used to bad guys trying to end my precious life. I am, after all, a very sensitive animal.

When a jet aircraft touches down, it is always a bit disconcerting to feel and hear the silken descent turn into a barrage of thumps, roars, screams and rattles. *(And those are just the passengers.)* We were back. Octavius was already searching for his seat belt buckle buried somewhere in his massive fur pelt. Rumbling to himself but, of course, unwilling to ask for help, he flailed away at the belt, the seat and anything else that was nearby. *(That anything else happened to be me.)* "Ouch, Bear, that hurt!"

"The minute I get off this roaring juggernaut *(it is after all, the Aquabear!)* I'm going to set up a UUI engineering project to make seat belts easier to open and close."

(Do I smell Noble Prize?)

Bearnice went through her party piece recitation. "Please remain seated till we come to a complete stop and the captain has turned off the seat belt light." The Concorde swung past the pagoda and up to the Roman Hangar and The Bear's Lair. I was watching the faces of the cats and the condor as they looked out the windows. Disbelief, puzzlement, admiration *(from L. Condor)* and perhaps just a touch of fear *(from the cats)*. Good, let's start off on the right foot.

Bruce piped up, "Gentlebeasts, welcome to the Twilight Zone," as he bounced out of his seat.

Octavius raised an eyebrow but said nothing.

As the forward door opened, there was some further consternation at the sight of two wolves and a porcupine standing at the bottom of the jetstairs.

"Welcome back, Herr Bear, Herr Maury. *(She ignored Bruce, as usual.)* I imagine you're hungry and thirsty. There's a keg of mead, some coconut milk VSOP and *(with a sideways look at the Wallaroo)* some beer in the library. Tell the Bearoness and the other bears there is champagne and fish snacks. She looked at the cats and L. Condor. What would your guests like?"

"To get off this supersonic seagull, for starters!" That was smart mouth Jake. He's going to be a problem.

After Octavius managed to gingerly maneuver his bulk down the semi-steady jet stairs *(he just trundles up the cargo ramp on the Ursa Major)*, the others followed, taking in the environment and the natives.

L. Condor stretched his wings and almost knocked over two of the ground crew. Howard Watt came up and held out his paw. "Bom tarde, Senhor Condor, I am Doctor Howard Watt. A pleasure to meet you. Maury has been telling me all about you. I hope we will have a chance to work together."

The condor searched around in his carry-on bag for a pair of text phones and proceeded to start a long conversation with the porcupine. There was one thing you could say about L. Condor. For a bird who couldn't talk, he sure could talk.

The Colonel came over to Bruce and myself and asked none too softly, "What's the story with the cats?"

I turned and waved at them. "Colonel Wyatt Where, meet the Spotted Band minus One. Lepi, Ozzie and Jake. These cats are the musicians who played with Chita down in Rio and São Paolo. A series of complications that arose while we were there gave us good reason to bring them along with us."

The Colonel nodded in their direction. "Any idea where Chita is?"

They looked at me. I looked at them and then back at Wyatt and said, "We were hoping you could tell us."

Octavius and Bruce joined the conversation. "Do we have any news, Colonel?" asked the Bear.

"Not much. Several false alarms at the New York airports. She often travels as a black panther covering up her spots. So it is possible she came in under a disguise. She probably has a dozen passports. My personal theory is she would approach through Canada, maybe just running across the border after she landed."

"You may be right, Wyatt," I said. "Imperius seems to have developed a recent affinity for the Great Lakes and the Midwest rivers, and there's no doubt she's after Imperius. Has anyone seen that hydroplane of his lately?"

"No, after those run-ins on the Chicago Ship Channel, the boat seems to have disappeared, although it's not the easiest thing in the world to hide. We don't know whether the baboon is with him. He may not have survived Las Vegas."

"Didn't that watchman up at Pondscum say there were three of them? One was an otter in a Coast Guard Officer's uniform. Whoever he is? Wasn't the other one Bigg Baboon?"

"He couldn't give us anything helpful on any of them. I assume Bigg was one of them."

"Well," said Octavius, "let's go inside. I, for one, could use some mead."

144

"And we could use some champagne," said the Bearoness as she walked up to join the group. "That's one problem with being an aircraft crew member. No bubbles except cola."

Hellos from Bearnice and Bearyl to the assembled entourage, and then we all headed for the mansion. If the cats and the condor were impressed by the outside, they were positively awed by the interior. Lepi was staring up the main staircase, no doubt imagining a grand entrance singing an aria from *Catterdammerung*. Ozzie found a comfortable chair and flopped. Jake turned to Frau Schuylkill who appeared by the door holding a tray of snacks and said, "I don't suppose you could make some Caipirinhas?"

"Si, Herr Cat. Would you like them made with cachaça, pinga, caninha, branquinha, malvada, vodka, rum or sake???"

The three cats stared at each other and at the wolf. Lepi recovered first. "Cachaça, please! We're just simple folks."

L. Condor flapped his wings, signaling he'd like one too. *(We may have a second Wallaroo here. The condor's massive wings were going to give Frau Schuylkill a few nervous moments for the furniture. The difference was: The condor was careful while Wallaroo was.....Wallaroo.)*

I turned my head, and there was the Frau with a tray of bowls filled with icy green fire. *(I haven't the slightest idea how, and I'm afraid to ask.)* This really spooked the cats. I could see the two wolves were going to have a restraining influence on our feline guests. Great!

Howard grabbed a drink for himself and one for the condor and led the bird down the stairs to the labs. That's the last we'd see of them for a while. I turned to the Colonel. "Any more noise from our friendly duck?"

Octavius who had been chatting with the three bears looked over, all attention.

"No more missives or Black Quacks. He's been quiet," said Wyatt.

Octavius frowned and said, "I want to be proactive on this. We saw in Las Vegas how close he can get to mass destruction. I don't want to be a sitting bear for that crazy duck."

The Frau popped back into the room. "Pardon, meine Herren und Damen, but there is a call from UUI for the Inspector." She looked sideways at Wallaroo.

Bruce thumped over to Octavius' desk and picked up the oversized phone. "Wallaroo here! Who? Says she's an old friend? Needs to talk only with me?"

Octavius was doing a slow burn. "Inspector, could you please have your personal calls come in on your own cell phone. I resent UUI's switchboard being used as a dating service."

"Rightcherare, Ocko." He gave his cell number to the UUI operator and bounced out of the room. The puzzled expression on his face gave me a clue. This was no ordinary call. I skittered out behind him.

"Who do you think it is, Bruce?"

"Not sure, Maury. Care to hazard a guess?"

"An old friend who wants to talk only to you but doesn't know your phone number. Sounds like a certain...

Bruce's cell phone rang *(Waltzin' Matilda, for gosh sakes)*.

...cheetah to me."

"Wallaroo here...Hello Chita. I'd recognize that purr anywhere. Speaking of anywhere, where are you?"

(And now through the wonders of literary license, I will reproduce both sides of the conversation for you.)

"Not a question I want to answer at the moment, and don't try to trace the phone. You'll be disappointed," she said. "I have a proposition for you and your Meerkat friend. It's going to take your best powers of persuasion to get that roaring furball to buy into it but I have great confidence in you, Brucie." *(Brucie? Oh boy, here we go!!)*

"Look, Chita, I doubt very much you're calling from Brazil, and I told you if you came to the States, all bets were off. You're wanted here for some pretty serious stuff including wanton destruction of a priceless jewel and accessory to attempted mass murder."

"You know damn well I had no part in that assassination attempt and actually helped you stop it. Don't give me that bad cop stuff."

"Well, sheila, the loss of the Deep Blue Sapphire wasn't exactly a college prank."

146

"Gee, guvnor! That's a fair cop. I'll come in and surrender right away."

"OK, let's stop the ruddy sparring. What do you want?"

"No, Inspector! What do you want?"

"Well, we've already done a number on your Brazilian mate, Pontius."

"Who???"

"Chita, you're a great actress. I'll give you that. But don't push it. I'm talking about your formerly high powered love light, Pontius Puma, or is it Paolo?"

"Paolo is Pontius Puma??" She really sounded shocked, "The Pontius Puma? How do you know that?"

"He's none other than, and you know it. Look, you didn't call to play 'Let's Pretend!' What do you want? We can chat about Brazil later."

"I'm reasonably sure that I killed or at least seriously wounded Imperius Drake. I left too fast to be certain."

(Bruce was signaling to me that she was talking about the duck. Flapping his arms and looking crazy.)

"Where did you kill him or almost kill him?"

"Oh. Now, Inspector, that would be telling. You wouldn't be trying to take advantage of a poor kitty-kat, would you? But that's one of many questions I'm willing to answer if we can come to terms, and that includes Octavius Bear and U.S. law enforcement."

"Chita, I can try to persuade Ocko to cut you some slack, but there's not much I can do about U.S. law enforcement, and I'm not going to get us into the soup by aiding and abetting."

"Well, I guess we've hit an impasse."

"I'm not even sure what you want, Chita, or what you have to offer. How could we have hit an impasse? I'd be rapt to see proof that Imperius isn't with us anymore if you tell me where to look. Maybe we can work out some kind of mate's rate."

"I have a couple of other things to offer, Wallaroo. I have a flask of Imperius' latest power potion and the lab notes to go with it, and I have his latest experimental subject with me. I'm willing to turn them over to you along with Imperius' last location, but here's where I play my trump card. This experimental subject, let's call him animal X, has been treated by Imperius with several shots of his genetic juice and it has taken effect. The problem is: it may kill him if he isn't injected with an antidote, and I don't know anyone else who could work out an antidote as fast as Octavius and his team. In other words, play along with me, or you'll have an innocent death on your hands. Luckily, you have a conscience that works full time. Mine only phones in periodically. That's it."

"Chita," said the Inspector, "knowing you, this could all be a furry tale. You're not famous for telling the truth. I'm not even sure you know what truth is.'

"And you do, I suppose."

"All right, don't get all wobbly. Let's save the philosophy for another day. You want a free pass out of the States…"

"And a pardon for everything that I'm charged with and a sufficient sum of money to set myself up elsewhere, and I don't come cheap."

"You wouldn't like to be named Global Benefactor of the Year, too, would you? I need some real dinkum before I even begin negotiating with you."

Long pause. "OK, you go talk to the Bear and your superiors. If they buy off, then I will tell you where to find animal X along with proof of Imperius' whereabouts. I'll hold onto the serum and the lab notes. This stuff could easily be the eighth genetic wonder of the world, but it's mine until you guys have worked out your scruples and have a plan I can buy. I'll call back in two hours. So long Brucie! You too, Meerkat." *(Of course, she knew I was standing right there.)*

Bruce swatted at his nose with both paws – a sure sign he was plenty aggravated. "Come on, Maury. I have to talk to Ocko. I'll fill you in at the same time. That spotted sheila is one tough cat. We need a war council."

Bruce walked back into the room where Lepi was now playing the piano and Bearnice was humming along. The Inspector signaled to Octavius that we needed to talk – in private. The Bear rose with great effort and trundled through the entryway and down the hall to his "war room." We were in close pursuit. Among other things, Octavius has the war room swept for bugs on a twice daily basis and the walls, ceiling and floor are all electronically shielded.

148

"What was that all about?"

"Chita!" said Bruce. "She's here."

"Where's here?"

"I'm not sure, but since she wants to bargain with us, I assume she's pretty close by." And he launched into a repetition of the conversation.

Needless to say, Octavius was not pleased on several counts. His sense of justice wouldn't allow him to give Chita a free pass and a reward to go with it. He felt ambivalent about the fate of Imperius, whatever it was. He was eager to get his hands on the serum and lab notes but he definitely did not like being "extorted by that cat" in order to save an unidentified animal we weren't even sure needed saving. On top of that, he had left his keg of mead in the library. I suspect it was this last item that really bothered him the most. He said, nay he roared, "No Way" and stomped from the room.

Clearly, Bruce and I had made a mistake. We should have come up with a thought out solution, instead of presenting Octavius with a series of problems. Incomplete Staff Work! To repay her for helping us twice against Imperius, Bruce and I were of a mind to let Chita take the first stage coach out of Dodge, provided she left the States permanently.

The showstopper was that we lacked the resources to let her go with a jingling purse over her shoulder. We could bring Animal X, the serum and the lab notes back to Octavius as *faits accomplis,* but there was no way we two humble servants of the law and of the Bear respectively were going to come up with the kind of money Chita wanted. There was also no way we were going to get her an international pardon, especially if Wallaroo's superiors found out she was Pontius Puma's mate.

A thought tickled the edge of my whiskers – a phenomenon peculiar to meerkats. Maybe she wasn't lying about Pontius/Paolo. It seemed unlikely, but…

The Inspector was having ruminations of his own as he bounced off the electronically shielded walls, upsetting a few Bearlini etchings in the process. "We may have to work this out without Ocko, Maury. I don't like going behind his back, and I'm sure you're not crazy about making him angry, but I want to get that serum and notes away from her. I want to find out if the duck is really dead, and I don't believe she's lying about this Animal X. I just don't think she

149

knows what long range effect Drake's super shots will have on him. As for the money, I think there's an ace we can play, but we'll have to be very careful how we pull it off."

We decided to rejoin the others in the library and wait for the cat's next call. As we entered, music filled our ears. The two operatic virtuosi, Bearnice and Lepi, were just reaching the climactic strains of the love scene from *Bearish Goodenough*, the famous Italian opera set in the wilds of the Hundred Acre Woods. I had to stuff an hors d'oeuvre in Bruce's mouth to keep him from harmonizing with them. A sparkling tear was flowing gently down Belinda's cheek, Juno and Frau Schuylkill were enraptured and Ozzie and Jake looked bored out of their minds. Octavius looked like…well, Octavius and surprise, he had fallen asleep.

Bruce whispered to me, "Here's our chance." He hopped over to Belinda, handed her a handkerchief to wipe her tears and said, "Could Maury and I have a minute of your time…outside?"

Chapter Seventeen

She's a knockout, the whole world agrees.

She's Belinda, a polar bear tease.

She's a Bearoness now.

So she really knows how

To give male bears the deep Arctic freeze.

Chita closed up the cell phone and looked around for the otter. Where had that little jerk gone? "Otto, hey Otto!"

"Here!"

She looked around, and he was standing behind her. She could have sworn he wasn't there a second ago. "Where have you been?"

"Right here!"

"No, you weren't. I would have smelled you." Something wasn't right here. Oh, oh! A feline epiphany! Suddenly, Miss Lee-Li-Li wasn't the only one hit by a ton of bricks. *(All right, a ton of stones. Let's stop this pedantic bickering!)* She stared at the otter and said, "Do me a favor. Walk to that shed over there and come back again."

"Why??"

"Humor me!"

"OK!"

"Well, go ahead!"

"I just did!"

"Do it again."

"This is silly. All right, satisfied?"

"Did you notice anything unusual?"

"Aside from the fact that you're asking me to do dopey things, no!"

"Otto, my little sweetheart. I don't know how to tell you this, but the Duck's super serum has kicked back in again. You are zapping back and forth faster than the eye can see."

"No, I'm not!"

"Trust me, Otto, you are."

"Trust you? You gotta be kidding. You kitnap me, tie me up, threaten me and dump me off at this creepy docksite after admitting you're a criminal, and I'm supposed to trust you? Give me a break!"

"Well, seen in that light, I can understand why you might be a bit dubious. But wait a second. What else can you do when the spirits are upon you?"

"I can make things move without touching them, but there's nothing wrong with me. That serum wore off a long time ago."

"You can make things move without touching them? OK, just for the fun of it, without touching it, toss that stone over there into the river."

"Cut it out, Cat. I'm in no mood for fooling around. Either let me go or…"

"Or what? Roowwrr!!" Splash! Cheetah suddenly found herself up to her nose in murky river water.

"Oh, gee, I'm sorry. I just wished I could toss *you* in the river instead of the stone, and I guess I did. Wow!!! Maybe you're right. Gee!! What do I do now?"

The snarling, soaking, sputtering cat crawled up over the jetty. Her first reaction was to tear the otter into little pieces. Her second reaction was to forget her first reaction. This needed some thinking and…scheming.

"OK, Otto, just stop wishing, or at least stop wishing about moving things *(and me)* around. Let's discuss this."

"I don't want to discuss anything. I want to get as far away as I can from you and that crazy duck and the ugly baboon and that whole house of horrors over there on that island."

"That, my dear Otto, is exactly what I have in mind with one minor variation. I'm going to use this situation to promote the well-being of an animal I've grown very fond of...ME!"

"I don't follow you."

"Whiskers, you are my escape vehicle out of this country." She proceeded to tell him about the negotiations she had started with the Inspector and Maury.

"That's just great," said the otter, "but you have one problem. I'm not buying it, and all I have to do is toss you back in the river and run like hell."

"True, but you haven't the slightest idea how that stuff is going to continue to work on you. Neither do I. And I'm the one who has that bottle along with the lab notes stashed away. The only guys I know who could possibly decode what that nutty duck has done are the geneticists at UUI...Octavius' crew.

Now, you can take your chances on whether you turn into a stark raving mad uber-otter like our duckish friend or maybe we can salvage something out of this whole mess. If they buy my proposal, you get a much better chance to return to normal, if that's what you want, and I also get a chance to return to normal, which for me is as far away as I can get from here. If they don't buy it, I leave you here, take the stuff as a security deposit and sneak my way back out of the country. And I'm very good at sneaking in and out of countries."

Resisting a strong urge to toss her back into the river just for the hell of it, Otto scratched his nose and whiskers and said, "OK, let's see what happens. But remember *(with his claws crossed behind his back)* I am not without my own resources." *("At least for the moment," he thought.)* "When do you call them back, Chita?"

"In about half an hour. Meanwhile, why don't you demonstrate for me what you can do."

"Oh, no. You just want to know whether the serum is working or not, so you can overpower me again when it quits."

"*If* it quits, Otto. *If* it quits."

*****

153

Bear's Lair – Same time except for a time zone change, but now I'm being pedantic.

Bruce, the Bearoness and I had slipped outside on the pretense of looking for something we had left on the Aquabear. When we had moved out of earshot, Belinda turned to us and said, "OK, boys, what's this all about?"

We told her, adding a small request for a temporary loan of enough money to bribe Chita, without telling Octavius.

She sat down, snorted and pierced us with an arctic stare *(a polar specialty)*. "Now, let me get this straight. All you two defenders of law and order want me to do is to collude with you in paying off a criminal wanted in a number of countries for a wide variety of felonies in order to get your hands on some kind of crazy genetic joy juice you think Imperius has cooked up. How do you know Chita's not conning you? That may be a bottle of fizzy water and the recipe for salmon stew she's trying to palm off on you. Who's this animal X??"

"We're not sure, but he or she may be the proof we need that she's playing straight for once. That and Imperius' dead body."

"So you intend to do what, exactly?"

"Tentatively agree to her conditions and offer her…what do you think, Maury?"

I scratched my nose. "I'm not sure, but she's not going to give it up cheap."

"This is my money we're talking about here...and I haven't agreed to a thing yet." she said. "Octavius will be in a super rage when he finds out, and I wouldn't want to be in your paws when he does. To say nothing of the authorities if they find out. You could be unemployed, in jail or both. I can always fly back to the Shetland Isles, but I was beginning to really enjoy our married relationship. He's a silly old bear but he's loveable."

"Once he considers the whole thing, I'm sure he'll come around, especially when it's an accomplished fact," I said, not believing it for a minute. Beneath Octavius' logical and bear trap mind *(sorry)* there still lurks a fearsome Kodiak and all that that entails. She was right. Octavius and the minions of law would have a major snit. And the snitees could end up in a lot of trouble. But we needed to get that stuff out of the cat's paws. If we could capture her in the

154

process, so much the better. But we would have to at least start out bargaining in good faith. And…if this animal X existed and was in the condition she said it was, we had an obligation to try to help it out *(and maybe get it to cooperate as an experimental subject…without doing it any harm)*. A moral dilemma!

"All right," said Belinda, "I could never resist a little intrigue. But we'll do it on my terms. I am willing to purchase – got that, PURCHASE – the formula and notes from Chita in the interest of science. I want a bill of sale. I will not press the point of whether she is the legitimate owner or not. Animal X can return with us or not as he or she sees fit. No coercion, no force, no capture."

"Return with US?" yelped Bruce. "You're coming along???"

"Look guys, if I'm buying this stuff *(and I must be out of my mind to do it)* then I'm doing the buying. Besides, I've never met Chita. In some ways she's a girl after my own heart."

"Oh, not you too, Belinda," I squeaked. "Octavius is going to swear we're all ganging up against him over this cat."

She looked at me and laughed. "Well, we are, aren't we? He'll come around, especially if that serum is real."

And, I thought, if anyone could wrap Octavius around their little claw, Bearoness Belinda Béarnaise Bruin now Bear *(nee Black)* was that someone. I said, "Chita will be calling back on Bruce's cell phone shortly. We'll tell her we want to get together. I haven't the slightest idea where she is, but I doubt it's that far away. I'll also open the negotiations on terms, conditions and money. That way Bruce can't be blamed." *(I know. A technicality! What do you want? I come from the French Meerkat strain. We live for linguistic and ethical subtlety.)*

"Yes," said Belinda, "you'll be negotiating with my money. Since I intend to go along on this little joy ride, you'd better tell her you're going to have company. Inspector. Maury, what's the best way to get to her?"

"As I told you, I don't know where she, is but we could check out one of UUI's corporate helicopters and use it if she's within range." I could see the maniacal light in Bruce's eyes when I mentioned "helicopter."

Those of you who have read the prequel to this book, *The Open and Shut Case,* know that Bruce adopts a symbiotic relationship with the churning chariots of the sky. Between them, they carry out unspeakable acts of non-stop, idiotic, aeronautical aerobatics that neither animal nor machine was ever meant to perform. I, unfortunately, have been a passenger on far too many of these joy rides and as a result my stomach and psyche have deteriorated way out of proportion to my tender years. "We will check out a chopper AND A PILOT, Bruce. Not you."

Before the Wallaroo could answer, Belinda growled. Loudly! She had our attention. "I am a qualified copter pilot as well as a jet jockey. Let's keep the participants and witnesses to this caper to a minimum. You get the chopper. I'll do the flying."

Bruce slowly closed his mouth without a sound. I wish I could get that result. So now, where's the cat?

We decided to stay near the hangar where the SST was parked. Then it occurred to the Bearoness that if we boarded the aircraft we could plug Bruce's phone into the Aquabear's comm system and all talk with Chita together. We climbed, skittered and bounded up the jetstairs *(ladies first),* and Belinda went into the flight deck to set up the communications. Bruce and I settled in until his phone rang, and we could patch the cat in. I looked over at him. "Do you think we can pull this off?"

"Don't know, but it's worth a try. That Bearoness is one dinkum sheila, I'll tell you, mate. I can see why Ocko is dotty over her. One minute she looks like a brainless bimbo, the next she's queen of the pack."

"Aurora!" I said.

"That's not her name."

"No, a collection of polar bears is called an aurora."

"Ah, Maury, you never cease to amaze. But as far as I'm concerned she could lead the whole animal kingdom."

"Ah," I thought, "yet another victim of the Béarnaise allure." She was just a bit too overpowering for me, but then I am a very small animal. Further evaluation of her bearonial charms was cut off by the ring of Bruce's phone.

"Hello? Hello, Chita. We are prepared to talk with you, but there are a couple of things you need to know first. Octavius has turned you down flat. Wait, stay on the line. He's not about to assist in giving you a pass with the authorities. Second, neither Maury nor I can do anything on that score either, except keep our mouths shut. Even that will probably get one or the other of us in the soup. But, and it's a big but, we've come up with a scheme that might get you most of what you want and get us most of what we want. Are you up for listening? Good! Now there's a third party to these negotiations, Bearoness Belinda Béarnaise Bruin *(nee Black. He didn't mention her recent wedded status, for obvious reasons)*.

Why is she involved? Because it's her money, that's why. Now, are you going to throw a feline hissy fit and kill off your chances of getting something out of this situation or are you ready to talk to the three of us? Octavius has no idea we're having this conversation, and Maury will be shopping for a new skin if he finds out. We're sitting inside the Bearoness' airplane with the doors shut, and she's ready to plug you into the plane's comm system so we all can have a nice chat. Is it a go? Ridgy-didge! Hold on while we do some patching and plugging."

Bruce and I moved up into the cockpit where Belinda was already ensconced in the pilot's seat. Bruce took the co-pilot's chair and I bounded into the engineer's jump seat. Belinda plugged Bruce's phone into a patch panel, threw a few switches, and we could hear Chita saying, "Stay here, Otto. This involves you."

So Animal X was a "he" named Otto. Maybe a German Shepherd. Then I heard a squeaky voice reply and immediately revised my judgment.

"OK, Chita," said Bruce, "we've got you. Maury is here, and let me formally introduce you to the Bearoness Belinda Béarnaise Bruin *(nee Black)."*

"Hello, Bearoness, I don't suppose we have to go through formalities, do we?"

"No, considering I probably owe my life to your scrawling a warning on a hospital wall. Can we make this a first name negotiation? I'm Belinda."

"You may call me Miss Catt. Just kidding! While I've accumulated a string of aliases over time, Chita's the one I'm comfortable with."

Bruce looked at me, and I stared back. We were probably having similar thoughts. We might turn out to be superfluous to this conversation. It could well end up being Ladies' Day at the bargaining table. Feeling left out so far, I decided to insert my no doubt, essential presence.

"Hi, Chita, Maury here! Welcome to North America, although if I were you I wouldn't consider staying very long."

"I'm coming to the same conclusion, Short Stuff, although that's not exactly the way I wanted this to play out. OK, what are your terms?"

"Simple," said Belinda before Bruce or I could get a word in edgewise. "Bruce already told you that an amnesty is off the table. Too many people would have to agree, and the odds against that happening are more than a gambler like you would want to take on. So, we get down to a simple transaction. While the Inspector and Maury look the other way to establish their deniability, you and I will work out the sale, notice I said sale of the 'merchandise.' If we can come to an understanding, then we will work out the transfer procedure. By the way, your friend, associate, captive, whatever, is another matter. As part of our bargain, you release him, and he makes up his own mind what he wants to do. I assume he's a he."

"You bet I'm a he. I used to be Hairy Otter, but thanks to Milord Mallàrd and Commandante Babaloo, I keep turning into Otto the Magnificent, high speed escape artist, teleportation specialist and all round confused and miserable river otter."

Stares and raised eyebrows around the cockpit. Bruce spoke up. "I assume Milord Mallàrd and Babaloo are Imperius and Bigg."

"You got it, Brucie," said the cat. "Last time he tried to use his serum on someone other than himself he was trying to kill me. Looks like he may have met with some success this time."

Otto interrupted, "I don't want to be anybody's experiment. For a few minutes, I thought it would be swell to 'cloud minds and send stuff sailing into the next dimension,' but I'm not even sure who or what I am anymore. It looks like I keep switching back and forth from stupid otter to super otter. All I wanted was a career in show business like my aunts and uncles. Not become a freak. I'm not even sure if the stuff the duck pumped into me isn't going to kill me."

Belinda's head snapped up at the mention of show business and I could hear ursine wheels spinning in her lovely cranium. Bruce jumped in. "Look, Chita, however this discussion turns out, you've got to let him go. You're going to want to travel light and not have to worry about His Magnificence."

The cat replied, "Not exactly true, Wallaroo. I've been hatching a few scenarios where the otter's talents might help me get over a few rough spots in my exit strategy. You're right, though. I've gotten fond of this little guy, and I don't want to do him any harm. I'm very selective about whom or what I choose as a victim."

"Speaking of which," I said, "what's the story with Imperius and Bigg?"

"We don't know, do we, Otto? I belted the duck pretty hard with a lab beaker and I thought I heard a few things break besides the glass. Bigg was too surprised to react, and I just grabbed Otto and ran like hell. We took the hydroplane, so if he is still alive, which I doubt, they're going to have a little trouble moving about. I sank the boat after we went upstream for a bit."

"That's another question. Where are you?"

"Not so fast, little buddy. I'm not the least bit interested in revealing my whereabouts, and even if you're trying to trace this phone, we're moving out even as we speak. Look, let's cut to the chase. Bearoness, what's your offer?"

"What do you want?"

"500,000 euros!"

I choked. Bruce shook his head but Belinda kept hers. "Nice try, Chita, but consider this. Otto, listen carefully. When Chita releases you, make your way to Northern Kentucky near Cincinnati and go to the headquarters of Universal Ursine Industries. Tell them who you are and we'll come and meet you. Now, Chita, unless you want to keep Otto as hostage and with his talents, I'm not sure you can, you just lost a small *(forgive me, Otto)* bargaining chip."

"Not entirely, Bearoness, not entirely. What are the scientists at UUI going to do for Otto if they don't have the serum or the formula?"

I jumped in, "Don't underestimate those guys. They're good."

"Sure, but time may be working against them. The serum and notes will give them a major head start. Besides, it's not even clear Otto wants to play, is it, Otto?"

"Yes, I do. Yes, I do. I want to become normal again and go live with my folks in the St. Lawrence River."

Belinda growled. "Let's not get sidetracked. Look, I am prepared to offer you one tenth of that amount – 50,000 euros – and not a cent more. I don't know whether I'm buying serum or ginger ale, and for all I know, those notes, if they exist, may just be the biographical ravings of the world's nuttiest duck."

My respect for the Bearoness was increasing with every minute. Bruce and I listened as they haggled back and forth and finally settled on 100,000 euros...not bad for a day's work. Imperius would be furious, of course, at being sold so cheaply, but with any luck, he was in no state to care. I wondered what had become of Bigg. I wondered how he survived Las Vegas. I wondered what this Commandante Babaloo thing was all about. While I was wondering, Belinda and Chita were arranging for the money to be put in an escrow account in the Cayman Islands that Belinda would authorize for release as soon as we had Otto and the genetic materials. All that remained was the pickup.

Chita said, "Belinda, it's good to deal with a tough business female. I doubt it will ever happen, but we might have made quite a team."

Belinda snorted, "No, I don't think so, dear, but I will say this has been a most interesting day, and I'm looking forward to tomorrow. I understand you're also a singer."

"It's one of my many avocations. Somewhere between con games and modeling. By the way, Bruce, do you know the whereabouts of the rest of the band?"

"Oh, indeed, my swindling sheila, we know exactly where they are. They're with us."

The unflappable cat was clearly flapped. "With you? What are they doing with you?"

"Let's leave that discussion till tomorrow. Where will you be?"

"Correction! Where will Otto and the serum and notes be? I'll be elsewhere on the end of a phone. I'll leave Otto with a phone too, in a place where you can find him easily. In fact, I'll throw in a bonus. He'll be right near Imperius' laboratory, the Duck Blind. You can check it out for yourselves while you're here. With any luck, you'll find his carcass."

The cat was obviously a survivor. Still trying to press for more information about the band, she gave us a set of coordinates just north of St.

Louis on the Missouri River. We told her and Otto to stand by tomorrow morning and we'd sync up an arrival time and we'd talk to her then about the band *(and Pontius Puma.)*

Belinda got on the horn to her financial manager, telling her to allocate 100,000 euros for a purchase of medical materials and to put it in escrow at Chita's bank in the Caymans.

I called over and reserved a chopper for 11AM tomorrow. The Bearoness would go over earlier and get checked out on it. St. Louis was well within its operating range. We then put our heads together to figure out how to pull this off without Octavius becoming any the wiser until after the *fait* was *accompli.*

We decided on the least complicated solution: Say nothing and just disappear for a while. There were plenty of distractions, provided Octavius didn't want to develop a romantic interlude with Bel or a not-so romantic encounter with me. No problem with Bruce.

When we got back to the library, the concert had just broken up, and the participants were getting ready for dinner. Frau Schuylkill who, no doubt, knew we had been out at the Aquabear *(nothing happens in that hangar without her knowing about it)* looked at me with a half inquiring, half knowing look but said nothing.

I grabbed a cup of fermented coconut milk VSOP and girded myself for this evening. I was counting on Bel to keep Octavius' mind off the Chita situation. There was no question of him forgetting or believing that we thought the issue was closed. I'm sure he assumed we were going to grab an opportune time and work him over again. He, of course, would revel in his immutable and unchallengeable position of rectitude. In short, he would be a classic pain in the ass.

Frau Schuylkill announced dinner, and the various parties drifted in. The three cats looked like they had been having some kind of argument. The three bears, on the other hand, came in looking delightfully lovely, their fur sparkling under the crystal chandeliers. Howard and L. Condor seemed to be making excellent progress on the bird's artificial voicebox. He could create a wide range of sounds but organizing them into words of more than two syllables still seemed to be a problem. The voice was also a sultry feminine purr, but he didn't seem to mind that.

Juno had found a bottle of champagne and was making large withdrawals from its contents. She sidled over and pinched me. "I love meerkats. You have the most adorable faces."

"Thank you, Mrs. Bear. You look adorable, too." I think I'd had too much coconut milk. "It's good to see you again. Are you planning on staying long with us?"

"I think Sonny Boy wants me to hang around while he and his geniuses sort out this teleporting thing. It's fine with me. I could get used to this place. I've talked with Florence, and everything is under control up in the Kodiak. She asked if she could come and join me. Poor dear, she gets out so infrequently. Maybe I'll ask Octavius to send for her and some of my clothes. Which reminds me! I want to go down to Cincinnati and do some shopping. Maybe I could talk the three polars into going with me."

"I don't know about Bearyl and Bearnice, Mrs. Bear, but I do know the Bearoness is going to be busy tomorrow. I heard her talking on the phone to her business manager." *(Well, it's the truth, isn't it?)*

"Oh, well! I'm sure the three of us could still do some real damage, but the Bearoness has such a wonderful eye for fashion. Maybe next time. By the way, please call me Juno. Everybody does, except of course, Tavi."

Speaking of whom, he had just re-entered the room after a serious bout with his keg of mead. He had won, paws down. Octavius asked the Frau where Colonel Where was. She seemed to have developed some telepathic bond with the wolf after their mutual journey to Transylvania. No sooner did the bear ask and the phone rang. Colonel Wyatt Where was on the line wanting to speak to Octavius. We all looked at the she-wolf but she just gazed off into space, oblivious to our quizzical stares.

"Yes, Wyatt, we're expecting you here for dinner. You're about to miss one of the Frau's culinary spectaculars. You will? Fine, fine!! *(He'll be over shortly.)* What's up? Well, who are they? Most important but extremely confidential?? Did you tell them who you were. Made them nervous, huh? They're still on the phone. No, I don't want to talk to them, but suppose you and I agree to meet them tomorrow at say, ten o'clock in my office. I don't want them anywhere near the estate. Did they give you names? No, I don't recognize them but I can guess what and who they are. After you hang up, come on over and join us. We're just having cocktails before dinner. Fine."

162

He hung up and turned to the waiting assemblage. "Do any of you know a couple of bulls named Belial and Brutus? From Chicago? No, Bruce, they're real bulls. I never use that term for the police."

As I looked across the room, it seemed to me that the three cats looked a bit perturbed. Maybe it was just the mention of cops. No one else seemed to be able to cast any light on the subject. Wyatt zapped in *(I swear)* and after a round of hellos we all went in to dinner.

Octavius obviously didn't want to discuss his prospective visitors or the Chita situation in front of strangers, so we kept the conversation general. Bel asked the cats about their show biz experiences but steered clear of the missing member of the band. Howard and the Condor exchanged technobabble.

Since the Frau had joined us at the table, she and Wyatt were fully occupied with each other. Bruce and I deliberately sat too far away from Octavius or each other to hold a conversation. I chatted with Bearnice and Juno. Bruce talked to Bearyl, and Belinda kept Octavius occupied. As far as we knew, he was unaware that she had become a genetic conspirator. And that's the way we wanted it. Gentle night settled in upon us all.

Chapter Eighteen

The grey wolf's from Europe, they say

The red ones are from USA.

But no matter which kind,

You should keep this in mind.

Stay away when you hear a wolf bay!

I awoke in my usual semi-stupor at about 8:30 AM. It took a few minutes to sort out the existential details of my life and current situation and arrive at an approximate definition of who and where I was. *(I never touch "why.")* I remembered that we had some tricky time management to work out today. Octavius was meeting with his bovine visitors at ten and Bruce, Belinda and I were taking off for St. Louis, Chita and Otto at eleven. We said we'd meet them at one o'clock.

I wanted to hear what the bear's meeting with the bulls was all about, but I didn't want to be there physically. I might get roped into something or steered in the wrong direction *(Yes, I know they're lousy puns. What do you expect? I just woke up.)* Somehow I had the feeling that what we were plotting with Chita was going to have an impact on his meeting with the bulls and vice versa.

After going through the Meerkat version of a morning shower and other ablutions, I got on the phone to Wyatt Where. He was already over at his office at UUI.

"Wyatt, Maury! Yeah, Hi! Look I have a favor I'd like to ask you. I had wanted to attend your meeting with the bulls, but I have to be somewhere else at ten AM. *(Liar, liar, tail on fire! I wanted to be anywhere Octavius wasn't.)* I assume you're going to be with the Great Bear, and you'll have the office recorders on. Could you patch in a portable recorder for me so I can listen to the conversations later on? How long is the meeting supposed to last? A half hour or until Octavius throws them out! Yeah, I know what you mean. I've been there. Suppose I stop by your office a few minutes before eleven and pick up the recorder. No, no real mystery, but I think these guys may be related to our recent activities in South America, and I'd like to hear it from the horse's mouth. All right, smart aleck, the bull's mouth! You will? Thanks. I owe you one. Hey, someday I want you to explain how you and the Frau hyperspeed or whatever it is you do. Oh, sure, "wishing will make it so." Now, I'll be humming that stupid song all day. Bye! Thanks again."

I buzzed Bruce and told him what I had done. He shared my suspicions about the bulls and Brazil, but on the other hand, Octavius was tied up in so many different ventures, we could have been way out in left field with our surmises. When I tried to reach Belinda, she had already left for the UUI heliport. I ran downstairs and grabbed a mouthful of breakfast before Octavius could find me. I hid down in the lab until the bear stopped roaring my name. Giving up none too gently, he stomped out the door to the transfer truck that shuttled him back and forth between the Lair and UUI. I sneaked up and watched at the window. When I turned around, I was facing Frau Schuylkill who could move up on you in perfect silence.

"Your pardon, Herr Meerkat, can I do something for you?" *(It sounded more like "can I do something **to** you)."*

"No, Frau Schuylkill, I was just looking out the window while I waited for the Inspector."

As you already know, the she-wolf and Wallaroo were not on the very best of terms. She sniffed, bade me a good morning and padded away. But that wolf knew something was up. We get along very well, but she is unbelievably loyal to the Great Bear, and if she felt anything was happening that he wouldn't have liked, she'd probably tell him. Careful, Maury, careful! You're getting paranoid. I wasn't cut out for a life of deception. Theft and picking pockets, sure, but not deception.

Bruce had also been evading Octavius, but I hated to tell him that, truth be told, the bear was also avoiding him. He needed to take Bruce's hyper-animated style in very small doses. I also noticed that the bear was a bit more irritable lately. Although it was tough to see the difference, if you didn't know him well. I wondered if his marital relationship with the Bearoness was causing some agita. Why those two don't just decide to live together in one place is beyond me. But they have both reached such a level of independence that the idea of compromising their lifestyles and changing priorities just doesn't seem likely. Of course, my strong preference would be for them to stay here in the

Lair. But I've never seen Bearmoral Castle. Who knows? It might be the place to be. Then again, I've never been married, either. Horrid thought!

Whilst I was musing, Bruce had dragged me into one of the staff SUVs, and we were hurtling out of the protective foliage around the Bear's Lair and down toward the Ohio River bridges to get over to UUI. "Bruce, for gosh sakes, don't make one of your outback stampede approaches to the HQ building. We want to approach nonchalantly, without causing any special interest on anyone's part. *(Of course, the word 'nonchalant' doesn't translate into Wallaroo Strine or Bruce's style, so he didn't have a clue what I was talking about.)* Just let me off in the parking lot and head on down to the helipad. The Bearoness should be just about ready to go. I asked Wyatt to make me a recording of the meeting with the Chicago Bulls, and since it's well past ten o'clock, it might be over."

When we had reached the parking lot, a large black truck-limo with shaded windows was tearing past us out the exit. I noticed a pair of bull horns on the hood. Ah, ha! Meeting over! Bruce let me off, and I headed for Wyatt's office. The wolf was just walking through his door when I arrived. He was alternating between laughing and looking concerned. Both expressions were scary.

"Well, my friend, we have been thoroughly threatened, given fair warning and told exactly how the world currently stands," said the wolf.

"And what did we *(or he)* say in return?"

"Octavius, with an occasional snarl from me, thanked them profusely for their warnings and told them if they tried to carry out any of their threats there would be a sudden glut of available steaks and hindquarters on the freshly killed beef market. He also took the occasion to call his friend Police Commissioner Daley in Chicago and ask if he could give us any references for our two guests. The commissioner did and they weren't good. They left unhappy. What a pair of characters! Right out of *These Horns for Hire.* One of them – Brutus, I think – had a large diamond ring in his nose and the other guy, Belial, had shiny stainless steel tips on his horns. I'm sure that goes over big in the Chicago Stockyards. Highly polished hooves and size fifty fedoras with cut-outs for their horns. Wait till you hear the conversation."

"But what's it all about?"

"Something happened in South America while you and Bruce were there. I couldn't follow the whole story, but you probably know it better than I do. Look, I now have a few more protective chores to do. Much as it annoys me, I have to take those jerks seriously. Here's the recorder. As you might imagine, Octavius has sent out an all points bulletin for you and Bruce."

"Thanks, Wyatt, you didn't see me. I'll be back at the Lair a little later."

"What are you up to?"

"I'll give you chapter and verse when I return." *(If Octavius doesn't kill me first.)*

I took the recorder and, taking back stairs and utility shafts, I managed to slink out of the HQ building, under and around a bunch of trucks and ended up breathless next to the skids on the UUI chopper. Belinda had the engine idling and Bruce, wonder of wonders, was strapped in. I clambered up the skid and into the cabin. Fortunately the helipad was on the opposite side of the building from Octavius' and Wyatt's offices. There was no way to leave quietly, but copter traffic wasn't all that unusual at UUI. And the way the Bearoness hauled us off the ground, if we couldn't be quiet, at least we'd be quick.

She headed out in a westward direction and got herself set up with air traffic control. While she was doing that, Bruce and I hooked up the recorder to the internal audio system and fooled with it until all three of us got a clear signal. Belinda had to keep one ear on flight frequencies and one on the conversation. Bruce and I were listening very carefully. Herewith a slightly edited transcript of the meeting of the Bulls and the Bear with Wyatt in a supporting role and occasional side comments *(in italics)* from me:

*****

"Good Morning, Gentlebeasts, I'm Octavius Bear. You wanted to see me?"

"Yes. Mistuh Beah, *(Mistake there. Should have called him Doctor Bear.)* Our cards."

"Brutus Taurus and Belial Taurus, Facilitators! And you're from Chicago. Interesting and an interesting occupation. Just what do you facilitate?"

"It is our privilege to represent some of da most influenchial individuals and organizations in da world on matters of delicacy and complexity."

167

"Which one brings you here today?"

"Poddun?"

"Delicacy or complexity??? Which one."

"Well, Mr. Beah, that sorta depends on you and your associates."

"No, I believe it depends on your telling me what you want as quickly, concisely and clearly as you can. I find guessing games rather irritating." *(I suspect Octavius or Wyatt made some form of movement that upset the bulls. One of them snorted loudly.)*

"That's what we like. An animal that comes right to da point, Mr. Beah."

"And 'da' point is?"

"A very important client of ours in South America has strong reason to believe dat you are in possession of a valuable piece of his property which disappeared over a week ago. He has retained us to recover said property in a most expedishus manner and to ensure that he does not sustain any further losses."

"In fact, *(second deep bovine voice)* he has reason to believe that certain business and financhial setbacks he has recently undergone are also closely related to the activities of you and your associates, and he wants us to firmly advise you that no further interference will be tolerated. What is more, he expects compensation for these losses and has authorized us to take steps to ensure that he receives it."

"What kinds of steps? Please don't tell me that you are threatening me. Colonel Where and I suffer from very strong allergies to threats. It makes us break out in the most unbecoming ways."

"Now, now, as we said, Mr. Beah, this complex situation no doubt calls for delicate negotiashun and trade-offs. Let's not use emotionally charged woids like 'threat.' We prefer to think of it as helpful protective advice."

"Mr. Taurus and Mr. Taurus, let me give you and your client a little helpful protective advice. There is a rather large number of very sorry citizens who have tried to intimidate me and my people. I'll be happy to provide you with references. Speaking of references, I'm going to make a phone call that may interest you. *(Sounds of speaker phone dialing.)* Snorting sounds from the bulls. Very low pitched, throaty growl from Wyatt.

168

"Daley, here."

"Commissioner Daley, Octavius Bear."

"Well, Octavius, what a pleasure to hear from you. We seemed to have lost contact after that sapphire thing."

"Yes, Commissioner, sorry that didn't work out more satisfactorily."

"Well, at least you kept that crazy duck from knocking off the genetics research community."

"It required more force than I like to use, but the rockets were effective. *(Subdued snorts from the bulls.)* I have Colonel Wyatt Where with me here. He was very instrumental in the operation. His Special Forces experience was just what was called for. But I'm afraid this is not a social call. I have two individuals here in my office who claim they ply their profession in your jurisdiction. Mr. Brutus Taurus and Mr. Belial Taurus. They call themselves 'facilitators' and they are here representing a South American client who believes I have done him wrong and also confiscated some of his property. Both patent falsehoods."

(One of the bulls started to talk, but the commissioner interrupted.) "Oh yeah! We're very familiar with your visitors, Octavius. They sometimes call themselves the Raging Bulls. Their definition of facilitation usually amounts to extortion, kidnapping, assault and other forms of physical negotiation. We've been running them in for years, and for years, their shyster lawyers have been getting them off on technicalities or bribery."

"That is slanderous, libelous and insulting, commissionuh," blurted one of the bulls.

"But probably very true," said Octavius. "Thanks a lot, commissioner, if we need any further assistance on this one, we'll call. The offer goes the other way as well. Regards to all the Daleys." *(Readers of* The Open and Shut Case *may remember that just about the entire Chicago Police Force is named Daley [Irish Setter] or Dzawlicza [Polish Retrievers and pronounced Daley.])*

Sound of phone connection being broken. Octavius' voice: "Now, back to the subject of helpful, protective advice. The best advice I can give you right now is to end all this bullshit and get your sorry bovine asses out of here. But before you go, just what is this property I'm supposed to have unjustly appropriated?"

169

"You know damn well what it is. It's Pontius Puma's pet cat – Chita. He wants it returned." (*Oops, I don't think he was supposed to identify his client. Trouble for the Tauruses!*)

"It?! Pontius Puma's Pet Cat?! The Chita I know is nobody's pet cat. If ever there was a feline that is her own very independent, larcenous and dangerous animal, it's Chita. And for your information, if she left Mr. Puma's bed and board she probably did it under her own power and cognizance; certainly with no persuasion from any of us. I don't know where she is, and frankly, my dears, I don't give a damn. Now, get out of here or Wyatt and I will show you the Kentucky version of the Running of the Bulls."

"Don't think we're going to drop this, Beah. *(No more Mr.)*. You're in for a few nasty surprises. And you better get that cat back down to South America, pronto."

"Colonel, please show these Chicago Bulls out of here. I've had enough conflict sports for one morning."

(Sounds of wolf growls, snapping and thumping of hooves. Recording ends.)

*****

"Well, that was certainly entertaining," said the Bearoness. "I never got the full details of what you two rover boys and your condor friend did down in São Paolo and Rio but it sounds like you certainly struck a chord with the puma." *(She winced at her own pun. So did we.)*

"As we told you, Bearoness," said Bruce, "we broke up Pontius Puma's industrial and military espionage apparat and did some substantial damage to his music business as well. He knows that I was involved along with an unidentified Meerkat and a bunch of my Wallaroo relatives. I'm sure that's enough to get him just a bit peeved at me and my law enforcement associates. I don't think he knew about L. Condor. What I don't get is why he thinks Octavius was a prime mover behind this and why he thinks the bear has anything to do with Chita doing a bunk."

"There's something else in this picture that's not coming into focus." I said. "Let's assume that he traced the wipeout of his systems to you and me, Bruce. Fine! But someone had to fill in the rest of the blanks for him. For one thing, our linkage to Octavius. Plus, nobody but you and I knew about L.

170

Condor's attack, and I can't imagine the condor left any traces but…there are three spotted cats I'd like to talk to again after we get back. The puma knows more than he should. One, two or all three of them could be feeding the whole story and relationships back to old PP and his thugs. That would explain how much the bulls know and why they threatened Octavius. Those cats *(or cat)* are playing both sides."

"But they were there when Chita ran out," said Bruce. "They know damn well we had nothing to do with her disappearance. In fact, the last thing we wanted her to do was to take off the way she did after Imperius. And above all, we saved their asses."

"Maybe yes, maybe no! It could all be a setup to find Chita, but the cats sure took a pounding in the process. Who knows, they probably just want to get back to Brazil, and the first thing they need to do is get on the puma's good side, assuming he has one. So they may be handing him a very convenient concoction, mixing truth and lies and stirring till ready to serve."

Belinda was listening to all of this with a pensive look on her face, pausing periodically to talk with the ATC's as we moved from traffic center to center. Before she could add her, no doubt, useful two cents, Bruce's phone rang. Chita??

Chita!! She was calling with Otto's phone number. We were to call him and use his GPS coordinates to land and pick him up. He would have the serum, notes and bill of sale. She had just checked with her bank and was happy to find that the money was sitting in an escrow account in her name waiting for the Bearoness to release it. She mentioned something dire would happen to me if Belinda didn't play straight. Neither Belinda nor I took very kindly to that.

Bruce shrugged and said, "Chita, don't hang up. There's a recording of a meeting Octavius had this morning with a couple of thugs that might interest you, and we never told you the rest of the story about what we're doing with the other members of the band. You listen to this while we contact Otto. and then we can discuss the situation."

Chita snarled, "Don't try anything fancy like trying to locate my signal, Brucie. I'm a hell of a lot faster on foot than any of you, and I haven't met a helicopter yet that I couldn't hide from."

"I've already told you that trying to capture you is more trouble than you're worth. But you may change your mind about what's next on your own agenda after you hear this conversation. Shut up and listen." He hit the play button on the recorder and started transmitting to the cat.

Meanwhile, I had called up Otto through the chopper's comm system and got a squeaky series of "hellos" accompanied by a picture of a twitching black spot.

"Otto, this is Maury Meerkat. First, hold the phone away from your face. All I can see is the tip of your nose."

The spot got smaller and was joined by radial spikes of whiskers and a trembling mouth. Then a couple of eyes and finally a complete face. "Good, I can see you. Can you hear me OK?" The furry head nodded. "Fine, now we've got your GPS coordinates and we should be getting near you in...what, Bearoness?"

"Ten minutes," growled Bel. The chopper had just hit an air pocket and she was trying to restabilize.

"Who was that?" asked an obviously frightened otter.

"That, my friend, is Bearoness Belinda Béarnaise Bruin Bear *(nee Black)*. She is, in a matter of speaking, your savior. She is a polar bear. I am a Meerkat as you already know and the third member of our party is Inspector Bruce Wallaroo of the International Counter-Espionage and Intellectual Property Protection Agency. No, you are not under arrest or in trouble. Bruce and I are both old playmates of Chita's."

I'm not sure Otto heard anything I said beyond Belinda's name. "Did you say 'Bearoness Belinda Béarnaise Bruin *(nee Black)*?'" he gulped.

"Yes, I did. *(I wasn't about to repeat that litany of B's again.)* She goes by Belinda or Bearoness."

"Wow, she's one of my idols. Her and the Aquabears. Can you imagine what it's like for a slapstick, star-struck animal who loves to swim and dive to be in the same company as show biz royalty?"

"Yeah, well, you'll be meeting her in the fur in just a few minutes. In the meantime, give us a description of where you are. We have your coordinates, but we don't know where we can land."

"I'm sitting on a dock on the Missouri river upstream from Pelican Island. We're not too far from St. Louis. I swam down there once while I was with Milord Mallàrd or whatever his name was. There's an ore loader overhead, and when you get closer you can also see the top of the duck's hydroplane sticking out of the river. Chita dumped a couple of tons of rocks on it and sank it. I can't hear your rotors yet."

"You probably won't until the last minute. This chopper is configured for stealth *(and combat, I might have added)*. Wait a second! Bearoness, is that the loader up ahead?"

"It could be. The GPS numbers are right. Otto, is there a clearing where we can land? I don't want to take a chance on an abandoned dock if I can help it."

"Yes, ma'am, Bearoness, your grace. There's a big parking lot on the other side of the loader."

"Belinda will be fine, Otto."

"Gee, Belinda, Wow! Gosh! First name basis with a legend."

The three of us were having a hard time holding in the laughter but Belinda toggled off the comm for a second, looked at Bruce and me and said, "I think he's sweet. It's more respect than I get from you two."

"Right-chew-are, your worship," chortled Bruce off-mike. He had been listening to us at the same time he was interspersing an occasional comment with Chita as she listened to the recording of the meeting over their phone link. Damned flexible, these Wallaroos. He said into the phone, "We're coming up on your little buddy, now, Chita, as I think you know. Meanwhile, listen very carefully to the end of this session. You'll find it very interesting, my pet."

That "my pet" would have gotten Bruce swatted into the next county if they were face to face. Wait till she hears it again on the recording.

We had spotted the loader, and as we came in closer, we could see the outline of Miss Lee-Li-Li in the murky river with just the top of the cockpit showing. We could also see a little animal scurrying for shelter from the rotors as we came down in the parking lot.

Bruce held his phone away from his ear. I could hear Chita snarling over the sound of the rotors and cabin vibration. That was one angry cat. "Property!

Pontius Puma! Pet!!" and assorted growls and nasty words in several languages. I'm surprised she didn't tear her phone to shreds.

"Chita, stop the earbashing and join the conversation here!" said Bruce as we settled into the parking lot. "I have no doubt you're nearby and can see us without aid of a picture phone. You don't have to show yourself on the screen either, if you don't want to. That's ridgy-didge, mate. Just give us a minute to get out of the helo and we can all have a nice calm chin wag without you throwing any wobblies."

I haven't the slightest idea whether she understood what he was saying, but the noise level at the other end of the phone dropped precipitously. So did the chopper noise as the engine whined down and wound down. Otto was sitting *(cowering?)* over by the shed. I got out and slowly walked over to him, paw extended.

"Otto? Maury! Good to meet you. Your rescue crew has landed. I hope you're up for a helicopter ride. We'll be heading back to Kentucky shortly, but a chopper cabin is no place for lengthy conversations. So we thought we'd get acquainted here on the ground. That's Inspector Wallaroo. He goes by the name of Bruce, and I need hardly tell you who the polar bear is." *(Especially since he had been staring at Belinda from the moment she cracked the door on her side of the cabin. He shook my paw, but I could have been a green and purple striped unicorn for all he noticed. The River Otter Chapter of the Belinda Béarnaise Fan Club had been founded and called to order and all attention was on that vision of ursine loveliness as she stood outside the chopper's door.)*

"C'mon over and say hello, Otto," she said. "We need to stay here so we can talk with Chita over the cabin speakers."

I'm not sure whether otters normally wag their tails, but he was doing a pretty good imitation as he half skittered-half waddled over to the ship. Bruce waved at him while he was still talking with Chita. Otto waved back, but it was clear where his attention was centered.

Belinda extended a paw that was about the same size as the otter, and he wavered for a moment and then took it in both of his paws and kissed it. This guy had just made a friend and ally forever. I thought I was something of a pro with the ladies, but little Mister Aw-Shucks-Gee-Whiz had me beat by a furlong. "I am speechless, ma'am," he blurted which, of course, he obviously was not.

Belinda smiled, which is not always a comforting expression since it shows some of her beautiful but largish teeth. The otter was too mesmerized to even notice. "Otto, I'm sure we'll get along just swimmingly," she said, which set them both off in gales of uproarious laughter. Listening to a polar bear and otter laugh in unison is a bit like listening to a steam whistle harmonizing with a fog horn. Interesting, but is it art?

"Now, little friend," she said loudly so Chita could hear over the copter's comm link, "we have some outstanding business we have to complete before we leave and I make a phone call to a certain bank. Where are the notes, serum and bill of sale?"

"I don't know," said Otto suddenly looking very frightened again.

"Chita???" we all chorused.

The cat was still muttering and snarling to herself about that no good Paolo *(Pontius Puma)* and his lousy Latin attitude. She was nobody's property. A lot of cats had already found that out to their sorrow. Sending goons after her and almost screwing up her business transaction in the process. "Yeah, yeah, yeah, I hear you. OK, the stuff is hidden up in the control cab of the ore loader."

The four of us first looked up at the decrepit crane and cab swaying slightly in the wind and then at each other. Neither Belinda nor Bruce was going to be able to make it up there. Cheetahs can climb trees and reasonable facsimiles thereof with ease, but in our group, I came the closest to a tree climber. And I was sure I had acrophobia. I'd never actually experienced it, but I was absolutely convinced at that moment that I had the worst clinical case ever recorded in the medical annals. I was prepared to get a note from my doctor, if necessary. Otto looked like he was a lost cause, too.

Bruce barked, "Very clever, you dumb sheila. If we can't get that stuff down, you don't get your money, and don't be too sure we can't track you down. You're good but so are we."

"What are you talking about, Bruce?" the cat screamed back. Then it dawned. "Oh, crap! It never occurred to me that you couldn't get up there. Well, I'm not coming back to get it. What about the Meerkat? You can climb steep obstacles, can't you Maury?"

"Are you kidding, Chita? I've lived in holes all my life. If something comes after me, I go down, not up. No way I'm going up there."

Silence. Then Otto piped up. "Wait a second, maybe I can do something."

"You can't be serious, Otto," said Belinda. "I'm a high diver but I couldn't possibly make it up that narrow, broken staircase. Have you ever gone up something that high?"

"Not yet, ma'am, but I don't think I have to. Wait just a second."

A swishing sound, and there by the door of the chopper sat a notebook with a sheet of loose paper hanging out of it and a beaker full of dark fluid.

"Hey, Chita," he screamed at the comm link, "the serum is still working. I just wished that stuff down here from the control cab."

Chita laughed hilariously on the other end of the link, and the three of us stared in amazement at the otter and the materials sitting in front of us.

"There," said Chita. "You have, before your very eyes, a demonstration of what makes Otto the Magnificent so magnificent."

I recovered first. "How do you do that, Otto?"

"I don't know, Maury," he replied. "It's that crazy serum. I just make a wish and I can move things and animals."

"Right," said Chita, "don't get him angry. I ended up in the river by just telling him to do something he didn't want to do."

My thoughts shot back to Wyatt Where and Frau Schuylkill. They seemed to be able to teleport and use telekinesis, too. What was that Wyatt said, "Wishing will make it so?" Oh, boy, welcome to *The Twilight Zone*. I think Belinda may have gotten off cheap if this serum really worked. But it could also turn the user into a stark raving nut. Speaking of which – "Hey Chita, what about Imperius? Is he dead, or what?"

The cat replied, "We don't know, do we Otto? I think he is. Why don't you go look in the Duck Blind. It's just down the river. Otto can show you. I'll call back in a couple of hours from a place far, far away, and you can fill me in. Meanwhile, Bearoness, you have a phone call to make, and I'm not kidding about getting even with you through Maury if you don't come across. A deal's a deal!"

"A Béarnaise Bruin's word is inviolable, my dear Ms Catt. I may have started out on the ice floes of Churchill, but I have taken on the full mantle of titled nobility. and I bow to its heavy responsibilities. Your filthy lucre will be in your hands shortly."

I felt like applauding. Sarah Bearnhardt couldn't have given a better performance, especially when she winked at us at the end. She broke the connection to Chita, dialed the bank and the four of us climbed into the cabin of the chopper, holding onto the notes, beaker and bill of sale for dear life – Otto's.

Frau Schuylkill

Chapter Nineteen

He's a faithful, good natured best friend.

He's a dog upon whom you depend.

See him striding along

Dignified and so strong.

The Bull Mastiff has courage no end.

Frau Ilse Schuylkill had just finished reviewing the Aquabear's maintenance schedules with Bearyl and was padding back into the mansion. "Such beautiful bears and so competent! Just like the Bearoness!" she thought. Frau Schuylkill was no slouch in the beauty and competence department herself and paired with the dashing Wyatt Where, would have made ideal leads for a TV adventure series – *Wolves of War* or *Tails of Fur and Glory.*

She had been approached more than once by cinema and TV producers working for UUI's entertainment division but she refused. "Show business types – a bunch of nutty squirrels." She made a great exception for the Bearoness and her entourage who, although they were up to their fuzzy ears in stagecraft, nevertheless kept their paws on solid ground or ice. Besides, they were all females.

She had less respect and affection for the three cats that Maury and the Inspector had brought back from Brazil. There was something about them that didn't smell right. The opera singer she could abide because he sang so beautifully. She was enthralled by his duets with Bearnice before and after dinner last night, but the other two, especially that surly drummer who liked Caipirinhas. The sooner gone, the better.

As she padded through the front hall, she could hear a feline voice in the background. She silently sidled over to the anteroom from where the voice was originating and listened. Whoever was talking was speaking Portuguese. Nothing unusual for three cats from Brazil. Before meeting Octavius at the *Schloss* at Breakurbach Falls, the Frau had spent much of her free time furthering her linguistic studies. Although she along with all of the UUI-related staff, had the

179

latest version of the Pea Pod Translator at her disposal, she insisted on working without it most of the time. *("I don't like those wires hanging from my ears." Female Vanity?)* She kept her studies up and added to her repertoire after joining the Great Bear. Now she could read, speak and understand twelve languages. Between her and Wyatt, Octavius had a team that could translate over twenty languages without technical augmentation. He himself could handle a few and so could Maury. But all of them, including the Pea Pod, had trouble with Bruce Wallaroo's Strine.

She listened. The language was no problem, but the subject matter was. Whichever of the cats was talking, he was keeping his voice very low, and he was talking very rapidly. "*Si, Si*, I know you sent the bulls but they met in his office, not here. I don't know what happened. No one has returned yet. *Si,* Senhor Puma, I understand. As I told you, Chita is not here. I don't know. This morning, the Wallaroo Inspector and the little Meerkat left together, but I don't know where they went. They've been gone for several hours. They took a jeep so they can't have gone too far. I'm sure they know where she is. I heard the Meerkat mention her name to the bear. I'm not sure they're holding her. She may be on her own."

"*Si,* I know that even if we can't find her you still want revenge for the attack. Funny thing, there's an Andean Condor who traveled with us from Brazil on the polar bear's plane. I haven't seen much of him since. He's working with some scientific genius porcupine here. I think they're trying to give him a voice. Yes, I know, a talking condor. Pra Caramba! But...that condor had a lot of electronic equipment with him."

"Now, Ozzie,' I say to myself. 'If they have this computer geek condor with them, could he have something to do with the terrible destruction that Senhor Puma's networks suffered?' And I answer myself, 'Ozzie, this is something you must investigate further.' And I am doing that, Senhor Puma. Even as we speak. I very much think you want to have your bull friends come here and not UUI Headquarters, although a little damage to the bear's business couldn't hurt. Come up yourself??? Is that wise, senhor? No, no, I meant no disrespect. It is just that you have always been reluctant to leave Brazil. *Si, Si*. I understand.

Well, I'm not quite sure where we are. Of course, you have my GPS coordinates. We flew in over a river and landed on what looks like a highway.

The house is huge and there's a Chinese and Roman temple. No, Senhor. I have not been drinking. *(Not any more than usual.)* This place is bizarre. All right, I'll call the Chicago Bulls and tell them to suspend the search for Chita and concentrate on destroying this place. It won't be easy. It's heavily defended. Of course, Senhor, of course! I didn't mean to imply…*Si*, I'll go scouting and call back with more information. Let me know if you're coming."

Frau Schuylkill overcame her canus lupus instincts to jump the ocelot and tear him to ribbons. Her military discipline kicked in, and she quietly backed away from the room. She needed to talk with Wyatt and Herr Bear immediately. This required a war council. She also needed to find Maury and much as she regretted it, the bouncing inspector. First things first. She called over to Wyatt's office and asked him to pop over ASAP.

No sooner had she hung up the phone than there was a "pop" and there stood Wyatt. *(They weren't quite sure how they did it either, but what the hell, it worked.)* Lapsing in and out of Switzerdeutsch and cursing with full military honors, she relayed what she overheard of the ocelot's phone conversation to the Security Officer. Although he agreed they needed to find Octavius *toute suite*, they knew that Maury, Bel and Bruce were playing hooky, and they didn't know where or for how long. Rather than get Octavius in a heavy duty rage searching for the elusive trio, he suggested they talk this thing through before calling him. Perhaps by then the three wanderers would have returned.

Wyatt started out by recapping the visit from the bulls and their veiled threats. Now the Frau had yet another target for her seemingly bottomless supply of spleen. Calming her down *(no mean task),* he suggested they sort out the culprits, real and or surmised.

Were all three of the cats involved, two or just Ozzie? Wyatt's staff was already busy getting all the intelligence they could on the bulls, and as soon as Wallaroo got back, he could fill in more details on Pontius Puma. Where did Chita fit in all this? Where the hell did Belinda and the boys take off for? A helicopter was missing from the UUI hangar, and they knew both Bruce and Bel could fly one. In the meantime, Action item number one: Stop Ozzie and get his cell phone. In fact, swipe all three of the cats' cell phones. They wouldn't dare to make calls to Brazil on the house phones.

What to use as a distraction? They had already eaten lunch. Lepi and Bearnice had gone off to the paddle boat Belinda B. to stand on the Texas deck and rehearse duets from *Show Boat*. They could hear Jake pounding away on a set of drums he and Howard had improvised from some materials in the lab and the hangar. Ozzie had disappeared. Find Ozzie!

Out of the corner of his eye, Wyatt spotted the ocelot pacing along the edge of the mansion. Probably doing a perimeter check for security systems so he could report to the Chicago Bulls and PP. He and the Frau approached the cat from different directions, keeping him up against the wall and between the shrubs. Ozzie looked nervous. His head pivoted from Wyatt to the Frau and back.

"Boa tarde! Senhor Ozzie," said the Frau. Continuing in Brazilian Portuguese, she asked, "Out for an afternoon stroll? The weather is very nice at the moment, but I think it may get very stormy for you."

Ozzie was shocked that the Frau was speaking such excellent Brazilian Portuguese, but he wondered why. "I can speak English, Senhora Wolf. You don't have to trouble yourself. I'm not sure the Colonel can understand us."

"Oh, I can understand perfectly, Ozzie," growled Wyatt, "and we both understand that you have been making a few phone calls that were not the sort an honored guest should be making. Frau Schuylkill overheard and understood your last conversation with Pontius Puma, and we are not in the least bit pleased. Now we would like you to come inside with us and wait for Octavius, Bruce and Maury to return, and we will all have a nice chat. We are also going to need your two band-mates."

"I don't know what you're talking about, you crazy wolf," hissed the cat in English. "What phone call? I didn't make no stinkin' phone call."

"Oh, Senhor Ozzie," said Frau Ilse, "didn't your mama tell you what happens to bad kittens that tell lies? I was standing outside the anteroom while you were talking to the puma and heard you tell him you would get more information about this place so the Chicago Bulls could strike at the Bear's Lair. A big mistake, incidentally. You don't know the half of how this place can be defended. I also heard you say he might come up to supervise the raid. We may just want you to call him back and tell him that you think that's a splendid idea."

"That wasn't me. That was Jake. I hate that puma."

"No, I don't think so," said the Frau. "I heard you give your name to the puma. 'Ozzie' doesn't sound at all like 'Jake,' even in Portuguese. Now, I'm sure you're a tough guy, although your paws haven't completely healed. Or were they ever damaged? Maybe you've been faking. Anyway, if you feel like taking on two combat trained wolves, feel free. Wyatt and I haven't had any real exercise in a while."

The ocelot tensed up, backed up against the wall and then…like a spotted missile, shot past them and headed out toward the road…running right into the front of the utility truck bringing Octavius back to the mansion. A screech, a yell, a yowl, a thud, a crunch. Not exactly the sounds Ozzie would have liked for a final riff, but dead cats can't be choosers.

Octavius trundled out of the truck along with the driver. Wyatt and Frau Schuylkill came loping up. No question. Ozzie was no more.

The bear looked at his driver, a Bull Mastiff named Charlie who had been on the mansion's security staff for years. The dog looked devastated. Not that he was crazy about ocelots but he had never before had an accident, much less a fatal one. Octavius said, "Charlie, he came out of nowhere. I was sitting right behind you, and I didn't see him till he was under the wheels."

Wyatt said to everyone and no one in particular, "He was trying to escape. Ilse caught him making a phone call to Pontius Puma telling him how to get here and promising him and the bulls the lowdown on our security systems. We had him cornered and were about to interrogate him when he ran for it. Charlie, that cat might have been responsible for your death and the death of all of us. I'm only sorry we didn't get a chance to grill him, but at least he won't be making any more calls."

Octavius looked at them. "Obviously, I've got a lot of catching up to do and quickly. Charlie, can you call the local police and tell them we had a fatal accident out here. We'll have to report it, but just say he darted out of the trees, which he did. No mention of him being chased. The three of us will confirm that it was an accident and certainly not your fault. I'll talk to the police chief or whoever they send and no doubt they'll have a medical examination. Keep me posted and don't worry about a thing.

From what I'm gathering, the accident might have been a blessing. It'll give us some extra time to defend ourselves, if we need it. After the police have left, go into the library and have yourself a couple of stiff drinks…but not until they've left. We don't want a DUI charge to contend with. Frau Schuylkill will have the sous-chef get you something to eat if you're hungry and not too shaken up. Thanks, old friend. I'm really sorry."

The mastiff held out a paw to the bear and growled his thanks.

"Now," said Octavius, turning to the wolves, "what the hell is going on, and where are Bruce and Maury?"

Sheepishly *(no pun intended)* Wyatt said, "We're not sure where they are. I know the two of them left the UUI campus between eleven and noon and it's almost five now. Maury just said they'd be gone for a few hours. I expected them back before now. We need to round up the other two cats on the double. We've got a bunch of things to sort out, and I'm not sure we can trust any of those Brazilians, including the condor."

"Where are they now?"

Frau Schuylkill said, "Lepi is down on the Belinda B. with Bearnice, and I think Jake is in the house. Oh no, he's not. Here he comes now. He must have heard the noise."

"Ozzie, Oz, what happened?" It was the first show of any emotion they had seen out of the jaguar other than a surly snarl or two at some minor inconvenience. He crouched down next to Ozzie's body and pushed at him, licked his face, put his head against his broken body and howled, "He's dead! How did this happen? Who killed him? Who? I'll get the lousy low-life for this! Oh, Oz. I knew you'd end up like this. I knew it."

The bear stood erect over the jaguar and said, "It was an accident. He ran right into the truck. We didn't have time to see him, much less stop. No one's to blame and you're not going to take it out on anyone. I can appreciate your feelings but this is all the violence there's going to be. Understand!?"

The jaguar stared at Octavius, said nothing, did nothing.

Wyatt asked, "What did you mean about 'You knew he'd end up like this?'"

"Nothing," said the cat, "Nothing."

"All right," said the bear, "everybody back to the house except you, Frau Schuylkill. I want you to go and bring back Bearnice and Lepi. Don't give them any reason except I want to talk to everyone. You come with me, Jake. Wyatt, find Belinda and Bearyl as well as Howard and L.Condor. We'll meet in the

184

library. Frau Schuylkill, after you get Lepi and Bearnice, find out where our two wandering heroes are and get them back here as well. I want answers and as of now, I don't even have the right questions."

The she-wolf turned to go and stopped. "Herr Bear, I'm getting a call from the Bearoness. She wants to talk to the three of us. It's an emergency."

"Patch her into the truck comm system! You stay here, Jake."

"Belinda, where are you, and what's wrong?"

"Tavi, I'm in a company helicopter, and we're heading back to the mansion as fast as I can get this thing to move. The Inspector and Maury are with me."

"What the hell are you doing out there with those two in a helicopter? What's the emergency?"

"Later, Tavi. Right now I need to know where's the best place to land for medical emergency treatment. UUI, the mansion or a local hospital?"

"UUI, definitely. They have a full medical staff on call over there 24/7 and they're discreet. We'll call and have them stand by. But who needs the help? Are you OK?"

"I'm fine. I'll explain as soon as I land. We're in the middle of a rainsquall and I have my paws full. Signing off!"

"Sometimes that sow is intolerable. I may need emergency treatment myself in another few minutes. Frau Schuylkill, call UUI medical and tell them to expect the chopper with an emergency on board. Then get down to the boat and bring back Lepi and Bearnice. Wyatt, lock Jake up before you get Howard and the condor. Charlie, call me when the police arrive and..." Large Magnitude Thud! Octavius fell over next to the truck. Frau Schuylkill raced to him and checked his vital signs. He was out for the count. Narcolepsy waits for no bear.

Chapter Twenty

Flying meerkats are really quite rare.

But when you represent the Great Bear,

The gyrations are few

That you cannot do.

Such as bomb-driven turns in the air.

Flashback: In the UUI chopper over the Mighty Missouri.

As we lifted off from the parking lot, Otto pointed down river to Pelican Island and said: "That's where Milord Mallàrd has his laboratory. He calls it the Duck Blind. It's an elaborate place."

I looked over at Bruce and Belinda and said, "Chita wasn't sure whether she killed Imperius or not. Maybe we should check while we're here."

Bel frowned. "Suppose he's not dead. I'm not too eager to fly right up to the front door of that crazy duck's fortress if he's still alive and quacking. Even if the baboon is the only one left, we could be asking for trouble. This helicopter does have an assault gun stowed away somewhere, but we need to land and then mount and operate it. Can either of you do that?"

Otto piped up, "I can get in there without stirring things up!"

Three part harmony – "How??"

"That's my other talent. The duck's serum has made me into an escape artist extraordinaire. I can get in and out of places even if they're locked up solid. Chita saw me do it, and I had the duck and baboon totally flummoxed during our test runs. Why don't you land the chopper on the far side of the island? Keep the rotors idling, and Maury and I will sneak around and up to the Duck Blind entrance. I'll zip in, and if it's all clear I'll signal Maury and he can call you two."

"Suppose it's not," said Bruce. "If one or both of them are still in there and alive, we may not be able to get you out again."

"You won't have to. If I can get in, I can get out. I'll just do a quick run-through. They may not even notice me. I can sneak in and out again in no time. What do you want me to do when I get in there?"

"You're a gutsy little critter, Otto. All we want is confirmation of Chita's claim that he's dead."

"Not fair, Bruce." I squeaked. "She didn't say he was dead. Chita said she clobbered him pretty hard and he fell over, but she wasn't sure what his state was."

"OK, let's not quibble. What do you think, Bearoness?"

"I think since we're right over the island, and we're making more than enough noise, if anyone's in there, they know we're here. We need to make up our minds this minute. I'm for chancing it. I like Otto's plan, provided you can do what you claim, Otto. Where should I land? I can't see anything that looks like a landing pad."

"There isn't any by the entrance, Belinda." *(There was a slight pause before the "Belinda." He still couldn't get used to calling this legend of the aquacade and paragon of beauty by her first name.)* "You can just make out the dock where they used to moor the hydroplane. It just looks like an old tie-up for fishermen. The doors to the lab are right near there, but they're carefully hidden in the underbrush and down a ramp. I used to practice breaking in and out of the entrance with all of its security devices. Once or twice I was slowed down a little, but I always got through. Going either way! There's enough of a clearing on the other side of the island to set down. Bearoness, stay in the chopper with the Inspector so you can make a fast getaway, if you need to. C'mon Maury, you're small enough to hide in the brush as I move up."

I wasn't quite sure about this particular aspect of his plan but I was somewhat reluctant to suggest that I wouldn't risk my furry skin while this hopped-up otter was gung-ho to stage a commando raid. For a cagey Meerkat, I am sometimes quite stupid.

"All right, Otto," called the Bearoness, "I'm letting down here. If they're in there they'll know we've arrived. I guess I could try to act innocent and pretend I needed to land to fix something, but this chopper has UUI plastered all over it and the Duck is no dunce. Anyway! Maury, you do a quick exit on the far side of the cabin while Otto gives us a short demonstration of his illusionist's powers. OK, Otto. Otto? Otto! Where the hell is he?"

"Out and back…twice," said the otter as he reappeared by the portside skid. The serum's still working. You didn't see me come or go, did you?"

Bruce grumbled to Belinda, "He's worse than those bleeding wolves. I'm getting damned sick of peek-a-boo entrances and exits."

Belinda chuckled. "You're just jealous, Inspector."

"Too right, I'm jealous. I'm the one who could really use that skill in my line of work. Maybe I'll chug-a-lug some of that fruit loop's serum myself."

"Well, if it drives you crazy, we'd be hard pressed to tell the difference."

"Very funny, Bearoness, very funny!"

I slid down the helicopter's undercarriage and sneaked off on all fours behind Otto. He was moving at my pace and kept looking back to make sure I was still there. We rounded a small hill and headed toward the makeshift dock. Otto stopped and waited for me to catch up.

"Now," he said, "I can get past all that security stuff, but you can't." *(File that under pretty damn obvious.)* "So when I get inside, first thing I'll do after I look around is turn off the alarms and open the doors for you. Then we can both investigate."

It was only then it occurred to me that neither one of us had any kind of weapon. *(except, of course, our natural animal cunning. Oh, swell!!)* "Suppose they're armed and hiding," I said, trying not to sound like the wuss I obviously was. "The duck used to have a ray gun."

"I didn't see any heavy armament the whole time I was in the Duck Blind. It's been less than twenty four hours since Chita swiped me, and I doubt he's gotten or made any in that time. But I must admit I didn't look everywhere while I was his guest. It didn't occur to me that they'd have weapons."

I was not greatly consoled.

"Wait here," he said. "I'll be right back."

I crouched down in some bushes near the entrance ramp and watched him disappear. *(Or to be more accurate, I did not watch him disappear since in the act of disappearing, he was no longer visible and therefore unwatchable. But, once again I digress.)* I checked my watch…ten seconds, twenty, thirty, forty…what's going on in there? Then I heard the sound of an electric door motor starting up, and as I was about to cheer, there was a thundering "WHUMP," and I discovered that I had a newly acquired talent. I could fly!!!

I had just enough time to scream, "Otto!!!" and "Help!!" before I…

*****

Four beautiful meerkats were tossing me up and down on an oversized beach blanket. Then suddenly I was taking bouncing lessons from Bruce on a trampoline. Now I was strapped in a seat in a careening helicopter. To my muzzy brain, of those three alternatives, the last seemed the least enjoyable and therefore the most likely. Worse yet, from the way we were bouncing, Wallaroo was at the controls. "Bruce, cut that out!" I shouted.

"He's awake! Cut what out, you mangy mongoose? I'm not doin' anything."

From the horrible thought that Bruce was at the controls, I jumped to an even more horrible thought. Bruce was not at the controls, but the Bearoness was. And she was not in control…therefore leading me to believe after five nanoseconds of analysis and contemplation that we were IN TROUBLE!

"What's happening?" I gurgled and yelped. Something nasty bit the nerves in my leg as I tried to move. I have a pain tolerance threshold that's way below zero.

"We are getting you and Otto home as fast as we can, and we've run into a ripper of a thunderstorm. Just hold tight and shut up. The Bearoness is doing a bang-up job."

"Bang-up" wasn't a word I wanted to hear. I looked across the aisle, and there was Otto, stretched flat in a reclining seat. He was out cold and actually seemed lifeless to me. "Bruce," I shouted over the rotors, engine, wind and the hail that was pelting the fuselage, "What happened to Otto? Is he alive?"

"Just bearly," he replied. "I think that ratbag duck had the doors booby-trapped. As far as I can tell, Otto must have gotten in. I found him up against a wall on the far side of the room. Out and hardly breathing. I think he has a concussion, and I don't know about any of his limbs. You look a bit bruised yourself, and you may have torn something in your leg, but all your bones feel

189

OK. There wasn't anyone else in there and no bodies that I could see. So, it's still a mystery as to whether the duck and his baboon friend are alive or dead."

"Somebody had to set the booby-trap!"

"Yeah, that's what I'm thinking but until we can talk to Otto or Chita and find out how that entrance control worked, we won't know. I'm betting the duck is still alive, and so is Bigg."

"Where are we?"

"Hold on, I'll check with Bearoness. Try not to move."

Now, half-sitting and half lying down in a helicopter that is getting batted all over the sky, it's difficult to take advice like "try not to move" seriously. I wished I could pass out again before motion sickness kicked in.

Bruce shouted back, "We're about twenty minutes out, according to Belinda. We're getting out ahead of the storm but after we land, we'll be right back in it again."

"Good. I could use a fermented coconut milk."

"Not likely, mate. You and your swimmin' friend are going to the medical unit at UUI. They have doctors standing by. Belinda hasn't told Octavius about Otto or Chita or any of our adventures. She just said she had a medical case on board. I don't know what's worse. This ruddy storm or the one Ocko's going to raise when we tell him about all of this."

For one brief moment, I held out the hope that my wounded condition might lead the Great Bear to be a bit restrained in his divine wrath. Then I realized that all it meant was I couldn't run away while he lit into me. Then I began to hope for a speedy and painless death. In the meantime I was feeling some exquisite pain *(what the hell is exquisite about pain?)* in my ribs, back and legs. Now I at least wanted to pass out. On cue, I moved my leg and fainted.

When I came to again, Otto and I were under spot lights, lying near each other on mini-sized hospital gurneys. Otto was still out and surrounded by several doctors and nurses. Obviously, since I was being tended to by the second team *(so what else is new?)* my wounds and ills must have been less serious. I looked around. Bruce was there. Howard was standing off in the corner talking to a nurse, but no sign of Octavius or the wolves. Strange.

190

I could hear Belinda on the phone. "You'll just have to wait for your explanation until we get over there. You need to hear the story from all of us. But, how come you're not over here? Your number one sidekick is hurt, and you're blustering at me over the phone. Sheriff? What sheriff? What are you talking about, Tavi? Ozzie? The little guitarist? Oh dear! So you and the wolves are tied up with the law. Then I think it's best we stay here till they leave. You agree?? It was an accident wasn't it? All right, we'll talk later."

I had obviously been sedated, but even in that state, my anxiety levels were rising rapidly *(along with my blood pressure reading and my heart rate blipping on the bedside scope.)* <u>I am not a hypochondriac</u> but my health has always been a great cause of personal concern. And after all, I had been blown up. I guess it doesn't take much in the way of an explosion to sail an erect, two foot, two pound mammal like me into the woods. Otto, on the other hand, probably weighs about twenty five pounds and is three to four feet long. It must have taken a fair size blast to throw him across a room.

I hadn't been able to make heads or tails out of Belinda's one-sided phone conversation with Octavius, so I listened to what she was saying to Bruce. Something about Ozzie being dead. Oh, boy! And Pontius Puma planning a raid. Even more oh, boy! And when we added our suspicions about Imperius Drake and Bigg and then threw in Otto and the Chita negotiations to round out the agenda, this was going to be a night to remember. The doctor was talking to me.

"I'm sorry, Doctor. What did you say?"

The medic, a white rat who specialized in small animals, was telling me that I had a nice collection of bumps and scratches and had torn a ligament in my left leg, but they had taken a vote and decided not to take me outside and shoot me. He and a nurse, another white rat, helped me off the gurney and over into a wheel chair. An attendant went out to search up a size 000 crutch. I also had a bandage over my right ear.

Pictures! I had to get some pictures to send back to the mob in Mauritius. My aunt would be fascinated. She alone had some affection left for the Black Meerkat of the family. Everyone else in the clan was into theft and larceny and here I was, for gosh sakes, working as a detective. They were so ashamed they couldn't even mention my moniker. She called me the Nameless Detective.

I asked about Otto. His doctors, in this case a group of orangutans, said they couldn't be certain until he came out of his coma. Bodily, he didn't seem too badly damaged, but he had obviously suffered a concussion and was still out for the count. I wondered if anyone had mentioned the serum he'd been taking. For that matter, what could they say for certain about it? Developed by a crazy duck geneticist to conquer the world and fed to an unwitting otter who wanted a career in show biz. This film is rated PG13.

I watched as Bruce and Belinda spoke with the doctors. They were telling them what little we knew about the serum. Chiti BingBang, the chief physician reached for a phone. I think he was calling the genetics lab. Bruce looked at Belinda and then hopped out of the room, probably going for the serum and the lab notes, wherever they had left them. Oh boy! Was Octavius going to hit the roof! What should have been treated as a top secret research program was turning into a hospital room soap opera. I called the chief physician over and explained the situation as best I could. All unnecessary personnel should leave the room when Bruce returned with the serum and notes. But wait a second.

The serum and notes were Belinda's property. It was up to her to call the shots on this one. And Octavius was completely out of the loop. I grabbed my cell phone but the Bearoness had beaten me to it. She was on the horn to the Great Bear again, telling him to get his big brown bulk over here ASAP. The things that lady could get away with. I guess the agents of the law had folded their tents over at the Bear's Lair, because Octavius was heading out to a shuttle truck while they were speaking.

The geneticist, Dr. Vark, arrived and the chief physician suggested that all concerned parties *(except Otto, of course)* adjourn to a conference room down the hall and wait for the bear's arrival. Otto was left with a resident and a nurse.

I wheeled myself into a space at the conference table with a little help from Howard, who had been taking all this in with a very quizzical look on his prickly puss. Bruce came through the door at the far end of the room, brandishing the bottle and the notebook. I noticed he handed a sheet of paper to Belinda. The bill of sale from Chita. As we settled in, waiting for Octavius to arrive, Bruce's phone rang. Ah, now the circle would be complete. Ms Catt was on the line. Checking in as promised

Bruce bounced to the back of the room and in as quiet a voice as I have ever heard him use, he proceeded to bring Chita up to date. Clearly, from the expressions that were crossing the Wallaroo's face, she was not taking any of the news too kindly. I couldn't make out if he was telling her about Ozzie. Of course, on this side of the river, we really didn't know what had happened to Ozzie except he was dead. We'd have to wait on Octavius for that bit of breaking news. Bruce was shaking his head and saying "yes" and "no" alternately. I was waiting for him to lose his Aussie temper. Instead he hung up. He looked over at Belinda and me and said, "I told her to call back in an hour. We'll have a conference."

Out in the hall, a series of growls and thumps announced the event we had all been waiting for. The door flew open with a 120 dBa roar, "What the Hell is Going On????"

Octavius had arrived.

Chapter Twenty One

The Orang-utan's really quite bright.

And his reddish brown hair's quite a sight.

He swings swiftly and free

From a ceiling or tree.

He's a high-flying brilliant delight.

Before he could get another sound out of his mouth, Belinda pushed back her chair and leaning her front paws on the table top, snarled, "Doctor Octavius Bear, *(this was going to be good!)* how dare you come stomping in here like a common boor? I have spent the entire day along with Bruce and brave little Maury here flying back and forth to St. Louis through abysmal weather. I have spent a substantial sum of my own money to secure what may be one of the most valuable genetic developments of all time. We have been booby trapped at Imperius Drake's hideout and both poor little Maury and that courageous otter have been seriously wounded in the process."

"What otter??"

"Don't interrupt. I did not fly all the way over here from my peaceful home in the Shetlands *(by way of Las Vegas and Churchill)* to be beaten, bumped and battered and then subjected to a harangue from you. Now either you climb down off your moral high ground and forget about delivering one of your tongue lashings or sermons or speeches, or I am walking out of here and flying home immediately, taking MY property with me along with poor Otto if the doctor says he can be moved. Read the riot act to someone else. We are all tired and our nerves are in tatters. Now, what happened to Ozzie?? Where are the wolves??"

I have seen Octavius with his mouth wide open before, usually roaring and scaring the hell out of an adversary. This time he was just gaping, hardly believing that he had been so summarily shut up by this polar tornado. She stared at him and growled, "Oh, close your mouth. Your teeth need cleaning!!"

I'm not sure what I expected. If anyone else in the room had gotten just one of those sentences out of their mouths, they would have been flying through the unopened conference room window.

"The wolves are back at the lair," he grumbled, "guarding the remaining band members. The condor and your two bears are with them. We may be under attack shortly. Wyatt and I had a visit this morning from a couple of Chicago Stockyards thugs threatening us if we didn't tell them where Chita is."

"I know," she said. "I listened to a tape of the conversation." *(Oh swell, Bearoness, you have just well and truly cooked my goose.)*

"How did you get that?"

"Never mind! Is Ozzie's death connected to that visit?"

"Since he got here, Ozzie had been spying on us and relaying all the information including our location to Pontius Puma. Frau Schuylkill overheard a phone conversation they were having and when she and Wyatt confronted Ozzie, he tried to run away. He ran right into our shuttle truck. Dead on Impact! We're not sure about the other two cats. That's why we have them in confinement. Bearyl and Bearnice are helping the wolves interrogate them.

The sheriff just left with the ocelot's body. He knows nothing about this Pontius Puma mess. I'm pretty sure they've decided Ozzie's death was an accident – which it was. The coroner's inquest is scheduled for Friday. We didn't tell them why he was running and not looking where he was going. This thing with Pontius Puma is escalating. Not only is he after Chita. He wants revenge for what we did to his operation. As you know, if you listened in on the conversation with the bulls *(I got a sharp and piercing bear glare)*, I haven't the slightest idea where Chita is."

"We do," blurted Bruce.

"Obviously! You've must have had contact with her if that bottle and notebook came from her. What did you pay for them, Bel?"

"Don't worry, Tavi *(we were back to Bel and Tavi again)*, you'll get the bill if you want them."

"I'm not sure what I want. By the way, Doctors Vark and BingBang, forgive me for not saying 'hello' earlier. As you could no doubt tell, I have been a bit preoccupied with a series of crises."

He was addressing Chief Geneticist Dr. Helix Oryceteropus Vark and Dr. Chiti BingBang, UUI's Chief Physician. Both of these animals are exceptional in their respective fields. Dr. Vark is a rather eccentric African anteater who has made many of the great discoveries that have put UUI's Genetics division in the forefront of scientific and commercial success. We have known each other for years, sharing, as we do, an African background and a crazy sense of humor. Like most of his friends, I call him "Odd." He flipped his large ears in Octavius' direction by way of greeting.

Dr. BingBang is an orangutan from Borneo who had met Octavius in his travels through Malaysia and sprang at the chance to head up UUI's Medical Unit. If anyone can get Otto back, Chiti BingBang can. He puffed his cheek and throat flaps at the bear and went back to hanging from a ceiling fixture.

"Now," rumbled the bear in the general direction of Belinda, Bruce and myself, "having heard a summary of my day, perhaps you'd like to share your merry adventures with me. And who is this otter??"

We took him through the chronology of the day, including a description of what little we knew of Otto and his mysterious powers brought on by the duck's potion. Chiti, Odd, Howard and Octavius all paid very close attention to that part. No doubt, this complicated the otter's treatment and his fate.

When we got to the booby trap, Octavius asked the obvious question. "Is the duck still alive?"

"That's the 100,000 euro question, Ocko. We need to compare notes and it would help a great deal if we could talk with Otto – that's his name – Otto the Magnificent – actually it's Hairy Otter but he's using his stage name. Clever little guy! You should see him teleport and go through locked doors. He's got a great career ahead of him..."

"Ooh, for God's sake, Inspector, spare me the headlines from *Variety*. Doctor BingBang, what do you think his chances are?"

"I'm not sure, Doctor Bear. *(He dropped onto the conference room table and stared at Octavius.)* This serum puts a whole new spin on things. It could be a crucial key to his condition, or it could be incidental. I'm sure he took a major blow from the blast and a concussion could leave him in a coma for days...or permanently."

No one spoke for several seconds and then Octavius *(surprise!)* picked it up again. Turning to the geneticist, he asked, "Do you think you could analyze the contents of this bottle and come up with any useful theories on what it is and what it did to the otter?"

"I'm going to have to take some blood and DNA samples from Otto for openers. I may also have to MRI his head and vital organs to see if there are any significant abnormalities that could be due to genetic alteration."

"All right, Doctor and Doctor, please get to it. Take the lab notes and serum with you and let's see what we can find out."

Belinda cleared her throat. "Excuse me, doctors and DOCTOR Bear, but you are forgetting that those items are mine. I have a legitimate bill of sale from the previous owner. Please do not play fast and loose with my property."

"But what could **you** do with them, Bel?" *(Oh, good one, boss! Right down the sexist alley! I sometimes wonder about you. Brilliant and dumb at the same time.)*

The Bearoness bristled and said, "I will do what I told you I would do. Take them and Otto back to the Shetlands. I will set up my own genetics institute and hire some of the best minds in the business to develop these materials, assuming they're worth anything at all."

She turned to the Chief Geneticist and asked, "Would you be interested in a change of venue, Doctor Vark, with an increase in earnings and broad freedom of action and decision making? Think about it. We'll talk later."

Before Odd could respond, Octavius said, "All right, I'll buy them from you. Half again what you paid."

"No, Tavi dear, you will not buy them from me, but I will consider a partnership in a new venture. 'Bruin and Bear Genetic Specialties' or some such thing. Fifty-fifty ownership, but I get top billing. I always get top billing. Now, just agree in principle before all these witnesses, and I will turn over the serum and notes to the good doctors so they can help poor Otto."

Buried in the midst of several cavernous grumbles, we all heard words of agreement. They might not hold up in a court of law, but Octavius was a Bear of Extreme Honor. So too, was the Bearoness. This would be interesting. Business partners, as well as life partners. Stranger and stranger.

197

"Now," said the bear, "what's the story on Chita?"

"She'll be calling back in half an hour or so," said Bruce. "Why don't we head back to the mansion and let Doctor Chiti get on with his work on Otto. If you want to come with us, Doctor Vark, some of the discussion might help you figure out what the doofus duck did. We can have a nice chin-wag with all the cats when Chita calls in on my phone. This Pontius Puma thing is getting out of hand and we need to compare notes and surmises about Imperius and Bigg. I should have stayed in Australia."

Here I sit in a wheelchair, swathed in bandages and doped half-way out of my gourd and *he's* complaining. It would feel good to get back to the lair and have a bowl of fermented coconut milk VSOP *(drugs or no drugs)* and maybe a snack or two from the kitchens of Schuylkill.

Boy, did Belinda shut down Octavius! In my next spare moment, I am going to form a brand new chapter of the Bearoness Belinda Béarnaise Fan Club complete with clubhouse. Maybe we'll call it "Octavius' Retreat." I am no doubt feeling euphoric due to chemical assistance. Tomorrow or sometime in the immediate future, I will still have to face the music with the Great Bear. But for now, what the hell! Actually, what Octavius needs is a healthy slug of mead. We filed *(I rolled)* out of the conference room and headed down to the carpool.

Bruce and Howard managed to get me into a different truck from Octavius, thus saving my fuzzy skin for the nonce. As our little cavalcade worked its way toward the river and over to the Ohio shore, I sat next to my folded wheelchair and contemplated new career opportunities for a down-in-his-luck Meerkat. Perhaps the Bearoness needed another assistant although it got pretty cold up there in the Shetlands. Who was I kidding? It gets pretty damn cold in Southwest Ohio.

Or…Or…Or if Sleeping Beauty Otto awoke from his snooze *(Should I run back and kiss him? Nah! I'd just make it worse)*, **and** if he's still Magnificent and not just dopey, maybe he could use an agent. I'd look great all in black with oversized sunglasses. I could hire those bimbo meerkats I keep dreaming about. "Yes, Mr. Maury, No, Mr. Maury." Or take telephone calls from theatrical impresarios - "Maury, sweetheart, what's shakin' babe? Have your animals call my animals. We'll do lunch. Bring the otter."

The truck came to a screeching halt, and so did my dreams. A small traffic jam at the entrance to the mansion. Octavius piled out of the lead vehicle

198

and roaring for a keg of mead, trounced into the mansion along with Dr."Odd" Vark. The Bearoness was in the second truck with Bruce. Howard and I had taken up the rear. By the time I reached the library, Octavius was already settled behind his desk. Lepi and Jake, looking none too happy, had one paw apiece chained to a chair, under the watchful eyes of Bearyl and Bearnice. On the other hand, they also had some of the Frau's hors d'oeuvres and a bowl of something at their side. Even as captors, those two bears exhibited style. *(Ah, life in the luxury lane with the Bearoness and her ursine entourage. It couldn't get that cold in the Shetlands. Maybe I could represent Otto while living with Belinda.)* I was once again shaken out of my reveries by the rumbling voice of the Great Bear saying, "So!!"

No one else I knew could make the word "so" sound so ominous.

"Let's begin with your rescue trip."

We laid it out, starting with the consensus observation that Octavius was being a moralistic stuffed shirt *(Guess who said that?)* for being unwilling to deal with Chita. Belinda stared down his protestations, so he cast his bearful gaze on me.

We told them about the otter demonstrating his ability to use telekinetics and to get past obstacles and closed doors. We said we'd pick that part up again when Chita called back in. As best we could tell, Bigg and/or possibly Imperius, if he was still alive, had booby-trapped the door to the Duck Blind, to catch anyone trying to break in using the entry system. Otto had simply bypassed the system.

"How?" asked Doctor Vark.

"We don't know." I said. "That's another question for Chita or for Otto if and when he wakes up. But when he attempted to activate the system to let *me* in, the door blew, sending me flying into the shrubbery and him to wherever Bruce found him."

"He was lying upside down on top of a specimen table inside the lab. I think he hit the wall and bounced off. He was all rigid," said Bruce.

"That's strange," said the geneticist. "I would have thought he'd be limp. I'll have to talk to Chiti about that."

"Her name is Chita," I said.

"No, Chiti! Doctor BingBang. That rigidity might be an indication of that serum at work. Although I do want to talk to Chita, too." *(Somebody has to change their name.)*

"So, Inspector, from what you could tell, there is no confirming evidence as to whether Imperius is alive or dead."

"I didn't have time for anything but a quick look about, Ocko. I'd just dropped Maury into the helicopter, and the Bearoness was running up the engines for a high performance getaway. So when I hopped back in there to check for Otto, expecting to see body fragments scattered all around, I was so relieved that his body was intact, I just grabbed him and bounced. It wasn't until we were airborne that I even determined he might still be alive. From what I could see as I sprang in and out, there was nobody else in there. No lights, no signs of habitation. Empty. Chita may have done Imperius in and Bigg may have buried him, set the trap and headed off for who knows where."

"Or," intoned Octavius, "he may still be alive."

"Senhor Bear, who is this Imperius Drake?" a low whirring voice asked. We all stared over to the corner of the library where it had originated from. L. Condor could talk!!

"*Si*, thanks to…Senhor Howard…and your talk, er tech staff, I can speak a bit through a modified Pea Pod. We're still working on it."

Bruce bounced over to the corner, upsetting a floor lamp and sending Frau Schuylkill into howls of aggravation. "Goodonyer! Way to go, mate!" He pounded the condor on the back and the bird in turn flapped his wings in involuntary response, sending an end table to join the lamp and sending the she-wolf into a spasm of frustration. The two cats stared at the condor in amazement.

"That's wonderful, Senhor Condor," said the Bear. "Congratulations to all of you. To answer your question fully would take a long time, but suffice it to say that Imperius Drake was once a great but erratic geneticist – correct, Dr, Vark??" The anteater nodded. "But he began experimenting in genetic manipulation to create über-animals and was cut off by the scientific community. He began experimenting on himself and created an avian monster. Perhaps the greatest evil genius the modern world has known. He and I along with members of law enforcement around the world *(raised eyebrow from Bruce)* have been engaged in an ongoing struggle that never seems to end. That's why I am somewhat dubious about this situation. If Chita is telling the truth about attacking him but he is still alive, then that would be the second near miss in the last few months. The last one was a direct hit by a heat seeking missile on a balloon he was in while trying to destroy most of the genetic science community, including the good doctor here."

It was clear the two cats had not heard anything about Imperius either. I was watching their disbelieving expressions as Octavius told his abbreviated tale.

"So, we may well hear from our two long-time adversaries yet again, or perhaps he may have finally run out of lives *(a sideways look at the cats)*, and Bigg may or may not make an appearance."

"Looks like we may have a two-front war on our paws," said Bearnice.

"Right, Bearyl," replied Octavius. He couldn't see which one had the ankle bracelet and had guessed wrong. She didn't correct him. "I am reasonably certain from what Frau Schuylkill picked up from Ozzie's phone call that Pontius Puma is going to try to get here to participate in the mayhem. That gives us some time. He'll need at least twelve hours or more to make it up here. Stupid on his part! Outside of Brazil, he's pretty vulnerable, isn't he, Inspector?"

"Too right, Ocko, but I think his Latin honor has been besmirched, and he's not thinking straight."

"That cat has a mean temper," said Lepi, "he sure showed it to us." Nod from Jake.

"Which brings us to the next subject," said the bear. "What did these feline fellows tell you, Frau Schuylkill, Wyatt?"

Wyatt looked at the Frau and the two bears and said, "We questioned them separately and then together. Jake had some idea of what Ozzie was doing. Lepi, here, seems to be completely at a loss. I think we all agree. For all practical purposes, Ozzie was doing a solo." Frau Schuylkill and the bears nodded affirmation.

"I don't understand," said Bruce, "We saved you blokes from the puma's paws and Ozzie turns about and plays the dipstick telling him where to find you…and us."

Jake responded, "Ozzie wanted to go back to Brazil. He has a girl friend there and his family. He thought he could get on the right side of the puma by setting you guys up and finding Chita. I heard him on the phone yesterday talking Portuguese, and I called him on it. He said he was talking to his family, but the conversation sure didn't sound like 'Hi, mom, I'm fine.' I asked him point blank if he was in contact with PP and he changed the subject. What made him believe that Pontius Puma would play it straight with him is beyond me. He probably didn't even level with Chita."

"So aside from having suspicions, you didn't have anything to do with the visit from the bulls."

"You kiddin, bear? I can't stand bulls. And I have no great desire to go back to São Paolo. I don't want to stay here either. I was hoping I could locate Chita and the four – now three of us - could get back together. Maybe play Europe. Chita knows Europe like the back of her paw."

"And you, Lepi? How about you?"

"Like I told your two friends, I have no ties to Brazil. I got deported from China and I'm strictly Asian. But if I try to go back to the Himalayas, I'll end up in a cage or worse. I want to do opera. I wouldn't mind teaming up with Bearnice here."

All three bears gave him a quizzical look. Something started spinning in Belinda's brain. For all of her *savoir faire*, her face was a dead giveaway when she was plotting and scheming. Hooray, more intrigue! Just what we need!

Octavius looked around the room, searching for someone who wasn't buying the two cats' act. No takers. "OK," he said. "The chains can come off, BUT I expect both of you to help us face off against whatever the puma and the bulls have in mind. You owe us that for getting you away from him. Anything that may happen with Imperius Drake, we'll take care of ourselves. If you don't agree, you both stay in confinement for the duration."

I half expected Jake to say something like, "I'm a drummer, not a fighter!" but to my surprise, he said, "I want a shot at that puma for what he did to me. It's gonna take a while to get my rhythm back. I'd like to practice on his head."

Lepi said, "In the Chinese Army, we learned the elements of paw to paw combat as well as singing fight songs. I can handle a weapon. That cat is a menace."

The Bear waved at Wyatt who started to unfetter them.

Frau Schuylkill looked over at Wyatt and then at Octavius. She had gotten the lamp and end table back into an upright position with apologetic assistance from the condor. Bruce as usual was oblivious. "Herr Bear," she said, "we managed to save Ozzie's video cell phone. A thought occurs to me. If the puma tries to contact Ozzie again after he lands here, we should have someone ready to respond with a story that will lead him into a trap."

"Wonderful thinking, Frau Schuylkill," replied the bear. "Now, which of you two most willing cats can do a credible imitation of Ozzie's voice if Pontius Puma calls?"

Lepi started to volunteer, but Jake interrupted. "I'm the one who speaks Portuguese with a native accent. Lepi sounds like he's ordering from a Chinese menu. If I whisper, I think I can convince him I'm Ozzie, and I'm trying to keep our conversation confidential. What do you want me to say?"

Wyatt looked at him and said, "We need to work out a trap, and you're the one who'll lead him into it. Let us think this through. I think we have a few hours before he calls Ozzie's phone. We'll have a whole script and scenario worked out by then. Of course, it would help if we knew what and who he was bringing with him. I can't believe those bulls are going to come alone, and I doubt they'll come without heavy weaponry. Maybe you can get a few clues from talking with Pontius. We'll prompt you through the call."

I looked over at Bruce. "Now, I guess we have to wait for the newly monied Ms Catt to call back. She claims she didn't know Paolo is Pontius, so she may not be any help there. What do we say to her? What do we want to know?"

Octavius intervened, "We need everything she can tell Dr. Vark about Imperius' experiments and concoctions. Most of it is probably in the lab notes, but I'm especially interested in how and why the serum affected Otto differently than it did Imperius."

"Well, for openers," said Bruce, "Otto didn't start out crazy or at least no crazier than river otters usually are."

Dr. Vark said, "Imperius has been taking his serum for a long time and no doubt he's been fine tuning it. He also developed a severe mental trauma from the loss of his companion. The serum may just amplify some basic genetic characteristics in each subject. Although I refuse to believe that Imperius had a show business career in mind for Otto after he finished the treatment, his performing talents may have been enhanced anyway."

Octavius said, "I doubt Imperius wanted the next Amphibian Idol. I suspect he may have been trying to create a replacement for Chita who oddly enough, also has show business talents. I'm not sure what she can tell us, but I wish she would call."

(All right, as you can see, this chapter is coming to an end, so I'll supply the last bit of business required to bring it to an appropriate climax.)

Just then, Bruce's phone rang. *(See, right on schedule.)*

Chapter Twenty Two

The lone Aardvark has claws that are strong.

And his tongue stretches ever so long.

Thus he gobbles up bugs,

Loads of insects and slugs,

But I still think his face is all wrong.

Stretched out in room 302 of the Cat Nap Inn near Granite City Illinois *(across the river from St. Louis)*, Chita scratched her nose and pondered. She had just finished a one-on-one conversation with Bruce Wallaroo and was resting up for the Bear's all-star review scheduled for the next hour. Everybody and his dog *(wait, not dogs – wolves)* would be on the line to mix it up with her over Otto, the serum, Imperius, Bigg, Paolo *(AKA Pontius Puma)*, those stupid bulls from Chicago and assorted other topics. Aside from telling her that Otto and Maury had been injured trying to get in or out of the Duck Blind, she hadn't gotten any new news out of her conversation with Bruce.

Nor did she tell him any new news - although she had some: As soon as the helicopter had taken off from the ore loader parking lot, carrying Otto and the serum along with Maury, Wallaroo and Belinda Bear, she started to slink out of the nearby underbrush where she had been hiding, observing and communicating with them by phone.

Suddenly she heard a familiar voice shouting: "Chita, Chita, it's Bigg. I know you're here somewhere. I saw that copter come in, and I came up here to investigate. I just saw it take off with Otto and the emperor's serum. You must have given it to them so you must be nearby. *(Bigg must be taking "smart" pills.)* C'mon out, Chita, I won't hurt you. *(But I might hurt you, yo-yo!)* The emperor is awfully angry with you already. *(Aha, he's still alive, dammit.)* You really hurt him. When I go back to the hospital *(!?)* and tell him you gave away Otto and the serum to UUI, he'll be furious. I'm not even sure I should tell him you sank the boat. That was a terrible thing to do. He'll lay an egg. Tell you what! Why don't we meet down at the Duck Blind and talk? I've got a big surprise for you. *(Oh, Bigg, the smart pill just wore off. I can just imagine what kind of surprise is waiting for me there. No way am I going near the Duck Blind.)*

Eventually, Bigg gave up trying to coax her out but not without having told her some important information, the dope. Or was he being a dope? Was he trying to ambush her at the hospital? Probably not. He didn't say where it was. But he did try to get her down to the Duck Blind for a nice surprise. Oh, sure.

Now for the choice! Should she follow him to see what hospital Imperius was in or should she head for the hills? She came all the way up from Brazil to knock that rotten duck off. While she had done some damage to him physically and operationally by swiping his serum, notes and Otto, she still hadn't really succeeded. He had tried to kill her with his serum. No, she had to be put him out of commission permanently.

She decided to follow Bigg. She could out-stealth him any day. But the stupid baboon had, of all things, a motorcycle. She could keep up with him for a short distance, but after that it was going to be a guessing game. On the other hand, the hospital couldn't be that far away.

She had followed Bigg at top speed for a short distance when she saw a blue road sign with a large H *(for Hospital)* on it. Not certain, but the odds were good that was where he took Imperius. He wasn't going to carry him any distance, if he'd been hurt. Imperius and Bigg in a hospital emergency room!! Now, there was an image. She wondered what cockeyed story they told the admissions people about his head injury. Or maybe, Imperius was still out cold. Well, she'd probably never know. She'd have to work up some way of getting at him in his sick bed. Maybe she'd dress up as a nurse. She always liked costumes. Anyway, she needed to get ready for the session with Octavius and Company. Imperius probably wasn't going anywhere. He could wait but...not for long.

Almost time to call. Should she tell them about the duck? Let's play it out and see where it goes. She wanted to get the low down on that low down Paolo first. His property!? Octavius had that right. She was nobody's property. Not only that, the lying sneak didn't even tell her he was Pontius Puma. They were supposed to be mates. She turned out to be his convenient little rest stop in Rio when he wasn't mixing it up back in São Paolo. Probably has a hundred little super star "hotcha" wannabes at his beck and call.

But the part that really griped her was, if Bruce and Octavius were right, he had a major global racket going and he hadn't cut her in on it. Now, that was unforgivable. Here she was, wanted by the police in any number of countries for all sorts of major cons and big money deals, and this jerk treats her like his pet pussy cat. Hey, Pontius, you're in for a big surprise. Chita is a big girl and a formidable foe. Hell hath no fury like Chita cut out of a major caper!!!

OK, time to communicate. She took out her cell phone, the one thing Imperius Drake had given her that she had hung onto. It was a technical marvel that had all sorts of stealth and covert capabilities. Came in handy when you didn't want to be tracked, and she definitely didn't want to be tracked. She dialed Bruce's phone.

All sorts of alarums and excursions on the other end. They plugged her into a speakerphone arrangement. She was getting a video feed from them, and all she was showing back was her face. All the usual suspects were introduced to her, plus a couple she had not had any contact with – a condor from São Paolo and wonder of wonders, he could talk. There were a couple of polar bears, friends of Belinda, no doubt, and an Aardvark named Odd Vark. Ah ha, he was a geneticist. And had she seen that porcupine before? Probably at Las Vegas or Rio. but she wasn't sure. Maury was all bandaged up and sitting in a wheel chair. Where was Otto? How was Otto?

She looked at Lepi and Jake as the camera swung past them. She needed to get the story on Ozzie. The camera rotated back to a wide shot of Octavius, Wallaroo, Belinda and one of the wolves.

"Well," she said, "welcome to Animal Planet. A nice representation of mammals and one bird to ensure political correctness. But no fish or invertebrates. Tsk, Octavius, you're slipping."

"As usual Chita, always lead with a quick offensive move. Or are you just being offensive, period?" retorted the Great Bear.

"Now, now," said Belinda. "We all have a number of common issues to work through, so let's concentrate on those and leave the snide remarks contest till later, OK?"

Chita thought she could really get to like this Bearoness if only she wasn't tied up with that self-important bear. They should get together and talk show business. One performer to another. However, there were one or possibly two assassinations waiting in line before any sociable chit-chat. Get your priorities straight, Chita.

"OK, somebody fill me in. What happened to Otto and to you, Maury?"

Bruce popped in front of the camera and related how they flew down to the Duck Blind with the resulting booby-trap explosion.

"So that's the surprise he had in mind," she said. "Ooops! Big mouth!"

"What surprise? What do you mean?"

"Oh, what the hell," she thought, "the cat's out of the bag *(whatever that means)*. I might as well tell them."

So she told them about her one-sided gab fest with Bigg.

"Imperius is still alive." I think the entire choir sang that line in four part harmony. Grumbles from Octavius. I thought Bruce would do a back-flip. Only a threatening growl from an obviously upset Frau Schuylkill stopped that. Belinda was obviously upset. She had been the Duck's primary target at Las Vegas.

"Let's get one thing straight immediately. He's mine," said Chita, "I came all the way back here to make sure he's history, and I'm not going to get all tangled up with a bunch of goody two shoes commandos. He's toast, and I'm the toaster."

Octavius growled, "You seem to forget he tried to kill all of us at the convention. I'm not sure there's much difference between being blown to bits and being injected with suicide serum."

"Yeah, but you guys will probably bring him before the bar of justice. The only bar I have in mind is a crow bar. Obviously his skull was thick enough to withstand a beaker. Let's see how good he is with iron."

"Chita," said Bruce, "I thought you drew the line at killing. Didn't you tell us that out at Vegas? You're in enough trouble as it is without a murder rap."

"It'll be self-defense. But this isn't getting us anywhere. I know where he is, and you don't. On top of that you don't even know where I am. One of the duck's inventions to keep snoops from tracking us down."

She was right. At the moment the bear's telecommunications source locator had her placed in the middle of Antarctica. Not likely.

Bruce signaled to the condor and Howard. He typed on the condor's communicator. "Get out of range of the camera. Good! Now can you techie geniuses track her down?"

The condor typed back. "Maybe, keep her on the line."

"OK, Chita," said Octavius, "let's table the Imperius issue for the moment. There's two more we need to talk about. Otto and the serum and Pontius Puma. Otto first! You were with him for over twenty-four hours. Can you tell us anything useful that might help us get him out of his coma?"

Chita said, "Let's go back. The first thing you have to understand, Dr.Vark *(ignoring Octavius)*, is that Imperius has been trying for years to create a method of genetic alteration to control the entire world. He's trying to create super beasts - hyper intelligent, physically powerful, swift, invulnerable to attack and most important, totally subservient to his will. He first experimented on himself, and he lost his mate who tried to stop him by drinking the formula. Since that time he's been dogged *(sorry)* by the problem that the mixture can't be generalized. It has to be adapted to the individual animal."

"Animal or species?" asked the aardvark

"I don't know. He tried to kill me by feeding me his own serum. Fortunately, I got away before he had the chance, but I don't know whether what he's been feeding Otto would work on all river otters. His own mixture certainly didn't work on Li-Li-Lee. She was a mandarin duck too."

"That's the other thing. The serum wears off. In his case, in as few as a couple of days, although I've seen him go for over a week. The transition process isn't a pretty thing to watch. Of course, he's been taking it for years and he's so far gone now, he's loony before, during and after. As far as I know, Otto has had four treatments. At least, that's what he told me. Three by mouth and the last one was a shot in his rump.

From what I could see and what he said, Otto's basic powers of illusion and performance magic have been enhanced but he's not the least bit subservient to the Duck or Bigg. Those are probably the mixture alterations that Imperius was working on when I swatted him and stole the serum and notes. Unless he can be made to follow the duck's orders unquestioningly, Otto is less than useless to him as a replacement for me. *(Yeah, that's what Imperius is trying to do!)* Bigg follows him because his brain is stuck at the bottom of the tree and he's also scared stiff of the duck. Think about that for a minute. A huge baboon scared of a scrawny duck. Imperius thought he already had me in tow, because I just enjoyed a life of crime and luxury. So, he didn't bother to work on my genes and psyche. That's where he made his big *(or one of his big)* mistakes."

"Did you see Otto go into a catatonic state at any time, Chita?"

"No, he was normal or normally abnormal the whole time he was with me. But the duck, on the other hand, would occasionally go rigid. He never admitted it."

Several eyes wandered toward Octavius, checking to see if he was awake. He was.

"Well," said the aardvark, "That gives me something more to work on. Doctor Bear, I'm going back to UUI and get together with Chiti."

"Who?" said the cat.

"Not you, Chita. Doctor Chiti BingBang is our chief medical officer at UUI. He and Doctor Vark are working together to save Otto. Yes, please, go ahead, Doctor Vark, and keep me posted on the situation."

As the aardvark moved off, Chita caught sight of the two cats on the screen. They had not said a word since the round of hellos and introductions. "How's it goin', cats?" she said.

Both of them looked toward the phone with "You talkin' to me?" expressions on their faces. When they realized that she *was* talking to them, Lepi said, "Not bad, considering we just lost our band mate."

"I'm truly sorry about that. I really liked Ozzie."

"So did we. Everything was great until that phony boyfriend of yours came along. We could have made it without his so-called help," snarled Jake.

"Wait a second. He conned me worse than he did you. I know, I know. I'm not dead and Ozzie is but I swear I didn't know Paolo was Pontius Puma. If I had, we'd have been playing in lot better places than those gyp joints in Rio."

"Well," said Lepi, "What's done is done. We can't bring Ozzie back."

"Hold it Lepi,' she said, "According to *Who's Who in the Animal Kingdom*, Himalayan Snow Leopards are pretty tough characters. Did all that time in a Chinese prison turn you into a wussy pussy?"

"It's a good thing you're on the other end of a phone line, lady or I'd show you how tough I still am. For your information, Jake and I are helping to set up your slick inamorato right now. He ain't getting away with anything. When he gets here, he's in for a big surprise."

"Paolo – Pontius- is coming here? Is he out of his mind?"

"We hope so," said the Bear. "You see, Chita, not only does he want you back, as you heard on that taped conversation, but he wants revenge because we put him out of business for a long while. I sure hope he's not thinking straight."

"I want a piece of this action," she said.

"We were hoping you'd think that way, Chita," said Bruce. "How about joining us?"

"Nice try, Brucie, but the minute I showed up down there *(Down there!? Where was she?)* Ursus Worsest would have me in irons. Wouldn't you, Octavius?"

"Chita, I can't let you get away with all you've done, even if my colleagues seem to be in a more forgetful mood."

"That's what I thought. Well, I'll think of something."

I had been sitting in my wheel chair being quite quiet. I know, a miracle!!! But I was still feeling pretty punchy from the drugs and the pain. However, at that moment, I felt impelled to speak. *(Ready? Here comes the big bright idea.)*

"I have a bright idea," I said.

Chita said, "Maury, sweetheart, I forgot you were there."

("Sweetheart!" Anything to annoy Octavius and get me into deeper trouble with him. What the hell! My ship is sunk anyway.)

"Yeah, Chita and you're there - wherever 'there' is. You can stay there and still play, if you want to. PP is supposed to call Ozzie back after he arrives. We assume he's coming up on a private jet and traveling with phony papers. He's probably going to meet up with the Chicago Bulls and their goon squad, but they all need to know how to get here and how to get around our security. Ozzie was supposed to tell him. In exchange, PP was going to fly Ozzie back to Brazil when he left."

Jake interrupted, "Yeah, but now I have Ozzie's cell phone, and I'm going to try and fake being Ozzie when the Puma calls. I think I see where Maury's going with this. When he calls, I hook you into the conversation, and you can lure him in. Right, Maury?"

"You got it, Jake. If he's so nuts about you, Chita, he'll probably make even more mistakes trying to get you back. In fact, you ought to give him a tough time about lying to you. That'll really get him going. Just as long as you don't decide to join up with him again."

Eyebrows rose around the room as this possibility sank in.

"Don't worry, Meerkat. I'm not playing house pet to anyone. He just wants his 'property' back. I like your idea. We need to set up how Jake and I communicate. I assume Paolo won't get up there before tomorrow morning. But he'll probably want to stage whatever he has in mind at night."

Wyatt chimed in, "That's our estimate, but we're ready for him right now. Anything you two can find out about his plans will make dealing with him a lot easier."

"What have you got in mind for him?" asked Chita.

"Now, it's our turn to play our cards close to the vest, dear cat," said Octavius. "You play your part, and your pals Bruce and Maury will fill you in on what happened after it's over."

"That bear is unbearable," she thought. "Well, Mr. Smug, we'll see about that!"

"OK," she said out loud. "Let's set up a comm link, and don't try to use it to find me."

Which is exactly what L. Condor, Wyatt, Howard and the Frau had in mind.

"All right, Chita, call us back in an hour and we'll have the link set up with Ozzie's phone. When it rings, yours will ring too." This from Howard.

"OK, prickle-puss, I gotcha."

She hung up. Job one at the moment was to find Imperius, but it was getting too late to be walking into hospitals asking for a wounded duck. First thing in the morning. She looked at a sign on the desk in the hotel room. "Visit the Cat Nap Inn's Cat Nip Lounge. Happy Hour and Free Karaoke every night."

She could use a couple of drinks and a howl or two just to keep in practice. But she'd go down to the bar as a panther. No point in being spotted.

212

Chapter Twenty Three

Cows don't just stand around and say "moo."

They eat grass and have lots more to do.

And don't pity the bull

For his life is quite full

In a field full of heifers? Hoo, hoo!!

A heightened state of alert was set both at UUI and the Bear's Lair during the night and would be maintained through the next few days. Wyatt, the Frau and Howard spent most of the morning checking out intrusion sensors, automatic barricades, patrols, weapons and beast traps. They had transferred several of the aircraft to other locations for their protection. The Aquabear and Ursa Major cost too much to move. Just running up the C-5A's engines was a budget stretcher. Besides, they wanted one or two attractions to get PP and his Pals to make their move. They were going to leave the doors of the hangar partially open during the night…but not unstaffed or unoccupied.

The objective was to *capture* Pontius Puma and as many of his henchbeings as possible. Bruce was on the phone to the FBI, Interpol and a variety of local constabularies. He also contacted military intelligence, since Pontius was wanted for trading in high security defense materials as well as backstreet warfare basics. The Chicago police staged a "routine roundup" of a large group of "the usual suspects" around the stockyards, but Brutus and Belial Taurus were nowhere to be found. Wyatt also alerted the air police at CVG International as well as several of the smaller executive jet airports in the area. They were ready to impound the Puma's jet on instruction.

All parties agreed that they wanted Pontius and his goons to actually stage an attack. An on-site, violent attempt on life, limb and property with a raft of witnesses would be a lot easier to prosecute and would avoid all the red tape of Brazilian extradition laws. Catch him in the act!!

Octavius checked with Howard and L. Condor. They had rigged up Ozzie's phone to ring Chita whenever the Puma called. Jake spent the morning trying to sound like a whispering Ozzie. They were all going through their prep routines for the umpteenth time when the phone on Octavius' desk rang.

"Bear here! Yes, Dr. BingBang. Yes! He did? Well, that's wonderful. Sometime during the night? How is he? Well, you'd expect him to be weak and disoriented, but is he fully aware of his immediate surroundings? Vital signs OK? Tell you what. I'm going to ask Bearoness Bruin to stop over and stay with him for a while. I gather he idolizes her, and she can fill in the blanks for him."

He looked over quizzically at Belinda who was just finishing her breakfast bowl of champagne and she nodded. It was apparent from the telephone monologue that Otto was back among the living but in status unknown. She liked the little guy. Although she and the other two polars were also getting ready to do battle, they had some time to spare, especially for a cute, stage struck, telekinetic escape artist. The Bearoness might even be willing to pick up where the Duck had left off guiding Otto's career. Minus the injections and enhancement drugs, of course! She was curious to see if his powers had survived both the blast and being without the serum for over forty eight hours. Topping off her basin of breakfast bubbly and waving for Bearnice and Bearyl, *(Wait till Otto sees them – two more pearlescent dreamboats.)* they left for the shuttle truck.

Juno galumphed after them. "Wait for me. I want to meet this little world wonder, too." Juno had a soft spot in her heart for cute and cuddly animals, especially the kind that could move furniture without any effort. Her maid, Florence, would love him.

Octavius shouted after them, "Are you ladies armed?"

Bearyl waved an automatic pistol at him as she passed and said, "We even took some target practice earlier this morning."

"Silly of me to have asked," said the Bear.

*****

Meanwhile, west of St. Louis, Chita was almost awake and shaking her hung over head. Her voice was sore from "singing" along with the karaoke machine. She looked at herself in the mirror. Her black panther disguise could use a little touch up here and there, but not bad for hospital visiting. After forcing some breakfast down her aching throat, she called for a cab and told the driver, "Take me to a hospital."

214

He looked concerned and said, "Are you sick, lady? Is this an emergency? Please don't die in my cab!"

"No, you jerk, I'm fine. I'm supposed to meet someone there, and I forgot the name of the place."

"Well, there's several! *(Oh great!)* Granite City General, St. Eucalypta, Missouri River Memorial and…."

"Which one is closest to Pelican Island?"

"Let me see, as the crow flies it would be……"

"No, as the motorcycle races!"

"Huh? Well, that'd be Missouri River Memorial."

"That sounds right. Take me there!"

Scratching his head and looking over his shoulder occasionally, the raccoon mumbled to himself, "I'll bet she's a lousy tipper, too."

She was. When they arrived at the hospital, Chita put on her best concerned friend of the family look and approached the Information Desk. What the hell name would that crazy duck have registered under? Bigg probably signed him in if he was here at all. Emperor Imperius? No, not even Bigg is that dumb. What did the otter call him? Milord Mallàrd??? That's it! Let's try that one. Pausing to put on her diamond collar and her haughtiest attitude, she primly walked up to the receptionist and said, "I understand Milord Mallàrd is a patient here. I should like to see him. I am from the British Consulate checking on his condition for some of his concerned family members. My name is Cecily Catt."

The receptionist, an overweight heifer, mooed and consulted her computer screen. "Milord Mallàrd is no longer with us." she said.

"He's dead??" exclaimed the cat, almost losing her cultured cool in the process. She felt a back flip of joy coming on.

"Oh, no, no, no! I'm sorry. I misled you. He was released this morning to a Commandante Babaloo, whoever he is."

"He's Bigg, honey," thought Chita. Out loud she said, "I believe he is a business associate of Milord. Did they leave a forwarding address where they might be reached? I'd like to advise him to contact his relatives."

215

"I'm sorry. We can't give out that information. Privacy protection, you know."

"Yes, I know. Thank you for your help."

"Now where the hell have they gone?' she thought, "Back to the Duck Blind? I doubt it unless they went there to pick up some stuff. Too many people knew about the Duck Blind now, including Wallaroo and of course, the Bear. Well, there's no doubt the duck is seething at me and at Octavius. As soon as he can, he's coming after both of us, especially the Bear. He wants to recover his research, and he knows I gave it to the polar bear. I'll just have to wait him out."

Reluctantly, she switched her thoughts to the other outstanding name on her dance card. Paolo/Pontius! So much to do! So little time! She had a pretty good idea where the Bear's hideout was from the GPS functions on her phone. That's where Paolo, the creep, was probably going to make an appearance. Those bulls working for him knew where UUI was, at least. That would be their start-off point. So, back she'd go to the Cat Nap Inn, collect her belongings and head for the airport. She'd stay in her panther guise for the time being. Black suited her mood.

*****

When they arrived at Otto's room, the otter was sitting up in bed trying to get one of the orderlies to "Pick a card, any card." As the three bears walked through the door, he dropped the cards on the bed spread and gaped. "Bearoness, Belinda, Gee, I didn't think I'd ever see you again. Wow. Are these your sisters?"

Laughter from the three bears. A number of shelves and medical instruments rattled. The orderly scurried from the room. "No, Otto, these are two of my associates in the Aquabear Review. And this lovely Kodiak lady is Juno Bear, Octavius Bear's mother. Bearyl, Bearnice and Juno, meet Otto the Magnificent."

"Not so magnificent anymore, I'm afraid. I think I'm back to being stupid old Hairy Otter."

"Why, Otto," said the three B's and Juno in rapid succession, "What's the matter? You took a terrible hit from that explosion. Are you all right? Can you move? Is anything broken? Any internal bleeding? Did you have a concussion?

Can you see straight? You're talking coherently! Can you get up? What do the doctors say?"

After this barrage, all Otto could do was catch his breath and blurt, "Physically, I'm fine. I ache in a few places where I guess I hit the wall or a table. But I think I lost all my super-otter powers!! That orderly was just cleaning up the floor where I dropped a glass of water after trying to raise it up."

"Well, Otto or Hairy, if you prefer, why don't we just wait and see. Have you met Doctor Aardvark, yet?"

"Yeah, he was in earlier with Doctor BingBang. What does he do???"

"He's the Chief Geneticist here at Universal Ursine Industries. Maybe I should catch you up on your whole situation, where you are, who we all are and what is going on. I know Chita told you some things."

"Chita," he said. "Where is Chita? How is Chita?"

"Chita's fine," she replied. "As to where she is, no one is quite sure. We've been talking to her over the phone. We'll update her on your condition next time we talk. Now, let's take a few minutes and fill you in on the big picture…

By the time Belinda finished her tutorial, Bearyl and Bearnice had returned from a trip to the rest rooms and the cafeteria. They passed a fish to Juno who had stayed behind with Belinda. They looked in and could see Otto shaking his head in disbelief.

"What have I gotten myself into?" He said to Belinda. "Maybe I should just head back to the St. Lawrence River and my family. It's not too far from here."

"Look, Otto, it's a little early after your experience to be making big decisions. Let's see what the doctors have to say. Doctor Vark has been analyzing Imperius' formula to see what he was trying to do to your genetic makeup. We pretty much know from talking to Chita that he wasn't going to make you into a showbiz sensation. He wanted a super creature that could help him in his quests for conquest. But you seemed to be resisting all of his attempts to change your basic personality and character. That's a very good sign."

"But, Belinda, if I have to keep taking that stuff in order to be a star, I'd rather just go back and be a clown cousin to the other kids in my bevy."

"No one has suggested you do, Otto. We know that Imperius Drake is a genius – an evil genius up in the 100th quartile of nastiness, but a genius nonetheless. What he's been doing may be salvageable for creating long term positive results for lots of animals. We don't want to destroy his work. We want to understand it and use it for good if we can."

"I couldn't have said it better, Milady." Dr. Odd Vark had just walked into the room. "Well, Otto, Dr. BingBang tells me you're greatly improved. No serious injuries besides a few bruises. All your reflexes, nerves and mental processes seem OK. You're alert and…"

"Anxious to get out of here, Doctor," said the otter. "This hospital reminds me of Milord Mallàrd's laboratory."

"Milord Mallàrd?"

"That's the name Imperius Drake was using, Doctor," said Belinda.

"Yeah, him and Commandante Babaloo," said Otto, shaking his head. "What a jerk he was."

"That's Imperius' long time assistant, Doctor. He's a baboon. Thick as a launch pad but strong and utterly faithful to the duck. By the way, you should know, Otto, that Imperius is not dead. Chita found out through an accidental meeting with Bigg that he was still alive."

"Chita met Bigg???"

"Not exactly. It was one of those 'I know you're out there somewhere!' conversations while Chita and he were both hiding near our takeoff point at the ore loader but in the course of it the baboon confirmed that Imperius was also in a hospital recovering from the wounds she inflicted on him when you two escaped."

"That whole thing is a blur," said the otter.

"Well, it seemed to have happened so fast, I'm not surprised," said Belinda.

"Anyway, when can I get out of here?"

"Otto, Dr BingBang and I will make you a deal. We'll let you leave the hospital if you promise to go with these ladies and stay for a while at Doctor Octavius Bear's Lair. We'd like to have you where we can reach you, but I understand about not wanting to stay in a hospital room. We're making great progress in solving what the duck was doing and how his process works, but we'll need to consult with you and run some tests from time to time. Are you game for that??"

"Yes, Otto," said Bearnice. "We know Octavius is anxious to meet you as well as a number of other animals who have heard about you. In a way, you are famous already."

Otto blushed, and his whiskers quivered. These bears were making mush out of his common sense. "OK," he said. "After you've described all these beasts to me, I'd like to meet them nose to nose, especially Octavius Bear. I also want to thank Inspector Wallaroo for rescuing me."

He got up and started to collect his one or two possessions.

*****

Back on Pelican Island, a baboon and a duck rode a motorcycle over a narrow pedestrian bridge from the mainland, along the hiker's paths and on toward a decrepit dock. With the baboon holding the duck unsteadily on his shoulder, they dismounted and walked into the scrub pine, down a ramp and through a door that hung precariously from its hinges. Fluttering over some glass and metal stripping, Imperius alit in the center of the anteroom.

"Well, Baboon, I see the booby trap worked, but where is the victim? Let's see if there is a body inside. There doesn't seem to be anything out here."

"I don't think Chita came down here, Milord."

"We can stop the masquerade foolishness now, Baboon. We don't have to fool that idiot otter any longer. You may return to addressing me as Sire."

"Yes Milord. I think she might have been following me when I got on the motorcycle, but I wasn't sure. But the helicopter headed down this way. The wallaroo, the meerkat, the polar bear and the otter were all on it when it left along with your serum and notebook. The helicopter had 'UUI' painted on it."

"All my old friends and that ungrateful otter. They probably stopped here. The otter must have shown them where the Duck Blind was. They couldn't have seen it from the air. Well, somebody got blown up, but who? Search around outside. Look for any sign of a body or the helicopter. I'll look inside. We're not going to stay. This place isn't safe anymore. I'm just going to get my own serum and a few other things, and we can leave. After we get back over that bridge, we'll have to get a car. Hanging off the back of that motorcycle in a high wind doesn't help my bandaged head or the rest of me, for that matter."

He waddled inside through another shattered door and looked around. Plenty of signs of the explosive impact but no signs of…wait…is that blood over there on that specimen table? Yes, it is. Let's see if we can take a sample and look at it under a microscope. He waddled/limped over to the table with a probe and then to the instrument. "Ah, ha! Otter blood. So it was Otto. But if the door blew when he was trying to get in, why is there blood inside the laboratory? Ah ha, again! He got in using his teleporting powers. The door blew when he tried to open it from the inside for the others to come in. So was anyone killed, I hope? But there are no bodies."

He turned as Bigg came back into the lab. "There was a helicopter on the other side of the hill, Sire. You can see where everything was thrown around by the rotors. But no sign of any bodies."

"Hmmmm! Well then, Baboon. We shall collect our necessities and head east to UUI headquarters. My serum and notes are probably in the despicable paws of that nut Odd Vark. Calls himself a geneticist. Ha! For the few months I worked there, he displayed himself as a complete idiot. He won't even come close to understanding my processes."

*****

Ozzie's phone rang. Jake picked it up and motioned to Bruce who was sitting next to him. They picked up another phone and called Chita. She answered on the first ring. Bruce whispered, "We have contact on Ozzie's phone. We're going to patch you in, but don't talk unless you absolutely have to. We're not even sure it's PP."

Meanwhile, Jake had said, "*Ola*" in a whisper and said, "*Si*, Senhor Puma, this is Ozzie. I have to whisper because they almost caught me talking to you yesterday. There are two security wolves here who can appear and disappear out of nowhere. One of them heard part of my conversation with you. *Si*. I'm not sure what they think. We must be careful. Where are you? In Cuba?? Trouble with the plane? Can it be fixed quickly? Tomorrow morning! I see. Where are the bulls? Waiting for you as well. Yes, everything is fine on this end. I'll give you detailed instructions when you all get closer. Well, call me again when you're in the United States."

Jake hung up. Bruce said to Chita. "You heard all that? He's coming himself." Chita snarled and cut the connection. They had just called her flight.

And so, as the day wore on, more and more creatures began, continued or ended their journeys, all heading for the same destinations…UUI and the Bear's Lair.

Chapter Twenty Four

A meerkat clan is known as a mob.

But most of them don't steal or rob.

But then there is Maury.

A whole different story.

The Great Bear nabbed him pulling a job.

It had to happen. Octavius cornered me. During the course of his tirade, he fired me three times and I quit four times. That was after he said he was going to dock my future wages *(non-existent, since I had been fired)* for the cost of all these defense measures against Pontius and probably the Mad Duck.

As you have no doubt concluded, Octavius Bear is the Poster Ursine for the Type A Executive. To call him a control freak is to be euphemistic. And yet, to be fair, he is not a tyrant. A swift pain, yes, but not a tyrant. In his more mellow moods, he is actually quite considerate even though the Bearoness wonders if he has a gentle or romantic bone anywhere in his massive carcass.

Anyway, I had sins of omission and commission written on my "naughty" slate. Not since he first picked me up in Mauritius for "aiding and abetting" my larcenous relatives had I walked so blatantly on the side of crime. I had let the side down *(although my recollection is that the "side" agreed with me on this one)*. I had bitten the paw that fed me, and the repercussions would, no doubt, be felt well beyond the next few days. *(Fair enough. Getting rid of PP and who knows, maybe the Duck **yet again,** would alter our lifestyles a bit.)*

Dragging a souped-up otter into our lives wasn't the brightest thing I had ever done. But I noticed he was quite concerned about Otto the minute Belinda had flown him into UUI's emergency unit. I also strongly suspect that I was a stand-in victim for the Bearoness upon whom Octavius would have really liked to vent his spleen *(but didn't dare!)*

Octavius finally met Otto in person when he was brought to the mansion. The Bear was cordial to him, saying that he understood what the doctors over at UUI required and he agreed. Otto was welcome to stay as long as he wanted, and

222

if he wished, he could be helpful in our upcoming conflict…providing he checked in with Wyatt, the Frau or himself beforehand. I noticed that Bruce, Belinda and I were excluded from that charmed circle. We'd live.

It was also more than likely that Octavius had the idea of adding Otto to our teleportation research team. This group was growing exponentially even before any of the UUI experts were roped in. Keeping it confidential, especially from General Turmoil was not going to be easy. But Otto seemed to be an ideal candidate. He represented yet another form of mind-driven travel.

I waited for the Great Bear to either wind down or hopefully, fall asleep. He did neither. The phone rang. It was Wyatt and Jake. PP had called in again. He and a small entourage were leaving Cuba very early in the morning, and they were planning the assault on the Bear's Lair for tomorrow night. He'd call again on arrival. Chita had not been on the call.

Completely forgetting that we had permanently parted company a total of seven times in the last half hour, he started shouting orders at me about keeping all non-involved personnel non-involved; keeping UUI in the loop and making sure Wyatt had law enforcement synched in. It would seem our relationship was back to normal, although I still had that little thought nagging in the back of my mind about working with the Bearoness. Octavius left, saying he was headed for the nearest tree to sharpen his claws.

I limped out. In a true show of Meerkat macho, I had ditched the wheelchair and was hobbling around on my crutch. Who knows, I might have to use it as a weapon. Maybe my aunt would finally remember my name if I turned out to be a big hero. Then again…

Meanwhile, Otto had gotten himself settled in, had immediately stolen the heart of Frau Schuylkill and had set about making up for lost time in the food department. He was stuffing himself and chatting with Howard and Wyatt about techniques of breaking and entering when the three bears made a grand entrance. They announced that first thing in the morning, they were going swimming in Octavius' Olympic swimming pool and that Otto was invited to join them. Perhaps the Bearoness was doing a little clandestine auditioning. The otter accepted with an eagerness that would have made a teenager on his first date look suave.

Lepi and Jake had said "hello" to Otto and explained a little more of the Brazilian caper that was in progress. The condor joined them, and Otto seemed fascinated by his artificial voice. L. Condor was getting more articulate with every passing day and the vocal support equipment he had originally been saddled with was getting smaller and less conspicuous. He said he was thinking of organizing a self-help movement for voiceless animals. He'd have to be careful. Mottoes like "Let Yourself Be Heard!" or "You, Too Can Have a Voice" might be interpreted by some South American governments as seditious. But governments had never stopped him before. He was talking to both Octavius and Belinda about some bootstrap funding.

Of course, this all presupposed that Pontius Puma was taken care of. L. Condor was convinced that the PP had either been told by Ozzie or had figured out for himself that the condor was involved in the technical carnage wreaked on his operation. The bird's life wasn't worth a plugged *centavo* as long as that cat and his cronies were free and active. Maybe he'd have to emigrate. He was sure Octavius could get him placed in a good, challenging job in the States, but he was an Andean condor and centuries of South American pride fluttered in his gigantic wingspan.

He was also enthralled by the stories of Imperius Drake. An avian genius gone off the deep end! L. was a genius, too. *(So was Octavius and Howard. A surfeit of geniuses! genii?)* Would he too end up plummeting over the edge?? Not likely, but the idea of a Mandarin Duck striving to become master of the universe both engrossed and repelled him. If, as seemed probable, this crazy duck was going to make an appearance, the condor wanted to meet him beak to beak. Curiosity and fascination, no doubt, overcoming his common sense.

Frau Schuylkill announced dinner. Otto had been eating since the moment he came into the house and showed no signs of slowing down. We all ambled *(I hobbled)* into the dining room. This had all the signs of one of Octavius' "working dinners."

He kicked things off in a somewhat unexpected direction. "Has anyone heard from Chita, and what is the situation with the duck?"

Chita was clearly a thorn in the Great Bear's paw. Like a ghost who refused to appear but kept making noises and mischief, she was occupying more of the Bear's attention than he was willing to spare. She had become the spotted maypole around which all of the players were merrily dancing. Pontius, Imperius, Otto all had ties to Chita. The two cat musicians had been teamed with Chita, and in Octavius' mind, Bruce and I were besotted with Chita. And the lowest blow. Belinda had done business of a very shady sort with that cat. Only Wyatt, Howard, Juno, the polar twins, the Condor and Frau Schuylkill seemed untouched.

"Fraulein Chita is a most interesting animal," said the she-wolf. *("Oh no," thought the Bear. "Not you, too!")* Wyatt nodded his head in agreement. "She's very clever and elusive but most of all, I really admire her attitude." *(Admire her attitude? This from a security officer. Was the whole world mad??)* "She would have been an excellent operative in military intelligence," continued the Colonel. "A loner, but a master *(mistress?)* at manipulating others."

Octavius could stand no more. "That sweet little pussy cat is a deceptive thief, an extortionist, a con girl, a blackmailer, a fraud, a liar and in the case of Otto, a kidnapper."

"I wasn't kidnapped…not really…I was rescued!"

"Don't interrupt, Otto. Have some more fish! She has murderous instincts that are going to get her killed and I for one will rejoice when it happens. I'd be just as happy as any of you, probably more than most of you, to see Imperius roasting on a spit and Pontius locked away for a million years, but that cat is a menace. Now, I ask again. Has anyone heard from her?? Where is she?"

Silence!!

Then L. Condor broke the spell. "I think she's traveling and staying out of contact. You know, silent running."

"What makes you say that?" asked Bruce.

"Well, we finally tracked her to the same area as Imperius' lab. She certainly made it tough. We had her placed everywhere from Antarctica to inside Mt. Vesuvius. If that evasion system on that phone was developed by the Duck, he is a first class electronics expert."

"It was, and he is," growled the Bear. "This is no mere maniac we are dealing with. This is a maniac who has managed to raise his IQ well beyond current scientific measurements. The only things that level the playing field are his crazy obsessions and impulses. If he was emotionally stable, he would be hideously difficult to combat. As it is, he's no teddy bear's picnic. Back to Chita! Any judgments *(Octavius never made or tolerated 'guesses')* as to where she might be going."

I piped up, if for no other reason than to re-establish my presence. I was beginning to feel like a piece of the dining room furniture. "I'll bet she's heading here. She knows Pontius is supposed to make an appearance, and she'll risk getting nabbed by you or by the authorities in order to take a swipe at him or at least see him get his comeuppance. *(Strange word, comeuppance! Wonder where it came up from!)*."

"She doesn't know where we are." said Howard.

"Don't be too sure. She certainly knows where UUI is, and there's been enough traffic back and forth between here and there that we ought to start putting up road signs. THIS WAY TO SEE THE BEAR!!"

"You're probably right, Maury," said Octavius. "Colonel, Frau, we're going to have to start behaving as if this mansion is no longer a clandestine location. Too many people, too many of the wrong people, can find it and alas, we cannot fly it away to some other spot."

I swear a light went on simultaneously in Howard's, Wyatt's, Frau Schuylkill's and the Condor's faces. No idea was too wild for them to contemplate. No doubt a new agenda item was being formulated by the brain trust. Flying mansion!!! Telekinesis raised to a new level! Not with me in it, thanks.

Anyway, as things often turned out with Chita, once again I was right! She was coming, and so was someone else.

*****

Imperius and Bigg flew into Greater Cincinnati/Northern Kentucky International Airport *(CVG)*, rented a Jeep and took a room in a hotel midway between the terminal and UUI. The Duck had taken to wearing a ski cap *(black with a gold pom-pom)* to cover his head bandage. As he stood adjusting it in the mirror, he said to Bigg, "Revenge, Baboon, revenge on that pretentious aardvark, on that treacherous cat and on those two bears and all their minions."

"What are we going to do, Sire?"

"Baboon, we must recover my valuable work and take punitive measures. But first, we need reinforcements. I shall call several associates of mine from Chicago and see if they are available on short notice."

"Who's that, Sire?'

"The Taurus Brothers. You remember them. They helped us with the trucks and plane at Pondscum and Las Vegas." *(See: The Open and Shut Case)*

(The following telephone conversation is brought to you in its entirety through the wonders of omniscient narration.)

"Yeah?"

"Ah, Mr. Taurus, we'd recognize that snort anywhere. How pleasant to speak with you again."

"Who is dis?"

"An old friend and patron. Imperius Drake!!!"

"Oh, Doctuh Drake! Hey, great to talk to ya. Dis is Belial. Brutus is on the other line."

"I have a rush assignment for you and your boys. Tomorrow evening, if possible. A little destruction, firebombing, breaking and entering, robbery, possible kidnap. Sorry, pretty much the usual stuff. I do prefer the more artistic performances, but this is a high priority event and we don't have time for finesse."

"Gee, dere's nothin' we'd like better than to do another job for you, Doctuh Drake, but tomorrow night we're all filled up. We have a heavy job in Kentucky and Cincinnati."

This struck the duck as passing strange and so he pursued the matter.

"Oddly enough, that is exactly where I wanted you to ply your talents. Could I make so bold as to enquire who the target is and who your client is."

"Now, now, Doctuh Drake, you know we never reveal our clients' identities, but in fact, the target is an old friend of yours – Octavius Bear."

Imperius was not religious unless you counted self-worship but he felt a certain outside influence had made itself manifest. Could he finally be getting a break after all the near misses, slings and arrows and cosmic collapses?

"This may indeed be your lucky day, Mr. Taurus," he said. "It just so happens that Octavius Bear is the target against whom we also wish you to exert your services. In one swell foop, you will be able to serve two clients and of course, collect two fees and perhaps even enjoy a little plunder."

227

"Well, I don't know, Doctuh Drake. We do have our business principles, ya know, but let me talk to Brutus and we'll get back to youse immediately. We have our own score to settle with the bear and his security guy – the wolf. Maybe we could work out an accommodation, but our other client would have to agree. Dis could work out to everybody's advantage."

"We're sure it will. Obviously, we also expect you will conceal our identity from your other client at least until we have all reached an agreement. Actually, angry as we are at the bear and as much as we would like to see his demise, there is some property of ours that he has stolen and we want it back!!! There is also an exotic cat named Chita that we want to get our claws on. She may or may not be on hand when you stage your raid."

"Funny you should say that. So does our client. He seems to think she is there but we don't know why. I don't suppose there could be two Chitas?"

"The world is hardly ready for one, much less two. This whole thing is becoming fascinating. You speak with Brutus and get back to us. Is your client going to actively participate in the event?"

"He's on his way up from South America as we speak...oooops. I didn't say that."

"Of course not, of course not. When do you expect him?"

"Late tonight or early tomorrow morning."

"Well, call back as soon as you talk to Brutus and then we can plan for meeting with your other client, if he is willing. We are in a hotel near Cincinnati Airport, and we assume he will be coming in the same way. Good-bye."

"Baboon, we may have even greater revenge than we originally planned. With two enemies at his doorstep, that contemptible ursine will suffer indeed. But above all else, we must retrieve the serum, the notes and the otter. If we can get the particle ray gun as well, that would be the 'piece de persistence.' "

"Gee, Sire, do you think Otto is still alive?"

"We shall see, Baboon, we shall see and perhaps, just perhaps, we can also wreak our justice on that treacherous cat."

"I wonder where Chita is, Sire.'

"So do we, Baboon, so do we!"

*****

As she sashayed along the moving sidewalks in CVG terminal, Chita reached for her phone and placed a call.

"Hi Brucie! Miss me? Sorry, I was out of contact. What's happening? Tomorrow night. Where is he? Hmmm! Well, when do you expect him to arrive? When he calls, patch me in. Where am I? Oh, Brucie, wouldn't you like to know. I may tell you. but not now. Don't go playing twenty questions. You're a big boy. No time for games. Bye!!!"

"Now," she thought, "let's find somewhere not too obvious to stay."

Chapter Twenty Five

The Chamois is a goat called "sham-wah."

"Shammy" leathers will polish your cah (sorry!)

Please don't mix up the two!

Because if you do,

That would be such an awful faux pas

.

The splashes and laughs coming from the Olympic pool could only mean one thing. Otto and the three polar bears were cavorting and showing off their aquatic skills, which were considerable. At one point, the otter broke the surface in the center of a circle the bears had formed and flipped over the top of Belinda's head and dove back under again. From the moment they had entered the water, the audience around the pool had grown, and now the two wolves, Juno, Howard, Bruce and I were all alternately laughing and applauding at the impromptu performance. Whether he had his super powers or not, Otto was clearly a showbeast.

He repeated the maneuver. Only this time instead of re-entering the water on the flip, he disappeared momentarily, reappeared on the high diving board and did a triple somersault into the center of the ursine ring. OK, that wasn't your normal run of the mill river otter stunt. How did he get up on that board? Had the serum kicked back in? When he surfaced, I yelled, "Hey Otto, do that again!!"

On cue and with all of us staring wide eyed he repeated the routine, only this time he threw a twist into the dive as well. I looked over at Belinda who had stopped swimming so she could get a better look at what he was doing. When he came back up, he said, "Bearoness, you broke the circle!"

"Otto," she replied, "do you know what you just did?"

"Sure, a triple somersault with a flip!!"

"Yes, but how did you get from the pool up the top of the diving tower?"

"I swam and ran, of course."

"Well, dear, no one else saw you do that part. You just disappeared and reappeared."

It didn't take the otter long to figure out the implications of what she had said. "It's back! Oh gosh, it's back! I'm going to go crazy."

"Steady, mate, steady," said Bruce. "Let's call the doctors and get them over here. Now they can examine you in your hyper state."

"But I don't want to be in my hyper state. Not if I end up like that loco duck."

"We don't know that's going to happen, Otto. He's been taking his serum for ages. And you've been in your normal condition ever since you came out of your coma. Even now, you don't sound crazy, but you sure can do some wild things."

"Lock that door over there," the otter said, "and tie me up. Then throw me into the pool. I'll try to appear on the other side of the locked door. Somebody stand outside and make sure it's locked. Let's see if it's really working at full power." He had teleported a rope from the opposite side of the pool while he was saying this. The two wolves stood gaping showing all five thousand or so of their teeth. Howard's bristles were standing straight up. Juno scratched her formidable head. L. Condor, who had just arrived, volunteered to stand outside on the other side of the door. I hobbled over and locked it from the pool side. The condor tried it, and it wouldn't open.

The bears had gotten out of the water. Bearyl dived back in and took up station to release him underwater if he needed help. Juno tied his hands and his feet. He could still propel himself in the pool with his tail, but he wasn't going to be able to walk. Best he could do was a hop.

Belinda said, "Are you sure you want to do this, Otto?"

"It's the only way I can see what kind of shape I'm in!"

"Well, we won't let anything happen to you. Bearyl will release you in plenty of time. How long can you stay under normally?'

"About two minutes!"

"Did you hear that, Bearyl?"

She waved a paw from the middle of the pool. Bruce and Belinda checked the knots to see if they were secure and then somewhat unceremoniously gave him the heave-ho into the water.

There was a splash as he went below the surface and then nothing for a few seconds. Then what looked like a waterspout appeared and disappeared, and we heard the condor's new electronic voice shouting "*Caramba!!*" Otto had been outside and then a few seconds later was standing next to us at poolside. L. Condor pounded at the still locked door to be let back in. I opened it. Bearyl was climbing out of the pool with a length of rope in her teeth. Wasn't this an interesting development?

"Now this is an interesting development," said Octavius, who had walked in with the condor. "Inspector, would you be kind enough to call for the doctors?"

"Already did, Ocko!"

"Fine. Now Otto, just stay calm. I'm sure that Doctors BingBang and Vark will want to examine you in detail as soon as they get here. Frau Schuylkill, Colonel Where, may I speak with you in private, please?"

The two wolves padded off with Octavius to the lab that was adjacent to the swimming pool. The bears went back in the water but were unable to coax Otto back in. Bruce, L. Condor, Juno and I sat with him trying to calm him down.

In the lab, the Great Bear turned to the wolves and said, "Now, look, you two! It has always been my policy not to intrude on the private lives of my employees, but I feel I must in this case. Otto's talents are not very different from some of the more esoteric stunts I have seen you both pull off. Appearing and disappearing in an instant. Making things like a keg of mead or an aircraft maintenance checklist suddenly show up out of nowhere. You tell me it's hyperspeed. Now, can you shed any light on this talent of his? Have you also been genetically tinkered with??"

"Absolutely not," said Wyatt, "At least I'm not aware of it. Project Sleepwalker didn't have any geneticists on its staff. None that I knew of, at least. Ilse is more of an adept than I am, but we are both practitioners of Transylvanian Meditation. It allows us to move our bodies at hyper-speed. It may seem like we are teleporting, but we're not, although we have been doing some advanced training. We are learning to move small things at will."

"*Ja*, Herr Bear, I have been a devotee for many years since my early life in the Alps. I took Wyatt back with me on our vacation, and he too has now learned many of the transcendent arts from the Transylvanian Chamois."

"Chamois? Don't you mean Shaman?"

"Yes, Shaman Chamois. He is a remarkable goat who lives on the mountain tops and has perfected the high arts and mysteries."

"I would have thought a bat would be a more likely candidate."

"A bat, Herr Bear? Where would you get an idea like that? Anyway, we have spoken at length with Otto, and he shows no signs of knowing any of the Alpine secrets. He is something else."

"That's for certain! Is there any physical state you have to achieve in order to perform these little marvels of yours?"

"Not really," said the Colonel, "although it comes a little easier if you remain calm. Ilse doesn't seem to need any kind of preparation."

"No, Herr Bear, it is simply a Triumph of the Will."

"If anything, Otto seems to be in a state of high excitement when he does one of his little party pieces. I wonder…well, I'll talk with the doctors when they get here. But as for you, Colonel. Is this related to your ability to transfer to other universes while you are in a state of deep sleep and metabolic stasis?"

"I don't know, Octavius. I think they're separate, but I just don't know. The Shaman Chamois didn't know what I was talking about when I mentioned it to him, and I didn't want to explain too deeply. This is supposed to be confidential, but at the rate different animals are getting involved, we might as well broadcast it on the six o'clock news."

"You're right. As soon as this nonsense with the puma is over we have to organize this project and put some real security around it. That'll be your job."

They were padding back to the pool when Wyatt's phone rang. It was a relay from Jake. Pontius Puma was on the horn. Wyatt pressed a button and brought Chita into the link. She and Wyatt were on mute.

A feline voice with a Portuguese accent. "I am here, Ozzie."

"Where is here, Senhor?"

"A small airport near Cincinnati…Lunkhead, Lumpen, Whatever!"

"Oh, Lunken! *Si* Senhor! I know where it is. I thought you would have come in at the international airport."

"We cleared immigration in Miami. I thought the Bear would have his cronies looking for us at the Cincinnati International Airport, so we chose this one instead. Where are you?"

"I am still at the house, Senhor!"

"Well, I want you to come and meet me. I have a very important meeting with another enemy of the Bear who is also looking for Chita, and I want you to attend."

(Think fast, Jake.) "Senhor, if I leave now, I'm not sure I can get back in. They have established a high level of security ever since those bulls threatened the bear. They're suspicious of everybody here. All the members of the band are under surveillance. I think I would do you more good if I stay here and give you last minute reports and directions to the Bear's lair."

"Perhaps you're right, but be available by phone. We must plan this to the microsecond."

"Of course. When will you be initiating the assault?"

"I will know that better after I meet with this other animal."

"Who is that?"

"The bulls are being very secretive about his identity. They tell me they are being equally secretive about mine. We two are going to talk by phone first. Then if we decide to meet, we will plan our two-prong attack for sometime late tonight. Make sure you keep up to date on their security! I will not tolerate failure."

"Oh, *si*, Senhor. Of course. After all, you are my ticket back to Brazil."

"Make sure you remember that, Ozzie. I could always cancel your ticket. Adeus."

*"Adeus...(click, buzz)...*you bastard!"

234

Wyatt and Chita were still on the line. Wyatt gave Chita a different number and told her to call back in ten minutes. He was going to get the group together, and we would have a war council.

Meanwhile, a shuttle truck with the two doctors sped up to the door of the mansion. They ran down the stairs to the swimming pool and greeted Otto, who seemed to have relaxed a bit after his shock. He was munching on some fish pate and occasionally scratching his head.

Wyatt came in and whispered to Belinda, Bruce, the Frau and myself that we were needed upstairs. Octavius and the condor had already headed up to the library. Howard had headed off to UUI. We left Otto with Juno, Bearyl and Bearnice in case the doctors wanted an aquatic demonstration, and we went up. Jake was sitting in the center of the room on a tufted leather chair, somewhat pleased at being the center of attraction.

Between them, Wyatt and Jake recapped the conversation for the rest of us. Eyebrows rose *(on those who had them)* at the mention of an additional adversary, especially one interested in Chita.

Belinda broke the ice. "It's him. Somehow Imperius has hooked up or is going to hook up with Pontius Puma."

Octavius said, "We can't be certain…"

"C'mon, Ocko. Who else could it be?"

"What difference does it make?" I said to Octavius.

"The difference is in the objective. We all know that if it's Imperius, he's going to attack the UUI lab looking for his serum, the formulas, Doctor Odd Vark and maybe even the gun. He and Odd definitely did not get along in the short time Imperius was working at the lab. If he can also find Chita and kill her, so much the better. Wyatt, where is the gun right now?"

"Howard disassembled it, and the pieces are stored in seven different safes at UUI and here. He even split up the weapon's lab notes and hid them in still other places. Imperius will have to spend a lot of time searching, breaking and entering to retrieve that weapon. *(We had all agreed to call the thing a weapon although Octavius still insisted it was an instrument for good.)*

"Pontius Puma is probably going to come here looking for Chita although I'm sure he wouldn't mind creating some serious wreckage over at UUI. After all, we did ruin his business, and he is an eye for an eye type."

"To say nothing about teeth for teeth."

The library phone rang. Chita was with us again on the speakerphone. Her opening remark was classic cat. "Well, I'm certainly the center of attraction!!"

Jake looked a bit embarrassed and annoyed that he was no longer the star act. "Hey Chita, wazzup?"

"Hey Jake, where's Lepi?"

"I think he's off with the two bears or Otto or somewhere."

"Enough of this small talk," said guess-who. "Let me call the roll for you, Ms Catt, and we can begin our discussion. *(Oh boy, Ms Catt! Is somebody feeling a bit annoyed?)*

After everyone acknowledged everyone else, Chita *(bless her demure little heart)* said, "Well, Imperius has reared his ugly little head again."

"How can you be sure?" asked Octavius.

"Who else, bear? One wants to kill me, and the other wants me in his harem! Who are those bulls Paolo mentioned?" *(She still couldn't get the Pontius Puma thing straight.)*

"The Taurus Brothers from Chicago," I said.

"Well, that explains it. Imperius insists on using those taurian twits every time he has some heavy lifting he wants done. If they're also working for Paolo, they must have all made the link somehow. I'm not sure when, how or why but it sure sounds like they could end up coming at you together."

"I thought it was you they were coming for, Chita." said Belinda.

"Touché, Bearoness, I have a feeling the nutty duck would like to make a clean sweep of the whole bunch of us and I guess my puma friend wouldn't mind a little wholesale mayhem, either."

"All right," said Octavius, "we'll know more for sure when the Puma calls Jake back again. In the meantime, let's assume it's Imperius, and they do pair up. What's our defensive position, Wyatt?"

"Not entirely defensive, Octavius. As Bruce will tell you, international law enforcement agencies are licking their chops at the prospect of catching PP outside of Brazil. I've already informed them that his plane is at Lunken Airport instead of CVG and they are planning to descend in force there, at UUI and here early this evening. You must be one hot number, Chita, to get him to come raging up here like that from Brazil."

Chita let out a loud satisfied purr and chirp. "He's a pushover for long legs. He would love my sister, Cyd. She's a professional dancer."

Several thoughts ran through my febrile *(feeble, feral, whatever)* mind. A sister! Who'd a thunk? Chita and Cyd! Maybe there's a smash variety act here. Chita and Cyd in *Chicago!* Talent Agent Maury on the scene. Something about "pushover" tickled me too, but I couldn't get a firm grasp on it. I'd have to talk with Belinda and Bruce.

"She's not the only attraction, Wyatt," said Bruce. "Remember, L. Condor, Maury and I yanked his tail pretty hard. He's out of business for a good long while."

"So," said Jake, "I guess since he doesn't have much else to occupy his time in Brazil anymore, he decided to go on a vengeance run up here."

"Enough on motivation. What are our plans?" bellowed the Bear.

"I have given Jake directions to the Lair that will take them off the main roads and over an old set of farm paths that haven't been used in years. Let them think they're sneaking up on us from some obscure backwoods position. There are several vehicle traps dug along the way, and if they miss that, they will set off a trip wire that will light up the area with super-bright spots and floods. We'll have a number of security and police along the route. There will be UUI helicopters airborne at both sites as soon as the alarms go off. They don't have to do any actual damage to warrant arrest. We just need to catch them trespassing with weapons and explosives."

"Suppose they split up and approach from several directions?"

"I hope they do. We have the whole perimeter of UUI and the Lair equipped with motion sensors and trip wires. Each location will have over 40 security types deployed to deal with them. The smaller the individual groups the better. Chita, how many goons can the Taurus Brothers put into action if they have to?"

"I don't really know," replied the cat, "It's not that big a deal to transport a large group from Chicago. They normally use gorillas, other bulls and I know they have some chimps who are arson specialists."

"So we're going to have to watch the trees as well as the ground," said the Bear.

"Oh, yes, and I'd watch the river too."

"For what?" I asked.

"An assault boat! If Pontius Puma is willing to spend all that money to come up here with who knows how many of his own gang, plus the bulls' entourage, he's not going to let a little equipment get in the way."

"And we haven't even taken that crazy duck into account," said Bruce.

"I think Imperius will operate in just the opposite mode," mused the Bear. A quick surgical strike at the UUI lab looking for the notes and serum, an attack at Odd Vark, if he's around, a brief search for the particle beam accelerator, and if he knows where she is, a run at Chita and/or Otto. As far as he's concerned, I'm sure the puma is just one big diversion. First and foremost, he wants his scientific materials back and the weapon if he can get it."

Chapter Twenty Six

In Chicago, the Bulls are a team.

But our bulls here are not who they seem.

They're a dangerous pair

With a criminal flair

And their eyes have a murderer's gleam.

"As far as we are concerned, this other client of the bulls will be just one big diversion. First and foremost, we want our scientific materials back. Let us see what he has to say when he calls. We may not even want to meet with him. Maybe we'll just let him and his thugs cover for our operation." Thus strategized Doctor Imperius Drake, partially to Bigg, mostly to himself, as usual. He still needed to get some more decent full time help. This outsourcing wasn't working out. And Bigg was…Bigg.

"Baboon, were you able to get wireless headsets so we can communicate with each other during our raid?"

"Yes, Sire!"

"What about the lab coats and fake ID badges? I want us to look like we belong if we encounter anyone in the halls of UUI."

"Yes, Sire, but Sire…"

"What?"

"Do you think it's wise to wear your ski cap? It looks a bit unusual, especially with the gold pom-pom."

"Baboon, you have not spent your life in laboratories like I have. Unusual dress is usual. In fact, get yourself a long multi-colored scarf and a lot of pens. We have to blend in."

"Yes, Sire, ball point or soft tip?"

Before the duck could break into another temper tantrum, the phone rang. "It is probably the bulls. Stand by, Baboon. Our plans will unfold shortly."

"Hello? Yes, Mr. Taurus! No, we did not set up a pre-arranged code word. Yes, I'm positive. Well, if you think it's necessary! Quack, quack, quack!!! Yes, I know it sounds like me. It is me. *(Note the absence of the Imperial "we" - such condescension in the face of necessity.)* Now, where is your other client?"

(Once again, out of constant concern for the needs of our gentle readers and through the power of omniscient narration, we present both sides of the following conversation.)

"*Bom dia! Quem esta falando?*"

"Well," thought the Duck, "Portuguese. Probably Brazilian!"

(The puma spoke only Portuguese out of sheer nationalistic pride, ego and laziness. If someone wished to communicate with El Puma Grande, they must speak his language. The Duck, on the other hand refused to use a Pea Pod because it had been developed by UUI.)

"*Bom dia* to you, Senhor. As to your question, why don't we remain unnamed until we see whether it suits our purposes to reveal ourselves. Surely, both of us are animals who value our security and anonymity."

"*Si,* I agree. Of course, the bulls can identify us, but that would not be advantageous, would it, Senhores Toros?"

Snorts in the background.

"Now, I understand that you too, have a grievance against this *urso arrogante*. He and his cronies have cost me much in money and in honor. I also believe he is harboring a, shall we say, protégé of mine, against her will, I am sure. I intend to recover her."

"Aha," said the duck, "and are you sure your protégé is indeed in the Bear's custody?"

"No, Senhor, I am not, but if she is here, it is my intention to reclaim her and return her to Brazil where she belongs."

Obviously, this didn't sit very well with Imperius, who thought the only place Chita belonged was covered over in a deep ditch.

"And what are your plans, Senhor?" asked the puma.

"The Bear has some scientific material of mine and an experimental subject. It has been my intention to attack his company's headquarters, retrieve my property and cause as much damage as possible in the process."

"A trifle! I really do not care a *centavo* about your Cub Scout Science Project. *(The Duck had to try very hard to control himself at this point.)* But any damage we can inflict on his company will be some revenge for my losses. I will be generous and share the resources of the Taurus Brothers with you to a limited extent. I plan to destroy him and his mansion and find my own property."

"Well then," said the duck, fighting back an imperial rage, "I see no reason for you and me to reveal ourselves to each other. *(You jerk! I hope they kill you!!)* We will continue our negotiations directly with the Taurus Brothers. When are you planning your assault? We certainly should coordinate."

"*Si, si.* Tonight at midnight, we shall bring the Bear a healthy dose of Brazilian justice."

"So you *are* Brazilian," thought the Duck. I bet I can get this egotistical idiot to identify himself." *(Narrator's note about egotistical idiots: Takes one to know one!!!)* "Well, Senhor," said the Duck, "I am sure you are aware of the immense power of Octavius Bear. He is a formidable opponent. Not one to be trifled with."

"Bah, who is Octavius Bear compared to Pontius Puma!!"

"Gotcha, you dimwit," thought Imperius, "We've heard of you and I think we are going to steer clear of you and yours, Senhor Pompous Puma. But thanks for creating a diversion."

Aloud: "I am sure he will suffer immensely. *Adeus*, Senhor. Please ask the bulls to call me so we can plan our side of the operation."

He turned to Bigg and said, "Baboon, it is time to refine our plan. That stupid puma and the bulls will be staging their attack at midnight both at UUI and the Bear's mansion which incidentally, we have yet to locate. But it should be no trouble getting that information from our friends, the bulls."

"And we join in the fun, Sire?!!"

"No, Baboon, that is exactly what we will NOT do! We will just follow the entourage over to the mansion, keeping hidden, observe but not participate. Then, assuming Pompous Puma gets his head handed to him as I expect he will, we will wait until tomorrow morning when everyone has cleared out, and they have relaxed their guard a bit. Then you and I will walk into UUI and collect what is ours, including Otto. Then, depending on what we find out about her tonight, we shall also see to that faithless cheetah, assuming she is anywhere to be seen to."

"But, Sire…"

"They will be expecting us over at the laboratory tonight. That detestable Odd Vark will be heavily guarded and our notes and serum locked away. They will probably have the otter under protective guard as well. We must wait and catch them tomorrow after they relax and are too busy congratulating themselves on capturing or killing a famous international criminal like Pontius Puma."

"Pontius Puma is famous, Sire?"

"Certainly not in our league, Baboon, but he has amassed a collection of international warrants for his arrest. He is protected by the Brazilian authorities and their no-extradition policy. We are surprised he left the safety of his own country."

"Maybe he got a good deal on the air fare, Sire."

Rolling of eyes. "Perhaps, Baboon, perhaps. Now let us wait to hear from the bulls, and we will let them believe that while they are storming the mansion and UUI, we intend to stage a commando raid on the UUI genetics laboratory."

"Which we're not going to do! Right?"

"Right, Baboon, there may be hope yet for you!"

"Then why don't we just leave, Sire?"

"I spoke too soon. Once again, we are going to infiltrate UUI's genetics lab tomorrow morning when they are back at work and probably have our notes and serum out and in use. We must stay here until then. We will also see if Chita is indeed on site. In which case we may have to improvise an assault upon her person."

"She's a pretty tough cat, Sire!"

"But where it counts, Baboon, with our profusion of intellect and cunning, powerful tactics and strategy, split second timing, undaunted bravery and flawless execution, we excel." Having said all this and looking at the baboon's vacuous face, a small doubt started to creep into Imperius' bravado. Shrugging his wings, he murmured, "Well, maybe two out of seven!"

His phone rang. This was probably one of the Taurus Brothers. The game was awaddle.

*****

Down at the Bear's Lair swimming pool, another scenario was unfolding. The doctors had arrived and were questioning Otto, Bearyl, Juno and Bearnice. Dr. BingBang was testing the otter's vital signs and re-examining his bruised head and other wounds from the explosion. Dr.Vark was getting a detailed description of exactly what Otto had done both during his performance with the Aquabears and his fabulous escape routine.

"Now, Mr. Otter, you are certain that from the time you regained consciousness in our clinic until you took your er, spectacular dives an hour or so ago there had been no other evidence of unusual capabilities."

"No, I was just plain old Hairy Otter."

"So, to your knowledge, this is the first manifestation of the serum's effects on you since your, um, accident."

"Right!"

"Now, let us review what was happening during the extraordinary events."

They went over the sequence splash by splash and then examined the entire "escape artist" stunt in the same detail. Nothing new surfaced.

"When was the last time you drank any alcohol, Otto?"

"You told me not to have any, so I haven't."

"Anything unusual to eat??"

"Just Frau Schuylkill's fish paté. It's to die for, but not enough to change me into a whirlwind."

"Now that you're feeling a bit calmer, do you think you could reproduce your actions for us again?"

"I guess. You'd better watch closely. Most of the time, I just think I'm acting normally. What do you want me to do?"

243

"Try the diving board thing. Ladies, could you assist in reproducing the event?"

Bearyl and Bearnice dove into the pool and began circling. Otto plunged in and headed for the bottom. He came shooting up like a rocket, flipped over Bearyl's head and flopped back into the water and started swimming toward the side of the pool. When he reached the edge, he climbed up the stairs of the diving board and did a triple somersault.

"Was that OK? That's what I did the last time!"

"No, Otto," said Bearnice, "you did everything at normal speed this time. No 'now you see him, now you don't!' "

"Let me try again."

Five runs later and no super-otter!

"Let me see if I can get through that locked door…Ouch!" He had run at the door which steadfastly resisted his attempt to get through.

"Gee, I guess I lost it again. Doctors, what's going on??   Am I hallucinating?"

"No, Otto," said Bearnice, "if anyone had been hallucinating, it was us. We all saw you pull off those tricks. You thought everything was natural. What *is* going on, doctors??"

"The effects of the genetic manipulation Imperius performed seem to turn on and off but we don't yet know what triggers the change. We also don't know whether the manipulation is permanent or not."

"You also don't know what else is happening to me," said Otto. "I may be going completely nuts like that duck. Milord Mallàrd, Hah! Lord Looney, that's who he is!"

"Let's not jump to any conclusions," said Dr. BingBang. "We're going back to the UUI lab and review everything we have and what you've all told us. Can you come over and meet us at our offices tomorrow morning, Otto? Plan to spend the day with us."

"Sure, what else have I got to do? I'm even afraid to go swimming anymore. Thank goodness, my appetite hasn't been affected. I wonder where Frau Schuylkill is."

Dragging his tail, he wandered off, unlocking the door before going through it and headed up the stairs toward the kitchen.

"Poor Otto, he's so sweet!" said Bearyl. "Do you think you can cure him, doctors?"

'First Ms Bearyl, we must figure out what 'cure' means in his case." They started packing up, and the bears jumped back in the water and started doing synchronized routines. Practice, practice, practice.

*****

Bruce's phone rang. "Hi, Brucie. Guess who?"

"Well, sheila, I was expecting a call from the Australian Prime Minister making me Minister of Justice, but you don't sound a bit like him."

"I hope I don't look like him, either."

"Naw, he's a dromedary. First immigrant prime minister we ever had. What delightful news have you got for me this time?"

"I just thought I'd tell you that I am close by."

"How close by??"

"Very close by! Stop scratching your nose!"

"Oh, that close by."

"Yep, and I'm looking for somewhere to hide. I'd normally just creep around in the woods, but the way you guys are re-working the landscape, I might back into a bobcat – the kind with the shovel attached. Got any idea where I can lie low without running into Octavius or the various and sundry members of law enforcement who seem to be descending on this place? I'm amazed Paolo hasn't caught wind of all this."

"He seems to be relying on what Jake as pseudo-Ozzie is feeding him."

"You know, for a powerful guy, he's not that bright."

"He just can't conceive of anyone being smarter, stronger, richer or faster than he is. I can't think of anyone more arrogant." said Wallaroo.

"I can! Two of them in fact. Wanna guess?

"Don't need to. Now, what are you doing here?"

"I'm not going to miss seeing my wannabe slave owner get his. I wouldn't mind seeing Octavius get his nose bloodied either. I am strictly an observer."

"Look, Chita! Maury, Belinda and I are on the edge of being in serious legal trouble over not turning you in already. Otto doesn't know any better. If you show up here and get captured, questions are going to get asked and I for one am in no mood to have to answer them. I'm sure the Bearoness and Maury feel the same."

"Don't worry. I just want to watch from a safe distance."

"OK, I'm crazy to tell you this. There's a paddle wheel steamer down on the river bank called the Belinda B. Octavius uses it as a pleasure cruiser. There are staterooms on the boat. I don't think anyone will look for you there. If they do come on board, there are a couple of small storage rooms below decks you can hide in."

"Thanks, Brucie."

"Oh! And Chita, do you really have a dancing sister named Cyd?"

"Why, Inspector Wallaroo, have I ever lied to you? Bye, bye. Don't you call me! I'll call you."

Chapter Twenty Seven

Our science has no explanation

To account for teleportation.

Since one minute you're here,

Then you just disappear,

It's a moving and strange situation.

Satisfied that preparations for defeating the pending assault were well under way and being effectively carried out, Octavius, ever the multi-tasker, decided to call a meeting of the members of the troupe who were to be involved in the alternate universe endeavor. The war room had been checked out for security in the last hour and the cast of characters was assembling inside its well protected walls.

Wyatt, Bruce and Frau Schuylkill, wearing headsets attached to optical cables that were connected to receivers outside the "dead" room, sat on alert for any Pontius-related defense issue that needed handling. Juno and Belinda sat to the side with a befuddled Otto between them. Howard and L. Condor were sitting up front along with Drs. Vark and BingBang and several selected senior physicists from the UUI staff. I was sitting on a table in the back with a clear view of the proceedings. Bearyl and Bearnice had stayed outside and were keeping the two spotted cats from becoming too curious about what was going on behind closed doors.

Suddenly, those closed doors opened, and a large black nose intruded itself on the proceedings. Attached to the nose was an outsized brown bear bearing a striking resemblance to Octavius and Juno whose jaw, incidentally, had fallen wide open. Another Kodiak!

"Is this the right place?" growled the intruder.

"Yes," said Octavius, "I'm glad you made it. How was your trip?"

"A twin otter isn't the speediest way to travel from Reno to Cincinnati but I'm here."

"Sorry, it was one of the few aircraft we could spare."

Juno, fed up with this transportation chit-chat, roared, "Agrippa, what the hell are you doing here. I thought you were holed up waiting for some *H.Saps* to do you in….Oops! Did I let a bear out of the bag??"

Octavius intervened before Agrippa could respond. "It's OK, Mom. I invited him. He's had one of the more interesting and exciting universe transfer experiences we've heard of, and we need him as part of our task group. Besides, he'll be a lot safer here than where he was hiding out. Everyone! This is my-half brother Agrippa, Juno's other son."

"Juno's other ne'er do well son!" snorted his mother.

"Hi, Mom. Nice to see you, too. Hello, everyone. Don't believe everything you hear about me except of course, if I'm telling it to you."

An assortment of grins, frowns and quizzical looks *(Otto)* presented themselves in response. Octavius looked at Frau Schuylkill, who had dispatched the plane to pick up Agrippa. "He'll be our guest for a while, Frau Schuylkill. I'm sure he'll be no trouble."

"No trouble at all, Herr Bear!" This accompanied by a loud snort from Juno.

"Now, let's get to the subject at hand. First let me apologize to some of you. We will be reviewing some data you've already heard. But to a few of you, some or all of this will be new. I want to hear all of your comments, reactions and most of all, recommendations. I believe this is a crucial situation that we must deal with rapidly and efficiently. If you disagree or hold differing opinions, let's hear them. I'm sure you'll all have questions. Now, let's go over what has happened to our happy or not so happy wanderers.

"I'm not even sure what to call your experiences, which while all relevant, have been different enough to defy being put into one neat category. My mother and Agrippa have reported stories of being transported – passively – to different environments while in hibernation. The general surroundings looked roughly the same at both ends."

"In Mom's case she ran into a mother bear who did not seem capable of communicating but who attacked her and took out a chunk of her hide for her trouble. Running back to her 'apparent den,' Mom passed out, and when she woke up was back in her own place along with her maid, Florence, who incidentally is on her way down here to help you, Mom."

"Thank you Tavi! You're so considerate!" Nasty look at Agrippa. He wasn't going to be able to catch a break from the old sow, no matter what.

"In Agrippa's case, he was hibernating outside Reno and was transported to what I'll call a Reno Prime. Gambling halls, hotels, show lounges and wonder of wonders, *Homo Sapiens*."

Agrippa piped up. "I *think* they were *Homo Sapiens*. I've only seen scientific sketches based on fossils that were dug up by faunapologists. I've always thought they were totally extinct!"

"So does the rest of the scientific world," interjected Dr. Vark. "I doubt very much that a city the size of Reno, populated with *Homo Sapiens* would have escaped detection in this world, Mr. Bear."

"But oddly enough," continued Octavius, "that world seemed to have *H.Saps* and sentient animals co-existing without any undue disturbance or conflict. Is that correct, Agrippa?"

"Well, let me put it this way. I was dealing a game of high stakes poker for a group of *H.Saps* and no one seemed a bit disturbed by the fact that I was a bear."

"Were you?" asked Doctor Vark.

"Was I what?"

"A bear? Did you still have the appearance of a bear, or did you look like an *h. sap*, instead?"

"Huh?"

"Consider," said the aardvark, "if, and this is all speculation on my part but if, when you teleport, you are momentarily reduced to your composite atoms, you could be reconstituted in many other forms. Likewise, *H.Saps* could also be among us in other forms if they can teleport."

"Wow," blurted Otto, "that's pretty wild, Doctor Vark. Maybe Agrippa's an *H.Sap*!"

"Well," said the Kodiak, "I know what I saw and I know what I am. I was dealing cards with my furry paws and looking out over my pointy black nose. I even remember seeing myself in a mirror. Except for the green eyeshade I had picked up somewhere, I was the same me. Now, I have no way of knowing what the *H.Saps* saw. Oh, wait, yes I do. I remember one of the more aggressive guys referring to me as a no-account bear."

"That was you, all right," shouted Juno.

"Mom, please," said Octavius. "OK, we'll go into the more grizzly details of the shoot-out and acquisition of the cash later on, Agrippa. Very interesting thought, Dr. Vark. Thank you, I think."

"Shoot-out?" Otto again.

"Yes, Otto, shoot out - which is why Agrippa is here and not still in Reno. Now let's shift gears. With the Colonel, we have a case of…I'll call it induced hibernation and semi-controlled teleporting…although I'm not sure it's the same thing at all. To compound the issue, he and Frau Schuylkill have developed another capability that gives the appearance of teleportation or telekinesis or both, but probably isn't. We're leaving Otto to the last in our discussions because we're not at all sure what his capacities are or how they happen. Colonel, would you describe Project Sleepwalker and your adventures since? Then Frau Schuylkill, I'd ask you to tell us to what extent you can match the Colonel's experiences and abilities and to what extent he can match yours."

"This is becoming quite complex, Senhor Octavius!" The buzzy tones of the condor emanated from his artificial voice box.

"Indeed, Senhor Condor, indeed and I'm not sure we have even clawed the surface. That is why all of you are here. This top-secret project that I am tentatively calling the Multiverse Program, a play on UUI's name, could become one of the most daunting and important developments for science and for civilization.

That's why I'm holding this meeting now, even though we have marauders almost knocking on our doors. I want everyone in this room, and I mean everyone, spending every available minute alone and in teams, applying their brains, experiences and technologies in trying to sort out all of the phenomena we'll be talking about. Remember, this is just *our* experiences. We haven't the slightest idea who else and what else is involved, and we have little or no knowledge about what's going on among the *H.Saps* who seem to be on the other end of some of these events."

250

Dead silence in the room except for a little rumbling sound which turned out to be my stomach.

Wyatt handed his handset to Howard and stood up in front of the group. "Some of you have heard this story, so I'll try to keep it brief." First he mentioned that Wyatt Where was not his real name. He described being recruited by the super-secret quasi-government organization without a name that some outsiders referred to as *The Business*. Insiders seldom referred to it at all. He mentioned General Turmoil, the chief of the agency, and Octavius interrupted.

"General Turmoil is a war horse, literally, with little in the way of ethics or sympathy for anyone he sees in his way. His avowed purpose is to constantly stay ahead in the development of defense technology, but I believe, and I think Wyatt agrees with me, that he has developed a sense of world conquest that goes far beyond national defense." Affirmative nod from the wolf.

"Unfortunately, he has many powerful friends to assist him and many weaklings to do his bidding. UUI and I have done work in the past for the *Business,* when it was headed by a far more rational and intelligent animal. Turmoil has a lot of the same characteristics as Imperius Drake, and he may be just as nutty. He's certainly not as intelligent. God help us if those two ever teamed up. The General and I are at a standoff currently, but I still look over my shoulder when his name is mentioned. As Wyatt tells you the rest of his story, you'll understand my concerns. Sorry, Colonel! Please continue."

Wyatt went on to catalog his experiences as an experimental animal in the *Business*'s Project Sleepwalker program. He stressed that although they seemed capable through physical and perhaps mental modification of putting him in a deep trance-state, while he was under, they were only able to get him to apply some basic telekinesis – moving small objects several feet. Attempts to get him to teleport himself only succeeded in having him fall off the test table several times. The ultimate goal was to reach a level where he might be able to transfer to parallel universes, if such existed.

The project never came near that point and was ultimately abandoned. They had applied a number of chemical as well as radiation based alterations to him, but General Turmoil decided it was pointless to try to restore him to his former state. Wyatt was convinced that he was slated for elimination. The only other member of the test group who had survived that far along with Wyatt disappeared without a trace.

That's when the Colonel decided to use his commando training, escape and get far, far away. But he also had another advantage that the experimenters didn't know about. They had actually succeeded more than they'd thought. Wyatt could teleport himself far enough to get out of the heavily guarded facility. He had discovered this capability during periods back in his quarters but never revealed any of it to his captors.

It didn't always work but considering the alternative, it was worth a try. He did try and after several failures, succeeded in getting free, changed his identity and headed to the other side of the world where he signed up as a mercenary. Then, after a few years, he came back to the States where he ended up working for the Bank of Lake Michigan and then got involved with Octavius and his crew. (*See The Open and Shut Case.*)

During that time, he kept experimenting on himself and gradually was able to induce the trance more predictably and in a small percentage of attempts, actually teleport relatively long distances. Then came the big moment – the first time he teleported to a place that seemed totally alien. It resembled our world, but then it didn't.

Most important, as he moved stealthily around his new surroundings, he came across beings that looked like the faunapological representations of *Homo Sapiens* he had seen in museums and books. They never saw him, although there were some close calls, but he saw plenty of them and the civilization they seemed to dominate. Later, he told Octavius about it and they both decided that all further experimental jaunts should be done in a rigorous scientific environment and under close monitoring and supervision. Hence this session.

"Thanks, Colonel!" said the Bear, "I'm sure all of you have many questions you want to ask Wyatt and each other, but we will handle them later or in subsequent sessions. Right now, I want Wyatt to stay up here, and he and Frau Schuylkill will outline their other talent which may or may not be related to teleporting. Then we'll get on to Otto, who seems to be a composite of everything we've been talking about."

"I don't want to be a composite," wailed the otter. "I just want to be a third rate magician and go back to the St. Lawrence River."

"I'm not sure we can do that, Otto, until we know that Imperius Drake is no longer around to threaten you and us. But you are among friends, and we will do nothing without explaining it fully and getting your permission."

252

"That's what that loony duck said, too."

"Otto," said Belinda. "Don't you think you can trust me? I'll be with you every step of the way."

That seemed to calm the otter down. His goddess had spoken and promised him protection.

Frau Schuylkill, still wearing her headset, stood up next to Wyatt and said, "While I lived in Europe, I travelled to Transylvania and studied with the Shaman Chamois. There, at his ancient feet I learned the art of *Höchstgeschwindigkeit* – hyperspeed. That is how I can appear to be several places at once and bring kegs of mead and other things so fast. If I don't stop during the process, it appears the things got there on their own.

But it isn't telekinetics. It's just me moving faster than your eyes can track. I'm also able through applied telepathy to anticipate what you are going to ask for and that's what makes it even more mysterious. But it's a different skill from teleporting, even though it may look the same. I have to be on solid ground and I can only run relatively short distances. And yes, I do get tired."

The group laughed. Then the Colonel chimed in. "On our recent trip to Europe together, Ilse introduced me to the Shaman, and he gave me some instruction in hyperspeed movement. I'm a rank amateur compared to the Frau, who is a class A adept. The Shaman knew little or nothing about teleportation although he implied that some of his ancestors may have been teleportable."

"Thank you, Frau!" She and Wyatt sat down and headsets were passed back and forth. "Now, as to our newest friend, Otto. Dr Vark has some ideas as to what the diabolical duck was trying to do. Knowing Imperius' specialty, he was trying to create changes in your genetic structure and rebuild you to his specifications which by the way were certainly not in your interest. We believe he was trying to build a super-otter but one who would be totally subservient to his every whim."

Otto's jaw hung open. He sputtered, but nothing came out.

"Actually, Otto, I'm not sure he was trying to build a super-otter specifically, but rather was trying to develop a generic serum that could be used on any animal, from an ant to an elephant. You were his first opportunity to experiment on an animal other than himself. Up to now, the serum was not transferable. An overdose of it accidentally killed his mate, Lee-Li-Li and Chita was deliberately destined for the same fate before she escaped. But once again, the crazy duck's ambitions outran his sense and he produced a result that was indeed a super-otter, but from everything we can tell, hardly subservient."

"You bet I'm not subservient. I'm not particularly brave or given to brawling, but if I can get my paws on that Imperius Drake, that'll be the end of him."

"I'm afraid you're going to have to get on the end of a long line of beings who have the same idea. Meanwhile, we're not going to let you anywhere near Imperius. We need you too badly to let you mix it up with him. He may look like just a duck, but he is formidable and faunacidal."

Pumped up by his anger, Otto turned belligerent. "Suppose I don't want to be protected. Suppose I just walk out of this room and head for the St. Lawrence River. Or suppose I do go out duck hunting."

"Let's take your last proposition first, Otto. We have spent too much time and effort trying to track down and stop Imperius to allow you to interfere. If you do want to return to your families, we'll happily put you in one of our airplanes and drop you, gently of course, in the St. Lawrence. Nothing could be easier."

"But," said Dr BingBang, "we'd strongly advise against it. Neither you nor we know what other effects that serum has had or will have on you. You, yourself said you were afraid you might turn into a loony. Imagine if you went back home and turned out to be a faunacidal maniac who starts wiping out all his brothers and sisters. I doubt that would happen but any number of other side effects may surface. Give us some time to analyze your situation. Who knows? The duck may have actually done you a favor."

"How???"

"By making it possible to become a show-business wonder, Otto." This from Belinda. "Think of the act we could put together. You as a single or with the Aquabears! A new sensation! Our routines need some freshening up."

This stopped the otter cold. The opportunity to work with Belinda and the Aquabears in top drawer show biz. How could he say no to that?

"And," Octavius rumbled, "you may also prove to be a key player in our Multiverse Project if you can truly teleport and apply telekinetics. Of course, if you really want to leave, unlike the duck, we are not going to hold you against your will. Frau Schuylkill can call over for a helicopter to take you to our Twin Otter airplane *(Ironic, huh!)* that we're housing off-site until this nonsense with Pontius Puma is over. What do you think?"

"I – I guess I'll hang on for a while but I reserve the right to…"

"Of course you do, and we'll respect that right if ever you decide to exercise it. Now let's summarize. We have several different types of other world travel here. Mom, Agrippa and Wyatt were not just dreaming. They actually brought back souvenirs of their journeys. In Mom's case, a gash on her behind…

"Tavi!!"

"…in Agrippa's case, let's just say he profited from the poker game and Wyatt has been collecting all sorts of material that we hope will help us to identify just where the hell he got off to. Frau Schuylkill, Wyatt and Otto all seem to have some unique powers of transit, and we're not sure how they resolve themselves into our picture, if they do at all. There seems to be sufficient evidence from this group at least, that somewhere *Homo Sapiens* or a reasonable facsimile thereof is not extinct but is alive and doing more than kicking. Bruce, have you had adventures of the type we've been describing?"

"Not me, Ocko, although I'd love to learn that hyperspeed thingy the Frau and the Colonel have picked up. You can bet your last can of Fosters that I could really use that."

"And Belinda, unlike your brown furred relatives, polar bears do not hibernate, do they?"

"True, with one small exception that doesn't apply here, Tavi!"

"So, can we assume that you, Bearyl and Bearnice have not had any adventures of the sort we've been describing?"

Affirmative nod from the Bearoness.

"And as some of you know, unlike my mother and half-brother, Agrippa, I have not been hibernating for many years.   I developed a pharmaceutical procedure that restrains the need for hibernation and allows me to work year round. I have never tested it on other bears and probably will not in the future."

No doubt, the same thought was circulating through several heads around the room: "Yeah, especially when the trade-off is a case of unpredictable narcolepsy that you, Oh Great Bear, ignore or vehemently deny when faced up to it!"

He then scanned the room and his beady eyes settled on me. I was wondering what, if anything, he had in mind for good old reliable, resourceful and reluctant Maury. I don't mind taking on bad guys here on *terra firma* but my personal jury is out and likely to remain so on gallivanting around parallel universes, especially if *Homo Sapiens* was involved. Although to be perfectly truthful *(which I seldom am)* I don't know the first thing about *H.Saps*. That was a gap in my African grade school education. I stared back at him.

"Anything you'd like to contribute, Maury?"

(Oh, yessir! I want to be the first experimental subject and defying all risk, go off to face the unknown in as many alternate worlds as I can find and bring back all kinds of new species and information and of course, establish permanent, peaceful relations with H.Saps. Indiana Maury! One small step for animal-kind! File that under Fat Chance, Bear!)

"Not at the moment, Octavius!"

Well, that leaves us to get ourselves organized. Howard, am I right in assuming that you have not been a direct participant in any of these teleporting exercises?"

"That's right, Octavius!"

"Then I would like you to take sole leadership of this project. Your scientific background is ideal, and since you have no vested interest in defending or explaining your own actions, I believe you can be a disinterested but highly interested party, if you get what I mean."

"I'd be delighted. Of course, I would want to work beside Drs. Vark and BingBang and I want to treat Juno, the Frau, Wyatt, Agrippa and Otto as colleagues, not as experimental subjects. There is a massive amount of data we need to discover, develop, sift, correlate and hypothesize from before we even think of plans of action."

"I agree, Howard, but we also don't know how much time we have before some event takes the reins out of our paws. This is not just a scientific study, important as that may be. It is also an action program, possibly a defensive action program, although we can't jump to conclusions. And let me be completely clear to all of you. This is a top secret project. Need to know only. If General Turmoil or any number of other groups or individuals get wind of what we're doing, we are going to have a conflict on our hands that will make tonight's episode with Pontius Puma seem like a school yard jape. Speaking of which…" turning to the animals with the headsets "…is everything going according to plan?"

Wyatt answered, "Everything is progressing on schedule and without any glitches, Octavius."

The Frau looked up at the Bear, "I just wish we knew if that *verdammte* duck was in the area. He could be a problem."

Octavius replied, "I hope our defenses can deal with him as well if he appears."

Wyatt shook his head affirmatively.

"Well, then, let's get back to work. Howard, you and I should get together later and put some more meat on the bones of this thing. You call how and when you want to have meetings with the concerned parties. Of course, we'll need highly protected and backed up notes of everything we say and do. I have access to a massive amount of theoretical notes about parallel universes and teleportation. I'll be happy to share and discuss them with you. Then we can plot our next steps."

"So much for being in sole charge of the project," thought the porcupine. "But that's Octavius and he has more knowledge and insight than I could ever develop. It's just that he can be such a pain in the ass sometimes."

As they were filing out of the room, Belinda grabbed the Great Bear's paw, pulled him over to a corner and said, "Just a minute, Tavi! I know and you know that I know about your narcoleptic excursions."

The Bear reluctantly nodded his head.

"Well," she asked, just where do *you* go when you're out??"

Chapter Twenty Eight

The Doberman's noble and sleek

With a powerful canine physique.

He can bring down a crook,

But behind his fierce look

Lies protection for those who are weak.

Back to the problem at hand. At about 8 PM, Jake/Ozzie had received another PP call. Wyatt and Octavius listened in. Since Chita had never been cut out of the automatic connection, unbeknownst to any of them, she silently eavesdropped as well. This time it was Belial Taurus who called, telling Jake/Ozzie that everything was set for midnight. One more check of the GPS coordinates, vectors, approaches and best place to go for dinner and they reached agreement. Jake/Ozzie was to sneak out of the mansion at about 11:30, make one final look around and then head out to the deserted pathway and signal "all's clear" to the marauders.

He would then wait for the utility vehicle carrying Pontius Puma and join him for the escape and trip back to São Paolo, with or without Chita. He was told to expect two trucks full of raiders and the special armor plated Hummer with the Puma. There would be another two trucks over at UUI. The principal weapons would be firebombs. An "old" mansion like that should go up in no time. *(Little did they know about the comprehensive fire, lightning, wind, storm and flood protection that had been expended on the Lair.)*

Of course, the Puma was anxious to know if Chita was there. He snatched the phone from the bull and said, "Ozzie, you have been very uninformative on one point. I keep asking you about Chita, and you keep telling me you don't know. Now I ask you one last time. Your trip back to Brazil depends on your answer. Is she there?"

Suddenly a seductive feline voice came on the line. "Oh, Paolo, don't be so mean to poor Ozzie. Of course I'm here. Come and get me. I'm waiting for you." She cut her connection.

Wyatt had to stuff a paw in Octavius' mouth to keep him from roaring over the phone. They listened as Jake/Ozzie came up with a *(pretty believable)* story for Pontius about Chita hiding away to avoid the police. After all, she was a wanted cat in the United States. She had made Jake promise not to tell anyone she was here until they were sure Pontius/Paolo was really coming. Now that she knew he was on his way, she'd be ready. As she said, she was waiting for him. Say what you like about Jake as a drummer. He was a hell of a skilled liar. Say what you like about Pontius. He was a gullible jerk.

Needless to say, when the connection was broken, and Wyatt had retrieved his slightly gnawed paw from the bear's mouth, Octavius went into super-snit mode. "She's here. Am I the only one who didn't know that she is here? Am I surrounded by plotters and subterfugists?" *(Is that a word?)*

"Calm down, Ocko," said Bruce. "We don't know where she is either. She may be around here somewhere, or she may be playing telephone games with Pontius. I can honestly say that at this moment I have no idea where Chita actually is." Australian sophistry at its best. He knew damn well where she intended to be in the next half hour…on the boat.

"We shall have the FBI and members of international police organizations here shortly. I will not stand for having to admit to harboring a criminal."

"Tavi," said Bel, "you're not harboring a criminal or anyone else the FBI may be interested in. Just calm down. If Chita appears, it will be on her terms and under her own conditions. Besides, she may not come at all. She may send her sister, Cyd, the dancer."

Octavius is obviously no dope. He can tell when he is being conned. But he can also tell when he is being conned to his own advantage. He looked at Bel, Bruce and myself. "Ah, yes, Cyd, the heretofore seldom mentioned dancing sister!" He apologized to Wyatt for chewing on his leg. He asked the Frau for a keg of mead and said, "Well, we may yet be able to rid the world of an assortment of ne'er-do-wells this evening if we play our cards right. That's worth something, I suppose."

Sighs of relief around the room. The drinks table appeared *(You know how!)* and we all relaxed in the quiet before the storm. Howard and L.Condor were over at UUI with members of the FBI. UUI was considered a national asset and was on the Bureau's critical "Protect" list. Oddly, the Bear's Lair was not. I guess it's because it doesn't officially exist. No matter! We had representatives anyway from local law enforcement, the FBI and Bruce's International Counter Espionage and Intellectual Property Protection Unit.

The wolves had spent the day with the Lair maintenance teams in installing and testing counter-offensive measures. Bruce and I, along with Juno, the three polars and Lepi, had spent an hour or two at target practice. Juno turned out to be a crack shot. Up there in Kodiak Island, sometimes it takes more than claws to mount an effective defense. It turns out Juno was quite an aggressive athlete when she was a juvenile. She played first Home on the Attack for the Kodiak Krushers Lacrosse Team. Highest record of scores in Alaska history. And this was a male team.

Octavius sharpened his claws for the second time. He kept mumbling to himself about ridiculous interruptions when he had so many other important things to take care of. Pontius Puma was not very high on his list of formidable foes, but if he could also get rid of the Taurus Brothers and possibly get another shot at Imperius Drake; it might be worth the effort. I wondered if PP and Imperius, if he was in on the attack, knew what they were in for.

*****

"I doubt if that stupid Puma knows what he is in for, Baboon. I can't imagine that wretched bear allowing his lair and his company headquarters to go undefended. I think our feline friend is going to get an unpleasant surprise. Better for us! As you know, I am a great devotee of the diversion. And that upstart puma is just the one to provide it. I do hope nothing serious happens to the Taurus Brothers. They have proven useful in the past but what must be, must be. Just as long as Pontius the Ridiculous is taken care of."

"If he's so dumb, Sire, how come he's so rich?"

"Was rich, Baboon, was rich. He has just recently lost most of his assets, probably courtesy of the bear. We are not entirely sure. You seem to forget all the wealthy idiots we separated from their money when we operated in Europe. Greed and arrogance – the seeds of downfall. Ah, those were the days. We were a team! We as well as you and…Chita! That treacherous cat. Ah, how we hope she makes an appearance. Vengeance burns deep within our spleen."

"Would you like a Bromo-Seltzer, Sire?"

A despondent rush of air escaped the duck's nostrils. "No, Baboon, thank you. Here is what we wish you to do. It's 9:30 PM. At about 11, you will join the Puma's attack force headed for the Bear's mansion. You will be our show of solidarity with him. We are sending our most trusted assistant to be with him in his raid."

"I'm your only trusted assistant, Sire."

"Too true, too true. Nevertheless, the Puma doesn't know that. We'll call right now and make sure the puma knows you're joining him at the mansion. Stir them to a fever pitch when they launch the attack. Think back to your days in France starting general strikes among the workers. Those were some of your finest hours."

"We also made quite a few Euros, Sire."

"True, true! We, meanwhile, shall muster the group assigned to attack the UUI headquarters. We shall stir them up with one of our peerless speeches to the troops on the eve of battle and once it is underway, we shall conveniently disappear…to fight another day, of course."

"But your assignment, Baboon, is most critical. You are **not** to participate in the fighting. You are to ride in front of them, rousing the raiders and cowing the natives and then…head for the trees when no one is looking. Your only job is to observe and relay information to us over your headset.

Your number one objective is to find out if Chita is there and if she is, you are to follow her wherever she goes. It is imperative we know her whereabouts at all times. If we have to, we'll come over and kill her on the spot. But we would much prefer to defer her death until tomorrow morning. We will use it as yet another diversion to facilitate our stealthy second approach to UUI to make off with our notes and serum. Under no circumstances are you to attack her. That's our imperial privilege. Do you understand all that?"

"Of course, Sire. I have committed it all to my flawless memory."

"Oh, would it were so, Baboon, would it were so. Go now and get ready to join the parade."

"I love a parade!!" hummed the ape.

"A figure of speech, Baboon, just a figure of speech."

*****

261

The Taurus brothers had split their resources. Brutus was on the back road near the Lair with Pontius Puma. PP had brought several of his toughs with him from Brazil. These were complemented by several gorillas and incendiary wielding chimps from Chicago. Across the Ohio in Kentucky, Belial Taurus was organizing his attack group in the woods south of UUI. Suddenly out of the trees shot a black feathered missile – Imperius Drake.

"Good evening, Mr. Taurus. I have come to join you in this mission of revenge. No doubt you and your brother are most severely inflamed by the unforgiveable treatment that arrogant bear and his toady wolf inflicted on you the other morning. I, too, have several scores to settle with him and I can think of no better vengeance than turning his pseudo-scientific Taj Mahal into a pile of burning ashes. I should like to address the troops."

"Well, sure, Doctah Drake! Who am I to deprive a longtime client of his full moment of glory."

"Very well phrased, Mr. Taurus, very well phrased. Attention! All you bringers of retribution! Yours is indeed a noble cause. *(The gorillas, chimps and bull didn't much care for nobility. All they wanted was to do the job quickly, get the hell out of there and collect their sizeable fees.)* For decades, the world of crime has been subjugated to the whims of an officious, overbearing bear who characterizes himself as the savior of animal kind. No hard working pickpocket, blackmailer, mugger, gangster, hooligan, thug, extortionist, thief, assassin or murderer has been safe to ply his or her trade in peace and prosperity as long as Octavius Bear and his slobbering sycophants have been free to harass them and take away their freedom. No more!"

"Tonight, you will take part in an exploit that will live forever in the annals of criminality. Years from now, you can tuck your youngsters in bed and tell them the story of the fall of Octavius the Tyrant, his obsequious minions and his cursed UUI. I envy you the pride that you will feel when animals passing in the street will cower and whisper, 'They were at the UUI massacre.' Once more we will return crime to the hands of the criminals, where it belongs. Stir up your courage! Bring forth from your spleen a rage that can only be satisfied by complete destruction. Attack and show no mercy. Decimate and obliterate! Let us go now and change the world." *(The assembled ruffians were beginning to wonder if they should have charged more for their services.)*

262

And so, at midnight, the fiendish forces formed to foment their fearsome foray. In the forefront, Belial Taurus, urged on by Imperius' hysterical exhortations, led the attack – two trucks with firebomb brandishing chimps, several armor clad gorillas and the bull - sped across the parking lot access ways toward the entrance pavilion of the labs and office building. The chimps jumped off the trucks and began tossing their lethal missiles at the structure, trying to soften it up for a quick bout of hyper-vandalism.

Suddenly, overhead, two helicopters appeared, dropping fire retardant loads of chemicals on the aggressors and their targets. A UUI security team opened fire with weapons and fire hoses. The gorillas smashed through an entrance barrier only to be cut down by hand- held rockets from the FBI. One chimp had caught fire and was jumping around trying to get in front of the oncoming stream of the high pressure hose.

The last thing Belial said before he was hit was, "Dammit, they knew we were coming!!" Before he could get on the radio to Brutus on the mansion side of the river, his truck blew up and him with it. Just as the trucks had approached the pavilion, Imperius had left the scene and landed on a tree top out of sight of the choppers. He watched the one-sided carnage with mixed emotions. He had predicted the result. He was just sorry so little damage had been done before the raid ended. Too bad about Belial Taurus! He had been useful. Perhaps his brother will be more successful and survive.

Reports vary after the fact but the consensus was the whole thing lasted less than two minutes. The FBI and police searched for the chimps and captured two. The rest were no doubt bounding through the trees at maximum speed. One gorilla was captured, another wounded, and two were killed. The bull was dead and both trucks were destroyed. Howard, the Assistant Director of the FBI from Chicago and the condor were checking on UUI casualties. Cuts from flying glass, some burned fur and a broken arm caused by a runaway fire hose, but nothing else. The raid had not even gotten close to the genetic labs. Howard was on the phone reporting results to the mansion. "What's happening over there?" he asked Wyatt.

"Nothing yet. Whoops, spoke too soon. Here they come. Hold on. I'll be back."

*****

263

Pontius Puma had gotten the "all clear" flash from Jake/Ozzie and gave the telephone signal to attack the Bear's Lair! He knew the UUI assault team across the river had already swung into action with Imperius stirring them on. The Puma's attention was concentrated on his own assault, so he did not know how rapidly and catastrophically the events on the other side of the Ohio had come to a conclusion. Over here, atop the first truck speeding up the deserted back road, that ridiculous baboon sent by the duck was jumping up and down and shouting, "*Viva La Revolucion*! To the Bastille! Death to tyrants! Hell no, we won't go! Free the Indianapolis Five Hundred! On, Wisconsin!"

From his position at the rear of the three vehicle column, the dark tinted, bullet-proof, rocket resistant windshields and doors of the Hummer made it difficult for PP to clearly see what was going on. The last thing he had heard on the radio link was a "Dammit" from across the river and then a "Watch Out" from the first truck in his caravan. Then he saw the taillights of the second truck rise in the air with the rear wheels spinning uselessly. A brilliant burst of light from overhead and the thrum of helicopter rotors gave him his first confirmed clue that things were not going according to plan. The trucks had fallen into vehicle traps, and the occupants were being shot at and rounded up as they struggled to get out.

He shouted to his driver, "Carlos, turn around, turn around. Let's get out of here!!"

As the Hummer began to execute a broken "U" turn in the close quarters, he saw a golden flash out his window. He saw it again, and then standing on the hood of the Hummer was a spotted vision with the longest legs he'd ever drooled over. Chita!!!

"Carlos, stop!" He started to open the door, shouting, "Chita, get in, get in!" but the Hummer started to rock from side to side. There, along the side of the vehicle were three polar bears, two big brown bears and the biggest brown bear he had ever seen and they...were...pushing... it...over.

With an appropriately dramatic crash the Hummer came to a rest on its side. Chita had jumped off the hood. Octavius had clambered up on the capsized SUV and was laying on it almost the full length of the cabin. Carlos took out a weapon, fired a shot and then remembered that the glass was bullet-proof both ways. The bullet ricocheted around the interior of the cab grazing Pontius. "Idiot, idiot, put that away!!"

264

"Good evening, Senhor Puma!" bellowed the Bear. 'Welcome to our country! The authorities will be along in a moment to take you and your gang into custody. Unfortunately, one of your trucks caught fire and exploded, so Mr. Taurus may not be able to join us, but you are surrounded, and I believe surrender is called for."

In what seemed like a split second, the cheetah had jumped up again next to Octavius, stared into the Hummer and said, "Bye, Paolo!" then to the Bear, "I told you he was a pushover for long legs." She jumped down and disappeared at super speed. *(Who was that masked cat??? OK, she wasn't masked but she does have long black lines running from her eyes to her mouth along with her spots.)*

The law enforcement officers were taking the marauders into custody as the helicopter continued to hover with its flood lights. Wyatt and the Frau had both seen Bigg on the first truck. How could you miss the stupid loudmouth? But now he was nowhere to be found.

As the FBI Special Agent from Cincinnati and the Chief of the International Counter Espionage and Intellectual Property Protection Unit took up their station, the six bears pushed the Hummer upright again. Jake and Lepi stood aside laughing as Pontius and Carlos were unceremoniously dumped out the door into the waiting paws of the law. "Senhor Puma," shouted Lepi, "you forgot to fasten your seat belt."

"By the way, Senhor Puma, I'm not Ozzie. I'm Jake. Remember the broken leg? Ozzie was killed in an accident. You've been talking to me all this time. Sorry, I guess if I go back to Brazil, I'll have to pay my own way. I don't think you'll be going back for a while."

The response from Pontius Puma was a mixture of feline screams laced with some very arcane Portuguese curse words.

"We've got him, and I think we've seen the last of the Taurus Brothers." said the FBI Special Agent, one of the largest Dobermans I had ever laid eyes on. *(These dogs held most of the major posts in the Bureau, just as German Shepherds seemed to own the Drug Enforcement Agency.)* "I know one of them was killed here and the team over at UUI reports a dead bull over there as well. Didn't you say you thought Imperius Drake would be joining the party?"

Bruce Wallaroo interrupted, "His hooligan baboon was up in the first truck. Wyatt, the Frau and I saw him, but he's not among the dead, wounded or captured."

"Baboons can just about fly through the trees, Bruce," I said. "He's probably long gone. But if Bigg was here, where was Imperius? And why here? I would have thought they'd be over at the lab."

"He might have been," said Wyatt, "but their exercise over there went sour from the get-go. Howard said he thought he saw the duck, but he wasn't sure. Imperius is pitch black, and there was plenty of pitch black night to disappear into if he was ever there. He'd better disappear. The FBI wants him, too, of course. He and Bigg are probably off licking their wounds right now and trying to figure out how to make a safe getaway from this part of the country."

"Don't be too sure, Colonel, don't be too sure," mumbled the Bear as he fell over into a deep narcoleptic slumber.

Chapter Twenty Nine

Is there really a cheetah called Cyd?

If there is, where has this sister hid?

She's a dancer, they say

With a distracting way.

Does she cover for things Chita did?

"You're sure it's her, Baboon?"

"Oh, yes, Sire. I followed her to this paddle steamer. She's here now. I'm up on the pilot house and I can see right down to the gangplank. She hasn't left. I'm pretty sure she's hiding out in one of the staterooms."

"Well done, Baboon. She's probably waiting until all the law enforcement animals clear out. She is a fugitive from justice, you know."

"So are we, Sire."

"Justice may pursue us, Baboon, but Imperius Drake is never a fugitive, never! Stay where you are, Baboon and I shall join you. I believe my wings are strong enough to once again sustain flight. Is the boat visible?"

"It's next to a grove of trees, Sire. Hard to see from land, but wide open from the river."

"Excellent. I shall be there shortly. Then you may also tell me of the Puma's misadventures."

Down below, Chita was stretched out on a stateroom bed. She had helped herself to a vodka from the stateroom's mini-bar and lain in the dark, contemplating the Puma's comeuppance *(there's that word again)*.

"Let's not get too confident, Chita, my dear," she thought. "I saw Bigg in that rag-tag invasion force. Where there is Bigg, can the Duck be far behind? He may have been killed off over at the lab, but I doubt it. Let me see. Time to call Brucie again."

"Hello, you long eared devil, you!!! This is your wake up call."

"Well, weren't you the showy sheila, though. Prancing right up there on the bonnet of that Hummer."

"It got him to stop. My legs always stop traffic. Are you alone?"

"Not really. Are you on the boat?"

"Yeah. Quick question! Did Imperius show up? I thought I saw Bigg!"

"Haven't seen him myself, but Howard and the wolves are sure he was here."

"Was???"

"The consensus is he and Bigg split after the invasion fizzled."

"Don't be too sure, Inspector, don't be too sure."

"Funny, that's what Ocko said to Wyatt just now."

"OK, if you could give me a call in the morning – no rush, a girl needs her beauty sleep – and let me know there are no residual law enforcement hangers-on and that Octavius is still cool with the Chita-Cyd thing, I'll be off and running."

"To where?"

"Oh Brucie, you never give up, do you? Call me in the AM. Thanks!!!"

"Thank you!" said the wallaroo.

Chita fell back on the bed. "I wonder," she wondered, "what Jake and Lepi are going to do now that this nonsense is over. I don't think it would be very smart to go back to Brazil. As far as I remember, Ozzie was the only Brazilian native. Poor Ozzie. Fat chance of Paolo-Pontius-Whosis ever taking him back with him. That lying sneak. On the other hand, I wonder who's going to run the puma's music empire now? If most of his number twos are as dumb as I think they are, there may be a place for a smart feline *(modesty forbids naming names)* to move in and take charge. Let us consider that, Chita. But let's not get killed off in the process. Let's consider that too, Chita."

The baboon had been sitting atop the pilot house and climbed down to the next deck where six staterooms were located. Listening at each door, he heard movement in the room next to the stairs leading down to the saloon deck and ultimately the main deck, engine room and the below decks holds. He heard a scratch on the door and bounded behind a stanchion just as Chita peeked out. She was all black again. Bigg liked her in black. He was leg enthusiast too, and black did wonders for legs...oh well.

The cat looked up and down the companionway and then headed for the stairs leading below. "Let's check things out, Chita, my dear," she whispered to herself. "Where to hide, if necessary? Bruce or Maury said something about utility storage rooms below decks. Let's go look."

As she slinked down the steps, the baboon swung down from deck railing to deck railing, always keeping a safe distance behind her. He waited until she had gone below the main deck and listened to her trying doors and latches.

"This looks like a good one," she murmured as she opened the door. "Off to the side and lots of stuff to hide behind. What's it say on that doorplate? Bosun's Locker. I wonder what a bosun is."

As she started to move back up the stairs, Bigg scampered away and after a few acrobatic displays landed back up on the pilothouse roof just in time to see a coal black Imperius emerging out of the equally black sky. He was flying, but just barely! Obviously the wing wounded in Las Vegas still wasn't as strong as it should be, and the head wound wasn't helping any. He dipped, swooped and spiraled just on the edge of control. He made a gooney-bird landing on the deck behind the pilot house and waddled over to look up at Bigg. "How did you get up there, Baboon?"

"I swung up, Sire. Would you like me to carry you up here?"

"No! Yes! No! Oh, all right! Ouch! Oof! Where is the cat?"

"In a stateroom on the deck below. She's disguised as a black panther again. Shall we go down and kill her now?"

"No, no. It will be morning soon and time for the execution of my great plan."

"Another great plan, Sire?" he winced.

"Yes, and you have an important role to play, Baboon. I wish to inflict vengeance on the cat not only for what she did to me but what she did to Miss Lee-Li-Li."

"But Sire, you told me she died in Tibet."

"Nepal! I'm talking about the boat, imbecile. Chita sank my boat!"

"Oh yes, Sire, with a pile of rocks."

"The same fate awaits the cat. I concocted this scheme as I was fluttering over here."

"You're gonna sink this boat?"

"Yes, Baboon, with Ms Catt trapped below the water line. We will even raise the alarm or more accurately, you will raise the alarm among the bear's subordinates...too late to do any good, of course. While those fools are striving to reverse catastrophe, I will have entered UUI unnoticed in my Mandarin Duck manifestation, will have gone on to the genetics lab and after dealing with that fraud Vark, I will have escaped with my property. I shall join you later. Do you understand all that?"

"Where do we get the rocks?"

"What rocks?"

"To sink this boat."

"Ah, baboon," said the duck, fighting back total despair. "I see I have not made myself entirely clear. Do you remember the hydroplane, Ms. Lee-Li-Li."

"Sure, that's your boat that Chita sank with rocks."

"Yessssss! She did. Now remember when you used to empty out the bilges and the other water that got in below the deck of the hydroplane. How did you do that??"

"I opened the sea cocks."

"Very good! But if you left them open too long, what happened?"

"The water started coming back in instead of flushing out."

"Does that suggest an idea to you, my dear Baboon?"

"If you're not careful, you can get very wet. Oooooh!"

"That's right, Baboon. I want you to go very quietly below decks and locate this boat's sea cocks. You will open them, and you will not be at all careful. In fact, you will be very careless, break them and leave them open. DO NOT OPEN THEM YET! When I get back over to UUI and transform myself into my Mandarin Duck guise, I will signal you by phone. You will call out to

270

Chita from the shore. Tell her you are the FBI and for her to come out with her paws up. She'll probably try to hide down below."

"Yes, Sire. She was down looking at a room called the Bosun's Locker."

"Splendid. As soon as she hides herself in the Bosun's Locker which I assume is well below the waterline, you will lock her in, open the sea cocks and get off the boat. Jump into the trees near the mansion and scream "The Belinda B. is sinking! *(Or whatever the name of this cutesy tub is.)* When they start running to save the boat, you take off. I will meet you further upstream, and we can get our car and escape. They'll never even know Chita has met her watery demise in their floating pleasure palace."

"It's kind of shame to sink a nice boat like this. Who's Belinda B?"

"That worthless glamour puss polar bear who thwarted us in Las Vegas. She is Octavius Bear's sweetheart. Do you see the irony in sinking a boat named for her after what Chita did to the Miss Lee-Li-Li, Baboon?"

"No!"

"Well, do it anyway! I'm leaving now. I want to get back across the river and onto the roof of UUI before it gets light. Then I need to find a place to transform. Keep your receiver on for my signals."

"Yes, Sire." Bigg somersaulted down the decks to find the bilges and sea cocks of the Belinda B. all the while murmuring under his breath, "This is the FBI. Come out with your paws up, Chita! Chortle, Chortle."

271

Chapter Thirty

Sinking boats seems to be right in style.

Yes, you really should give it a trial.

Find a river that's free

And just go on a spree

With a waterlogged, mischievous smile

.

Otto had watched the excitement of last night from a second story window inside the mansion. He wasn't sure what was going on until Frau Schuylkill raced by beneath, stopped and looked up. "Are you all right, Herr Otto?"

"I'm fine, Frau Schuylkill but I'm confused. What's happening?"

"We have been under attack here and over at UUI. We know that verdammte puma from Brazil is behind it. He's angry because Maury and the Inspector ruined his espionage business, and he is also up here looking for Chita."

"Is Chita here?" asked the otter.

"She's here somewhere. She's been talking to the Aussie and Colonel Wyatt on the telephone. I think she helped us capture that *schweinehund* cat." *(The miracle of selective breeding that this epithet would have required seemed to escape the she-wolf.)*

"I never got a chance to thank her for putting me in your paws. Do you know where she is?"

"I saw her for a minute before they toppled the Hummer and captured the puma, and then she disappeared."

Since all of the action had taken place outside of Otto's field of vision *(except for the helicopter's spotlights)* he wasn't quite certain what a toppled hummer had to do with anything. He wasn't sure what a toppled hummer even was. You could never tell with Frau Schuylkill.

"I must go, Herr Otto, there is much to clean up!"

"Thanks, Frau!" Back to bed.

Otto re-awoke after a short snooze, welcomed the dawn and thought he might go down to the kitchen for a pre-breakfast snack and then maybe a swim in the pool. He was supposed to be doing more work with Dr.Vark today, but with the excitement at UUI, it might be delayed or canceled. He hoped not. He still wanted to get to the bottom of what was happening to him.

He padded over to the massive refrigerator. "Let's see, a few fish to cheer me up and oh look, that wonderful Frau Schuylkill has gotten in a supply of kelp juice. I haven't had kelp juice since I was in Reno. That crazy duck kept feeding me those strange concoctions that tasted like tainted sea water. Well, if nothing else, I'll get a chance to catch up on my eating." After one or two not very restrained burps, he turned and started looking for the pool.

As he was walking out of the kitchen, he ran into the condor. Picking himself up and apologizing to the bird, he asked him what he knew about last night's adventures. L. Condor related the details of the raid on UUI, the casualties and the clean-up process under way. No damage had been done to the genetics lab or the hospital wing and business was going on as usual.

He was heading over to the lab shortly. Wasn't Otto due over there as well? Did he want company in the shuttle bus? The condor was fascinated by Otto and his apparent preternatural abilities. The otter was likewise enthralled by the bird and his progress in producing a high-tech voice box.

(Forgoing the swim but what the heck!) "Sure, Senhor Condor. I'd love the company. Maybe you could fill me in on all your electronic exploits. Did you really hack the puma's network to pieces?"

*****

Bruce and I were comparing notes. We both knew Chita was hanging out on the boat waiting for the coast to clear. Jake had been pestering us about where she was. He wanted to team up again. We waved him off with shrugs, but Bruce made a mental note to tell Chita about it when he called her in about half an hour. Bruce had already made his report to his superiors and was basking in the new light of being a hero once again. That loss of the sapphire in Chicago still hurt, but Pontius Puma in flames was a pretty good recovery act. Now if they could get that damned duck.

273

The wolves had chased after Bigg but had lost him. Wyatt along with Octavius was now finishing up exchanging evidence with the law enforcement units, and Frau Schuylkill was appearing six places at once, managing clean-up and repair activities at the mansion.

The polar bears were down at the pool again sans Otto. Juno was rocketing off the diving board and splashing all and sundry. Agrippa was lolling in a beach chair munching on a fish. Pushing over large cars was fun. He'd have to do more of that. Jake was nowhere to be seen, but Lepi was there. He had developed something of a crush on Bearnice and had spoken to Belinda about coming back with them to her Shetland Island estate to work up a singing act with the bear.

The three bears wanted Otto to come too and the otter was showing signs of being interested if he could get rid of the effects of the serum. She never came right out and said so, but I believe Belinda wanted him to keep his special powers. There were plans for a spectacular multi-species act forming in that lovely white head. As for me, I also had to work some kind of agent angle with her while still sticking with Octavius. This would take some thought and delicacy. In the meantime, let's check across the river.

Howard answered the phone at the lab. "Hey, Maury! How's it goin' over there?"

"Fine. I think you guys took more of a hit than we did."

"Mostly cosmetic. Everything is functioning. It's just not as pretty as it was over here. I lost a few quills in the ruckus. I think a couple of them are sticking in a gorilla's rear end. What's the story on Imperius Drake? Was he here or not?"

"We think he was and still may be. We saw his baboon thug over here or at least we thought we did. Keep your eyes open. What's going on in the lab?"

"We heard from L. Condor. He and Otto should be here any minute. The two doctors are here and we're just getting Imperius' stuff back out of the safe to start experimenting again when Otto arrives. He's a game little character."

"Don't be too casual about keeping those notes and serum in the open. Until we know where the Duck is, it could spell trouble."

"Gotcha, but Dr. Vark is not going to let a little thing like security stand in the way of science. He's waving at me. Talk to you later."

*****

Imperius had returned to the roof of UUI headquarters, slipped into one of the air conditioning housings and gone through the ritual of transforming himself into mild mannered Yu-Aul-Kum, nerdy looking but clearly homicidal Mandarin Duck. He took the lab coat out of hiding, adjusted his black and gold ski cap, put on his spectacles, patted his geek pack of pens and turned his ID tag wrong way around. It was a good counterfeit, but why tempt fate? The morning shift was just coming on in the building, but he knew from past experience that in the lab, most of the staff was probably there already or hadn't left from the night before.

As he waddled confidently along the hall, no one seemed to notice an unobtrusive duck. His ski cap blended right in with the lab's other sartorial oddities. As he neared the genetics lab, memories returned of past encounters, including his fight with Octavius Bear in which he had actually wounded the ursine with a flying sharp instrument. A shame the bear probably would not be here this morning. As he turned a corner, he saw the smart-aleck porcupine just about to close up his cell phone. The last words he heard him say were, "Dr. Vark is not going to let a little thing like security stand in the way of science."

"Good old Vark – 'plus ça change, plus ça meme chose.' – well, he'll be sorry." Then he opened his cell phone and called Bigg. "Commence with the operation, Baboon!" Hoping against hope that the baboon remembered what the operation was.

"Aye, aye, Sire," said the baboon. "On my way over the side."

Imperius swiftly fluttered up to the top of a tall file cabinet and hid out of sight behind a plaster anatomical model of a moose head. From his vantage point, he could look into the lab cubicles and the work area. Vark was there. So was the porcupine. And someone he didn't know, a bird, maybe a vulture. And sitting on a table swinging his feet over the edge was Otto. Where were his notes and the serum? Vark moved over to the wall, pushed aside a picture of a Tyrannosaurus Rex and proceeded to open the laboratory safe. He took out a number of vials and beakers and ah yes, Imperius' notes, his precious notes. They were no doubt incomprehensible to that intellectual pygmy. A sacrilege that they were even in his paws!

Which beaker held the serum? There seemed to be several that looked the same. Actually, what difference did it make? The otter was useless to him now. He would never be subservient to the Great Duck. He must start again with a more malleable species. Since the serum was tailored to the otter, it too was useless.

A plan of attack formed. But first he must determine the best route of escape. A small gurney was sitting by the door big enough for a raccoon or a squirrel or a...duck! If he created enough momentary chaos by smashing glassware and throwing several lethal missiles such as scalpels and broken vials at Vark, he could grab the notebook and propel himself down the hall and out the door to freedom before they gathered their wits. If the confusion was great enough, he might be able to snag the particle accelerator, as he left, provided they were keeping it in the same room as last time. But speed was all.

He stood behind the moose model and shoved hard. It came crashing down on several glass shelves shattering everything in its path. Otto ducked under the table, but Vark stood there open mouthed. Imperius struck him in the chest with a scalpel, and the aardvark fell over on top of the porcupine. The condor hopped over to assist the wounded aardvark and in the melee, Imperius threw a broken beaker in their general direction, grabbed the notebook and jumped on the gurney, giving it a shove away from the wall with his feet.

L. Condor and Howard stayed in the lab and tended to Dr. Vark's wounds until a doctor arrived. Howard shouted, "He has the notes. After him!" Otto yelled for security and bounded off after the duck.

"Don't bother about the notes," gasped the seriously wounded geneticist as they placed him on the table that Otto had vacated. "I made copies, and they're really not all that useful. He's probably flown off by now. We'll never catch him, the murderous fowl."

"Maybe you can't, but I can," said the condor and headed for the nearest exit.

*****

Bigg jumped off the gangplank, cleared his throat, turned to the boat and roared, "Chita, this is the FBI. We have a warrant for your arrest. We know you're in there. Come out with your paws up, and no one will get hurt."

276

On reflection, Bigg thought he sounded pretty convincing. In fact this whole operation was his brainchild. Oh, maybe a suggestion or two from the emperor. The Emperor!! Why couldn't he be the emperor sometimes; Why was it always the Duck? He was bigger and stronger than the Duck and he had ferocious teeth and a scary face. Why couldn't he give orders, too?

"Duck, we are displeased with you, Duck! You have failed again, Duck! We shall see to your punishment, Duck. You may address us as Emperor Bigg, Duck!"

Yeah, he liked that! He would be "we" for a while. Again he shouted, "Chita, this is the FBI. We have a warrant for your arrest. We know you're in there. Come out with your paws up, and no one will get hurt." The second time was even more forceful. A fitting sound from the Emperor Bigg.

Chita heard him the first time and opened the door of her stateroom on the opposite side of the boat facing the river. No other boats or anyone else on that side that she could see. She ran as rapidly as she could in the tight stairways and made it down to the Bosun's Locker, closed and locked the door and hid behind a large pile of spare parts.

She was black and unless they broke in and did a detailed search of each room, she could probably stay hidden or use her speed to run past them, down the gangway and into the woods. Damn that wallaroo! He was supposed to call her and tell her what was what. Not like him to forget - unless he was double-crossing her. Or…maybe he didn't know about this. There was something very familiar about that FBI voice. She had heard it before. Who? Who?

Bigg had sprung from the shore to the below decks hold and watched from a darkened corner as the cat ran into the Bosun's Locker. He pushed a large, heavy generator in front of the door and piled a table on top of that.

Chita heard the noise and slipped out of her hiding place, unlocked the door and tried to crack it open. It wouldn't budge.

"Chita, this is not the FBI. You're trapped in there. Guess who this is?'

Of course, it was Bigg. "Let me out of here, you stupid baboon."

"Oh no, You will address us as emperor and Sire. We are no longer Baboon. We are Emperor Bigg! Resistance is futile!"

"Is Imperius dead, Bigg?"

"No, I have just taken charge. Time for your bath."

He ran off and proceeded to break the bilge valves and the seacocks, tearing some of them right out of the hull. The water started to rush in. Then he ran back up to the main deck, swung up the railings to the pilot house and looked for Imperius. He could see a bird flying in his direction, but something was wrong. There was another bird, a very big bird, not far behind him and someone familiar was swimming across the river very rapidly. Time to get lost.

*****

Back at the mansion, Bruce and I were just getting ready to do a final walkabout, checking for the fuzz when his cell phone rang. All he heard was "Help!!" and the phone went dead. "Chita! Something's wrong!" he said.

I climbed up on his shoulder. My leg was still game and he traveled a lot faster than I could. As we ran down to the river bank, we heard a screaming voice shouting, "The boat is sinking, the boat is sinking!" We looked up and saw a baboon – Bigg- swinging through the trees and heading north. I looked around as we bounded along and saw Wyatt, the Frau and Octavius all heading for the boat. When we got there, the water had just risen above the main deck and The Belinda B. was settling in about twelve feet of water.

"Chita's on board."

"The staterooms are still above water."

"I'm not sure she's still in a stateroom. She called for help on my cell phone but then it went dead before she could say anymore."

"The phone may have gone underwater and her with it! She may have gone below decks for some reason. I don't know why. I didn't call to warn her."

"I'll bet it was Imperius and that baboon. They psyched her out."

"How do we get to her before she drowns? There's not a diver in the bunch of us."

"Yes, there is," said a squeaky voice from the river bank. Otto had dragged over the cheetah and was trying to give her artificial respiration. "Are any of you any better at this than I am?"

Frau Schuylkill ran over and started pushing on the cat's lungs. Water was dribbling out of her mouth, but she didn't seem to be breathing.

Chorus of voices. "Otto!! How did you get here? What did you do? What happened?"

The otter was also spitting out water and trying to recover his breath. Octavius shouted, "Give them both room and let him recover before you give him the third degree. How's the cat, Frau Schuylkill? That is Cyd, isn't it? What's the black stuff on her pelt?"

Belinda had just come up and said, "Of course it's Cyd, Chita's sister. Tavi, give the Frau a break, too. She hasn't got time to answer you either."

Just then the cat shuddered, coughed, gasped and spit up a small river of water. She looked up at the wolf, scrambled to her feet and wobbled away for about five feet. Then she collapsed.

"Look up there," Wyatt growled, pointing to the pilot house. "There's a duck, but he's not black. Can that be Imperius? He's holding a notebook. He doesn't have the weapon, though."

"That is Imperius!" growled the Bear. "He's in his Mandarin disguise. I guess he came to inspect Bigg's handiwork."

Suddenly, a large shadow fell upon the drake, and as he looked up he saw L. Condor in a power dive heading straight for him. He ducked *(!?)* down the other side of the pilot house as the condor came swooping in overhead, turned and rose for another pass. The wolves and Bruce jumped on board and came bounding up the stairs heading for him. If he stayed on board, he'd be trapped. Those wolves could follow his scent anywhere. And that dumb Wallaroo might just fall on him. If he flew, he might be able to get away from the condor by heading into the trees. Swimming was out. He'd be a sitting duck. Not much choice.

He waited until the condor made another unsuccessful pass and was rising back into the sky. Then Imperius broke out, flapping, wobbling and swooping, but heading for the woods. He was almost there when he looked ahead. Coming right at him on a collision course was the condor. He flipped over and headed out to the river with the huge bird in close pursuit. He looked over his tail feathers. No condor! Where was he?

A wing the size of billboard smashed into him from above and he spiraled unconscious…down, down into the river. L. Condor circled the spot where Imperius went in, but there was no sign of him coming to the surface. No bubbles, no nothing. The current was swift, and the condor swept back and forth in large patterns. Was Imperius a dead duck? Otto was in no shape to dive and search for him, and no one else was much of a speed swimmer.

Octavius knew better than to take anything for granted as long as they had no avian cadaver. "One of these days, I may believe he's finally gone, but not yet. Where's the baboon?"

"Somewhere in Indiana by now," said Wyatt. "Well, at least they didn't get the particle accelerator. I guess we have to call the FBI and the police back here again. More explaining. Hey, Otto, great job! How're you feeling?"

"Hungry!!"

Epilogue

We have come to the end of our tail.

Pontius Puma is sitting in jail.

The Imperius Duck

May have run out of luck,

Or his fortune perhaps, didn't fail!

Close to thirty-six hours had elapsed since the Imperius-Bigg show had reached its violent climax and once again, things were getting back to normal, whatever that is. Wyatt and Octavius had called back law enforcement, and they had spent the better part of the day and night crawling all over the partially sunken Belinda B. and gathering evidence of the assault over at the UUI genetics lab. Dr. Vark had been very seriously wounded, and it was still not clear whether he would survive. The phones had been very busy over the last day, checking on his condition. Dr. BingBang, along with several other members of the UUI medical staff, was tending to him.

Needless to say a warrant was issued for Imperius *(if he was still alive)* and Bigg for attempted murder, assault with a deadly weapon and wanton destruction of property. We deliberately did not mention the baboon's attempt on the cheetah's life to the FBI or police because we deliberately did not want to mention the existence of the cheetah to the FBI or police. We simply explained away the sinking of the Belinda B. as an irrational act of revenge by Imperius and Bigg.

Chita *(Cyd?)* was secretly recovering in one of the remote bedrooms in the mansion, and she told Bruce and me how the baboon had tricked her into seeking cover in the Bosun's Locker. From what we know of Bigg, he couldn't have come up with a scheme like that on his own, but the cat insisted that he was claiming now that he was the emperor. But we were pretty sure that it was Imperius that got clobbered by the condor so Bigg may have just been having delusions of grandeur to match the duck's.

281

Later, we were getting ready for dinner, and Otto had gone up to see how Chita was doing. He crept down the stairs, looked all around and approached Bruce and me. "She's gone!!!" he said.

"Chita??" I blurted.

This was followed by a chorus of "Shhhh's." One or two policemen may still be in the house.

"Yes," said the otter. "I went up to her room, and it's empty. I went looking for Jake and Lepi to see if she was with them. Lepi's here. He's practicing scales in the library, but Jake is also missing and Lepi doesn't know where they are."

"Well," I said, "I'm willing to take a small bet that they're on their way to yet another round of musical stardom, but not in this country. Jake kept talking about Europe and Chita was a big hit in Europe. Who knows? Maybe she'll team up with Jake and her sister Cyd and there'll be a Spotted Band II."

"Do you really believe there is a Cyd?" asked Otto.

"Why, Otto," we said as we pulled our chairs out at the dining room table. "Would Chita lie to us?"

Belinda, Bearnice and Bearyl made a typical grand entrance with Lepi taking up the rear. Looking around to see that the guardians of the law had left, Belinda came over to Otto and gave him a hug that had his eyes popping. I'm not sure whether it was the strength of the hug or just being squeezed by his goddess, the "most wonderful animal in the world," but Otto just lost it completely. He took a few minutes to gain back his composure. Then for good measure, Juno gave him a motherly hug. All the while, the three bears were telling him what a clever, brave, magnificent otter he was. Yes, he was indeed Otto the Magnificent. Even Agrippa was impressed.

"Otto, now that things have quieted down *(again)*, suppose you tell us how you pulled off that rescue. Oh, by the way," said Octavius, "Senhor Condor, that was some of the most skillful flying I have ever seen. I never imagined a bird your size could be so maneuverable in the air."

"Oh, *si*, we condors don't just soar. We can dive and swoop up to 55 miles an hour. We are not birds of prey, but when we scavenge, we still have to get in on the carrion pretty fast before someone else gets away with it first. I keep up my soaring license and aerobatics rating."

The aviating wolves were staring at him with a mixture of wonder and respect. "I wonder, Senhor, if you would be willing to get together with Frau Ilse and me to discuss aerial tactics," said Wyatt.

"Most certainly, senhor and senhora wolf, it would be my pleasure."

Octavius turned back to the otter. "Sorry about interrupting myself, Otto. Now that you've had a moment to think, how *did* you do it?"

"Same answer as always, Doctor Bear. I don't really know. I just remember running after Imperius and swimming across the river, and after I heard the boat was sinking and that Ch…that is, the cat might be trapped, I started running, then swimming and diving and searching and lifting heavy machinery under water and breaking down the door and grabbing Ch…er, the cat and bringing her up to the surface. I guess the serum had kicked back in."

"It must have. There was no way any other otter could have done what you did without major augmentation. But why did it kick back in? You've been 'normal' ever since your performance with the Aquabears the other day."

Howard had just arrived from UUI and was seating himself when he heard the end of Octavius' question. "We may have been on the brink of discovering why it happens when the duck staged his rampage."

"Could you save anything, Howard?" asked the wallaroo.

"Not unless you'd like a collection of broken glass and lab furniture. That duck must get super strength from his version of the serum, although he appeared as a mandarin, not his usual dark and despicable self. He took the notes but Dr. Vark had the foresight to copy them. Otto's serum is a total loss!"

"That's fine with me," said the otter.

"However, the doctors have a theory, and as soon as Dr. Vark is recovered, he'd like to study you further, Otto."

"Is he going to recover, Herr Porcupine?"

"Dr. BingBang thinks so, but it's going to take a while."

"Well, in the meantime, I'm planning to fly Otto back with me to Bearmoral Castle for a working vacation. Serum or not, I think we can work up a routine with you and the bears that will be a comic smash."

"Gee, that'd be great Belinda, but I still want to know if I'm slowly going nuts."

"The doctors didn't think so, Otto,' said Howard. "Yes, the serum did alter some of your genetic structure and if you kept taking it, it might have had a similar effect as it had on Imperius. But their belief, and they still need to prove it, is that the thing that changes you into Super Otter is a simple surge of your own adrenaline. Every time you go into your hyper mode, it's after you've just undergone an exciting moment. When you calm down, you're back to Hairy Otter or whatever your original name was."

"Well," said Bel, "if that's really true, things are certainly looking up. If show business isn't one gigantic adrenaline high, I don't know what is. We'll have you flying and diving and escaping and bringing in the audiences by the thousands."

A flash of light crossed my Meerkat brain. This was the hook. I would persuade Belinda to allow me to "handle" Otto in his show biz career, being very careful not to cross any of the bears *(especially Octavius)* in the process. Agent Maury, the toast of the backstage world, wheeling and dealing! I'll have to call my tailor and start ordering up those Hollywood blacks.

Belinda turned to Octavius and said, "I'm so sorry about the paddle boat. We never did get to take a real cruise, and we have to leave at the end of the week."

"It'll be afloat again the next time you come back. I promise. I'll be looking forward to all of your returns."

"Oh, no, Octavius Bear, the 'we' includes you. You promised you would come back with me to the Shetlands and I won't take no for an answer. All of you are invited if you want to come."

Octavius was still trying weasel his way out of the trip, so I helped by saying I would be delighted to come along and take over all of his "administrative burdens." The two wolves and Howard immediately chimed in with assurances that while he was gone, everything would run on an even keel.

(Not the best simile in the world, considering) Otto could return with Belinda and Octavius on her next visit back and catch up with the geneticists and doctors.

Howard was organizing the Multiverse Project and had set up a work schedule with Juno, Agrippa, the wolves and the UUI science team. Hopefully, Dr. Vark would be able to join them as he recovered from the duck's assault. And of course, the Great Bear would be monitoring and sticking his big black nose in the proceedings electronically. Needless to say, an ocean wasn't going to get in Octavius' way.

L. Condor allowed as how he might stay a little longer until he got a clearer picture of how things were in Brazil after PP's capture. No doubt, he was also getting caught up in all the scientific activity and opportunities at UUI. I have a feeling he'll be around for a bit. Bruce was heading back to Aussie Land to bask in glory and rest on his re-established laurels. Lepi had been adopted by the bears and was coming to the Shetlands with them.

"What language do they speak in the Shetlands?" I asked.

Bearnice laughed and said, "That's difficult to say, Maury. It's English, but then again, it's not. The Scots speak Scottish or Scotch or Scots depending on whom you ask. You never refer to the people as Scotch. They're Scots. Scotch whiskey or Scotch broth is OK, but if you go to Edinbeargh Castle, you'll see the Scots Guards. And that's just the national names. A lot of what they say is indecipherable. I'm not sure they understand each other. Bruce, you'd have a field day getting everything misunderstood."

"Hold on there, Ms Fairy Floss. We Aussies speak English the way it should be spoke."

"Scotch, Scots, Scottish" I said. "Sounds pretty bizarre to me."

"Wait till you meet the folks who speak it."

Dinner was served. *(There was no Haggis on the menu!)*

End of

The Case of the Spotted Band

Volume Two of

The Case Books of Octavius Bear

About the Author

Harry DeMaio is a *nom de plume* of Harry B. DeMaio, successful author of several books on Information Security and Business Networks as well as *The Open and Shut Case – Volume One of the Casebooks of Octavius Bear*. A retired business executive, consultant, information security specialist, former pilot and graduate school adjunct professor, he whiles away his time traveling and writing preposterous articles and stories.

He has appeared on many radio and TV shows and is an accomplished, frequent public speaker.

Former New York City natives, he and his extremely patient and helpful wife, Virginia, and their Bichon Frisé, Woof, live in Cincinnati (and several other parallel universes.) They have two sons, living in Scottsdale, Arizona and Cortlandt Manor, New York, both of whom are quite successful and quite normal, thus putting the lie to the theory that insanity is hereditary.

His e-mail is hdemaio@zoomtown.com

Also from MX Publishing

MX Publishing is the world's largest specialist Sherlock Holmes publisher, with over a hundred titles and fifty authors creating the latest in Sherlock Holmes fiction and non-fiction.

From traditional short stories and novels to travel guides and quiz books, MX Publishing cater for all Holmes fans.

The collection includes leading titles such as *Benedict Cumberbatch In Transition* and *The Norwood Author* which won the 2011 Howlett Award (Sherlock Holmes Book of the Year).

MX Publishing also has one of the largest communities of Holmes fans on Facebook with regular contributions from dozens of authors.

www.mxpublishing.com